THE FIRST DOOR IS THE FINAL EXIT

Timothy Kenneth O'Neil

ACKNOWLEDGEMENTS

I nearly drowned swimming in the memory pool trying to rescue those memories of Vietnam from disappearing into the abyss, and keeping me afloat was a cast of friends who offered their reading expertise, their insights and critiques into the book, and mostly. . .their support.

This book would not see the light of day without the hard work and talents of the book cover creator, Chris Urban, who was a joy to work with and accomplished getting this book published, which I couldn't have done alone.

My readers who simultaneously were both editors and supporters. . .nothing but kudos !
First, my long term supporter, Steve Flaum (author of *The Prussian*), Janet Ayres, my three "brothers" from San Diego: Bill Bennett, Rusty Morse, and Bill Beaty, Prof, Andrew Popper (author of *Rediscovering Lone Pine)*, Stu Mattson, Roy & Sandra Schumacher, Reneé & Kevin Jones.

I also need to thank my sweetie Kathleen Spaine, for tolerating the hours spent writing, and I need to thank my kid brother, Kerry O'Neil, for saving my life so many many years ago.

◆ ◆ ◆

This book is dedicated to all my brothers and sisters who gave it all for their country and checked into the Big Hotel so many years ago, and to all of us that survived and cannot forget...and pray history does not repeat itself.

It is with profound humility this novel is dedicated to those that shared the other side of tragedy, all the girl friends, wives, sisters, and mothers who were seriously scarred by the war and have wounds that truly never heal.

GLOSSARY

*Definitions of commonly used Vietnamese
words, GI slang, and military acronyms*

AO
>   *Area of operations*

Bic
>   *To understand*

Boom-boom girls
>   *Young prostitutes*

Cansa
>   *Vietnamese for marijuana*

Charley
>   *A Vietnamese soldier, either a NVA (North Vietnam Army) or a VC (Viet Cong)*

Chieu Hoi
>   *Usually meant "to surrender" or one who had surrendered*

CP
>   *Command Post*

DEROS
>   *"Date of Estimated Return from Overseas Service" The magical date all GIs looked forward to... the last day in Nam*

Di di mau
>   *Literally "go quickly" but often used to tell someone to get lost*

Dinky-Dau

"Crazy"

Dum-dum round

A bullet upon hitting its target begins to spin creating a larger wound

Dust-Off

A helicopter ambulance used to pick up the wounded or slain

Eagle Flight

Usually nine, but sometimes less, group of Huey helicopters who would pick up troops and deliver them to their combat destination

Gook

The racist slang term used to describe the enemy. As in all wars, a racist derogatory demeaning term was used towards the enemy

Ho Chi Minh sandal

Made from a rubber tire. Named after the leader of the North Vietnamese

Klick

1000 meters

Laager Site

A held over word from the Boer War, a camp en-circled by defensive wagons (or sandbags). A main camp often with recon units.

Lister Bag

Olive drab in color, made of a canvas fabric that "weeps", holding 36 gallons of drinkable water, enough for 100 GIs

LP

Listening Post

Lima Charlie

Loud and clear
Loomy-loomy
Luminescent artillery, an extremely bright flare on a small parachute
Looey
Slang for a lieutenant
LBJ
Slang for the Long Binh Jail. The cells were often underground, with just enough space for breathing and a rat to get in
Mess
Meal
Mos
Military Occupation Specialty
MPC
Military Payment Certificate. Army printed money, low on the totem pole of accepted payment
Number One
Anything good or great
Number ten
Anything bad or terrible
PZ
Pick-up zone
REMF
Rear echelon mother fucker. The 90% who weren't in the field, wearing starched fatigues, eating hot meals, and sleeping inside covered barracks
RTO
Radio telephone operator
Section Eight
Category of discharge for a service member.

One mentally unfit for service (a dishonorable discharge)
Spooky
A C-47 gunship armed with powerful miniguns. Also called "Puff the Magic Dragon"
Starlight
A night scope enabling one to see in the dark. It had a krypton green lens.
Ti-ti
(Pronounced tee-tee) meant little or soon
The "World"
What America or home was called

CHAPTER ONE

The Hallmark Gift
Wrapping Comes Off

January First, 1969
Vietnam

It was the cheering that was so mystifying. As they got out of the plane, the roar of the crowd was if they were some rock group just walking on stage. It was deafening.

What a welcome !

After some fourteen hours in the air, crossing enough time zones one didn't care what day it was, everyone was both exhausted and strung out. The flight was a near perfect cross section of humanity in crisis, although it was far too close for anyone on the plane to pick up on

at the time, some feelings, even under the emotional microscope were invisible.

There were men on the verge of tears (they were "men" whose average age was twenty...they were babies, but soon they would be soldiers), and then there were those who crossed the verge. The fear of death is far mightier than dying itself.

There was the group of guys who were ready to conquer the world and kill some gooks (the common derogatory term nearly all GIs used referring to the enemy) and no one was going to stop them. This war was for them and they were here to fight and to kill, and to save Democracy and the Free World. They laughed and joked about killing gooks like drunken Indians with a teepee full of fresh scalps. War was going to be an adventure, intoxicating exhilaration; and they couldn't wait to get their hands on an M-16.

They were the immortal ones.

The majority had a stoic funneled perspective that when the plane takes them home, one year from today, some would be traveling in the cargo hold dressed in a body bag. Looking around at everyone, Winston, our hero, could only wonder who it would be and hoped it wouldn't be him. It was the beginning of Grim Reaper roulette, a game that would last the entire year. For one and all this was a turning point in everyone's life but they were all too naive and too

ignorant to realize what a strange concept survival would be.

Meanwhile the cheering outside provoked a great feeling. As they each pulled down their brand new duffle bags, everyone wearing new starched fatigues, the sounds of hooting, laughter, and giddy cheering brought odd smiles to their faces.

What a welcome!

Their first day in Vietnam and they were greeted like heroes who were about to save the world. After such a long flight it seemed like such a relief, and what an odd feeling it was, eager to exit the plane, leave the womb, and enter the unknown universe of the war. The entire flight was one of trepidation...of having *to leave* the plane and face the reality that was Vietnam...and now they were about to be greeted by cheering throngs!

As they exited the plane they mindlessly waved to the crowd, intoxicated by the warm feeling that they were loved by strangers. The rebellious crowd had a nervous side to it, they were more than just a little bit eager to see them get off the plane. As they walked down the steps, all nervous grins and stomachs a basket full of butterflies, they formed a long green line across the tarmac...of just so soldiers. The clapping, yelling, and laughing became more raucous. As exhausted as they collectively were this was a psychic tonic...and invisible hug from their own

kind.

What a hello and good morning!

It was too good to be true!

And then the wheel of reality began to roll over them. They weren't rooting for them...they weren't tossing bouquets...they weren't the new brigade heralded to save the day, they wanted them out and the faster the better...

they wanted their seats!

And the welcoming committee was not without its cheerleaders straight from the Marquis de Sade.

"Move it you cherries. You're slowing us down. That's our Freedombird out there!" This was followed by a wave of raucous reinforcement.

"Thanks for keeping my seat warm!"

"You're going to love your year suckers!"

"We're free! It's your time in Hell now!"

There were some, as they filed past, who said nothing. They nodded, they gave the peace sign, they put their fist to their chest and their eyes told it all...God be with you and good luck.

The Hallmark gift wrapping had been removed; they were the new fodder in town, and what they had to offer to this group was an empty plane, which for all of them was the ticket they had been waiting for, praying for, in complete anticipation for, all year.

The sympathetic looks and sporadic handshakes mingled with the cold hearted greet-

ings evaporated in an instant when the last man exited from the plane. The crowd roared in unison, strong enough to echo in the valleys of Valhalla...it was soul-numbing deafening. The ultimate short-timers picked up their gear and began their quick and short walk to freedom.

The plane was being refueled and there was no formality of cleaning up the inside, and with virtually no down time this group of soldiers would only look back once, and from then on it would be only memories and nightmares.

CHAPTER TWO

A Short Goodbye Begins the Long Wait

Veronica, Winston's fiancée, and the love of his life, had just got off the phone with him from Oakland, and it would be a year until they would speak again. It was a very terse rushed call, there was too much to say in too little time, like packing a entire scrapbook's memories and emotions into a pocket-sized paragraph.

Edith, her best friend and Winston's best female buddy as well, was waiting for her downstairs in the kitchen speaking with Veronica's

mother.

Her mother began, " I know she's upset, but she'll get over it, get over that lazy piano player, and find a real man with a real future, a career ahead of him..."

Edith interrupted, " I love Winston almost as much as your daughter. They're a perfect match, and I wouldn't worry about his career, he's a brilliant piano player and far from lazy. She's not going to abandon him."

" Well, we'll see. A year is a long time, and a lot can happen, most of these long-term relationships don't last..."

" Once again I have to disagree with you, but no matter... this bond isn't going to be broken. I think Veronica is lucky, at least she's found a soul mate, I keep dating men who just can't meet my standards or can't cut the mustard. I'd wait a year for Mr. Right, any time..."

Veronica came downstairs, wiping the tears away, said a curt goodbye to her mother and they left to their favorite private hangout, an off the way bar where women weren't hassled.

" I'm numb Edith. I don't know what to do, fortunately I'm in the nursing program which will keep me busy, but mother never liked Winston, and you know what she's going to do..."

" Yes. She's going to be a relentless match maker and make your life Hell. You may have to sleep on the sofa in my apartment."

" Fortunately we never talk much, private

lives in the same house. Too bad dad divorced her and started a new life no where near here, but I can't blame him. He'll be paying alimony forever."

" Forget her. It's about you. You and Winston are both going to have to be tough to survive. It's going to be separate wars in separate worlds, and through your letters, which is all you got, you are going to have to feed each other's strengths. You both, I know, can do this. Every letter increases that invisible bond...no one can *see* love, but you know it's there."

" Edith you're my best friend. I don't know what I would do without you."

" I'm not the only one in your support group, don't forget our other nurse pal, Elizabeth, and nutty Helen, the future accountant. Besides, once Winston returns, " she laughed, " you'll forget my name."

Veronica laughed, " Sure Betty, I doubt it."

Edith giggled.

CHAPTER THREE

The Oral Farting of the General

The "cherries" didn't look back either as the processing for in-country would soon begin at the huge airport complex at Long Binh. It was dark as they separated into antique buses, some with no seats and very few windows; that reeked of years of dank human odors, as they began their journey to their barracks where they would have a one week respite getting a general indoctrination about their "tour" in Vietnam.

The "chauffeur " was a real piece of work. He was portly and unshaven and smoked a cheap

cigar as he yelled at them to get on the bus, " Hey girls and grunts get your dead asses on my bus ! And I mean now privates ! You're going to love the ride." He laughed a cough infused arrogant laugh. As they entered he would spice up their ignorance with such quips as..." You girls are going to love it here. I've got two months and two days and you all have your lifetimes ahead of you !...hear those mortars in the distance ? Everyone has got a number on it and maybe one of you has the lucky number !" He laughed his sickly chortle, " I'm the short-timer here, now hurry up and get on the bus !"

Shortly after their "chauffeur" started his hell bent ride over roads rough with potholes it began to rain. With no windows the rain was soaking them and the odors picked up in intensity. It was a Johnnie Blue (a porta-potty) careening precipitously around dark slippery corners, and they all knew this scumbag for a driver was doing this deliberately. There was a moment when the bus began to lurch on its side and they were as one praying to get to their destination. It was easy to understand why the bus smelled like it did.

Since the "chauffeur" was a lance corporal, just a hic-cup in rank above the rest of them, when he finally stopped at their destination surrounded by sergeants ordering soldiers to do this and do that; he became a perfect gentleman. Here and there was a second lieu-

tenant bobbing his head in agreement with the NCO's as if he knew more than a manikin. The atmosphere was *so* military, and everyone was *so* busy, and they were herded into alphabetical zones to register into their new "homes."

They would inhabit the barracks for a week before the Army would divvy them up into their various units.

The meal in the mess hall was an exact replica of the cuisine served stateside, and was heartily welcomed, and all wet and tired and hungry this was a respite of lightness. A nameless GI speaking to no one in particular, " I never dreamed I'd get to Vietnam and nearly get killed by a bus driver, and that moron was on a suicide mission. How in the hell did he ever get that job ?"

There was an immediate breakout of medicinal laughter. The long tables where they dined facing each other became filled with complete strangers from all stripes of life talking and joking with each other. It was a great feeling.They could enjoy this meal, which Winston as an 11 Bravo should have savored; and among the tables there seemed to arise at least one comic, the proverbial class clown, some one who once they got you going could say anything, and eventually there would be more than a dozen of them totally ravaged by humor reduced to tears.

It was 2:30 in the morning, dinner was over, and reveille was three hours away. They

were shooed out of the mess hall like lambs into their barracks where one by one they fell into bunks, trying to fall asleep to the sound of what they thought was mortars , but was really artillery, making a statement somewhere for some one. Being naive Winston kept waiting for some mortar round to land on the barracks, but Long Binh was a very large well protected area, it hadn't happened in a long long time, but of course Winston didn't know that. As soon as he nodded off, the lights went on and the sergeant in charge began yelling, " Let's go gentlemen ! Hit the showers, and I mean now ! You have ! Breakfast at 0600 hours ! You have ! The general at 0730 ! You will be ready ! Do you read me Lima Charlie ?" The sergeant repeated this message in non-stop yelling. They were in a fog and numb...a perfect combination. Following breakfast an hour was devoted to a "police call" searching for renegade cigarette butts. They were dressed in clean starched fatigues, and at 7:30 in the morning it was in the high 80's and sauna high humid, for this would be the most important part of their indoctrination, listening to the "man."

When the general approached they stood in unison and saluted. As they sat in the sun in the blistery hot bleachers, He began, " Welcome to Vietnam. I have just a few words for all of you. It's going to be a long year but hopefully a fruitful one, in which you all will perform your duties as

you were all trained for with the end result that we will win this war and we can all go home. We are winning the war gentlemen but it's been a slow difficult process, and each and everyone of us has an important part in bringing peace to this country, whether your MOS is in infantry or driving a truck or being a military policeman. Everyone's part is vital to the team effort of destroying the North Vietnamese Army and ending this conflict. Every Private here will have a week in training with the M-16, even though you soldiers headed for an infantry unit have already had plenty of training in a variety of weapons. How many of you went to Tigerland ?"

About ten percent raised their hands.

" Great ! I have nothing but strong memories of Tigerland and it helped to make me the soldier I am today."

Fort Polk, Louisiana aka Tigerland was a hellhole, a perfect place to train for Vietnam, since the climate was similar and the mosquitoes were the size of your hand. Only morons, masochists, and crayfish thought it was a decent place.

The general ranted on about how important the mission was and how they were saving America and ended his sermon with a rousing, " the war will probably go on for another year. After all we don't want to deprive you all of all the good training you received." And with a huge grin and a hi yo Silver he wished them luck, and left.

While they stood at attention saluting and sweating, a bevy of "donut dollies", all cute and alluring in their candy striped uniforms offered them drinks of kool-aid. To a man there wasn't one of them that didn't want just a little bit more than a cool drink.

That afternoon was the beginning of the depressing reality. They were in Vietnam but not part of the experience. After lunch they were issued their assignments and Winston, with an 11-Bravo MOS(infantry) was headed to the Wolfhounds of the Electric Strawberry (the 25th) Division. Nine out of ten would wear starched fatigues and only hear war stories and these REMF's (rear echelon mother fuckers) were only too glad to tell those headed for the field how easy their year was going to be...seeing movies, drinking beer, getting boom-boom...getting "over." The huge difference between the Nam and stateside was that the REMF's would do less and make more money. They got the same hazard pay as infantry.

A brief bio of Winston...
He grew up in a small village in Ohio that eventually would be Kettering, learning to ride a bike on a gravel road, playing Little League baseball and knocking in the winning run in extra innings to win the city of Dayton championship, winning the spelling bee in sixth grade, and being an acolyte in the Episcopal church. Many a summer he

would break an arm, wrist, or shoulder emulating Tarzan, his boyhood idol. It would take years before he realized that swinging from branches worked best on the silver screen.

Ohio in the '50's was an idyllic place to grow up. No one locked their doors, there was no such thing as drugs, girls were from outer space...just a specie that happened to be in your classroom, and Winston and his friends played sports and went hiking when the weather was warm, and played Winter sports and board games during the cold months. Dad worked, mom stayed home. He had two younger brothers. Watching the Walt Disney show every Sunday night, eating popcorn and drinking 7-Up was the pinnacle of entertainment.

His world took a dramatic turn when his father got a fabulous job and they moved to an affluent suburb of New York City. They lived in a fifteen room mansion overlooking a nine acre field with a pond, quite skate-able in the Winter. Life lesson number one was that not everyone on the planet is white and Protestant, and he began to make new and different friends. Every weekend, he and his brother chaperoned by their mother would explore the unbelievable and vast cultural terrain, especially the theatre, of New York. At thirteen he had an epiphany with the disgustingly rich church, and much to his mother's consternation, never went to church again.

To intensify and proliferate the cultural shock he got a piano, and piano lessons and life changed forever. The world of music had made a home in his soul, and his life was going in a different direction...he was learning a new language where the muses spoke to him.

In the middle of his Junior year in high school he was uprooted from his beloved cultural womb, and his father took the family to the suburbs of D.C. He and his mother could not stop crying or hating their environs; but soon he would be off to college and yet another world. His father shortly thereafter lost his job, beginning the checkered career of rags to riches and back again, over and over until one last trip at the 19th hole finally did him in.

Winston played in a band in college, but majored in literature and not music. He had the perverse idea of education stifling his creativity, and read books instead. It was a rainy day, and perfect for coffee and a book at the Student Union, when lightning struck...and he saw Veronica in line...and she saw him. All shyness instantly dissolved away and conversation began as if they had known each other their whole lives. In less than an hour they were laughing about stuff they couldn't remember or care to, and spent the first of many afternoons together. She had long brunette hair, but it was her brown eyes and smile that set her apart for Winston. She was a sophomore pre-nursing student liv-

ing in a dorm, but due to his family's finances (dad currently unemployed) he lived in a migrant worker's quarters in a greenhouse, where he worked. It was a one room operation: kitchen, bedroom, and living room with a separate bathroom, and at 6'2" he couldn't stand up, but it was free rent, and college couldn't have happened without it. Several gallons of paint, new sheets and a bedspread, and many hours of cleaning and he cooked dinner for her, beginning the next phase of their relationship...the one that makes the world go round.

College thereafter, before hindsight was discovered, was the perfect forum for a romantic relationship. They wouldn't know how perfect it was until it was over. They spent endless weekends wandering naked at night in the greenhouses, often strolling outside in the adjacent fields. The owners drank, fought, and slept...and loved Winston. He delivered the truckloads of flats of flowers all over Cleveland and beyond, which kept them in the black, and Winston with a roof over his head. It was a win-win. The low ceiling was an inspiration for Veronica that when they graduated they could actually move into a place where non Hobbits could flourish. There was always so much to talk about concerning their future...but Winston kept getting drafted...and kept using his college deferment. He was drafted five times in two years, having to personally appear before the Selective Service

Board to prove he was *actually* in college, pursuing a degree, and that it was not that far off. For reasons unknown, they wanted him. A future President would sham out of it with bone spurs (and then being a real trooper go skiing).

Winston intensely explored the option of Canada, but he thought being a college grad he would probably end up being a clerk.

He had no idea how the military worked...the high school graduate who re-uped for a year and couldn't write his name was the company clerk, and an English major with a minor in philosophy was going to eventually walk point. His military education was going to be both painful and mind-numbing.

Winston was drafted three weeks after graduating. For Veronica it was the saddest, most hopeful day of her life. Nothing would ever be same, but their love was bound together like a valentine in stone. They made a vow they would marry when he returns and begin a life *together*.

Winston couldn't believe he actually was going to go.

Back at the barracks in Long Binh the sergeant informed him that due to a shortage of soldiers in the field he would be skipping the rest of the week's indoctrination and tomorrow he would be headed out to the Wolfhounds. Tonight was bunker guard and the afternoon was for sleeping...but before the sandman could make

contact...the commanding voice of the sergeant in charge began yelling, " Let's go gentlemen ! Your country is calling you ! You're going to the field *right now* ! There is no time, the bus is waiting," and screaming louder, "and I mean now !!"

Winston was as awake as he ever wanted to be.

"This is your day gentlemen. You all are going to get your chance to meet Charlie face to face, and real soon."

Winston could feel the cold hands of adrenaline on his shoulders, as he looked around at everyone...those that were going with him, and those that remained...their different expressions...all of them leaving were about to hitch up with the Four Horsemen of the Apocalypse...and the others just nodded good-bye. It was a long cold silent moment as they exited the barracks, each clutching his duffel bag and their brand new freshly minted M-16, and took their seats on the bus. Within seconds they were gone and out of sight.

For security a Jeep with a mounted M-60 machine gun led the way. They were going to Dau Tieng, a base camp large enough to hold two companies, which was reachable in daylight about fifty miles away. The Jeep had the opportunity the bus didn't in maneuvering around the major potholes, and it was meandering at as fast a rate as possible down the road creating a cloud of wearable dust.

While they watched, the landscape changed from rice paddies and water buffaloes to jungle, which grew denser with each passing mile. With twilight approaching the pace picked up, the jungle got closer...and there was no visibility beyond the wall of greenery, which seemed nearer and nearer. They were now in snipers alley and the bus soared like a ship over stormy seas, the road was diseased with mortar pockets, and if they weren't so scared they would've been seasick. Some of the leaps and falls of the bus were life threatening, and the driver would yell back to hold on to their seats. The jolts were so severe it was a miracle one didn't break one's neck on the roof or get thrown, exiled out an open window.

Nevertheless, the GI next to Winston, firmly gripping the seat in front of him began a staccatoed conversation as the bus rose and fell riding the waves of potholes. " My brother told me, back in the world, that you should never get close to anyone, it's only going to screw you up. If you get close and they die you're not going to want to trust anyone any more. You won't want to have friends again...it's too mind blowing."

"That's probably real good advice, but how do you spend an entire year living in a shell ?"

"You just don't get close, that's all...you just don't get in with anyone." As he spoke he had that faraway look, peering into the window of nowhere, while Winston looked out at the darkening jungle and wondered if he was going to

use his virgin M-16 cradled on his lap. He knew they had to be getting closer as darkness, that big black blanket in the sky was enshrouding them. The bus would never turn its lights on no matter how Stygian the circumstances.

The explosion to his right was mind boggling, about fifty yards away a mortar round detonated into the trees, and what seemed like a nearly simultaneous event a loomy-loomy round exploded like the Fourth of July creating a new sun, drifting on a parachute above the jungle top illuminating the area in a most surreal light...a blinding brightness. The driver put the pedal to the metal and yelled back at them, " Keep an eye on the perimeter, Charlie's out there !" He would be taking the bus to its vehicular limits.

Trying to focus on the perimeter was like trying to throw darts at a moving target from within a washing machine. The bus was more a place to survive in, than one to mount an attack. The eerie light from the loomy-loomy was dissipating as it burned out in the jungle but before it became extinguished another took its place and the brighter it got the faster the bus driver went. The only sounds they heard was from gunfire from far away, and as complete darkness dominated the landscape the Jeep and the bus flashed their lights as they entered the base camp, and with nothing less than a collective gasp of relief they floundered from the bus and entered the world of the Wolfhounds...as jellyfish.

◆ ◆ ◆

It was the beginning of 1969, a year in the "world" where a cultural tsunami was taking place, flooding the landscape with new ways of doing things, looking at things, and believing in new ways. There was a lot more to 1969 than Vietnam, although this was the year with the biggest troop deployment ever as well as the biggest anti-war demonstration.

Women's liberation, turbo-boosted by the pill and that women's rights have been suppressed too long was becoming a movement forever to change how men and women would communicate with each other.

Civil rights and gay rights were making a sea change. The music was not bopping with Benny Goodman, the new rock'n'roll was becoming part of the fabric that everyone young was wearing. There would be hippies getting high and astronauts landing on the moon, and while the Beatles sang "Come Together", Charles Manson and his "family" showed the dark side...helter skelter...of the peace/love movement. For many Vietnam was a TV show, but for Winston and his fellow draftees it was their world, a very narrow tunnel with but a dim light at the end.

CHAPTER FOUR

You're in the Wolfhounds now, not behind a plow

When he got off the bus he expected to see a mass of wild and ragged creatures, men who would gnaw the meat off a living thing, men who would kill a baby if it cried too loud. Wolfhounds ! Just the name was worth its weight in goose pimples. They were legendary. Their reputation was like a rumor that knew no bounds, and the war stories were endless...no group had killed more gooks than them or paid so dearly. The life span of a second lieutenant was about

two months and if you survived walking point, intact, you were on your way to becoming an old man.

The Wolfhounds thrived on being Wolfhounds...it was the image...the legend that simultaneously could give them courage, and give them hope.

The base camp was multi-company size with a full compliment of artillery and large enough to have a mess hall. There were no barracks, just a few pathetic wooden buildings, which Winston would never see the inside of. They were the war rooms where destinies were brokered, where the game of killing gooks was planned, and the fate of every Wolfhound was entwined. The place was set up within a tight circle of sandbag bunkers connected by sandbag levees with a single entrance and exit which could be rapidly closed with huge circles of concertina (barbed) wire. Outside of this inner circle of command was the main base camp itself, surrounded by a fortress of sandbags, with huge pieces of artillery located between the sandbag bunkers. On the outside were three rows of concertina wire (barbed wire, the first line of protection from a human wave attack.

Inside were lots of scraggly shirtless GI's mostly sitting around smoking or eating the dinner mess, A sergeant, an E-5, approached them with a clipboard in hand, read off a few names, Winston being one of them, and ordered them to

follow him, " My name is Sgt. Glover. Welcome to the third herd of the first platoon of Charlie Company. I'm your squad leader. If you want something to eat you got just enough time before you go on guard duty, so hurry up. The lister bag is over there, you need to fill your canteens now, so hurry up and meet me at the bunker in fifteen minutes." Glover was short, stocky, and muscular, wore a small Errol Flynn type mustache and appeared to be a low-key serious type of guy.

" What about smokes ?" The guy behind Winston popped up.

Glover responded, " There's a pile of SP's behind the mess hall. Just help yourself to whatever cigarettes, candy, and toothpaste you want; although it's been pretty well picked over."

They all moved over to the mess hall, which was merely some tables with a roof over them, where the cooks could ladle out food and advice of equal quality. It was the end of the Salisbury steak, mashed potatoes, and stewed carrots with white bread and butter. Winston didn't appreciate it at the time, but there would be days ahead that he would dream of meals like this.

As he washed down his supper with a tin of grape kool-aid, Winston looked around at his new world. The complexion of the group was the opposite of those who create war: there was a mixture of Hispanics and soul brothers, with a dash of hillbilly, Native American, and urban

white. He felt no kinship with the camaraderie that was apparent throughout the base camp. He was still a stranger in a land a long long way from home.

Glover motioned him to come to the bunker where he had dropped off his gear and weapon, and curtly told him this would be where he would spend the night and have guard duty. He further informed him to be sure and get some sleep because the entire company would be on an eagle flight at 0700 in the morning. It would be Winston's first day in the field, and his first day in the Michelin rubber plantation.

He mumbled "Sure," in his vaguest tone of voice, as if he had a clue what was happening. It was a total out of body experience, he really didn't know what was happening or what was a rubber plantation doing in Vietnam.

He lit a cigarette and entered the dark and musty interior of the bunker, where camouflaged in the shadows was a soul brother quietly mixing a coke and some 45, a Japanese whisky. He looked up at Winston, his eyes the only brightness in this Stygian fortress, and asked, " Hey cherry where you from back in the world ?"

" I'm a New Yorker transplanted to the suburbs of D.C., how 'bout yourself ?"

" Whoa man, you're small townin' me. I'm from the home of the nitty gritty, the capital city...color me from Anacostia."

" Wow, that is close. I'm called Winston,

and you are...?"

" Rufus, and spell me why you're called Winston. You got relations with the Churchills ?
"

" Well man, it's kind of a family name. My grandfather was called Winston."

Winston had a momentary flirting fantasy of having a piano in the bunker, and then poof ! It was gone.

" Don't mean nuthin' here. Winston, you want a hit off this Jap 45 ?"

" Sure."

" Don't mean nuthin'."

One swig was enough for him, he'd had moonshine milder than this devil's brew, " I'm good. The rest is yours."

" Only ti-ti left anyway."

"I hear the Wolfhounds are some really mean dudes."

" Some need a roscoe to get their rocks off. Some really dig it, but most guys same-same you and me. It's not my world, man. My mama never raised me to kill. Can I get a roger on that ?"

" Yeah man, absolutely." Rufus stuck his fist out, introducing him to the Nam handshake, and Winston hit the top of his fist with his, then Rufus hit the top of his fist, ending hitting fists together on the knuckles. A greeting as old as the gladiators.

" Everybody outside ! Un-ass that hooch ! I'm not talking for my health people !" It was Ser-

geant First Class Daniel McAllister, the platoon sergeant. He was a lifer all the way curse the civilians type of guy, a man whose voice would have tremendous reverberations for Winston.

" If he spoke for his health, he'd be Charles Atlas," murmured Rufus, and they went outside and merged with the platoon.

The squad leaders, of which there were three in the first platoon passed out mail as McAllister spoke, "Everyone got any mail that's getting any mail ? Okay. Tomorrow we eagle flight out of here at 0700 hours gentlemen, wake-up is at 0530 and chop-chop at 0600. Don't go anywhere you can't be reached in ten minutes, the second platoon is pulling a bush tonight and might need our help. Okay, keep your shit together gentlemen, we're going to the big bad Michelin rubber plantation tomorrow. You older men know what I'm talking about, you new men watch some of these older men tomorrow. Okay ! Don't get drunk, it'll sure as hell will be hot as hell tomorrow afternoon. Any questions ?" McAllister was a medium height white guy in great shape, whose home was Georgia, but he had just a whisper of a Southern accent, and with his full black mustache reminded Winston of a Neanderthal three musketeer.

Winston thought to himself as he and Rufus retreated to the bunker, "Where could I go and not be ten minutes away ?"

" Since I'm a new man, I guess I can get

away with a question like this...but what's an eagle flight ?"

" Oh man, there's a whole new world out there," and Rufus started to laugh, " an eagle flight is a mission by helicopter. They fly in formation, any where from four to nine of them always fast and low, and drop you off somewhere and then pick you up later somewhere else. The ride is a real trip, it's just the gettin' off that's a real bummer, but the ride home is always a groove, especially if you catch a J in the wind."

" Yeah, I can imagine. I've never flown in a helicopter."

"Look like tadpoles of the sky. Tadpoles in a sea of blue...lookey here Winston, you ever get down with some Mary Jane ?"

Winston's thin face (his whole body was wiry) formed a wry smile, " Why yes, I've been known to touch the evil weed."

" I think I can roll some up, can you dig it ?"

Atop a deserted weapons platoon bunker behind the circle of the main bunker line, Rufus and Winston began emptying tobacco out of some Salems. Rolling paper was non-existent and cigarettes were free to the infantry.

" Did you ever roll up your J's like this back in the world ?"

" No. I always stuck to the Zig-Zag man, but this system isn't too bad. The filter will get the impurities out, and this J has got a lot of

smoke in it."

" Oh my man. I know you will dig it. Salems are number one, menthol marijuana for the first time is a real trip."

" You sure this place is cool. I'm a little nervous...my first day in the field is tomorrow. God, I'd hate to get busted my first night in the Wolfhounds."

" Pretty soon, the smell of Cansa...that's gook for pot will be everywhere. Some nights it really gets out of control, but it don't mean nuthin'. We're cool here and the third herd is all heads. What they goin' to do ? Send us to the Nam ?"

" I can dig it. You married, Rufus ?"

" No man, no queen for me. I'm real short on sugar reports, besides the Nam is a widow maker. I pity the guys that are married with kids. I pity the dudes that passed the ring. I be so single...and, all I want to do is get through this year."

" I'm not married, but the girl of my dreams, my future mate for life is waiting for me. When I return we start a life together. It's what keeps me goin'." Rufus did not respond, Winston continued, changing the subject, " How long you been in country ?"

" About six months, a lifetime man, a whole lifetime. I've seen my share of shit," and Rufus continued taking the empty Salem cigarette tubes and scooping the open end into a pile of grass cupped in his hand, filling it up, tamping

it down, twisting the end, and throwing them into his helmet. " I guess you've heard a lot of stories about the Wolfhounds."

" Enough to fill a good sized anthology of gore."

" Yeah, I was scared when I first got here...I didn't know what it would be like. There's been a lot of boss brothers that have crossed this way...they were tough, they talked big...and they went back to the world in a body bag. Nam don't play pretty, and when your numbers up all you can do is cash in your chips, your room in the Big Hotel is available...and a lot of great Wolfhounds have checked into the Big Hotel. I don't want to scare you Winston, it's been real cool lately, we haven't seen contact in two weeks, but then, oh Lord have mercy...Tet is coming in a few weeks."

" When does it start ?"

" The end of January, and it could be bad shit, but nobody knows...it's the third Tet...it could be nothing."

" Do you think the Peace Talks will come to anything ?"

" Fuck the Peace Talks ! I don't count on nuthin' !" Rufus' voice had a hot razor's edge to it, " or anyone ! I expect the worst, and that's what's happening. When you're an 11Bravo, an infantryman, you learn you be fucked over all day. My morale is so low I'm lookin' at the bottom of my boots. Those Peace Talks will go on forever...we'll be gone by then...one way or the other, but those

fuckin' Peace Talks !!" And Rufus leaned over and poured the words into Winston's ears, " there's not enough dead GIs, man. The Great Society has a quota to meet and not enough young Americans, black or white have checked into the Big Hotel. That's the scene, man. That's what the war is all about." They both pulled deep on their J's, he continued, " the times you have over here, " and Rufus reeled his brain a little, he was beginning to feel the grass,

" you'll never forget 'em, and you can have some good times. It's hard to believe sometimes, but I've had some boss times, party all night on the bunker. Once you get to know the guys, and get tight with them you can have some number one times. It's hard to believe...even harder to tell your people back in the world the shit that goes on...who would believe it ? I've been in this bad Jose for six months and I've seen some shit I'll no way ever forget and I've had some boss times no forgetin' that either. After awhile, you get hip to what's happening. You can make it."

" Rufus, I'm so down I can't imagine digging this place at all. I don't know if I could hate Nam anymore than I do now..."

"...and you ain't seen nuthin' yet. Hold on brother, wait 'til you've been here about three months, Winston. You'll learn to hate the Nam...you don't even know what hate is yet."

" Wow. I've got a thousand days to go...I'd give anything just to set my piano up somewhere

and play, and play, and play.

" I'm hip, man. I get the feeling. I'm a blues singer, and there's beaucoup blues here, but I never sing. I can't get free..."

" This Nam weed is setting me free, but I'm leery about getting stoned too much. I want to be ready for anything and wow, tomorrow is my first day in the field."

" No sweat man. You fly up...you crash down, and the sound of a bullet cracking over your head will snap you out of anything. Believe me, a thousand volts of adrenaline will snap you out of anything, and combat is a trip that's like nuthin' else. I hope I never see another gook again. Goddamn, I don't never want to see contact again !...but live for today, that's all you go by...day by day. Lookey here Winston, there is no tomorrow in the Nam. All you got is todays and yesterdays."

" It already seems like a long time since I was a musician, of sorts..."

" I wish we could jam together, but we're trapped...with time to pay for our freedom. Over here you need to forget everything about the world, 'cause big daddy has got you by the ass. The Army has the power of God over you, and you're not breathing without his say-so."

" Whoa Rufus, that's a heavy trip," and he thought to himself "God help me this is my very first day." He changed the subject, " I guess beaucoup guys blow the evil weed over here ?"

" Got to. It's the only way to see the Nam...to unwind...'though some units have got no heads in it, they follow the drinking gourd...but our platoon is total heads except the sarge, who's straight, and no one drinks except me and Juan, and that's just ti-ti."

" How does Sgt. Glover feel about his squad being potheads ?"

" He's cool, but don't be blowin' no J's outside of base camp."

If the moon were a poet and wrote only in star language, the sky was a beautiful, luscious poem, bright with mystery.

" I wonder what the world is doing tonight ?"

" Lookey here Winston the world don't no way care what you're doin' tonight..."

" I know someone does..."

" Amen to that," and looking up into the endless canopy of stars, he mused, " don't get too lost in the stars. Remember the tally isn't up until there's enough guys buy the farm. The difference between a big war and a little one is the amount of ghosts it produces...the cats that pull the strings want this to be a big one," Rufus exhaled like the Cheshire Cat, " we're be pawns in a cruel game, and dig it, the Army would just as soon see a dead GI as it would a dead gook. A dead GI goes to the glory count, and glory is what the Army digs...lookey here, get the whole scene...the youth are out of tune with the establishment.

34

They want the opposite of what we want, but they are in control and they're doin' what comes natural...they got the power, and they want to hold on, so fuck the little man and draft anyone that might resist...it's all about power, and all legal, and all you can do is pray for the Freedom-bird to some day take you way. I hope one day you're out of this bad Jose forever."

" And you before me...I got one whole entire year."

" You can make it. I got a hurtin' feeling in my soul and I see myself comin' back to the world in a bag...don't mean nuthin'."

" Don't talk like that. I'm too new, you're too short, you'll be sending me candy from the world and I'll be mailing you some cansa."

" I'm goin' to die, Winston. I'm goin' to die...I can just feel it. I know it. It's a number ten horrible feeling. I've seen too many guys go and someday it'll be me. " He shivered.

" What a downer ! I know you're going back to D.C. to sing. You're going to make it. I know you are. Man, don't ever say you're not going home."

" I'm amazed I've lived *this* long...but everyday is a day, and I gotta dig it," he took a final drag and threw the doobie outside the bunker, " I'm sorry, man. I never should've brought you down...sometimes I just can't be stoppin' myself. Let's go back to the bunker, we need to get the 411 on when we have guard duty."

Beneath the eternal infinite sea of stars, always on perpetual galactic guard duty, just another night in Nam, the two souls did the Nam handshake. It was a stoned conversation, with wisps of verisimilitude woven among the passing clouds and idle chatter.

The squad consisted of nine guys including their squad leader, and there were three squads in the platoon, and equal number of platoons in the company. The Wolfhound battalion was comprised of four companies, but for Winston his world would rarely go beyond the company, and tomorrow's little foray would consist of two platoons.

Most of the men slept on top of the bunker, several had hammocks strung up inside, and a few slept on the ground inside. The bunker had all the ambience of a dead elevator with broken doors. It was a cold sepulcher...sometimes a protector, a defense against the forces of death... sometimes a crypt, part of the smorgasbord for the Grim Reaper.

The guys with the most seniority got early guard duty or could sham from it, his was at 2AM, and "Gorgeous" George tapped him on the shoulder, waking him as his head slipped off his towel "pillow" hitting the sandbags, and handed him the watch.

"Just stay awake and keep your eyes open. If you see something wake up the sergeant. Wake

Dylan in one hour. He's the machine gunner," and pointed to this big stocky blonde headed kid drooling on his towel, deep in sleep.

The stars hid behind a dark cloak of clouds and occasionally the sky would explode with distant fire works, accompanied by the echoes of far away artillery. The war in the realm of the Wolfhounds was a 24 hour operation. There was always time to kill gooks.

Winston was nervous...his mind kept telling him he was seeing the NVA creeping through the concertina wire. The shadows in the night were trying to escape from the jungle, the chiaroscuro of dancing forms blending with the vague visibility of the concertina wire were like ghosts trapped within writhing in torment...and then an explosion in the distance colored by tracer rounds mindlessly proliferating erased the palette and a new gray darkness shrouded the jungle perimeter and a new cast of horrors filled his eyes as Winston stared and stared seeing nothing, but imagining everything threatening. He prayed no actual reality would appear. At 3AM, after five minutes of shaking, Dylan came to life, and Winston handed him the watch. He was exhausted, and closing his eyes he felt the adrenaline drain from his body into the sewer of his soul and he oozed into a comatose camaraderie with a dreamless sleep.

Private Wheat, nicknamed "Prince" was the other cherry in the squad. He was fullback

big, and simply emanated strength. His hands and arms could be licensed as lethal weapons, and with the breadth of his shoulders, standing about 6'5" he demanded respect. In Detroit he earned his nickname because of his size and strength, although he felt it was due to his handsome looks. He eschewed fighting and sports, and was nearly righteous religious. His job at the furniture store was a perfect fit. He loved it and planned to make a career working there, plus the taste of money was addictive, and with his childhood sweetheart , they were going to have a future and a family together, when all of a sudden the draft fairy came by and adopted him.

He was six months shy of twenty, and towering over Winston he was trying to wake him.

Winston looked up into Prince's eyes in total ignorance, as in who are you, where am I, and where is the yellow brick road ?

" Hey buddy, it's chow time, reveille, chop-chop," Prince spoke in his customary low voice, " I'm Greg Wheat, but everyone calls me Prince. I'm the other new guy." He couldn't bring himself to call himself a "cherry."

Winston looked at this dude and wondered how they got a uniform to fit him. His shoulders were like Atlas, he must be wearing an XL to the fourth power...the biggest black man he'd ever seen.

"Thanks Prince, God knows I'd sleep 'til

the sun baked me awake."

"I hear ya brother," and as Winston got up they did the Nam handshake, " so you got a name for that face, he politely asked.

" Have I ever," and Winston laughed, " it's an old family name...no relation to Churchill...call me Winston."

Sgt. Glover was issuing orders pretending to sound like an authoritarian lifer, "Gentlemen ! Hit the mess hall and get a quick hot one ! Get your gear together and C-rations for two meals. Dylan, you and Juan are going to need 20,000 rounds so share with everyone, and check in with munitions, they want you to sign for it." He smiled.

"Gorgeous" George interjected, combing his black brylcreemed hair, " They think if you don't sign for it, you're going to steal it." They all laughed.

Glover continued. " Make sure ! Make sure you grunts ! That everybody's weapon is clean, we PZ in one hour, and it's a day at the plantation." Glover didn't fool anybody with his gruffness. He was a draftee, not a lifer, and what set him apart was he liked the rank, the extra money, but he felt the same way as the privates he led. A good ole boy from a small town in Massachusetts he had blue collar roots and blue collar attitudes, except his patriotism didn't jive with his parents. This war was a disaster and he would do his best to make sure the men he

commanded survived. He had been in-country too long to adopt the mythology of winning the war...it was all about getting on the Freedombird and going home.

" Why we need C-rations for two meals, Sarge ? This is supposed to be a day trip, right ?" Juan, the assistant machine gunner, was of Mexican descent and heralded from San Antonio. He was short and wiry with a pencil thin black mustache, and his eyes seem to sink in his face...very beady tiny eyes. He had some peculiar "homemade" prison tattoos, and no one knew too much about him...what kind of work did he do, did he have a wife ? As the assistant machine gunner he would carry 5,000 rounds of ammo, which he draped over himself Pancho Villa style, but only one clip for his M-16, and seven to eight grenades. His nickname was the "frag man" and there never was a firefight that he didn't chuck at least one frag, if not them all. He loved grenades and liked what they could do to gooks, but Juan was a scavenger and sometimes he'd do too much damage and there wouldn't be enough human to find even a watch or a ring. Jewelry and drugs were what he most wanted to find, but the Vietcong and the NVA rarely wore more than a necklace. Once he got lucky and peeled three gold rings off of a severed hand. He laughed when he picked up the hand and joked that he'd just found the whole jewelry store. Besides the frags, there was "Pancho" a Bowie knife that he kept perpetually

sharpened, which he brought from the world. When he was honing the blade he would tell the others how sharp and quick his "Pancho" was, and that his knife was born to carve and many a dude back in Texas would always remember this "Pancho." His true past was a blank, Juan didn't reveal much. He didn't trust anyone.

Glover answered his question, which was obvious, "If the shit hits the fan we might not get out 'til next morning, so bring extra C's."

Meanwhile, Winston and Prince sat down at a picnic table and wolfed down scrambled eggs and slabs of bread and butter, potatoes and gravy and sausage links. It was a feast. They were in the middle of the jungle and if they closed their eyes their taste buds would think they were back in the world.

Prince in his naturally low voice talked to Winston hoping Dylan and Juan sitting nearby wouldn't hear him, " Do you think we'll make contact today ? I'm kind of nervous...I hope I don't see no gooks...I'm about to shit in my pants. I'm so wound up, Lord, I can't wait for this day to end and it hasn't begun yet."

Winston was about to answer when Sgt. Glover sat down next to him, and Rufus across from Prince. Rufus just looked at his food, moved it around with his fork and lit up a cigarette. He didn't feel like eating or talking and stared out into the jungle.

" Winston, you and Greg..."

Winston interjected, " The dude's name is Prince."

" Prince is cool," Glover smiled, " we're not used to royalty out here in the boonies."

Prince's voice was so low you could barely hear him,
" That's what I've always been called."

Glover's eyes took in the expanse of this giant, " Then Prince works for me...anyway, you two guys PZ with me and I want you to stick close to me."

"Remember you're cherries !" Dylan smirked at them from across the table.

" Shut the fuck up Dylan ! Everything will be cool. Just watch the old guys like this asshole across the table from us."

Prince stared at Dylan and putting the tin dented coffee cup in his left hand crushed it like a gum wrapper, then nonchalantly tossed it into the trash can. Juan mumbled something to Dylan about some cherry being a KIA and no one knew his name, and Dylan, the poster boy for the All-American surfer (but until he went into the Army had never left Las Vegas), lightened up a bit, " Hey you guys, we all got one goal, and that's to get back to the world in one piece. Can I get a roger on that ?" And Dylan stuck out his fist and Glover, Winston, Prince, and Juan touched flesh like gladiators. The Nam handshake.

Sgt. Glover finished his breakfast, every-one was leaving the table as if an invisible alarm

clock had gone off. " You guys fill your canteens, get your C's, get all your shit together and I'll see you all on the PZ outside the perimeter in ti-ti time."

Prince and Winston got up and followed orders. Both of them wished they hadn't eaten so much, the butterfly population in their stomachs needed a migration. The choppers would be coming in a few minutes to take them where there was no cocoon, no safety net...where the man of the hour is always the Grim Reaper.

Winston and Prince were glued to the hip. " C'mon brother, can you possibly dig it that we're about meet brother Charlie today ?"

" Maybe not Prince. These guys said they haven't made contact in awhile."

" You're bad jammin' me Winston. Do you know the song "Any Day Now" an oldie from Chuck Jackson ?"

" Of course, but it's not *today. The 'blue shadows aren't falling all over town.'* It's just a song..."

CHAPTER FIVE

An Eagle Flight is not
a flight of eagles

After picking up their C's and filling their canteens they followed the crowd, a meandering group, outside the base camp. Some were joking as if they were going to meet some girls on a date, some wrapped tighter than a mummy, just smoking and walking, while the various squad leaders motioned and yelled for their men to get into position for the arrival of the eagle flight.

Sgt. McAllister was not in a good mood as he yelled at his three squad leaders, " Now you

can clusterfuck ! Glover ! Get your men away from the others and together ! These birds aren't going to wait for you !" His voice was all booming, all righteous, all lifer.

As everyone shuffled in the dust in the early morning hot sun there wasn't a breeze in the air, nor a sound to be heard. They clotted together in groups and waited.

McAllister knew they were coming before anyone, and he had the habit of checking out the safety on his M-16 and perversely switching it on and off then rubbing the barrel like a pet dog.

Winston lit up another smoke and Prince kind of shuffled and stared around...they were coming...for even the pretentiously laid back the adrenalin began to pump...the joking ended...the talking was over...they were coming...and the sound before sight petrified Winston and Prince and solidified everyone else. The roar and magnificence of nine helicopters surfacing out of nowhere literally exploding above the treetops was a photograph that belonged in the trauma section of one's mental scrapbook. They were just skimming the surface of the treetops full throttle before terrorizing the dust laden PZ as the horrible sound and fury began its dervish descent. The bellies of these giant metallic tadpoles with wings were canted at a slight angle as they descended spraying a blinding dust in which the GIs had to cover their faces with their towels. When they saw where each Huey was going to

land each cluster separated so they could board from both sides, six to seven to a copter.

The sound of an eagle flight as they hovered above the ground, never quite touching, was deafening; the air was blinding, their senses were numb as two platoons of Wolfhounds in perfect synchrony flopped into the copters, feet dangling over the edge immediately in the trance of the magic carpet ride. In seconds it went from all numbness and pain...to "Disneyland."

The breeze was cooling, the feeling of flight was exhilarating...flying in a stripped down chopper...no walls, no windows, no seats, was like riding a motorcycle in the sky with no helmet. No military group in history prided themselves as being as wild and crazy as the helicopter pilots of Nam. It was always how fast, and how low you could fly without crashing. Normal humans would experience a heart attack doing the same thing. But it went beyond how fast and how low...what made it spooky was how close together they could fly...the ultimate factor...while they were nipping the treetops going at full tilt boogie. Winston could not believe how close by the Hueys were on both sides of him. It seemed like these eggbeaters were auditioning to turn Wolfhounds into coleslaw.

The scenery looked like Prehistoric times, there was not a sign of civilization anywhere...everything was jungle, fields, and small rivers...not a man-made structure as far as the eye

could see...but what distinguished this pristine scene from the Paleozoic era was the landscape looked like it had been bombarded by monsters from Mars. The fields and forests were filled with bomb craters from B-52 strikes. Some had filled with water, and some imitated the acne of the Moon, and parts of the jungle looked like a punishing hand had crushed or maimed it. Only the insects were spared the killing reach of the military, but that too would soon end as in the South they were dumping Agent Orange, an untested poison more powerful than any minefield, where ever horticulture seemed a threat, which was everywhere. It was then just a brutal way to eradicate the environment, for its future danger was unknown.

Winston looked at Prince, who returned a weak flaccid smile. Rufus was completely lost in himself, and Dylan and Juan were trying to light cigarettes in the intense wind of the open sky. The sarge was playing with his map trying to guess where they were going...all they knew was they were going to the Michelin rubber plantation. "Gorgeous" George waved at him, he was holding his helmet in his lap, letting the cooling breeze run through his brylcreemed hair. He was totally enjoying the ride. He was always into himself.

Unfortunately the flight of freedom and fancy was about to come to a conclusion, the eagle flight began separating and descending,

the two machine gunners on each side made sure their string of ammo was in order and clamped in securely. In a few moments they would enter the Michelin rubber plantation.

Meanwhile, back in the world, the Peace Talks were being postponed due to a debate over the size of the table. There would be no peace until an agreement about table size had been made. It was Paris in Winter, not as festive as Spring, but still the "City of lights." There were a lot worse places to hold a meeting. The reality of both Americans and Vietnamese being maimed and killed on an hourly basis was not as important as deciding rapidly on the size of the table, and in a true *tres noir* sense, Fashion could be the Fifth Horseman of the Apocalypse. The snow was like lace on the Champs Elysees...what's an arm or a leg here or there...dinner at Tour D'Argent...champagne and pressed duck and a view of Notre Dame...all in a days work...and some soul empowered by a bullet was making its way to his special room in the Big Hotel...but the debate would continue...even in January some of the shops had their Christmas decorations up and they looked elegant...there was plenty to do.

Sgt. Glover yelled over the din of the helicopter blades to Winston and Prince, " It's not going to land, you have to jump ! When you hit the dirt hit the ground !" He tapped the side of his helmet as a sign they got the message. Neither one heard a word or understood the sign, but caught on quickly as Glover shoved the two of them out of the copter at an altitude of three feet. They hit the ground like professionals and aimed their weapons at...somewhere...at trees...at the perimeter. The awful crush of the song of the helicopter was replaced by the other fearful sound...total silence. The eagle flight had evaporated and was throttling over the jungle and as the whirr diminished, voices surfaced as it appeared the coast was clear. You never knew until the moment you landed whether it was a hot LZ (landing zone) or not. This was cool.

Everyone was quiet, no one moved until Sgt. McAllister stood up. He was the go ahead man, and after looking around, confidently ordered his sergeants to direct their men to the perimeter. " And be quick about it !"

There actually was a lieutenant (per platoon) theoretically in charge at the other end of the field, attached like an umbilical cord to his RTO (radio telephone operator)who needed to know where this mission was going...the Michelin rubber plantation was huge...there was more than one secret village among the rubber trees,

not to mention the underground camps that were like small cities. The NVA were genius at survival.

The two platoons fanned out in a line and racing to the perimeter, each squad leader prodded his men along in the tersest of military dialect. There was a small ravine separating the field from the plantation and the word came down that they would be there awhile, perhaps the ambush site for the day.

Winston, Prince, and Rufus laid across the top of the ravine and looked out towards the field, which was nothing but a sea of grayish green grass.

Glover looked down the row at them, " Just because we didn't get shot at when we landed doesn't mean Charlie ain't out there waitin' for just the right moment..."

" Just a veritable fuckin' snake in the grass..."

" Roger that Rufus, and one of you has to be all eyes on that picture out there. Work it like guard duty, this could very well be home for the day."

Rufus shuffled into the ravine, " I can dig it, this is a number one spot." They could feel him mellowing out.

" Rufus, why you dig this spot ? Where's the cool here, my man ?" Prince looked him in the eyes as if he were a prosecuting attorney.

" Yeah man, what makes this number

one ?"

Winston and Prince were both sweating like fevers in the summertime...they were watching the field intensely and feeling real nervous. The grass was so thick and so high that if there was anyone within ten feet they wouldn't know it...not until the first shot was fired.

" Jump with this gentlemen," he cleared his throat very softly, " cherries ! Rule number one is the less you move around the greater your chances for survival are. Stayin' in the same place, any place, is always better than bein' on the move, and I doubt there's any gooks out there in the field. We'd be fuckin' with them already if they were that close..."

" Man, aren't you nervous the little man is goin' to smell the smoke ?" Prince never looked away from watching the field, which was a perfect still life, not even a breeze altered the picture.

" Prince, if you wanted to make a scene, and like wanted everyone you knew was comin' to town, could you name one thing louder or more outrageous than a bunch of helicopters ? Dude, the gooks know we're here, they're waitin' for us to make the next move." Rufus exhaled mightily into the air, sending a cloud like a short-lived balloon into the Michelin. Prince and Winston continued the stare into the green void imagining things moving.

Prince responded, " When I want the

people to know I'm comin' to town, I order a parade."

Winston laughed, "Back at you Rufus !"

Before Rufus could reply, the sarge was coming towards them looking like an apostle of death, " The Lieutenant Just gave the order, we're movin' out to Village 13. The second platoon think they spotted some NVA moving around. Saddle up !"

" Shit. I knew it was too good to be true !" Rufus stepped outside the ravine, turning his back to Winston and Prince and took a leak, tossing the cigarette into the stream.

Winston could feel the adrenaline pumping through his veins. What next ? He felt like the new kid in school and it was his first day and he didn't know where the next classroom was. " So what's Village 13 ?"

In a somber voice, Rufus explained, " Once upon a time it was a normal village when the Michelin was a thriving plantation and the peasants probably spent all day suckin' rubber out of the trees for the French, but it's been deserted for a long time now. It's always been a free fire zone as long as I can remember. You see a gook, you shoot a gook. Mostly it's a stopping off place for the NVA as they're making their way south. There've been a lot of firefights at Village 13, a lot of good dudes have checked into the Big Hotel from that place."

" Let's move gentlemen !" The rough voice

of Sgt. McAllister set them in motion, with the third herd taking up the rear as the entire platoon single filed into the rubber plantation. Lt. Osgood and his RTO were strategically located in the middle of the pack, McAllister was about the fifth man from the front. He liked to be near the front to call the action. The other platoon was parallel about twenty feet from them.

"Winston," Glover barked, " you pick up the rear, then you Rufus. You keep an eye over your shoulder towards the front, but your ass is marchin' backward. You can take your weapon off safety, and if you see anything just hit the dirt. If you see anyone wearing black pajamas shoot first and ask questions later. Dig ?"

Winston nodded his head. No one was talking. The price of being a cherry was if you weren't walking point, you got rear security.

The Michelin plantation was gigantic. There were rows of trees all perfectly symmetrically lined up for as far as the eye could see. Interstices among the trees was a network of small dirt roads once used to transport the raw latex, now a conduit for death under the aegis of the highway department of the Four Horsemen of the Apocalypse. Of the thousands of trees, all identical in size, not one had escaped being scarred from the war. Every tree had either been shot or mutilated by artillery, their broken limbs oozing a white goo. The place was a maze of broken branches making it slow going, but it was

easy to visualize this was once a pristine productive plantation.

After an hour plodding through the
brush, McAllister motioned back to the Lieutenant it was time to break for chow. Everyone
squatted down facing in various positions so
that all flanks were covered, while the ubiquitous
P-38, the tiniest weapon in the Army's arsenal,
was brought out by one and all as they opened
their C-ration of meatballs, scrambled eggs and
ham, beef stew, or whatever canned cuisine that
each was humping. Rufus popped the back of
his Claymore mine, which was about the size of
an average purse, and peeled out a couple wads
of C-4, threw one to Dylan and rolled the other
into a ball and lit it. This tiny bit put out a tremendous amount of heat with a brightness like a
welder's torch, and in less than a minute, Rufus'
can of meatballs was boiling.

" Juan, toss me your bottle of hot sauce."

" Sure bro, anything for you." It was extremely difficult to discern whether Juan was
joking or serious.

Prince looked at Winston in amazement,
but didn't want to say a thing. He was afraid of
looking stupid.

Winston, on the other hand, felt he knew
Rufus and didn't care what he said anyway, " So
Rufus, what happens when you have to blow that
Claymore up ?"

" Don't mean nuthin'. Don't mean a fuckin'

thing. I'd say it won't do too much, 'cept I'd have to eat my chow cold," and he laughed, " there was this one unit they set up their claymores all around the perimeter. It was some kind of night ambush, and sure as shit, the gooks showed up and when they detonate them, they were as useless as fireworks. It seemed everyone had been cookin' with C-4 but I guess the smoke scared the gooks off as they di-di maued out of the territory and no GIs got hurt. "

Dylan threw in his two bits, " All a fuckin' Claymore is good for in my opinion is for cookin'. Half the time they don't go off, and the other time the back blast, if they're not buried right will blow your head off."

CHAPTER SIX

Village Thirteen

The field where they landed was now out of vision and being in the Michelin was like being in the middle of the ocean, everywhere you looked the view was the same, and after awhile your sense of direction becomes obliterated. Horizontal vertigo.

Winston and Prince were both nearly out of water. It was a hundred degrees and equally as humid, and both were working overtime fanatically searching the cloned forest for signs of life. They were completely caught in the game...look-

ing for the invisible soldier who was preying on the unknown soldier. It was the dead hot center of the afternoon, not a leaf was stirring, and the only sound was the quiet roar of mosquitoes, when they came in sight of Village 13. It was a shamble of beaten down shacks. No one had cared for this place anymore, by default it was the transitory home of killers, and it had been many years since this village heard the voice of a child.

By reputation it was the halfway house for Hades, but it was no more than a dozen shabby shacks bordering on a single road. It was quiet, austere...reeked of mystery and intrigue, and emanated a peculiar unique odor.

There was a ghostly allure to the place. It was *so* quiet in the middle of nowhere, and then the shots cracked over their heads, but there was nothing to see, no signs of smoke, no sense of direction of where the bullets were coming from...but shit was happening...McAllister was yelling at the squad leaders to get their men to crawl up in line facing the Village. No one fired in the first platoon, everyone was crawling getting into position for an enemy they couldn't see...McAllister yelled for the machine-gunners to watch the flanks...the Lieutenant was on the horn reporting.

The cracklings sounds of AK-47's, erupting in fits and starts seemed much more distant now. Winston looked at Prince. They both were

polarized. They should be watching the rear, but they were like moths at a candle with nothing to see in the entrancement...the Village hadn't moved a bit, there wasn't so much as a puff of smoke anywhere. The war was getting closer, but it was still as if it was on television.

Sgt. Glover turned to Winston and Prince, and snarled," You two ! Watch the rear ! That's your duty!"

Their blood was coursing with adrenalin, as they simultaneously pivoted around on their stomachs, their M-16's ready for action, as once again they stared into the static nothingness. Once all became situated and focused, McAllister yelled down the line to move forward and stay low. Crawl like a snake. For the two on rear security it was impossible to crawl backwards.

The platoon seemed to moving quickly slithering around the trees and through the broken limbs...there was another crackling of gunfire...this time much farther away, but the platoon froze to the ground.

Sgt. Glover whispered to his squad, " No one fires. The second platoon is sweeping on the other side of the Village...the word is there's a sniper in the area, but no one can find him...everybody keep moving." And the crawling continued, " Winston ! Get up here and walk point !"

Winston looked at Prince with eyes of desperate disbelief and not saying a word started

crawling towards the front. As Winston got ahead of everyone Sgt. Glover whispered to him, " You can walk now, but keep a low profile, and watch for the point in the second squad. Keep eye contact."

The squads would enter in two files, they were soaked in sweat, and Winston was frantic trying to keep an eye on the other point man, and look to the immediate future at the same time.

When they got to the perimeter of the Village they took a break and emptied canteens like a chug-a-lug. Village 13 was never checked out by a platoon sized unit, that was exposing the group too much. It was always a squad that was sent in to check out each hut and make positive no NVA were hiding inside. Trapped animals have a way of being fierce.

Glover looked imploringly at Sgt. McAllister, " Isn't it the second squad's turn to check out the Village ?"

McAllister's voice was cold and military-like, " Tell your men they can chamber a round, but make sure they know where they are." The fear of friendly fire was always there. " the second platoon is far from here chasin' down a sniper. Get moving Sergeant."

"Winston ," Glover addressed the entire squad, " you and this here Prince are both going to be checking out the hooches, on both sides of the road. Everyone keep a round chambered, but look before you shoot and be ready. Don't cluster-

fuck !"

Winston and Prince felt like targets in a carnival game as they cautiously walked to the rows of dilapidated huts. It looked like no one had lived there in twenty years, as they paused at the entrance to the hooches.

Glover could practically read their minds, " You have to get down on one knee, stick your weapon inside and look around. If anything moves, pull the trigger."

"Gorgeous" George was right behind Winston, " Be cool and get a good look around. If Charlie is in there you gotta get low real quick." He could afford to be aloof, it wasn't him poking his head in there. Winston scowled at him as he approached the entrance to the hooch, crept down on one knee and stuck the barrel of the rifle in the doorway. The stench was an aroma he would never forget. It was partly human, partly animal, and had been ripening for a long time...a raucous bite to the senses. They both looked deep into the huts...not a shadow moved, but there were archeological remnants: empty cans, broken straps, and miscellaneous unrecognizable trash.

Rufus, who was wound as tight as piano wire whispered to Prince, " Get beyond the funk brother, that smell will make burnin' shit seem like barbecue...and stay low, man. Charlie like da dark meat."

Prince played it cool, looked hard inside

the hooch, gagged on the smell, his finger on the trigger, then moved to the next hooch. The rest of the squad were poised to act if anything moved out of the ordinary, or Prince or Winston reacted to something, anything.

" Don't clusterfuck gentlemen...move slow..." Sgt. Glover was all eyes everywhere.

" Got my frags ready, Sarge. Love to blow one of these motherfuckin' hooches back to fuckin' Hell." Juan was at his usual, more than willing to destroy anything.

" Put a zipper on it, Juan. You don't do anything 'til the little man starts talkin'." Sgt. Glover's voice was as soft as back stage at the opera...but firm.

" Don't get sloppy my man," "Gorgeous" was like white on rice with Winston, who was now checking out his third hooch, " if Charlie is inside and he thinks he's trapped it don't mean nuthin' for the fuckin' bastard to suicide you."

Winston looked back at him in an angry turmoil, "What do I do ?"

"Gorgeous" looked at him with a stupid grin, " Stay lucky." He had his moments where he was on the precipice of being easy going.

Just as he and Prince were about to move forward Sgt. Glover barked out a terse order, " It's a halt gentlemen ! The mission is over, we're goin' back. Winston ! You and Prince are now rear security, we're heading back to the PZ. Let's move !"

Prince and Winston looked at each other

in befuddlement. The sweep through Village 13 wasn't half complete, who knows who could be hiding inside those hooches ? The painful confusion was exasperating, but this was only the beginning...this was day one.

The squad rapidly regrouped with the platoon and this time made their way standing up instead of crawling, as if the circumstances were totally different, and meandered through the maze of the Michelin more like hikers returning from camp, then soldiers whose mission was to create gravesites.

The platoon moved at a jogger's pace, no matter the broken bramble they had to overcome and what seemed like no time at all were back at the ravine by the field waiting for the copters.

" Just ti-ti time Winston, the eagle flight will be takin' us back to the land of Coca-Cola."

" Rufus, we heard shots, we're checkin' out the Village, and before it's all over they pull us out ! It doesn't make sense ! Why the fuck would they stop us when there were more hooches to check out ?"

" Winston, my man, welcome to this man's Army. Makin' sense is like makin' babies...there is no sense, it just happens. Today was a good day, the Village rang no bells today, brother, and believe me plenty of GIs have checked into Village 13 and never left walkin'. We were lucky today."

It was simply his very first day in the

field...the long road to the Freedombird was paved with the nebulous weight of eternity.

In moments, those tornadoes of dust were above the tree line and descending upon them. In moments, on the magic carpet ride the swirling air cooling their bodies was like instant amnesia, in a few moments it could seem like the mission never occurred. The eagle flight was like a womb, as long as you didn't get out, nothing could happen to you.

This base camp was large enough to have a water truck, which meant one could take a shower and get clean fatigues. Most camps got clean clothes air lifted in once a week.

" C'mon Prince, let's hit the showers, and I'll buy you a coke." He laughed. There was an ebullient atmosphere in the camp, but before everyone went off to get high, get clean, or both, Sgt. Glover informed them tomorrow would be a three day jaunt in the shadow of the Black Virgin Mountain, north of the Michelin in an area mostly jungle, and it would be a company sized ambush.

After a shower and scrounging through a mountain of cleaned clothes (he pitied Prince, it would take him awhile), he sat down and wrote a quick letter to Mom & Dad, and a longer, but more obtuse letter to Veronica. He was not going to scare her or cause worry, so everything was going to be watered down "...it was a beautiful day seeing an abandoned village in an old rubber

plantation, etc....".

Hearing the sound of gunfire for the first time gave him the sense the war was getting closer, but it didn't seem quite real, and he was too naive to know the Grim Reaper was sucking him into his world, one intoxicated with death, which Winston was about to enter...heart, body, and soul...willing or not...the only game in town.

Meanwhile, back in the world, Lyndon B. Johnson remarked upon leaving office that his biggest disappointment was his failure to achieve peace in Vietnam. The North Vietnamese, the South Vietnamese, and the National Liberation Front finally agreed upon the shape of the table at the Peace Talks, and promptly rejected the American proposal to restore neutrality to the De-Militarized Zone. It was as if school children petitioned the flu virus not to come to their school.

The Viet Cong were launching extensive mortar attacks on South Vietnamese cities with the horrible consequence of a huge number of civilian casualties.

These were good times for the Grim Reaper, who was flying high. The last bridge between Jordan and Israel was destroyed in a duel of gunfire, Sirhan Sirhan was going to trial for

the assassination of Robert Kennedy, Boris Karloff stopped going to the movies, and the Saturday Evening Post was writing its epitaph after a hundred years. As Bob Dylan was saying "The times, they are a changing..."

CHAPTER SEVEN

Veronica's War Begins

"Veronica dear. Guess who's coming home this weekend ?"

Veronica was in her room, and did not respond. It was her mother.

" Chuckie is home from college, and his mother has invited us over. It might be fun..."

" I'll think about it...I have studies..." she would rather be nibbled by ducks than have to spend an evening with Chuckie, a boring boy from her high school days who always wanted to be her "friend". The kind of person who believed

they would be better "friends" if she wouldn't mind disrobing.

" It's the week-end," her mother persisted, yelling from the downstairs living room, " you know he always had a soft spot for you..."

Veronica thought to herself, " I'll say he has a soft spot...in his brain." It was only a few weeks since Winston left and already her mother was playing matchmaker. She knew her mother didn't care much for Winston, but to start the war this early, with a year to go. It foretold of battles yet to come as Veronica knew her mother was not going to give up. " Mother, tell good ole Chuckie hello for me and that I'm having female problems. I'm sure he'll understand." She laughed to herself.

"Never mind." Round one was over, her mother retreated to the kitchen. She was not surprised at Veronica's response. There was plenty of time left.

Veronica looked in the mirror. She was the reflection of Venus with long brunette silky hair, big blue eyes that were hypnotically enchanting, perfect complexion, and high cheekbones like a queen, and with bee sting lips, and the figure of a goddess. She never had a problem with men, or at least no shortage of suitors. Winston was her perfect match...tall, handsome, a swimmers body...but it was his sense of humor that won her heart. Although it was love at first sight...some-

times that feeling was camouflage for a moment-ary infatuation, but this was pure serendipity. She knew she had met her soul mate. He could always make her laugh, but gazing at her reflection she didn't feel beautiful nor feel like laughing.

Ohio was a territory of small towns. Even the cities seemed like overgrown small towns. Although they seemed homogenous in character, each town had its own personality, and Veronica (until college) had spent her entire life within the idyllic environs of Masonville. Her father was the town vet, so it was a home of pets of all kinds, and as an only child, a surplus of pets was more than fun...it was being immersed in a fur lined cauldron of unconditional love. The drawback was that humans don't offer unconditional love, and Veronica evolved into an animal person and away from being a people person as she progressed through elementary school and into high school. She was too beautiful to be allowed to be a hermit, and to counter her journey to isolation she decided a career in nursing would save her as hopefully she could save others.

In high school she dropped out of the cheer-leading squad. She really didn't care who won at any game, and she wasn't looking to date the star quarterback. The older she got the more determined she became to say farewell to Masonville, and college was her only exit to a new life. Most of her classmates would stay and clone their parents lives, but Veronica was ready and eager to

cut the umbilical cord...unfortunately, there was a glitch. They couldn't afford the school in California she desired to attend, and ended up going to a small liberal arts college just an hour away, and worst of all commuting from home. She knew meeting Winston was destiny. Why would someone with a cosmopolitan background go to a small school located near the parking lot of absolute nowhere?

As nursing school had just begun there was always some book to study, but tonight she would begin her project, or at least make the necessary plans. She was going to make a private scrapbook with Polaroids they had taken of themselves and various events, with private text from her diary.

The first thing was to buy a scrapbook with a key lock and then call Winston's mother to get photos from his room. Fortunately they got along beautifully. She already thought of Veronica as her daughter-in-law. She would need a project beside school and interning at the hospital. Other than her cadre of girlfriends she wasn't planning on a social life, no matter her mother's determination.

The next day should she would have lunch with her future mother-in-law and get the necessary supplies to begin her year long project. They both tried to keep the conversation to nursing school and general idle chatter, but the war was everywhere and un-avoidable. The common

thread they shared...their worry for Winston, was truly a hopeless exercise, but it did bond them together, and therein lay the value.

Locking the door to her bedroom to avoid another intrusion from her mother Veronica pulled out a series of Polaroids when they surreptitiously rendezvoused at the beach last Summer. They both came with a couple friends, and beer, bathing suits, and a bonfire was the perfect trifecta for an evening of passionate romance. They looked like the king and queen of Summer, perfectly buff, young and vibrant, and Edith had captured the precise moment when they were looking into each other's eyes, and the entire galaxy had shrunk into their own private world.

Veronica laughed to herself looking at the volleyball pictures. The boys were more concerned with bouncing boobs, than winning. Sometimes the beach can be a category 5 of a hormone hurricane. Great memories. The scrapbook would be great therapy. The photos where she and Edith and Elizabeth face painted Winston and his cohorts were ridiculous and hysterical. Winston, looking like a transvestite clown had to dive into the surf to avoid scaring young children. Some day she'll look back, and remember those were the good ole days of Summer, an idyllic page in the memory book. While daydreaming, looking at the beach pics, Veronica; in the back of her mind wondered who would be the next victim her mother, Cupid's middleman,

would bring for her to meet. The war with her mother was just beginning.

Tonight she would lay in bed with Louise, her Irish Setter, her devoted friend, and compose a letter to Winston. He would refer to this as a "sugar report."

CHAPTER EIGHT

The World Shrinks

" Hey man, how 'bout that Coke ?" Prince's words, like a genie escaping from his lamp, awoke Winston from his letter writing trance.

" We're the only cherries in this squad, so what did you think ?"

Prince looked at him with the sad eyes of a collie, " I was scared to death. When I heard those shots I didn't know what to do, and I didn't know if that bullet had my dog tag on it."

Prince, I don't think we were alone out there. The only difference between us and the

rest of the squad is they've been in the movie longer. I think they were scared too but in a different way."

Prince looked down at the ground, "I don't think so, man. Those dudes knew what to do. I was waitin' for the little man to pop out of one of those hooches and blow my shit away. Are we called cherries because we're on top of the sundae ? First to get eaten. We're the sacrificial lambs, straight from the Bible, and I amen to that !"

" Amen, brother."

"Winston, tomorrow is a three day trip to the boonies. I betcha we see some action this time. I'm nervous...maybe I shouldn't tell you this, but I'm too big..." he laughed, " I'm too pretty to walk point."

" If it's one thing you don't have to worry about here, it's winning any beauty contest. Besides, eventually new guys will come in and they'll be toting their M-16's with the safety off, and we'll probably get lucky," he laughed,
" and carry the machine-gun."

Overhead a Chinook was beginning its descent bringing a hot meal, supplies, and returning shammers from the division base camp.The rain of dust totally nullified their showers, coating their skin in a bath of fine talc dust. Dylan and Juan were cleaning their weapons and used their towels to protect them from the killing dust. Bad timing, they would have to

re-clean their weapons. Sometimes, a speck of dirt, especially with the M-16, could paralyze it.

Prince went atop the third herd bunker and began his letter writing, while Winston had no problem locating Rufus, inside the "head" bunker rolling J's. When he walked in he scared Rufus into throwing the pot in his hand on the floor, " Brother, say something before you come in, how am I to be knowin' you're not Top or McAllister ?"

" Okay man, sorry to put a daze on you."

" Those kind of surprises can make you dinky-dau. Beaucoup dinky-dau." Rufus was laughing.

In the dank and darkness of the inner sanctum of this bunker, where some corners never see light, Winston could make out another soldier next to Rufus. " So who are you ?" Directing his query to a shadow.

" I'm Blackie Payne," and he moved his face forward into the light where Winston could discern an old man's aged features on the face of a young man. Blackie wore thick glasses, had jet black hair long enough to comb (which had nothing to do with his name), and he was *so* thin. The shadows of the bunker accentuated this reality, that only a skull would reveal more skeleton, his cheeks were so sunken.

" Blackie here is one number one dude, from Chicago,'though he don't talk much...and I believe your ass is a two-digit midget."

Blackie dropped his chin down, as if he was talking to the ground, " I got 56 more days in this bad Jose."

" You are flying with the big bird now my man. Whoa, 56 days until the Freedombird takes you back to the world ! I wish I could trade dog tags with you, brother." Rufus couldn't look him in the eye.

"Keep cool man, your day is comin'...how much time you got left ?" Blackie had a very low voice, Winston had to strain to hear him, " I thought you got about four months to go."

" Lookey here my man, my mathematics says I got six more months of Hell..." but my calendar says I got nuthin' to worry 'bout..." he looked wistfully out the small bunker window and blew smoke rings through the hole.

" After you're gone, I'll still have six more months in the field. Be cool ! After all, I'm the cherry here !" He sat down across from the two of them, " So Blackie, how many eagle flights have you been on ? Today was my first and riding in the sky was wonderful. I loved it." Winston grinned at him like a child does talking to his father.

In his perpetual monotone Blackie responded, " Over a hundred."

" Winston felt a little numb, " So do you like them, or hate them ?"

" If I had to make a choice ..." he dragged the words out slowly and quietly, "...I always

hated getting off more than I hated getting on, especially when it was a hot LZ."

Winston's brain curdled at the thought of being fired on getting off a copter. It was something one could imagine all too easily, but it was a distant dimension apart from his reality.

Rufus was diffusing Blackie, " Lookey here my fellow Wolfhounds ! Let's get back to the nitty gritty..." he opened up an envelope, " you guys want to send some ants back to the world ?"

Winston laughed, " Do I want to send some ants home ? Not even."

Rufus continued his stoned dissertation on ants and why someone would be interested in getting a letter filled with them, until they heard the words..."Un-ass that hooch !" It was Dylan doing his imitation of Sgt. McAllister, laughing as the three bolted out of the "head" bunker, "hey you guys, it's chow time."

" I hate surprises." And Rufus crushed his J in the dirt.

Mess was cuisine straight from the world...fried chicken, mashed potatoes, corn-on-the-cob, biscuits, cake for dessert and all the cartons of cold milk one could inhale. A great meal was uplifting, for Winston it was still routine, and if the fried chicken was a little on the greasy side, it was okay with the Wolfhounds, it absolutely surpassed C-rations. After dinner each soldier picked up extra C's, ammo, and canteens, then scrounged through the SP pile for smokes

and candy. Each Wolfhound had a preference where to crash for the night, inside, outside, top-side of the bunker, so you always knew where to wake the next guy up for guard duty.

The night air was cooling, breezy, still fraught with mosquitoes, but as darkness like a leaden blanket began to tuck them in Sgt. Glover set up guard duty, nagging each one to know where the person ahead was crashed. He hated being awakened because some moron couldn't find the next guy due for guard because it was too dark. A moonless, starless night was like operating inside a closet .

The heads of the third herd gathered on the top of the bunker as Rufus took off his helmet and unveiled his treasure of J's. The wind would tell the gooks what they were smoking, not the officers; though they to a man could care less... what are they goin' to do ? Send them to Nam ? Dylan was already feeling stupid, laughing about something private between himself and Juan. Perhaps it was because he was *his* assistant machine gunner, Dylan was one of the few guys who got along with Juan. At night Juan took out his knife, which was both his companion and therapist. "Pancho" liked to carve, and recently, oddly enough he was whittling a wooden knife. Blackie, "Gorgeous," Prince, and Winston filled out the circle.

Rufus tossed a J to Winston and Prince, " C'mon in out of the cold."

Prince tossed it back to him, " No thanks man, that's not my thing." Rufus nodded assent...it was cool.

Dylan, who was wearing a grin the Cheshire Cat on helium would envy, popped in, " So man, I hope you're not a drinker, 'cause this is a head platoon. No booze freaks."

" I don't drink, smoke, or take the Lord's name in vain." Prince was as somber as a pastor in a pulpit.

" That means you can still say fuck, right ?" Juan could be terse and crude at the same time, and Dylan laughed.

" Prince, I think you're the smartest dude here, but...I can't believe it but I'm going to get stoned tonight, even though there's a big mission tomorrow." Winston felt lost at sea.

" Well brother, this will be the last time for days," "Gorgeous" spoke up, " can I get an amen on that ?"

" Roger that !" And Blackie stuck his fist out to do the Nam handshake, and simultaneously Rufus added, " It don't mean nuthin'."

" So what should we expect tomorrow ?" Winston posed the question to no one in particular, I hear those jungles are the routes the NVA travel."

" Since they don't have wings," "Gorgeous" looked at him like an idiot, " they take the thickest jungle to hide in. There are entire hospitals and base camps beneath the ground...been there

a long time, and every now and then some lucky GI gets lucky and steps into one...like goin' to Hell." "Gorgeous" talked as if he was looking into a mirror and the mirror could reply. He should've had a tattoo he could look at "Vanity I am thy servant "but he probably wouldn't have got it.

" And don't forget those booby traps with them bungee sticks. That bamboo is sharp enough to go right through jungle boots." Dylan smiled and Juan whittled.

" Love to see some of those bungee sticks, they must be beaucoup sharp." He artfully peeled a thin strip of wood honing his wooden knife.

" You crazy, Juan !" And Dylan nudged him nearly disturbing his carving. Anyone else but Dylan would've got a free tattoo, courtesy of "Pancho."

" You never know," "Gorgeous" was dusting off his clothes as if readying for the prom, " being in the shadow of the Black Virgin Mountain has been bad luck, but...it could be three days just campin' out, or three days of Hell. We'll find out tomorrow."

Blackie left the group and laid down on the sandbags in a corner of the bunker top, wrapping his head in his towel to repel the mosquitoes, put his head down on his helmet like a pillow, and was asleep in moments.

" Rufus, where are you going to crash ?" Winston lit up a straight, " I got first guard duty, you're next."

" Don't mean nuthin', I'll stay up with your bad self. I'm not ready to crash yet."

"Gorgeous" motioned to Rufus where he'd be, and each in succession let the man before them know where they'd be.

" Rufus, I'm so glad I've got first guard, I'm too tired to get to sleep, not like those other guys...I'm nervous about tomorrow. I'm thinking it's going to change the dial for me, it seems pretty intense. God, I hope we don't make contact, but I guess I'm dancing to that different drummer now, whether I like it or not."

" You're going to be fine...cool. There's no tellin' when we goin' to make contact, but this area tomorrow is a bad Jose. It's the kind of jungle the gooks grew up in, and we, lookey here, are like babes in the woods. But this mission is an ambush, and that's a whole lot better than search and destroy...or walk 'til you die. A three day bush can rattle your nerves, but if we don't see nuthin', everything is cool. Can I get a roger on that ?"

They did the Nam handshake. Winston stared out at the perimeter through the concertina wire, and as clouds crossed the moon and the stars they made shadows jump across the monolithic darkness of the edge of the jungle. It was like the ghosts had come out to play. Eerie. The more you stared, the more you saw things move, " The name Black Virgin Mountain sounds ominous, where'd it get its name ?"

" Centuries ago, or so I been told, some young girl was sacrificed to the gods, or "whatever" the man might have wanted to call himself and the mountain went "black" with rage and exploded upon the people, and no sacrifice was ever made again, but the mountain is forever fixed in the people's minds that it's a place not to be messed with. You know, you don't cross the gods, but the man from the North knows it's the perfect hideout for everything. It's hard to imagine they are all the same people, but the gooks from the North love to kill and they got the power of determination on their side."

" Just like the Irish, they look the same, talk the same, eat the same food...the whole bit, but throw religion into the mix and they're at each other's throats...but hey ! Back in the world a whole lot of people are getting real fed up with the war, the protest movement is getting bigger all the time."

" Too bad it don't mean nuthin'. It's going to be too late for us Winston. You'll be back in the world and they'll still be protesting. It's like the fuckin' Peace Talks !"

" But you got to have hope. You got six more months, Prince and I have a year. Beaucoup time. I got to believe something will happen, maybe Nixon will try and end the war. Who knows ? After all, he's a new President, it would look good on his record."

" Unfortunately I got some really bad

news about Santa Claus. He bought a frag somewhere over Hanoi and he isn't comin' back...the
war isn't over until enough GIs have checked into
the Big Hotel. It's just that simple."

" I am the kind of guy who always needs
the carrot at the end of the stick, I'm never going
to ever so much as touch the carrot, let alone get
a bite, but it's always something to chase after.
C'mon, can you dig it ? There's the Freedombird
coming for you, it's just one day at a time, just
one *long* day at a time."

Rufus did not say a word, just stared out
into the black hole of the perimeter of the jungle.

" I wonder what people back in the world
are doing tonight ?" Very few would be spending
the night baffled in a panoply of stars stationed
in depths of darkness that seemed so impene-
trably rich. Winston thought he was seeing the
sky for the first time.

" Winston my man ! You're trippin' on me !
I hope everyone in the world is having a boss
time tonight. It's the least they can do for us !"

Winston started laughing, muffling it in
his towel.

" My man, you can crash now, it's my turn
to watch the big screen."

" I'll stay up awhile longer, I'm too wired
to crash now. I can't stop thinking about tomorrow."

"Well my man, that's cool with me. I can
always dig the company, but you better crash

soon, tomorrow has a real hurry-up to it." They talked about their past lives; for Winston it was life in college, avoiding the draft and having a great time, while Rufus was *supposed* to go into the military and one year out of high school he couldn't escape the long arm of the draft. His father was a Top Sergeant, a total career lifer of the highest order, which truly surprised Winston, as Rufus was quite the opposite. He had spent his entire life moving from one base to another, and now lived with his mother in Anacostia. He hated the Army, and deep down Rufus believed that somewhere out in that jungle was his destiny.

" Does anyone know your father is a lifer ?"

" A few guys, but Top Buchschell doesn't know it, and I want to keep it that way. Right now he hates me because I've bought so much sham time with my glasses. Now he keeps an extra pair on hand. I hate his guts."

" I can roger that. He really likes to rub it in that I'm a cherry, and shit has higher status than I do. Loves the fact that I'm a college grad walkin' point, can't fail to let me forget that."

" That's Top for you. His favorite expression is that he wants you to be lookin' up to his boots. He does nuthin', never goes out in the field...likes to think of himself as the Napoleon of Vietnam. It's amazing the 'assassin' hasn't got..."

" The assassin ? Who's the assassin ?"

" When he wants you to know, he will let you know. He's a dude no one messes with. He's mean. He killed one lieutenant who was a little gung-ho for the group. He would place a frag under the looey's helmet in his sleeping quarters and pull the pin. The first time he rolled over in his sleep, probably the last sound he would ever hear would be the popping of the spoon...and then his shit would be all over the bunker."

" And he calls himself the assassin?"

" He's a real loner, hardly talks to anyone. No one knows where he comes from, or much about him, but he sure likes to kill. He'd nail a coke kid if you let him. He shot a water buffalo one time, which I guess caused a big stink with the gooks. They love those buffaloes. When he looks at you...you can see evil. He loves a firefight."

" And everyone knows who he is ?"

" The officers don't know, or the sergeants, but guys that kill their own, that kind of thing gets around. Don't worry, he's in another platoon. You'll meet him."

" I can't wait."

" You should crash my man. I've got just ti-ti minutes until I wake 'Gorgeous' up."

Winston put on another coating of bug repellent on his face, wrapping his towel over his ears, and like his fellow comrades had short difficulty in falling asleep on the sandbags, but what seemed like just a wink of the eye, Sgt. Glover's

young military voice was waking them up.

"Get your asses in gear gentlemen! Breakfast is right now, we PZ in one hour so get moving!"

Prince mumbled to Winston, "Can you dig it. Hurry up and wait...my stomach is in knots. I don't think I can eat this morning."

"I'm with you brother, nothing but coffee and a cigarette for this GI."

"You've got a stronger stomach than I do. I'm heading off to the shitter," which in this base camp was a 55 gallon drum cut in half with a board over it with a hole cut out in the middle. Usually they were situated in the center of camp. The shammers and those that crossed Top would have the privilege of adding diesel fuel, "and burn the shit." It would take hours and had to be constantly stirred. If no one was serving punishment duty at the time, the cherries got to do it.

The platoons of Charlie company began migrating to the PZ area, as there would be multiple pick-ups.

They waited.

In the hot sun.

The Captain studied the map, while his RTO's talked that radio jive.

Just as the eagle flight broke the horizon, the CP group, the Captain and his entourage started to return to the base, followed by the second and third platoons. The situation became numbingly puzzling.

The mission had been aborted, it was now changed...the first platoon was going to do a day of road security for some engineer outfit, the other platoons would get the day off.

By the time the other platoons were back in, they had been picked up and deposited on a white-gray chalky road, that was once a civilized route of transportation, built by the French to carry the rubber to Saigon for processing.

As they disembarked from the choppers, Sgt. McAllister yelled over the departing din, " We're on road security gentlemen. Let's spread out... Winston you got point, Prince you got the rear. Let's keep a distance here. Let the engineers do their job."

CHAPTER NINE

Chicken Little Was Right

Sgt. Glover, trying to be more helpful than military instructed Winston to walk on the side of the road and keep his eyes peeled solely to the right. The job of the engineers was to sweep the road for mines, which went at an exact pace, and military protocol was that an infantry unit always escorted them on a road sweep. Holding up the rear was an APC (armored personnel carrier) which was completely gambling these engineers were being thorough in their search...one miss from the metal detectors and this mighty be-

hemoth would be another rusty dinosaur waiting for Godot, *and* the engineers would have to hitch-hike home.

"Let's move out ! This isn't a picnic ! " Sgt. McAllister had a war to fight.

Winston chambered a round and put his M-16 on automatic, taking the safety off; the privilege of walking point. In the already stifling heat and humidity, Winston began to wake up.

First, he began to see more and faster, and his step became more conscious and deliberate. His hearing was keener, and his perspective became more poignant as the only factors in the universe were him and the unknown environment, and nothing else...it was reduced to a one-on-one situation. If there was someone out there, who would shoot first ? Who would have the first opportunity to play God ? Winston kept pace with the engineers, slow and steady; and his eyes never strayed from absorbing the jungle, taking it all in, all the time, waiting for some stranger to appear out of the foliage. Life was being measured in steps, just like a baby, one footstep at a time; and although Winston knew he was a point man for the platoon, the one most likely to receive a bullet, the ordained front man, the ultimate sucker, the first candidate for death, that after a couple hours it was becoming the new routine. No big deal.

On the opposite side of the road was the second squad echoing his actions and the first

squad was guarding the engineer cadre.

Lt. Osgood, the platoon leader, was riding in the Jeep with the looey from the engineers. It was strictly against protocol, but he didn't feel like walking. McAllister scoffed to himself and spit in the dust. This young punk had more rights, made more money, and did squat. He was proud to be a sergeant, a leader of men...and a real soldier. Without the likes of him there would only be some pansy officers worrying about their golf games.

It took forty-five minutes for the engineers to sweep a mile, waving their metal detectors over the dirt looking for the invisible surprise, and after every mile they took a break, and one and all sat in the dirt and quietly waited to begin the dance anew. Winston sat in the shade along the side of the road and enjoyed a cigarette. It was over ninety degrees and equally as humid, and the engineers soaked their heads with their canteens, sitting in the sun in the chalky road totally drenched. This was their life, for months at a time they would do nothing but sweep roads for mines, doing the same roads over and over again, and occasionally some group of Vietcong would ambush them, and the infantry unit would be there to rescue them. It was during the fourth mile that the engineers, who were reduced to robots swinging their metal detectors back and forth, brought things to a halt when one of the machines began to buzz.

" Get down gentlemen, and hug the tree line. This could be Charlie's set up. " McAllister put his belly to the berm as the entire platoon fanned out and hit the dirt aiming their weapons towards the jungle. The Vietcong used this ploy often, the mine was strictly a lure to get them to stop in a cluster, and when Winston heard the loud pop it was if a nerve snapped in his spinal cord. It was followed by another loud popping noise, and the adrenalin began to pump like lava through his veins.

"Gorgeous," who was behind him, screamed, " Get down, there's no place to hide !" And someone from the second squad across the road yelled, " INCOMING !" And Winston followed the trail of the sound. After the pop was a short whistling sound, then the noise disappeared... just a very faint whirr as if it was evaporating in the atmosphere.

Then came the long mile of silence, ...

The eternal wait.

A deep quiet. No sound. No movement. No place to run.

At first softly the mortar's descent began as a soft whistle, an innocent sound, as innocent as the coo of a dove, although this charade was Satan's sick hello...and what sounded like an eternity, a screaming piercing high pitched wail began to crescendo from the sky as the sound stretched out in the folds of time, becoming a deafening scream getting louder and closer.

" Holy Jesus I've been hit !" It was some-one from the second squad about fifty feet away from him. Among the cries for medic, the squads began firing into the jungle, and he intuitively emptied his clip from his M-16, injuring some trees and plants. There was nothing to see, no one saw Charlie release the mortar rounds. It seemed to originate from the jungle opposite Winston's side of the road, but it was so quick it seemed to come from nowhere. They had prob-ably di-di maued out of the area and were eating rice in some hole in the ground.

The word came down the line to cease fir-ing. There was nothing to fire at. "Doc,' the com-pany medic immediately shot the wounded man up with morphine, and began taking the man's bootstraps off and tying them around his leg where his foot was blown off.

" Doc !" He was screaming, "I'm not going to make it ! I'm dying !" A buddy was holding his hand, and they both talked to him. " Don't worry GI, you're going to be drinkin' beer in the world in no time." "Doc" gave him another shot of mor-phine and paused what to do next. The man had a hundred holes in him from shrapnel each ooz-ing blood, each oozing life. "Doc" looked at the guy's buddy. They knew the score. He would be dead before the dust-off arrived.

" Winston ! Get out in the road ! We need to secure this area for the dust-off !" Sgt. Glover yelled to his men to move forward as they raced

to positions on the road, staying low, literally eating dust.

" Keep your eyes open out there ! And stay apart ! " McAllister had a booming voice, " We know the little bastard is out there. Let's kill the fuckin' gooks !"

They waited in the heat of the dust.

Winston rolled over and lit a smoke. He had a straight clear view of the chalk, the road. If anyone stepped into the road he would have a shot at them.

Except the murmuring of the RTO's maintaining contact with the dust-off, and the slow breathing of the wounded GI, the air was perfectly quiet and peaceful. There was another Wolfhound who had been hit, but he needed no morphine, the shrapnel ate through his body like a virus from Hell. He was dead seconds after the explosion. Not a breeze could be bought, and Winston and everyone else listened to the heavy labored breathing of the wounded man. As the Grim Reaper pulled his invisible chariot alongside the jungle, Winston became educated in another sound of the war. The man's breathing stopped for a second, there was a gasp and then a cough with a staccato rumble that tumbled inward...it was the death rattle. His soul was on a new journey, the tired bloody remains of his human form was abandoned, and the Grim Reaper was again off collecting his never ending due.

The dust-off didn't want to land where McAllister popped smoke, and was settling down in front of Winston, his vision completely blinded by this dervish of dust. Medics raced out with gurneys and within seconds, helped by men from the second squad the two KIA's were whisked away by this helicopter emblazoned with two huge red crosses, the flying ambulance of the war.

Once the dust had settled, there was still the problem of dealing with whatever the VC had planted in the road. Based on their experience it was small, in fact could be just an empty mackerel can used as bait, or a buried grenade. The engineer platoon sergeant ordered everyone to get back and gingerly placed a Claymore mine face down on the spot. Everyone hugged the earth and held their ears, and the chalk acquired a new pothole.

" Let's move out ! You men in rear security, watch your asses ! This mission isn't over yet ! He's watching us." McAllister cradled his rifle Davy Crockett style and Winston, once again, slowly led the way...never taking his eyes off the static jungle. Now things were different...they were walking targets. The entire mission had changed and everyone was paranoid...the engineers stepped up the pace, the most important thing now was to end this mission...and one and all were waiting for that sound...but Charlie had dealt his hand for the day and was no where near,

himself afraid of being pursued.

Eventually, from out of the depths of the torturing sun, the eagle flight landed on the chalk and picked up the First Platoon of Charlie Company of the Wolfhounds and returned them to the base camp. The engineers piled on top of the APC and led by the jeep raced back down the road to the security of their own base camp, one that was battalion size, and over beers that night they would recount how they almost got their shit blown away by Charlie.

Getting off the eagle flight was euphoria ! Prince looked at Winston and they both smiled. It was weird. Two guys had checked into the Big Hotel...but they were alive ! They had survived !

" Prince, when you heard the scream of the mortar round..."

" It was louder than any siren I ever heard..."

" ...I thought for a moment, brother, the sky was going to fall on us."

Prince extended his fist for the hand-shake, "...oh Lordy," and he laughed this immense laugh, "...I thought Chicken Little was right. I gotta be grateful those rounds didn't have my name on it. I feel for those dudes though that bought a ticket for the last train..."

" ...fifty feet in the other direction and we wouldn't be having this conversation. Two guys from our platoon won't be going into the field with us tomorrow..."

Sgt. Glover interrupted them, "Stay away from the second squad bunker. Lt. Osgood is over there now, talking to them, as if the moron knew his ass from a hole in the ground. He's probably trying to comfort them that war is Hell, that at least they died as Wolfhounds defending their country. The first platoon hasn't lost two guys in the same day in quite awhile. We've always been the lucky platoon..."

Prince jumped in, "Sarge, was one of them a new guy ?"

" Yeah Prince, one dude was lookin' at five months, O'Shaughnessy, a great guy, and a married dude. A cool grenadier, and other guy was a cherry, didn't know his name..."

Which meant he was no more than a face passing through. If it were Prince or Winston no one would care either. The passing face brought no mourning. If you haven't spent the time playing the jukebox no one would loan you a quarter for a song. Lt. Osgood was giving his spiel...which was primarily directed to O'Shaughnessy's best friend, " Gentlemen ! This was a tragic day for the First Platoon. For O'Shaughnessy and...a...Jones, this was the most heroic day of their lives...they gave their very lives ! For their country ! It was horrible what happened today ! Nobody thought the VC would get lucky and pop some rounds on us...they paid the heaviest price ! It was horrible, but we got to get over it, because gentlemen we have to get even ! These guys didn't make the sac-

rifice for nothing, we still have a war to fight to-morrow, and until we all return to the world we must always think of the future and not the past. We are Wolfhounds !" He paused, "This has been a sad day for the First Platoon."

The soldier who held O'Shaughnessy's hand when he died left the bunker never looking back at the Lieutenant. He was a soldier through and through, a kid tough as nails, a short-timer who should have been long past being an ob-server on death's row, with but forty days until DEROS (date of estimated release of service), the day the Freedombird saves a seat for you. He walked until he found a space, lonely and iso-lated, behind a bunker; and had an honest cry. It was a heartbreak. O'Shaughnessy was his best friend and they should've been going back to the world together...now, he was wrapped in a body bag, awaiting his widow.

Back in the USA they were dancing to Motown, and watching the Super Bowl on TV, with "Broadway" Joe Namath leading the under-dog Jets to victory. The economy was good, un-employment was low...if you didn't turn the TV on, no one would ever know a war was going on. For some it was evil, sinful, and others just a nuisance. Forty thousand had checked into the

Big Hotel with thousands of more rooms waiting for check in. There were more thousands who lost a leg, an arm, their sanity, and went from dynamic youth to wheelchair jockey, wishing to dance with angels.

At the Peace Talks, the debate went on...

CHAPTER TEN

Wine, Women, and Friendship

It was Monday night, girls night out with her gal pals. A good night to go out at their favorite watering hole, a bar that didn't cater to college kids (no pitchers of beers or loud music), where Veronica and her three best buds could commiserate, congratulate, or simply converse.

Edith and Elizabeth (not a Liz or a Beth, but Elizabeth) were both in nursing school with Veronica, (a juggling of academia mixed with interning) and Helen, had all been friends since their freshman days. They had shared a lot of laughs and a few tears together, and now with

busy schedules this once a week rendezvous was a precious treat.

Helen, in grad school for accounting (no surprise that in 1969 she was the only woman in the class) ordered a cocktail and the others would share a bottle of Mateus (a light fruity rose wine from Portugal), or two.

Helen began, " Before you three regale me with your adventures with blood and vomit, I need to tell you my latest "man" stories. It's amazing there aren't more audits done, but then all the auditors are men...anyway, Gerald, who is in all my classes, and wants to be my best friend, even though I told him he needs to place his hormones in column B until they accrue maturity, sent me a note...just like third grade." They laughed. It was hard to imagine her being a mostly serious young woman looking for a career. " I really shouldn't reveal the contents..."

" But we know you will, " Veronica would be Helen's straight man.

" My dear Helen, and fellow student. I've sent you this note, as this is a private matter, and I don't want anyone to know..." The three were on the edge of their seats. " but I was hoping we could meet at McDonald's and share a bite to eat. (A Big Mac cost 49 cents) I have things I'd like to talk about."

Elizabeth started them laughing, " Wow ! What a big spender ! He really knows how to impress a girl !"

Edith, a beauty comparable to Veronica joined in, " So what does he look like ? Is he cute ? A stud ?"

" Just your type. He's got eyes like a turtle, if they were any deeper into his skull, they'd be in the back of his head, and with those furry eyebrows...he wouldn't need a mask on Halloween..."

Veronica jumped in, " So what did you do ?"

" I sent him a note saying Big Macs are poisonous. No, I wrote him thanks, but I have a boyfriend..."

Edith continued, " That might only work for awhile..."

" Just because Helen doesn't have a different flavor every other week, doesn't mean she *couldn't* have a boyfriend..." Elizabeth, who's venture into nursing school was a means of meeting a young doctor and made no charade about her motives, needed these meetings as much as Veronica. She worried too much...about everything.

Edith grinned, " I don't have a different flavor every other week..."

Veronica laughed, " It's at least one a month."

" Yes, thank you," she laughed, " I'm looking for Mr. Right, and so far none of the interns, or none of the patients have been too appealing."

" Amen to the patients ! They're too old, too young, or too sick !" Elizabeth downed her glass, and poured another round, " I'm going to need some food to go with the next bottle."

" Excellent ! I have nothing to go home to but Louise, my dog, and my mother who's already trying to match me with some loser..." Veronica threw her hair back and finished her glass.

Edith, looking at Helen for corroboration, " So...have you heard anything from Winston ?"

Elizabeth chimed in, " You know we all think about him..."

" Just probably not like you do..." Helen perpetually amused herself, " so what's going on ?"

" I guess no news is good news, I'm sad to say. I think it takes awhile for a letter to get here...8000 miles is a long way away. "

" We are all praying for him," Edith raised her glass, and Helen raised a toast, " To Winston ! May he return safely even though he won't be able to attend these private girls rendezvous."

Veronica grinned. As the wine lubricated the laughter, and fueled Helen's comic repartee the conversation shifted to a heavier topic: the Pill.

Elizabeth began, " I know you're on the pill (to Edith), as you have a reason..."

Veronica interjected, " I'll be ready in about a year ! Can't wait !"

Elizabeth continued, " ...so Edith, have you heard about all the possible side effects including a loss of libido ?"

Edith smiled, " I sure have, but my libido is still working like the little engine that could. It comes from that book by Dr. Seamon..."

" Semen ! " Helen was almost yelling, " what

kind of female doctor writes a book like that and is named after sperm ?"

Veronica was laughing, " That's good Helen. I think Dr. Intercourse was already taken..."

Helen continued, " OK, OK, perhaps I was exaggerating slightly, fortunately for me the men I hang out with think 'the Pill' is an aspirin."

Edith, " Don't worry Helen, before the year is out I bet you find a man that believes a woman is not just a tax deduction..."

Veronica and Elizabeth both seconded the motion, "Amen sister ! After all, someone is reproducing accountants. There's an accountant born every day..."

Helen, finishing her cocktail, dryly responded, " More than half think their mother is a very nice person, but without the stork they wouldn't be there !"

Veronica was truly enjoying this kind of repartee, " I don't think Helen needs us..."

Elizabeth joined in, " I'm worried I'm going to miss my chance. There are only so many doctors, and so many opportunities."

Edith refilled her glass, " You shouldn't treat worrying as a pastime. Don't worry, you're a hot babe, something will happen."

Elizabeth: " You're the one they want, and you don't seem to care..."

Helen interjected, " Time out ! ! New conversation !"

" I agree," Edith took a deep breath, " There's

going to be another massive protest in D.C. It's about a 6 to 7 hour drive, which is not bad. Maybe we should go and support the cause..."

Veronica's voice was soft and low key, " Helen is the only one who doesn't work week-ends, and we'll never get time off being interns. Of all of us I'm the one that *should* go, but it's too early to get time off..."

Helen concluded, " I spend my weekends studying how amortization works for small businesses..."

" And keeping your classmates from pounding down the door..." Veronica laughed. Having good friends was one of the great therapies in life.

" If you see me with a man in McDonald's, please shoot me." Helen, was joined by the trio as they finished their drinks, and agreed same time, same place, next week.

Tomorrow, Helen as stocky as a fullback, dressed like plain Jane, would resume classes in her all testosterone world struggling to find a niche, Elizabeth would return to worrying about her hair, her classes, her future, and maybe even the weather, and Edith would smile and float through the hospital like an angel that every man wanted to love.

Veronica would start in earnest on her scrapbook and besides school and hospital time, would pen another "sugar report" to Winston.

CHAPTER ELEVEN

The Dead Baby Omen

It was a long night's sadness sinking into Hell for some, and for Prince and Winston the reality of the war had crept into their souls like a cancer that can never be removed. This was the first for both of ever being that close to death, and hearing O'Shaughnessy's dying good-bye, a cruel hello to the Grim Reaper was a memory that was like waking up the next morning with a tattoo that won't go away with soap and water. A difference of about fifty feet of Planet Earth was all that separated them from permanent room service in the Big Hotel.

" Prince, when I first heard that sound I didn't know what it was. It just seemed weird..."

" Oh brother ! I was buried against a tree as soon as I heard that pop. I thought that whistling scream was coming down on my head. Lord, thank you !" Prince bowed his head.

" Believe me, I'm very glad to be alive. I already hate being the constant target...this is going to be a long year."

" Amen to that, and Winston, my man, we gotta keep together. We became Wolfhounds on the same day, and we leave together for the world on the same day."

When nightfall arrived they were numb. Rufus was wrapped so tight he had fallen into that hole inside himself. Dylan, "Gorgeous," and Juan all got stoned and crashed after dinner. No one, not even the oldest man in the field could escape that a death was one more burden in the experience, and the weight can crush you. It's more than you're another day older, it's that you're getting closer...

Winston's memory of being a college kid not that long ago was slipping away, he was becoming a soldier, like it or not.

In the morning Sgt. Glover woke up his squad, while McAllister was yelling at someone to step it up and get their shit in order. The aroma of coffee and cigarettes mixed with the conversations of what the day ahead might bring. Business as usual. Today the First Platoon was going

to do an easy sweep through a friendly village. Everyone had been there before except Winston and Prince. It was a weekly check-up. The looey had lobbied for the platoon doing base duties instead of going out in the field, but this was the next best thing.

Sgt. Glover addressed his squad, " Well gentlemen, today is the usual stroll through the village, so just canteens and ammo, we should be back by lunch, but I'd bring one meal of C's, just in case..."

"Gorgeous" interrupted him, " You'd think after yesterday we would get the day off." He was angry, " we lose two guys and get the shit."

" Listen George..."

" You can call me 'Gorgeous' if you want, Sarge," as he smiled and ran his fingers through his brylcreemed hair.

"The other platoons are going for a sweep on the far side of the Michelin, near the jungle. This is gravy duty, a few hours walking through a friendly village."

" As long as we don't get shot at, it's gravy." Dylan piped in.

" Yeah man, roger that," and Juan grabbed his crotch, " and those fuckin' gooks can roger on this." Only Dylan thought he was humorous, and as the squads lined up they were joined by the "Kit Carson", an ARVN, a South Vietnamese soldier who acted as a scout and an interpreter, much like the olden days of the Indian wars. His

true name was unknown and he answered to Chuck.

" Let's get it together babysans, the sooner we get started, the sooner we get back to base camp." McAllister was not in a good mood. This was an unnecessary mission, but it was not his role to complain. They would just do it, and he would insure that the first platoon would do it in proper military fashion.

It was a single file walk through the sparse woods to the village, with Winston walking point as usual and Prince picking up rear security. The men from the second squad were in a tight gloom, and Dylan and "Gorgeous" in their own style were trying to lighten them up, " Hey Bixie ! Should be some good boom-boom out there today, you know you love it !"

McAllister scowled at Dylan, " Shut the fuck up soldier ! Let's move !" The village was a series of bamboo shacks of indistinguishable age wedded to a single dirt road connecting to rice paddies adjacent to it. To Winston it was a strange new world that all the movies and training hadn't prepared him for. From out of the hooches with its dirt floors, the babysans, the little Vietnamese boys and girls came running up to Winston.

" GI, babysan want chop-chop. Give babysan chop-chop."

" Keep moving Winston," Sgt. Glover yelled at him, "they go away after awhile."

He felt odd about the situation, but the village like all villages was nothing but babysans and old men, and women of all ages. In Winston's mind, this just didn't seem like a place for children, but then this was their country, of course there would be children.

Sgt. Glover continued, " Di-di mau babysan, GI no have chop-chop." They stood there, some wearing the tops of pajamas and some wearing the bottoms, with their hands held out. At a very young age they had learned that they had nothing to lose being persevering. When one tot the size of a large teddy bear demanded of Winston, " Give babysan lifer bar," Winston laughed and tossed the kid a tropical chocolate bar. They were developed so they wouldn't melt in the tropical climate, and were affectionately referred to as lifer bars or shit bars. When the bar hit the ground the babysans were canine about it, fighting to get a bite.

McAllister from the middle of the line yelled to Winston, " Keep your ass moving ! Fuck those babysans !" He didn't care the Kit Carson was with them, his job was not public relations.

Sgt. Glover in soft civilian terms kept repeating as he walked, "Di-di mau babysans, GI no have chop-chop."
A man from the second squad screamed at them, "Fuck you babysans ! GI got no fuckin' chop-chop !" The kids scattered into their hooches, disappearing like a breeze, as if they were never

there.

As Winston walked on the path he couldn't ignore the ground covered with cigarette butts, water buffalo shit, cow shit, pig shit, chicken shit, empty C-ration cans, straw, and amongst it all the footprints of a variety of small people. He walked passed a hooch with the stench of pigs that if the nose could hear would be deafening. There were miniature graveyards with small tombstones clustered together and chickens scratched at the graves as they meandered through the village foraging for scraps. These hooches had the constitution a common wolf could blow over. Winston was inundated with the smells and sounds of the village, and then he saw it. Hanging from a tree over the road was the North Vietnamese flag, the NVA banner. He hit the dirt and the rest of the platoon went down like bowling pins. Sgt. Glover ran low up to Winston, then yelled back to the RTO, " Tell the platoon leader there's an NVA flag up here, could be an ambush."

Everybody stayed real low, but began to relax hearing "Chuck" interrogate the old men and the women. There had been NVA soldiers in the village last night, but they had left. The villagers knew nothing. At least that was the official word from "Chuck." Before they resumed walking, a woman came down the road, running and sobbing, carrying a dead baby. It had been dead for days, the mother had refused to give it up

and bury her child. It was a puzzling omen for Winston.

Sgt. McAllister ripped down the flag and had the villagers walk on it as they passed by, then they resumed their mission. Winston made his first decision as point man and started walking on the side of the road, which was slower and more difficult. It was more like a maneuver through an obstacle course. Everyone followed suit as if Winston knew what he was doing, and as disgusting as the debris was to wade through, it seemed safer to avoid walking the obvious path. The NVA were here last night, somewhere was a booby trap waiting to happen.

Eventually they exited the village into a long open field cleared on both sides about fifty feet from the wood line. The Army Engineers had painstakingly bulldozed the trees away, under orders from Army Intelligence (one of the great oxymorons of all time) creating the perfect set up for a sniper. He could do his business and be sippin' tea in Hong Kong before they could do anything about it.

Winston kept a fast pace, being the perfect target, until they reached a camouflaged space where the engineers had ceased their demolition.

The three squads kept their distance as they took a break for some C's and some smokes.

" Rufus, can I get a ball of C-4 from you ?" Winston was making himself a cup of C-coffee.

" You must have a strong stomach, Winston, to drink that shit."

" What can I say ? I love coffee."

" Speaking of strong stomachs, lookey what's comin' down Main Street..." Rufus laughed, " it's 'Gorgeous' girlfriend."

" Don't be gettin' all righteous on me brother." "Gorgeous" was laughing.

Winston was about to be introduced to road culture, life on the outskirts of the village. Sitting astride her Honda mo-ped wearing clean white skin tight pants and a polka dot blouse was a girl whose face could melt the lines of the Sphinx. No amount of make-up could disguise the rapid aging she wore on her face. The scars on her soul were evident in her eyes, she was twenty going on fifty.

" GI, you want boom-boom ?" She was directing her words to Winston, and smiled and spread her legs on the seat.

Winston just stared at her.

She got off the bike and approached him, " Sally, boom-boom girl...make dick wake up !" She grabbed his balls and started fondling them. Winston backed off. He had never seen a girl this ugly, this bold in his life.

" How much babysan ?" "Gorgeous" was interested.

Winston saw Dylan with his poncho liner, his tropical camouflage blanket flung over his

shoulder, walking with the other boom-boom girl into the woods with Juan's M-16. Juan baby-sat the machine gun. It seemed to be a set pattern. Winston looked to Sgt. Glover, his eyes asking what was going on.

The boom-boom girl was now directing her attentions to "Gorgeous", " Me sell pussy...GI want pussy ? It cost you five dollah. I number one fuck, no sweat GI, you want fuck ?" "Gorgeous" grabbed his poncho liner and his weapon, " Sarge," he smiled, "will you watch the fort for me ?"

" Sure," and he looked at Prince and Winston, " if you or Prince are interested in getting the clap, now's the opportunity."

" I think I'll pass." He paused, " Sarge, aren't you worried that if something happens these guys would be in a real bind in the woods ?"

He just shrugged his shoulders. Right or wrong this was how things have always been. It was life in the infantry.

" What about you Sarge, do you ever do boom-boom girls ?" Prince asked.

" Never. I hope I don't get *that* horny, besides my R&R is coming up next month. I can wait."

"Gorgeous" was back already wearing a guilty but not quite ashamed smile. There was a war going on and he just got laid. Tomorrow he could be dead.

The boom-boom girl looked at Rufus, GI

want number one fuck ?"

" Di-di mau babysan. Lookey here, the last fuckin' thing I want is sloppy seconds from 'Gorgeous'." All she understood was di-di mau, and when Sarge repeated it, she and her girlfriend got on their scooters and headed down to the next squad. Next came the "coke kids", little boys around 12 or 13 who sold bottles of iced cold cokes for a buck apiece. They were bare footed urchins on bicycles who each humped a cooler of ice cokes.

" Hey GI, you number one, want coke ? Coke number one." Winston gave him a MPC dollar. " Hey GI, you got American dollah?" Real greenbacks had a greater currency, but Winston only had Military Payment Currency.

Winston turned to Rufus, " Where do these kids get ice out in the middle of nowhere ? We're miles from any civilization."

" Black market everything my man. Some REMF probably is selling both the cokes and the ice, which should go to us...to these kids...but you got me man, *where* does it come from ?"

While Prince and Juan were buying cokes, almost in front of Sgt. Glover's eyes, Dylan was buying a kilo of cansah, no seeds or stems for twenty bucks. The "coke kids" could get you anything you wanted. Sometimes they carried a cornucopia of illegal pharmaceuticals, Saigon speed being a big favorite, and sometimes they could fill your order in ten minutes. The black market

was always everywhere, and always close.

Blackie, who rarely spoke, he was so serious and insular, very softly asked the Sarge when they would be returning to camp. The RTO gave the word they would be camping out for a while longer, the NVA could still be in the area.

Rufus scoffed, " Hey Blackie" putting out his fist, " do you think the tooth fairy is still in the area ?"

" Why do you say that Rufus ?" Asked Prince, " We all saw that flag back there. What makes you think they have di-di maued out of here ?"

" 'cause when the NVA are around you don't see no 'coke kids'. The whores still come out. To them it don't mean nuthin', but the kids are too smart, they don't want to get shot...can you dig it ?"

Prince nodded his head, " After yesterday," which now seemed like years ago, "...I'm not takin' anything for granted. Charlie is the invisible man, and this is his country. I'm a believer, and I just hope my number never comes up but I'm goin' to try and keep my big ass as low to the ground as I can get."

" Whoa brother !" And Winston started to laugh,
" I didn't want to be the bearer of bad news, but when the shit hits the fan, I was planning on hiding behind that derrière of yours."

Prince guffawed, then stifled it. He could

laugh like a giant hyena if he let go, "...then you better carry an entrenching tool with your bad self 'cause you'd be a foot beneath the ground."

" Get down brother." Rufus interjected and did the handshake with both of them.

Juan, looking at Prince, who was a foot taller and wider than him, snickered, " You do make a really big target, dude...someday I bet you will be carrying the machine gun."

Prince half smiled at him.

" Prince," Dylan spoke up, his face had that goofy look like someone who was on something all the time, "don't pay no never mind to Juan, he thinks he's a real joker."

" Yeah, a real fuckin' comedian." Rufus lit a smoke, and blew a cloud over Juan's head.

" Yeah dude, I'm just fuckin' with you. Just remember, you don't fuck with me," and he laughed, and Prince absolutely knew he wasn't joking.

While Dylan positioned themselves to watch down the chalk, they made idle chatter.

" Rufus, those boom-boom girls sure looked ugly," Winston was savoring his soda, " I'd hate to get caught with my pants down if an NVA squad decided to ambush,"

"Gorgeous" was making a little tent with his poncho liner to protect himself from the sun, " In about six months from now, or maybe ti-ti time, those boom-boom girls won't look so bad."

Prince started to laugh, " Hey brother, I've

seen better faces on the south end of a mule going north. Ugly. At least my man Rufus can take his glasses off and pretend. You must want it bad."

" Back in the world pussy just came my way. They don't call me 'Gorgeous' for nothing."

Winston just looked at Blackie trying to suppress a laugh.

"'Gorgeous', why don't you admit you don't care who or what it is, or whether you get the clap, and you've had the clap before." Blackie spoke in his usual monotone voice. He could've been reading a stock report.

" So Blackie, you ain't no saint." "Gorgeous" was busy adjusting the sticks of his one man tent.

" Yeah, but I never got the clap...

" So what's that make you...?"

Winston interrupted, " Hey you guys forget it...what did you think of the woman coming down the road with the dead baby ? That was pretty weird don't you think ? That baby was pretty dead, like a rock."

Never looking up from his whittling, Juan threw in his two cents, " Don't mean nuthin'."

" Has anything like that ever happen before ?"

Rufus looked at him, " Seen beaucoup crying women, but never one with a baby been dead like a rock. Could be her only child, didn't want to give it up. Nothin' in Nam is too weird, this place

116

be a womb for strange shit."

" I feel sorry for these people. They're just simple peasants. Their lives would be so much better without us..." Prince was falling into "preacher" mode, " Lordy, these people probably had the same existence for thousands of years until we came along and brought war into their lives..."

" Not true Prince, before us were the French who treated the peasants like slaves, and now the North Vietnamese seem like they want to enslave them."

" Winston, you sound like a real believer in the war, " mumbled Blackie.

" Not a chance, you can put a flower down the barrel of my M-16 any time. We should all be back protesting this war instead of being in it, and these poor folks maybe did alright with the French, but who knows what'll happen next. America has never lost a war and I'm sure this is no exception, even though there's nothing to win. It has to end some day, I wish it would be soon."

"Amen to that brother !"

" Not in our lifetime !" "Gorgeous" was angry, "...that new President, Nixon, he's no better than LBJ, he won't do no fuckin' shit either. We're in it until DEROS day. A whole lotta GIs are going to go down for nuthin'...let's hope it's not any of us."

Rufus was about to say something when

Sgt. Glover brought them back to life, "Let's saddle up gentlemen ! We're going back to camp." Winston and Prince would bring up the rear, someone from second squad would be walking point for a change of pace.The return back was always faster, and this time it would be quicker as they would by-pass the village and cut through the woods to the camp.

"Gorgeous" seemed to be elated, " Hey Winston do ya wanna race back to the base ?" As if he got a vote. The entire platoon was in turbo-trot, forgetting the heat and stifling humidity; there was total unity in this mission...get back, and get back fast. It seemed like a stroll through the park, although it was a simple narrow path, and the essential mission had been accomplished...time to go home. Blackie was whistling under his breath, barely audible. The day was going to end as it was supposed to...they would be back by noon, lunch and siestas for one and all. Follow the yellow brick road...

" Hey Winston, let's play some cards when we get back, maybe some gin rummy."

" Now you're talkin' Prince. Ready to get your ass whooped ?"

" Be blest I'm not a gambler, you'd hate walkin' point without shoes."

" Lookey here civilians, Blackie and I can play some poker !" Even Rufus was feeling on the up. A short day, a short mission. Everything was cool.

Dylan yelled up ahead to some of his buddies in the other squads, " Poker game ! Bring your balls and your MPC to the third herd bunker when we get back. I'm going to thank you now for your money !" As usual he had that ubiquitous grin...nothing was going to harm this guy, and Juan, thinking because he was the assistant machine gunner did his version of a Laurel and Hardy bit and pumped up his voice, "...and you can keep your balls, we'll take your money."

" Let's move it gentlemen ! And cut the crap !" McAllister was high stepping also.

Sgt. Glover was smiling as they briskly walked across the chalk to the woods. It was a stroll through Disneyland.

And then it happened...Winston's ears were ringing, singing a million chimes...screaming banshees filled his head. Everything was sound, that all permeating ringing, he could feel it in his stomach.

The sound was accompanied by a gigantic flash. It was a subterranean happening. A huge mine had exploded where the road met the woods, and a cloud of dirt was now raining upon them. Time had come...gone...lost...it was over as soon as it happened. Winston and the entire platoon had hit the dirt immediately, his head seemed outside and beyond his body...his thoughts were melting in the din of the noise, mental waves transcended emotion. The noise seemed everywhere. The men were electrified.

What was happening ?

Amongst the cloud of smoke, the smell of gunpowder, the fear, and the rain of dust...someone fired.

In the background you could hear the RTO yelling into the horn for a dust-off. "Gorgeous" eyes beneath his furry eyebrows looked like they were bleeding dirt, his look was the glare of hate, as he emptied another clip into the wood line. Winston could barely hear the click of his safety as it went off, and then came the pounding in his ears again as the bullets streamed out of his M-16, an eighteen round clip as fast as you could pull the trigger. Magazine after magazine went into Winston's M-16. His trigger finger was stuck in the war, that vast void of civilization. His ears were screaming...he could hear nothing, nothing except the flashing of his weapon.

He felt nothing. He was numb.

The wood line was a pepper pot of smoke as the platoon madly fired at invisible targets. It was chaos until the booming voice of Sgt. McAllister roared out to stop firing. There had been no return fire.

" Separate on both sides of the road, the dust-off is on the way ! We need to provide security, we got a badly wounded man down here !" McAllister's voice was like Moses', they followed orders without question. The second squad had a man with his hands holding his guts. He was in complete shock, he couldn't believe he had his

intestines in his hands, which he could barely hold on to, his entire body was shaking so intensely. He was too numb to even scream, his whole world was concentrating...on one breath at a time. There was another man of the second squad where the earth had exploded and taken him in. He was gone. The blast, which he detonated from being in the wrong place at the wrong time had taken him heart, body, and soul back to where he came from...there were nothing but bloody fragments scattered everywhere. While the "Doc" covered up the wounded man with a poncho liner to protect him from the swirling dust about to be disseminated from the dust-off, one of the few survivors from the second squad searched for the man's dogtags, the final legacy to return to the world.

The grisly job of gathering up the man's humanity fell to the third herd. When Winston picked up the man's arm, perfectly in tact, he started to cry and vomit at the same time. There was blood and body parts everywhere. Dylan pulled the man's intestines from a tree branch and stuffed it into the body bag. This soldier's job was done swiftly and no one spoke a word.

The doctors in the rear would've never found enough skin to cover up his wounds. The man died of shock in the dust-off. The very next day he would be shipped in a body bag, along with his buddy, in the cargo hold of an air-liner bound for Oakland, and eventually home.

No one in the Wolfhounds would ever hear of him again...he had gone from a person, and soldier...to a statistic.

After the dust-off evacuated, they continued looking for the man's dogtags. They were about twenty feet from the explosion. Now they were moving slower, the distance to the camp was but a couple football fields away, but it seemed like an eternity. No one spoke. Donovan, who lost his best friend yesterday was joining the squad.

When they finally entered the base camp, Sgt. Glover, always cool, calm, and collected started screaming, throwing his helmet on the ground, " I shoulda known when we saw that NVA flag we should've called in the engineers ! They could have swept the road and two more guys would still be alive ! They left us an omen and we were too stupid to pick up on it !" Glover was seething.

" Sarge, it wasn't your fault..." Dylan was sincerely compassionate, "...you're only the squad leader. Sarge, you couldn't know what was going to happen...no one did. C'mon Sarge lighten up on yourself."

Winston, as a cherry had literally no right to make a comment came up to the Sarge, " You're a fool if you think you can predict the future.."

" I should have ! !" Sgt. Glover screamed at him. He was enraged and ready for a fight, totally out of character for himself.

Rufus and Blackie both came to him and put their arms around him, " You be too right-eous a dude Sarge. No one could know what was going to be. Don't take it out on your bad self."

In the dead monotone of the undertaker, Blackie told him, quite coldly, " If you had told McAllister to turn back once we saw the flag, what do you think he would have told you ?"

" It's the fuckin Nam, Sarge..." "Gorgeous" had to pitch in his bit, " if you had told McAllister you thought there were booby traps you know he would've never listened ! You *know* he would've told you to mind your fuckin' business, stay with the mission, and keep moving !"

" But I never said anything !"

" Sarge," Dylan's voice was pure inno-cence, " Not you, or anyone else could have pre-dicted what happened today...please, let it go..."

Sgt. Glover picked up his helmet and threw it inside the bunker, screaming over and over, " I hate you gooks !"

War creates strange bedfellows, and Sgt. Glover got into his hammock inside the bunker, and just stared at the ceiling. Deep in his soul he could have made a difference had he thought to act in time, but hindsight won't bandage these wounds. He rocked in his hammock, alone in the bunker, staring at the ceiling, torturing himself until

" sweet sleep that ravels up the sleeve of care," as Lady MacBeth so eloquently put it, closed his

eyes.

Winston and Prince went in search of sodas, his ears were still ringing...some lost soul from Hell was trying to tell him something...but he didn't want to listen, he was being deafened by the chimes of combat, and he could barely hear.

" The Sarge," Winston speaking to Prince, " really lost it. Hard to be cool when you lose your marbles. It was a bad scene today, one second it's a party going home, and the next it's for real...someone's truly going home. We've been two days in the field and four guys have died...I don't feel like any cherry. (Pause) When the woman came down the road carrying the dead baby...that was an omen of what was to be...she was the harbinger of death, the point man for the Grim Reaper. She was telling us all what was to be, but we mortals could never read the signs until it was too late."

" You're crazy Winston. I can't remember ever feeling this much 'mortal', but I don't buy it. It's just one freaky thing after another. It's soldier roulette out here, and let's hope..." he stuck his fist out, "...that our numbers don't come up. I'm goin' to make it, myself. I think God is with me. I believe it..." He paused, taking a deep breath, " and it's goin' to be a very, very long year.

" If I ever see another woman with a dead baby I'm going to run the other way."

" You better move fast, or I'll run you

over."

◆ ◆ ◆

The world is always in turmoil...fighting broke out in Istanbul, and as many as 20,000 clashed over a visit by ships of the U.S. fleet. From the perspective of Vietnam the world seemed more curious, more distant every day. Yassar Arafat was elected leader of the Palestine Liberation Organization, and Henry Cabot Lodge was appointed by Nixon to be the new chief negotiator at the Peace Talks...and the talk would go on and on...between 200 and 300 GIs were dying each week...and the mightiest government in the world talked and talked. McNamara said things were going well, we're winning this war...and the talk would go on and on...while the bell never stopped tolling.

The pitcher, Tom Zachary, who threw the low fastball that Babe Ruth hit for his 60th home run, back in '27, was getting a second chance to pitch to the Babe.

◆ ◆ ◆

CHAPTER TWELVE

A "Sugar Report"

"Dear Winston,
I never dreamed I'd miss you so much and that I'd dream about you so much. Every day I worry, I worry like every other girl who's man is over there, and maybe he's not coming back, but I *know* you are. I'm counting on it. I'm counting on us getting married and having babies together. I'm counting on a lot of things. I'm counting on you taking care of yourself. We get nothing but bad news here, but the protest movement is growing stronger every day, so we all hope maybe an end can come sooner rather that later. I'm praying Nixon will do something, as you

know my parents voted for him, and they believe in him, but I never liked him. I'm counting on the protest movement, the will of the people to overcome the war.

Tell me what's it's like being a grunt. Why are you called a grunt ? Sounds gross.

Every time it rains I think about you, and I know you won't forget that time in the rain. I hope no one else reads this letter, please promise me that, although I bet there are guys with nude photos of their girlfriends, but not from this girl ! I will never forget that night in the rain on that hot, hot day in July. The only thing hotter was us. I laugh when I think we could've been caught, and then what ?

Still see my gal pals every Monday night. Helen still a card, never a day without a laugh with her, Edith is still gorgeous and every doctor at the hospital wants her affections, while Elizabeth still is worrying whether she'll land a doctor, her reason for being a nurse. I've enclosed a picture of the three of us. Don't you think I look cute in my nurses' uniform ?

I wish I could send you something, besides my love, which you already got. I worry. Write me soon so I know you're OK.

Love forever,

Veronica

P.S.   Is there anything you want me to send to you ? I know your mom will be sending you snacks and crossword puzzles. Do you want

something in particular ? "

She walked to the mail box to start the letter on its journey.

Veronica had held back describing how she cried herself to sleep some nights, depressed that he wouldn't make it back. Not being alone in this predicament was little satisfaction. Maybe others were crying as well, and the news on the TV was never good. Americans were dying in mass every single day, and the images of the wounded were horrifying.

Every night she prayed, and by day she concentrated on her studies and kept busy at the hospital. Every morning she awoke with the sparkle of hope that *they* were one day closer, one day nearer to being re-united. There was a reason Pandora kept Hope inside the box.

Winston's return letter had vignettes of what characters his squad mates were, how they had actually seen some enemy soldiers, but nothing happened, how wretched the climate was and large the mosquitoes; and that C-rations weren't that bad.

The important thing was his determination to survive and get through this year and get back to her. His love for her was what kept him going...and eventually they would be in each other's arms.

All they wanted was each other, and it gave Veronica strength...love conquers all.

There were probably a 1000 letters written every day blessed by Cupid. Some would be intercepted by the Grim Reaper, and some would be harbingers of matrimony.

◆ ◆ ◆

CHAPTER THIRTEEN

Outpost on the Edge of Eternity

The NVA regular, stationed on outpost, watched the eagle flight bring Winston's unit to a large open field. He took note as they combined into two files, plodding along the side of an antique road. They were coming directly to his location but would pass him by. Heavily laden down, sweat pouring into their eyes, walking like they carried the burden of Mankind created a very hostile look. The NVA could read the inscription on the camouflage cover of the point man's helmet, they were that close. It said, "Where have all the flowers gone ?"

He could have easily sprayed the file, but he didn't have a rifle. He normally humped a mortar tube but today he was on outpost, just waiting and watching. Less than a click away in the middle of the jungle was a major underground base camp, with a half a battalion resting before they continued the march south. Tet was coming.

Winston was swearing with every step. It was to be a four day mission, and they were humping everything. He had a case of C's (10 meals), six canteens (which he knew wouldn't be enough), a double load of M-16 ammo, 60 ammo for the machine gun (everyone carried 2000 rounds for Dylan), two claymore mines, and a couple of frags. Juan, the frag man, was carrying eleven. Winston felt if they made contact and had to hit the ground, they would hit like Humpty Dumptys. After a hundred meters he already downed a canteen, his eyes were burning from sweat, his towel and shirt were sopping wet.

There was a small berm between them and the wood line, and the entire company spread out behind the green sanctuary. The NVA soldier watched patiently and took it all in.

Every leaf of foliage was embalmed in dust from a B-52 strike a few days ago and everyone was a short breath from a sneezing fit, as the Captain discussed with his lieutenants what the game plan was going to be for the next four days,

where were the outposts going to be positioned and where to put the main base camp. Essentially there was to be little movement once they encamped, it was a company sized ambush.

" So Sarge..." Winston propped up his head and lit a smoke, his shirt had turned to mud in the dust, "...so this is home for the next four days ? Looks like a nice place to visit."

Everyone was gathered together including the new guy, Donovan, " According to the Captain, this is like a secret mission. Once we make camp, nobody moves..."

" I'm diggin' that" Rufus interrupted.

"Some squads during the day will be used as outposts, the scouting party..."

" And that would be us to be first ! Am I right on that Sarge ?" "Gorgeous" had to exercise his temper.

" Roger that, we're just waiting on orders, so until then someone has to watch the wood line and we'll work it like guard duty, starting with you Prince. There's no telling how long we're going to be here."

Just then the sky was filled with the roar of a Chinook as it lowered a pallet of empty sandbags and some entrenching tools. The Army had a special way of making its leadership look like assholes. The guys smiled. Any gook within ten miles knew where they were now...nothing like a secret mission.

" So Sarge, about that secret." Winston

was laughing.

Glover smiled, " Do you think we should set off fireworks ?"

The Captain did not like to be made a fool of, and was furious. He radioed back, irate, that their position had been disastrously compromised, perhaps the entire mission. Now the company would have to re-locate, and carry the additional baggage of the empty sandbags, which he thought was stupid and unnecessary, but which they *had* to hump, as it couldn't be left for Charlie. He was as angry as a hornet caught in a spider's web.

The company picked themselves up, trudging forward, and by mid-afternoon totally exhausted from carrying well over a hundred pounds worth of gear and ammo, the Company fell into their final position like a school of jelly-fish.

As exhausting as their trek was, those not going out on outpost began filling sandbags. Glover and his squad felt lucky going out. They would only be going a klick away, and amongst the magnificent verdure, the fields and patches of bamboo, the squad became encased inside a hedge of old thick bamboo, offering them a good viewpoint and excellent camouflage. Sarge whispered into the radio their position, there would be no further oral communication, only squeezes on the handset.

" What a thrill ! If outpost isn't too bad,

this could be alright. I've never been too crazy about filling sandbags. " Winston laid back and made a niche in the bamboo.

" I'll take sandbag duty any time. I don't like this Robinson Crusoe stuff any way you cut it. If we see any gooks..." Rufus was tightening up.

" We do nothing. We don't fire unless we have to. Our mission is to report back if we see anything. Hopefully they'll walk into a trap, the Company ambush, but don't shoot because you see them. Everybody got that ?"

" How long are we out here for, Sarge ?" Blackie asked in his usual droll tones.

" We come back when the sun sets, so lay back and relax, and since you asked, Blackie you have first guard..." and before he could finish his sentence Dylan and Juan both fell asleep, as if in a coma..." we'll only be out here a couple hours, so everyone gets a short shift."

Rufus and Winston were both exhausted but joined Blackie in watching the perimeter of the wood line.

"...and no one speaks above a whisper, and keep it to a minimum, and if you have to smoke, keep it in your helmet." And the Sarge covered his eyes with his towel and laid back.

After an hour they formally relieved Blackie, who joined the rest of the squad in a deep afternoon slumber. Winston's voice nearly squeaked he was talking so softly, "Rufus, is this

going to be *it* for the next four days ? I wish I had the trilogy of The Lord of the Rings with me, I could finish it by the end of the mission."

" If we don't make contact it's sleep, eat, and watch...and that's cool." He curled up in a ball, got low to the ground and lit up a smoke, exhaling into his helmet, where it would slowly disperse.

Donovan neither slept or talked, but listened, as the RTO he was in communication with the Company's main camp, and the three other outposts. If anything happened anywhere he would hear it first. It was his first day as an RTO and he loved it, it totally captivated him, he could think of nothing else. Cocooned inside the huge clump of bamboo, when the air became still, you could hear yourself sweat.

On the edge of the wood line, a small soldier dressed in black pajamas and sandals, armed with an AK-47 and an extra clip, watched the group, too terrified of being seen if he moved, waited patiently for darkness. A most trying patience was the demand for this soldier, just recently turned eighteen, the same age as many of his enemy only yards away, not old enough to vote, but obviously perfectly eligible to die.

Winston was thinking to himself this new life was now the norm, and whatever he used to do back in the world was a memory growing more distant by the moment. In the Nam you never worried about what to wear, or

money or what you could do with it. You'll never starve, you're never alone and most of the time one's community is shrunk to about six people.

One's reason for employment was to kill people, so frowned upon back in the world. Winston imagined if he was Peter Pan and these were the Lost Boys and this is what they would be doing for eternity ? It would be splendid if a crocodile with a clock inside it would stop by and save the day. Winston and Rufus both succumbed to the heat, the stress, and the boredom and took naps as Dylan and Juan took the last guard. Sarge gave Donovan a spell on the horn, and the NVA soldier continued to watch, never moving.

It looked like the sun had about fifteen more minutes before calling it another day in Vietnam when the appropriate clicks on the horn told the Sarge it was time to return to the Company's outpost. They were over the hills and through the woods in no time. The young soldier in black pajamas finally stood up, and when they were out of sight raced through the darkening forest to his base camp.

McAllister greeted the squad with an abrupt, " Well gentlemen, you could've been filling sandbags all day," he was wearing no shirt and covered in grime, "...so tonight this squad has extra guard duty. Some of these guys have sweated all day in the hot sun filling these sandbags for YOUR PROTECTION ! They're going to

need their sleep gentlemen, and because you think you got it hard being on outpost, you're going to be on it tomorrow !" He gave Sgt. Glover his instructions, and the squad took position in a corner of the camp.

They were devouring their C's like canines escaped from the pound. " That scumbag McAllister !" "Gorgeous" was ready to scream, "...he thinks fuckin' sandbags are more important than standing outpost ! That lifer piece of shit ! And look what they did !" He wanted to laugh hysterically, the perimeter was two sandbags high all the way around, except for the CP group which was twelve and growing. The company RTO's would dig themselves to death if it would stop one round.

" I can't believe we're the lucky bastards that DON'T get to fill sandbags !" "Gorgeous" was still on a rant. His temper was non-stop explosive.

" George, do you think I should carve Sgt. McAllister into a clothes pin ?" This was Juan's audition for humor.

" How 'bout a fuckin' voodoo doll ?"

" Whoa dudes," Dylan seemed like he was awakening from the dead,"...this whole fuckin' mission is one big outpost, so what's the bitch ? We don't spend all day digging in the dirt filling sandbags. That's cool. I'd rather sleep than fill sandbags all day, and let's get hip, all the sandbags in the world don't mean nuthin' to a mortar

round, so I'll take outpost any day, sandbags are for the birds."

" Don't mean nuthin'," Juan held out his fist for Dylan, then extended it to Blackie and "Gorgeous".

Prince, whose shyness belied his bigness asked Juan, " Have you been on many outposts ?"

" Beaucoup amigo, beaucoup. It's always one day at a time, no matter what George thinks..."

" Hey amigo !" "Gorgeous" couldn't stop himself, "do you remember when a battalion of NVA...and yes, right from this very area, attacked a company of Wolfhounds, just like ours and they became overrun and called in an eagle flight for escape ? A hot LZ no less, every helicopter pilot's dream scene...the outpost never made it back to the main camp. How do you think a squad of six guys stands up to an army of gooks ? Where do you think our shit is going to hang if the gooks decide to attack the company bush ?" He took a deep breath, " Goddamn, I can't wait to get back to the world. No one will ever believe the stupid jackass shit we have to go through. Four days looking for gooks that are coming out of the woodwork...it's going to be Tet in a couple weeks, this entire country will be a hell-hole...too bad McAllister isn't going out on outpost...he'd probably want to hump some sandbags for protection."

"'Gorgeous" !" Dylan laughed, " Fuck it !"

As twilight evaporated into pure darkness they took their positions for guard duty. With double guard, no one slept more than two hours at a time, while the scenery transformed into an opaque view, no real forms, just stationary shadows.

The Command Post RTO's took turns looking through the "starlight" (a telescopic viewer that penetrated the night in a krypton green kind of glow), hoping nothing was moving.

Deep beneath the woods, not far away, a battalion of NVA slept in their subterranean maze, although some camped beneath the trees. Their mission was to hit Saigon at Tet, nearly forty miles away, and they couldn't afford a firefight, ammo was precious. They would be moving away from Charlie company before dawn hoping before nightfall to be in another underground base camp.

For the American GI it was a one-year tour, except if you were either a lifer or the gung-ho type; but for the NVA it was a lifetime commitment. You would not come home until the enemy was defeated, which fortified their determination.

In the morning there was the smell of cigarettes and cooking C-rations, and the sounds of coughing and farting. They were lucky the NVA were not down wind. They were long gone. The men urinated just outside the sandbag perimeter.

" Get inside the perimeter soldier !" McAllister yelled at Prince, " we have a shitter in the center of the camp, I suggest you use it !"

Prince was like one of a bunch of schoolboys who all wrote something horrid on the chalkboard, but only one kid gets caught and takes the blame...that would be him.

" It won't happen again, sir."

" Don't ever call me sir again private !" And he got right in Prince's face, " I work for a living. Just how long have you been in the Army, cherry ?"

" It's an old habit, s...s...sergeant. I'm sure I'll break myself of it." Prince looked like the gentle giant, the big dumb bunny...but still waters run deep, McAllister would be wise not to push him.

" Sgt. Glover, see that your men are ready in ti-ti time, there's a rumor that a huge battalion of NVA are camped out nearby...let's trap them."

" We'll be ready Sergeant McAllister."

As soon as he left, "Gorgeous" spoke up, trying to suppress his anger, " While McAllister is filling sandbags, who watches our water and C's ? How do we know the CP group might want to help themselves to some extra canteens ?"

Rufus was going to puncture his balloon, " It don't mean nuthin', there's not enough water to last for three more days."

" Rufus, I started with six full canteens, and now I've got four..."

"...and you believe brother that you are going to survive on two canteens a day for the next three days ? Got a hump like a camel ? This mission be a bust one way or the other, you dig ?"

Dylan was intellectually awakened, " So do we drink the blood of our enemies to stay alive ? Are we going to die of thirst ?"

" Rufus has dialed the right number, we're either going to get out of here early or be dreamin' 'bout root beer floats all day." Blackie, never smiling, had made his speech.

" Yeah, we'll see," and "Gorgeous " stomped his cigarette butt out in the dirt, " this fuckin' Army could give a fuck if we dry up out here."

"Get your gear together 'Gorgeous', we're moving out." Sgt. Glover was non-plussed.

While the entire company minus the three other outposts began filling sandbags, the third herd following a serpentine path through the field made their way to their outpost a klick away. It was behind a bamboo hedgerow, and Dylan's machine gun was in excellent position for anyone leaving the tree line. The machine gun was the most powerful weapon in their arsenal, and the entire squad made sure they all had plenty of ammo for him, and he made sure his weapon was clean and ready to go .

" Blackie, you got a deck of cards? It looks like it's going to be a long day. " Winston was getting antsy and it was still early in the morning.

" No poker, and no shuffling, this is a quiet mission, remember ?" Sgt. Glover leaned over on his side and went back to writing letters.

Juan tossed Winston a well-worn dog eared deck of cards, not saying a word...he was about to take a morning nap.

" Prince," he whispered, " how about some gin rummy ?" He nodded and Winston dealt, " can you imagine what you would be doing today back in Detroit."

" Not really, probably going to my job at the furniture store I guess. What about you ?"

" I graduated from college and three weeks later I got drafted for the fifth and final time. I didn't have time to think about a job, I mostly wanted to spend time with Veronica, my future bride, the love of my life, but I'm a piano player so I'll probably look for some band to join. Who knows ?"

They whiled away the afternoon whispering idle chatter, as did the others...only sleep made the time pass with ease. It was as hot as a playground in Hell, their clothes were drenched from sweating, and the clock was moving on lazy dials. The scenery was static as stone, nothing moved, not even a leaf. Donovan got the word they were to return early, as the sky began to blacken and the temperature dropped. A rare tropical storm was soon to liberate them from any form of guard duty.

Last of the outposts to return to the laager

site (a word held over from the Boer War, a main base camp protected by a circle of wagons, or sandbags in this case) as soon as they were ensconced in their corner, the wind and the rain joined forces to beat them up. Winston felt like he was being whipped by a fire hose. The rain was as dense as a wall of water and painful like hundreds of angry stinging bees. The sandbag fortress that the company had spent days filling was slipping away in the mud, the ground was saturated and Winston and Prince found themselves sitting in pools of water. He wondered if his M-16 would still fire, but only a lost NVA would be out tonight.

When the deluge ended it was night, the trading of one darkness for another.

The morning warm sun was a welcome feeling after a shivering night, and their day would be an echo of yesterday. The third herd was ecstatic to be on outpost rather than refilling sandbags in the mud, and by mid-morning they were dry...but a small difficulty was coming their way, and a large catastrophe was incubating in the sun.

Donovan informed Sgt. Glover the Captain and his entourage were paying them a visit. He was angry that the site Sgt. Glover picked was too close to the laager site and he personally wanted to set him straight.

The Captain escorted by his CP group, the first squad and Sgt. McAllister, was carrying

a shotgun and two shiny pistols special ordered stateside, gleaming Wyatt Earp style. He strutted like Teddy Roosevelt as he approached the third herd, angry as a wounded bull, " Get up soldiers !" Screaming loud enough that an NVA a klick away could've heard him, " do you consider this outpost a klick away from the laager site, Sergeant ?" Glaring at Glover.

Cowering, he looked at his map and meekly replied,
" I must have read the map wrong sir."

" Then perhaps I will personally show you where I want you to set up," he paused looking at the sweaty grimy soldiers freezing them in his sight, " do you feel capable of establishing a suitable location, or should I find someone else to lead your squad ?"

" I can do it sir, it won't happen again."

McAllister would've rather been filling sandbags...this kind of exposure, with the company commander as prime target, made him feel vulnerable, "You heard the Captain ! "Get your asses in gear gentlemen !"

They walked about five hundred meters, with Winston leading the way to a spot with less protection, less shade, but greater visibility.

" Set your Claymores up on all sides, and you..."pointing to Dylan, " ...aim your machine gun in the direction of the wood line." The Captain took a huge swig from his canteen.

" Sgt. Glover, I'll put my Claymore towards

the West." Rufus spoke like a model soldier.

" Good job, soldier." The Captain liked it when his orders went into action immediately.

"Gorgeous" and Juan had to hide their faces to stop from laughing, since Rufus' Claymore didn't have enough C-4 to blow up a yo-yo.

The Captain surveyed the scenery, his domain, his fiefdom, swelled up his chest and with one hand on a pistol...motioned to the others they would now return to the laager site.

" Nothing like a secret mission, huh Sarge ?" "Gorgeous" had to get the first bite.

" But thanks Sarge, for trying to keep us close to the main camp as possible." Dylan was sincere.

" Well, it was worth a try, and closer is always better..."looking at the ground, "...don't mean nuthin'."

" Well, if the gooks don't know where we are now, they never will..." Blackie paused, "...or there's none around nowhere."

" Amen to that !" Rufus put out his fist to Prince to meet the handshake, " that fuckin' Captain shouldn't be messin' with us. He lucky the 'assassin' don't walk with the First Platoon."

" He took a big risk with us," it was the first time Donovan had talked to anyone besides Sarge, " that John Wayne bit showing us where to be on outpost exposing himself as well as us was pretty fuckin' stupid. I've never heard of such a gung-ho Captain risking his life to teach some-

one a lesson." Donovan was from Virginia near Tennessee, and his words drawled out slowly, rich like syrup. Back in the world he was a school teacher.

" Donovan, you been in the Wolfhounds long as me,"
Rufus wanted to spit, "...this Captain be crazy, he's worried the gooks know our position and then...lookey here, he's Wyatt Earp and he thinks carrying shiny pistols is going to protect him from the gooks ? Blackie is right, if there are any gooks in this territory we wouldn't be having this conversation. This is no *quiet* mission. I don't know what is with his shit, but he's pushin' for trouble...he moves the company, he comes out into the field to personally tell the Sarge he's too close to the base camp, and for what ? He's lookin' for shit, and a hard rain is gonna fall."

In that Southern drawl that captures words so particularly, and gets one hanging on every syllable, Donovan added, " I believe you're right. I think the Captain is lookin' for a fight, and with his ad-ver-tise-ments (the word seemed to elongate in space) we should be lookin' Charlie in the eye real soon."

" Blackie's right, any NVA with a brain would be braggin' right now he got a Company Commander...we're in luck, this time they have di-di maued somewhere else..." Dylan yawned, "...it's cool...I bet there's not a gook around for miles and miles."

" I hope you're right, but we're on this out-post to be on the lookout, and that's what we're going to do," and Sgt. Glover made guard assignments.

The day was picking up heat, by noon it seemed it had never rained.

" So Rufus, what do you think, any gooks out there ?"

" I think the Sarge is right, you never fuckin' know...but my guts tell me they have di-di maued out of the area...what I'm worried about is what happens tomorrow morning and the entire company is out of water."

Winston licked his lips, " I'm already dreaming of a tall cool glass filled with ice. The water is so cold it gives you a headache when you drink it."

"Gorgeous" had to throw in his opinion, " I've never been in the field when we've run out of water, and knowing the Company Commander, Mr. gung-ho John Wayne, we'll run out of water and just live with it. I bet he's rationed his water so he won't run out," glaring at Winston, "...you know if you go without water long enough it'll drive you dinky-dau, people in the desert without water go..."

Rufus interrupted, " Lookey here, I seen what can happen in the heat without water, heat stroke can fry your brain like a hamburger," and with that he took a big swig from his last canteen, " don't mean nuthin'."

Back at the laager site, there were some GIs already out of water and refilling the sandbags in the hot sun was lowering morale by the minute. Conversation about the "drought" was becoming more vocal and vehement. They wanted the Captain to overhear them. There was still the night and the next day to go on this mission, an impossible task without water. The loudest to complain was the "assassin", and as the Captain approached the group, shirtless, but still wearing his pistols, all eyes were upon his last canteen, which was attached to his belt.

" So you men think the soldiers at Bataan ever got any water...they survived on a cup a day and not much more food. Remember you are Wolfhounds ! You can make it ! Pace yourselves filling those sandbags, take a break and make some shade with your poncho liners...and if the NVA attack, and our sources say they are travelling in this area these sandbags could save your life. No one ever said being a Wolfhound was easy, and remember...only the strong survive !"

The "assassin" had barely enough saliva to spit, and he couldn't take his eyes off the Captain's canteen. As the Captain walked away he could hear the soldier spit, loudly. The Captain turned and looked at him, and thought to himself there would always be someone that needed a little extra discipline.

Winston and Rufus were staring at the wood line, the blank inevitable, calmly nervous,

waiting and hoping no strangers from humanity would stumble, like grotesque blasts of fate, into their vision. Mother Nature was torturing them with the heat, and the sweat was like they had a new skin. There was still some water left among them, but they would wait until one step ahead of delirium, which was approaching fast...

Rufus, his head aswirl with a whirlpool of sweat, was numb to the immovable situation, and dehydration was beginning to take his mind down another road..." Lookey here,Winston, what would you do if a snake came crawling up to our position ?"

Winston was feeling a little droll in the heat, his eyes were losing their sense of three dimensional view from the constant staring, " I'd probably say hello, and let him crawl on his slithering way."

" Whoa brother. Everybody got hang-ups and mine are snakes. I can't use no snakes. They just break foul on me. A snake is just all wrong." He lit up a menthol, next to water it was refreshing,"...a snake started the world off wrong. It started the world in trouble when it talked Eve into biting the apple, and ole Adam's snake...whoa, that's a snake that can get you in beaucoup trouble...I can remember all those horror movies in my childhood...the snake always brings death. They bring evil, man. Can't use them. Every time I see one I know it's doin' wrong. Do you remember that snake on the flag ? That's when my

people were really down, that's when slavery was really big, and the Saigon River runs like a snake through the heart of Nam..."

" You're trippin' on me Rufus."

" You bic I hate to lose, although I know my day is comin', and I could never be a doctor, 'cause doctors lose, you can't stop death...and you ever see the symbol of doctors ? It's two fuckin' snakes wrapped around each other. You gotta lose with that...everybody got hang-ups and mine are snakes.."

Mother Nature was cooking, and they were on the menu.

The wait made the oven feel hotter.

Time had been suspended, moments dangled in the atmosphere awaiting their final punishment.

The picture never moved.

They stared. They waited.

The static scene was hypnotic.

And then they saw them...

Rufus' breath was an acid whisper as he rolled over to nudge the Sarge, keeping his finger to his lips. Everyone got real low as Donovan clicked back to the laager site they just sighted some NVA. It was a fast moment, and if Sgt. Glover hadn't seen them himself he would've doubted Winston and Rufus.

There were four of them, dressed in traditional black pajamas, all armed and moving quickly. There was a path from the field to the

woods and they just appeared from nowhere and then disappeared into the woods. They were a scouting party for another battalion of NVA on their way to another destination at Tet.

The four popped into Winston's consciousness in surrealistic injections, one at a time...and then they disappeared into the ubiquitous anonymous.

The entire squad was charged up and the word was to stay in place, keep your eyes open, and don't shoot unless in actual danger. It was still early in the afternoon, and the fear, the adrenalin, and the suffocating heat emptied every canteen, one by one.

"Gorgeous" was furious at the Captain for putting them there, Blackie was stone cold quiet; and the rest of the squad was hypnotized watching, staring at the never moving wood line. The afternoon was eroding in very long seconds.

When they returned to the sandbagged camp, the first GI they saw asked for water. It was not a friendly question. Winston took the cap off his canteen and held it upside down to illustrate the situation.

" Hey man, I was hoping there would be water here."

" This place is a desert. There's not a drop of water in camp, nada." And he walked away.

McAllister had protected their C's, as things were beginning to get a little rough around the edges, and some dudes would do any-

thing for a can of sliced pears or fruit cocktail, anything with any liquid to it."

Sgt. Glover smiled, "Thanks Sarge, appreciate that." He had been dreaming of sliced pears.

" Chuck was out scouting for a creek and saw a battalion moving through the jungle going south. He thinks they're gone, their objective is not us, and I hope so, the troops are exhausted from filling sandbags all day in the heat, waiting for Charlie to show up. It's going to be brutal here tomorrow without water. We're going to lose some people if something doesn't happen," McAllister was returning to the CP group,"...and your squad will be on outpost tomorrow."

"Gorgeous" was fueling the fire of his hate for the Captain, while the rest of the squad ate their C's. Prince was famished, " I'd give anything for a big glass of milk right now."

Juan piped in, " I'll take a beer, but that Captain better do something soon or he's goin' to have some crazy people on his hands." He took Pancho and made a sharp thrust across the piece of bamboo to emphasize his point.

The assassin, on the other side of the perimeter, was making plans. He felt he was being messed with.

" Lookey here, we should've been puttin' out our poncho liners last night and helmets and anything else that could catch the rain water, and we wouldn't be dreamin' about sleepin' under Niagara Falls."

" Shit, one thing for sure," "Gorgeous" could never stay out if a conversation, " if we make contact with Charlie, we'll be going' after his canteens."

Juan, always carving, never looking anyone in the eyes, " Too fuckin' bad Rufus, your crystal ball wasn't working last night."

" Too bad Juan," Rufus was trying to suppress a laugh, "you don't know where Niagara Falls is."

Juan did not like being made fun of, even if he didn't know how it was being done, " Some time you talk too much. Some time you watch what you say."

" Juan, it don't mean nuthin'," Dylan knew how to assuage his assistant machine gunner, " you know Rufus likes to fuck with you...be cool !" Juan never looked up from whittling.

" Hey Juan," Prince's innocent shyness was disappearing, and with his size he would be someone anyone would listen to, " I've been to Niagara Falls, it's not too far from where I live, and let me tell you...it's the World Series of water...if we could just get a trickle from that we'd be in hog heaven."

" Meanwhile our Company Commander thinks we Wolfhounds don't need water !" "Gorgeous" was irate righteous," he's like a fuckin' slug under a rock. he couldn't do what we do !"

" Lighten up a bit, 'Gorgeous'," Sgt. Glover was nearly as droll as Blackie, "the last thing I

want to do is to defend this man's Army, like I didn't get my lesson today, but no one's died of thirst, and it's not over yet, so stop bitchin'."

" Sgt. Glover," Donovan began, "...this Captain risking his own life venturing out into the field like he did, also put all of us in deep jeopardy today. Pure and fuckin' simple, and please pardon my French (he was rare on cursing or bad language) but he's a cowboy, and *all* cowboy; and cowboys get people killed...sometimes themselves...they like to take risks. I was beginning to feel like a short-timer, but with him I feel there's a long way to go."

" Lookey here, brother, you got a ticket on the Big Bird, and me..." Rufus abruptly ceased speaking, and stared out in space.

" C'mon Rufus," occasionally Blackie spoke up,"...we're going to make it. We're Wolfhounds ! Remember ? We're going on outpost tomorrow...and we will not die of thirst...let's hope the Kit Carson is right and the gooks have di-di maued the fuck outta here."

No one spoke, then their platoon leader, Lt. Osgood approached, " Hey you guys, guess you got a little close to some NVA today..."

" Lieutenant, when do we get some water ?" "Gorgeous" sounded like a disgruntled patron in a diner barking at the waiter.

"Let's hope soon. I know it's driving everyone a little bit crazy. You're just going to have to hang in there..."

" What happens if I *do* go a little bit crazy ?...""Gorgeous" continued, but was interrupted by Juan, " What happens my man decides he wants to drink someone's blood ? He's got a pretty bad crazy streak."

Lt. Osgood faced him. This conversation was going like a balloon letting the air out. " If George here feels the need to drink someone's blood, maybe you'll slash your wrists for him."

Juan was taken aback. He wasn't expecting that kind of retort from the Lieutenant.

"Gorgeous" looked at Juan, " You better be careful with that knife, my man, I could be a vampire."

The evening went by uneventfully. The entire company was of one mind...dreaming of swimming in a pool of ice cold water, drinking freely.

And life on outpost would have unraveled sanity at a faster rate, but their throats were too parched to speak continuously. Just as they en masse felt the Grim Reaper was turning the oven up to broil, at one in the afternoon they were summoned to return.

The mission was over, a new company was replacing them, and they were giddy with just the thought that water was soon to be cascading down their throats.

After downing a couple canteens, and several sodas Winston got the mail. It contained a "sugar report" from Veronica, and he felt like he

just won the decathlon.

CHAPTER FOURTEEN

From Sock Line to Listening Post

" UN-ASS THAT HOOCH !" And with a thunderclap of dissonance, the gossamer strands of conversation abruptly turned to stone and crashed, as the reality of Army smoked steel through their brains. It was Sgt. McAllister.

" Jesus ! What a voice !" Winston crushed his J into the dirt.

" That motherfuckin' McAllister is definitely the number one downer. What a God-damned cock suckin' lizard breathing douche-bag !" "Gorgeous" was furious.

" I want one straight line and I want every swingin' dick in line. I want to look down that

line and see one man. Let's move Charlie Three-...we don't have all day," his sharp succinct words and the pale expression with eyes of fire upon the men was an invitation to anger. Sgt. McAllister relished the medium, "...Can I have your attention...I want your Goddamned attention, gentlemen !" He had a special way of making gentlemen sound like "pig."

There was a slow pause as the men silently filed and merged into one line. There wasn't enough humble pie to go around.

" You are all getting one pair of white socks...just one pair to each swinging Richard." Winston looked at Rufus in total disbelief, as he continued, "...they've been donated by the Red Cross and the line companies are getting them first, that is why we are getting them first. Take care of them gentlemen...they're yours. You can't wash them in bath soap, they're made to be taken care of. We're lucky to get them, men, so take care of them."

So this was the purpose of the afternoon's call to arms...the giggle muse stomped on the bellows of hilarity, and Winston and Blackie began laughing.

" Now keep it quiet and file up and get your pair of socks."

That brought hysteria. Winston thought he was going to cry trying to hold back the laughter, and Blackie was buckling.

We're passing out hunks of gold today, so don't

wash it.

Winston turned back to Rufus and Dylan, " We're only getting one sock...and it's the left one." They howled.

Perhaps it was the lack of water or the excess of pot, the situation and the hot sun, but Sgt. McAllister or not, they just fell out.

" Winston ! Blackie ! You two get your young asses over here ! You'll get your socks last. Stand right over here, I want to talk to you two."

They couldn't look at the Sergeant, and they couldn't stop laughing. The others, Rufus and Dylan especially, were feeling rather punchy, but hid behind dark sunglasses and kept a straight face.

The gold was passed out.

" You two men are heading straight for the stockade, and I'm the one that's going to put you there. Blackie, your attitude has been off track ever since I've been here, and you ! You're a new man. You had better get your shit in order and get it quick. You two are going on listening post tonight."

While Blackie was ready to walk away and accept his fate as a soldier, Winston was beginning to lose his sense of humor, " You're using your personal power, your personal revenge...to screw us...and for what ? We laughed..." he didn't get to finish, as Sgt. McAllister put his face right up to Winston's. Winston could smell his breath and taste his spit, " You put yourselves there

gentlemen ! You put yourselves there ! You're dismissed."

There was nothing more to be said as far as the Sergeant was concerned. Tonight, being just days away from Tet, a human wave attack, according to intelligence, was expected. They were the perfect sized base to be overtaken, and those on listening post had a 50/50 chance of making it back inside if there was an attack.

As they were leaving, Winston said to Blackie loud enough for the Sergeant to hear, " The man's a sadist."

" I heard that ! And I have the stage here !" McAllister was erupting, his skin was bristling, " You will do as I say here. I'm the platoon sergeant here, and that's to get a job done !" Everyone in the sock line holding their treasured pair couldn't avoid his booming wrath, "...to keep you men alive, to get the job done, and get you home. You're all the same to me, every man looks alike, no one is special to me...I treat everyone the same. You *know* that young Lieutenant would be lost without me. Lost ! He's a young man like yourselves...not much time in the Army. I've got sixteen years experience behind me. This is my second war gentlemen...I fought in Korea and came out without a scratch, and with the grace of God I'm comin' out of this one the same way too. Your lives depend on me. When you get home, you're going to thank me. I didn't put you here gentlemen, I didn't bring you here, the gov-

ernment did...to fight communism...so we don
't have to fight on our own shores back home.
Would you rather fight in California ? Communism has to be stopped gentlemen, and you are
here to do a job and I am here to see you do it...
*Thank God they got a whole pair of socks, instead of
just a left sock.*
"...there'll always be a war, the Good Book says
so...from the start to the finish...there's nothing
you can do about it and there'll always be a draft.
Every man should serve his country and you two
are going to serve yours..." he paused to drink
from his canteen,"...I could get both of you for
insubordination to a senior non-commissioned
officer, but I won't. I'll give you another chance.
Your lives depend on me gentlemen. I can make
you or break you. If I want I'll take you to the
Company Commander and I know the Captain
will back me to the T, gentlemen, to the T. You'll
be courts martialed so quick you won't know
which end is up." Winston realized there was no
dealing with lifer craziness, this was the military, and began to walk away, but Blackie was
awakening out of his trance,
" I'm not going on any fuckin' listening post tonight, there's a human wave attack expected. No
one's going to survive on any listening post if the
gooks hit us like that !"

Just one pair of socks ?

McAllister exploded, " I said you're going,
you are going ! You got a problem with that ?"

Blackie scowled at the Sergeant and backed off. He got it. It was a losing battle, and to refuse to go into the field was a straight ride to the LBJ, the Long Binh Jail, clusters of cages buried beneath the ground, only allowing a few inches of daylight inside. It was a magnet for rats.

" I judge you by the way you are, and you got a surly ass attitude, and you better change it quick…or I'll get it changed for you just like that !" McAllister snapped his fingers and threw his pair of socks into a cardboard box.

" Do *you* have any questions ?" Glaring at Blackie. "Do *you* have any questions ?" Repeating the glare at Winston. If they were considering answering, the option was not available, as the Sergeant continued, " Korea was worse gentlemen, Korea was much worse. We'd go on LP in the Winter, and we didn't have any of those poncho liners or blankets, and the only cigarettes we got were in C-rations, and C-rations were the only food we got. There were men then, fighting Communism. They were men then." He tried to burn his words into them, "…not like the stuff that's coming out of that so called free U.S now…you're lucky. You're lucky you're not in Korea. You are both dismissed."

Are they passing out socks in Hanoi today ?

Blackie and Winston returned to the squad's bunker where Sgt. Glover informed them that "Gorgeous" and Prince would be joining

them on listening post tonight.

" The good news is that tomorrow you guys will have light duty." Sgt. Glover was smiling, " You guys really set off McAllister's fuse today."

" If there is a tomorrow ! We're going outside the wire on a night when the gooks are supposed to attack with a human wave attack, and that's not a suicide mission ?" "Gorgeous" was furious, "...there's going to be artillery, there could be guys on guard duty with a starlight, but no. The Army always has its way of doing things...send GIs out so they can be converted into cole slaw."

Donny, a rather goofy looking guy, the Company's candidate for a Section Eight (category of discharge for a service member mentally unfit for service) , who liked to live the look, passed by "Gorgeous", " So why don't you put on a dress ? Something pretty with polka dots and maybe you can get out of listening post tonight." "Gorgeous" just scowled at him as Donny skipped past him,

" I'll loan you my purse !"

Winston and Blackie started laughing again and the release from laughter was a strange but wonderful therapy that wouldn't let go. They continued to laugh long after whatever humor there might have been was forgotten.

This was an extremely small, company sized fire support base, reinforced with a mortar

platoon, and two artillery pieces and an FO who could call-in co-ordinates.

Tonight the two pieces were pulled up to the perimeter aiming straight level with the ground, and the battle hors d'oeuvres were beehive rounds, set to explode upon ignition expelling thousands of shrapnel randomly and forcefully. The entire company was adrenalized...the NVA had an amazing track record, no matter how overwhelmed they were militarily, they always got in.

When it became dark, the four of them, each armed with an M-16 and one extra clip, a canteen, and a poncho liner were escorted over the perimeter by Sgt. Glover. There were three rows of concertina wire and they were supposed to be between the second and third rows, but Sgt. Glover figured the race would be long enough just to make it back through one row of barbed wire if they were attacked.

Prince counted the steps from the hole in the concertina wire to their position, a distance of about twenty feet...in the dark they would never find it, and he knew that. He would barrel his way through if he had to. The ground out-side the base camp had some sloping features to it and they found a niche where they couldn't be seen from the perimeter, had a dim view of the outer rows of concertina wire, and a clear path to the hole in the wire.

Prince carried the radio and checked in

that Lima Papa 2 was in position. There would be no further conversation unless they saw something, and the CP group would let them know if the listening post on the other side saw anything, which was two clicks on the handset...and then run like hell.

Winston whispered very softly, " Prince, I know why Blackie and I are here, sorry about you and "Gorgeous"."

" Hey man, luck of the deal...don't mean nuthin'. I figure the two of us will get every rotten duty there was...until someone new comes in, I guess we're still the cherries."

Outpost by day was bright and hot, by night it was clouds playing God with the Moon...one moment everything is illuminated brightly, the next it's reduced to shadows, but all the while the view was pierced by the weaving of of barbed wire, an eerie surreal camouflage for the man on the other side. A twisted view of the night could not be more truer.

" Prince, how much time do you think we have before we see the gooks and the time we can get back inside the base camp ?" Winston was murmuring in Prince's ear.

" God help us brother there's just enough time, that's all I can say, and if I have to take a little barbed wire with me to get back in, so be it !"

There was no more talking, and the darker it became the more powerful the silence. No movement, no sound...like a black hole had de-

voured the base camp. The Captain was hoping the NVA would not be able to grope through the jungle and find them..it was a moonlit night, but cloudy. The NVA had perfected guerrilla warfare.

It was around 3AM, the time when all God's chillum should be asleep, that a GI on guard duty within the perimeter heard the "crunch" and yelled back to the mortar unit to fire a loomy -loomy. That "crunch" was the sound of the first wave laying their bodies on the out-side ring of concertina wire, so the next wave walking over them could do likewise. They were running, and when the loomy-loomy (a Kleig light broadly beaming gently descending on a parachute) became effective the final wave were laying down on the last row of concertina wire.

They *would* be getting in.

The Looey from Second Platoon was screaming to get the artillery piece in better position, as machine guns strafed the challenging wave of NVA, who fired back with their AK-47's, their single machine gun, but mostly grenades, which the camp was defenseless against. The loomy-loomys were bursting in the sky like the Fourth of July, and the eerie light earned shadows a new respect for the fear they could induce...they could mimic a reality that was not there, and colorize a fear that was truly there. Looking at the descending incandescence was like viewing an eclipse of the sun, the closer they got the brighter they grew, but when they

hit the ground they shattered into darkness. The sky was nothing but artificial stars...and at the sound of the first pop the four were ready to race back in, but it was too late...Sgt. McAllister's stern voice was crystal clear, " Stay where you are ! The attack is from the opposite side, stay down ! If you attempt to enter you'll be killed by someone !"

From the other side of the perimeter they could hear the cacophony of weaponry exploding in unison...the recoil noise of artillery was deafening, and the roaring aroma of gunpowder that ensued burned the eyes and enraged the nose.

Despite the firepower aimed point blank at them...the artillery, machine guns, grenades, M-16 fire, aided by the erratic illumination, the NVA through a barrage of grenades got the precious seconds to climb over the sandbag fortress and once inside the perimeter where everything was dark they were as invincible as rats. They could hear the cry for medic over the din of gunfire, and Winston looked at his cohorts wondering who was actually winning. There was no communication on the horn, only static, they were isolated on an island of barbed wire, cut off from everyone, with very little ammo.

Prince kept talking, louder and louder into the horn, trying to get a response...there was nothing.

" Jesus fuckin' Christ !" "Gorgeous" was

167

ready to claw someone to relieve his frustration, "...we're on fuckin' listening post and they've stranded us."

" Keep it down 'Gorgeous ' ! We can't risk moving ! The gooks are everywhere, and we can't move." Blackie was serious as an apostle.

They laid back and watched and listened to the fireworks while the loomy-loomys were falling all around them, with no rhyme or reason, exploding in momentary brightness when they hit the ground. Inside the base camp it was screaming madness...there were dead gooks and live ones, and the Wolfhounds were paralyzed with fear of shooting their own...in the chiaroscuro of moving shadows when someone aimed, there would be a moment of truth to fire or not to fire...and hesitation was often fatal. There were three medics attending to the wounded, some of whom were screaming in mortal agony, and the Wolfhounds retreated into and on top of their bunkers. Dylan replaced the machine gunner from the Third Platoon, whose body had fallen in front of the bunker, and was burning up a barrel repelling the NVA from further entry. Inside the CP, a Lieutenant felt his hair rise and curl inside his helmet, as an NVA regular stormed in shooting. The Lieutenant emptied his entire clip into the soldier, they were amazed no one had been injured, and all eyes and weapons were aimed at the entrance to the bunker. The next person to descend inside wouldn't

have the opportunity to identify himself. Inside another bunker GIs engaged in hand-to-hand combat, something they thought would only ever happen in the movies. The mortar platoon, already experiencing injuries, were terrified and hiding behind sandbags. They stopped firing the loomy-loomys as their vulnerability was erasing their courage, and firing mortar rounds meant complete exposure.

There were now just three NVA regulars within the perimeter, and the base camp was completely dark, except for the random bursts of gunfire. Juan grabbed Dylan and had him turn around, and he sprayed two of them with enough lead they could be donors for an iron lung. He was a careful, not fanatical marksman, and no one else was shot. The last gook turned into what was easy target practice as he jumped over the sandbag perimeter and began to race towards the concertina wire. The human wave attack was over, the NVA were retreating at a rapid pace dragging their wounded and the dead. Those that could move that had laid upon the barbed wire to be a bridge for their fellow soldiers unstuck themselves from their thorny bed and disappeared with the others into the jungle. From the far side Winston could hear them retreat and the loomy-loomys had returned via artillery from a neighboring base camp. They started sooner and higher and would fizzle before they hit the ground, and the light they

brought enabled some sanity to return. A dust-off was on the way, and finally McAllister's voice came over the horn, "Lima Papa 2, this is Foxtrot 43, roger this transmission ?"

Prince was ecstatic, " This is Lima Papa 2, can we come in ?"

" Negative. We have KIA's here. We think the situation is under control, right now there is a bunker to bunker check. Until we are sure there are no NVA within the base camp, you are to remain in position. Roger, over."

" What the fuck is going on ?" "Gorgeous" was steaming, " how many got through ?"

" How in the hell did they get through ? Those artillery pieces with the beehive rounds can turn a picnic into cole slaw." Blackie's voice was back to the usual monotone.

" How could they get through all that barbed wire, that's what amazes me, and through all that firepower ?" Winston was truly perplexed.

The loomy-loomys continued to burst into the air, their tiny parachutes making a popping sound as they unfurled. A dud screamed over their heads and landed outside the last row of concertina wire, about thirty feet away. The scream was piercing.

" I love it !" "Gorgeous"took his hands away from his ears, " now we're getting bombed by our own guys."

While Prince kept his ear to the horn, they

saw the dust-off leave and another one land. It was not a good omen. Soon it would be dawn and the loomy-loomys would be ceasing, so Winston lit up a square, " Blackie, was this the way it was last year ? Human wave attacks all over Nam during Tet ?"

" Last year was pretty bad I guess, beaucoup GIs died..."

"...and a whole lotta gooks too." "Gorgeous" interrupted.

"...and if this is the beginning, we're in for some real trouble. Charlie doesn't think like we do, a suicide mission for them is part of being a soldier, although the Vietcong are different...they'd rather snipe at you."

Prince jumped in, " The Sarge said there's KIA's, but he didn't say how many."

" I guess we'll find out when we get back in."

" Whenever that'll fuckin' be," "Gorgeous" lit up a smoke also, he was dying for a butt.

They were exhausted, and when the dawn's rays began to burn them with sunshine, they were finally allowed to come back in. The base camp was a mess and still in turmoil. When Winston put his hands over the sandbag perimeter he could hear the sound of safeties snapping off. He yelled, " Hey ! It's the listening post ! Don't shoot ! " The men from the Third Platoon had lost eight men, they were on edge and ready to shoot anything. They wanted revenge.

Once inside Sgt. Glover greeted them, " Good to see you guys made it."

" No thanks to the fuckin Army !" "Gorgeous" was ready to get into someone's face.

" Did anyone get it from our platoon ?" Blackie spoke like an undertaker.

" Donovan has joined his buddy, and checked into the Big Hotel."

" Oh man, that's a bummer, he was a good dude."
Winston looked up in the sky, as if he could actually see something.

" He was about to leave the bunker, help some guys from the Third Platoon and a bad luck frag landed in his lap. He never knew what happened to him."

The men from the Third Platoon were carrying in the bodies of the men from the other listening post and laid them next to one another. Their bodies were grotesquely mutilated, by no telling what kind of firepower. It was their uniforms that positively identified them. The Platoon Sergeant was crying, as tough as he was, when he removed their dogtags, and had them put in body bags immediately. The image of a friend, a comrade, once normal now barely recognizable, was put in freeze frame in the memory bank. It would haunt them in the nightmares yet to come...

Winston and the others *did* stare at them...Winston wanted to cry, and there but for

the grace of God it could've been them. If the NVA had chose to attack their side of the perimeter someone else might have been looking at them, wondering who they were and how did they get that way.

" How many gooks got killed ?" Winston was shocked that he asked that question. Was he that much into the war?

Sgt. Glover looked to the outside of the perimeter as he spoke, " As soon as some unit does a sweep we'll know how many outside, but ten motherfuckers bought a one-way ticket back up the Ho Chi Minh trail."

" Ten ! How did that many get in ?"

" Before we could move the artillery piece in the right position they were in...they were tossing grenades and shooting everywhere. It was insane, it was a miracle more didn't get in."

" But how did they get through the con-certina wire ?"

" They're running Winston...they don't stop to cut through the barbed wire...they *lay* on it, one wave at a time, and they were probably in and throwing frags before we fired a single shot."

Winston, looking at Prince, " I guess the other LP never had a chance."

" They radioed in, I guess, as soon as they could...no one will ever know. It happened pretty fast."

Winston joined Rufus, hoping to mooch a ball of C-4 from him to heat up a cup of coffee, "

" Hey man, good to see you made it…must have been real hell last night." He sat down next to him.

" Lookey here Winston, it was unbelievable once they got in, we just hugged the top of the bunker and kept an eye out. Dylan replaced the machine gunner from the Third Platoon, who bought a mean frag from the gitgo, and the rest of us kept watching…everywhere. With the fuckin' flickering of the loomy-loomys , you couldn't tell who was a gook and who wasn't. You couldn't take a shot…there were guys running all over the place. Dylan killed two gooks on the inside, no counting how many he got on the outside. It was a brutal night…I really felt for those guys on listening post, they didn't have a chance. When the gooks got near they were tossing grenades and shooting everything they got. When the frag went off inside the bunker we all knew Donovan was dead. He didn't speak, when we yelled at him, and no one could leave the top of the bunker to check him out. It was horrible knowing he was just beneath us and could have been helped."

" Glover said he probably never knew what hit him."

" It was a bad scene. Those NVA always seem to get in, no matter what. We all worried about you guys, but since they attacked from the other side, we knew after awhile you guys were better off than we were."

" There was zero communication over the radio. All we heard was gunfire, explosions, and yelling. We felt like we were adrift on a raft, lost at sea…no communication, nowhere to go, waiting for someone else to decide what's happening with our lives. I'm exhausted, there was no sleep last night."

"Winston, my man, beaucoup shit to go."

Mornings in Nam always seemed to get too hot too fast. Dylan was sound asleep on the top of the bunker with his head on his helmet. Juan was whittling mindlessly, his incessant hobby and Blackie and "Gorgeous" sat and talked to each other, or Blackie listened, while Prince laid back and wrote a letter to his mother.

The Third Platoon, which had suffered the most casualties, as a result of the night's horror had created a "crier" and a "screamer", two twisted muses of insanity. One GI, who lived bullet by bullet through the night, totally adrenalized, never wavering…true as Sir Galahad, jumped over the perimeter, the first to go out. He had to check on their Listening Post, and he didn't have to go far to find his best friend.

There was only half a head, but he recognized his body. The other three members of the LP were next to him strewn on the ground like broken GI Joe dolls, except real. The platoon sergeant asked him to help carry a body back inside the base camp, and of course he did what he was told to, he was a good soldier. When he placed

the body of his friend down upon the ground, he could feel things crackling, falling apart...it was a feeling more wordless than a broken heart... more depressing than the giving up of hope...it was a crippling sadness...he started to cry...and couldn't stop...the river had to run itself dry. The "screamer" on the other hand was psychotic, seeing the four bodies set his compass on "all kill" and he screamed and strutted and screamed all around the perimeter for revenge...he was ready single-handedly to go after them, until one of the "Docs" gave him a little morphine to ease the madness. The next day he would awaken to an all day duty of burning shit. Today he would sleep. The "crier" eventually stopped, the well ran dry, and he curled up inside his poncho liner against the side of a bunker, and likewise, sweet sleep remedied his shattered soul.

McAllister approached Sgt. Glover, " Get your men together, we're making a sweep outside the perimeter. We are looking for "live" ones."

It was very demanding for Dylan, he was weaving back and forth like a drunk. Total exhaustion. McAllister yelled back, " George, you walk point." He was very nonchalant.

He stormed up to the front of the line, while everyone else stopped. Turning to McAllister, never stopping, "Fuck you ! " He kept moving briskly, " Fuck you ! I'm not walkin' point. I'm tired of this shit. I'm tired of all you fuckin' with

me. Harassment. That's all it is, harassment."

" Shut up boy."

" Don't call me boy, you see a boy..."

" Shut up George ! There are no individuals in this man's Army. It's your turn, and that's it. Start walking."

Sgt. McAllister merely folded his arms.

" Oh don't give me that shit. There are a lot of guys that haven't pulled it yet...beaucoup guys. I know. I know. You're just fuckin' with me. Okay. I'll walk point and there better not be anything out there...man, woman, child...I'll shoot them. Nothing better move out there. You guys get your shit in order...'cause I'm firing at first sight of anything." "Gorgeous" stomped to the front of the line, weapon on automatic, shoulders hunched over and eyes angry and ready to go.

Winston turned to Dylan, who was smiling in a stupid tired sort of way, " My God, you'd think we were storming the Bastille."

" That's 'Gorgeous ' for you." Dylan had seen this movie far too many times.

Winston was walking second, and they were barely outside the perimeter, when "Gorgeous" yelled back, "Here's a body ! He's a kilo." The first of many to come.

Circus time.

Feeling that he shouldn't, but wanting to, Winston moved closer to the dead body, pretending to be oblivious, while Juan and "Gorgeous "

were on him like white on rice.

Rufus was standing over them, " I wonder if he's got any stuff on him ?" He always wanted to know if the NVA were all heads.

" Well, we won't know until we search him," "Gorgeous" looked at the body. The NVA regular had been shot in the head, his mouth was goldfish like, and his hands, frozen in rigor-mortis, were as in prayer clasped against his chest.

Juan was going through his pockets, and looked up at "Gorgeous", " Get down on it Jack. What's holdin' you back ?"

" Nuthin'." "Gorgeous" was just staring at the body.

" I thought you liked to search bodies." Juan had turned him over looking for more pockets.

" My mother didn't raise me to go scroungin' for stuff in the pockets of a dead man."

Juan was completely nonchalant as he finished going through his pockets, " Oh wow ! How you gonna act ?" He pulled out a bag of white powder and some small photographs, the size kids use to exchange in school. "Number one smack ! I know some guys in the rear who'll pay beaucoup for this shit."

" Do you want to check some more, maybe you missed something ?" Juan was immune to "Gorgeous's" sarcasm.

"Hey look at this ! There was a MPC dollar folded up in a tiny cloth purse.

Winston watched aghast, he felt nauseated. The corpse looked so pale and stiff, his brains a jigsaw puzzle lying on the ground, the bullet hole through his head told the story that at least he didn't suffer.

And what did you do in the war, daddy ?

The figure once had life, felt love, felt hate...danced as a child and grew to be a person, now laying still awaiting the flies and the ants. How strange to end up being searched for dope by renegades of a macabre Easter egg hunt.

McAllister made his way up front, " You men find any thing ?"

Juan held up two scrawny photographs. " This is it Sergeant." McAllister glanced at them for a moment and then tossed them on the ground. Only Winston was curious enough to pick them up. They were two indistinguishable oriental faces, their significance now perished.

" Let's keep moving gentlemen, maybe we'll booby trap this gook on the way back."

There were bodies everywhere. The ground was strewn with body parts as if some mad surgeons were playing sport with cadavers, and tossing their mistakes on the ground. There would be a corpse with no insides, and another bereft of a complete side. There were parts everywhere of the human anatomy hanging from the barbed wire...symbols of the last insane effort to get nowhere. It was a carnal clothesline, a circus of gore, and to the guys of the third herd of the

First Platoon of the Wolfhounds this was a trip with Alice through the bloody glass.

Winston looked at what looked like an ass hanging on the barbed wire. It was just protoplasm, lost flesh chewed up by the war machine.

It was very bizarre, very sad, death's secret ragged remains.

How far did this man journey to end up anonymous on the battlefield, unrecognizable and unknown ? How much misery and fear did he go through before he took that one step beyond ? It was just an ass and nothing more, only God knew where the rest of him was or who he was, and in a strange and twisted way this gory flag was the true banner of battle.

Lt. Osgood, who had felt compelled to join them was having a heyday. He felt like it was his body count, although he was stashed in the CP bunker last night, and the reality was mostly what he heard and saw through the bunker peephole. He never fired a shot nor gave an order. With posture correct, arms arched just right, the twenty-four year old who looked nineteen burped out orders to his men, "Winston, you and Rufus check out those NVA over there, George, you and Prince go to the opposite side."

There was a sea of carnage between the perimeter and the second row of concertina wire...nothing but blood and bodies everywhere. Overhead a Chinook was dropping off a backhoe. Tomorrow would be the grisly funeral service. It

was such a simple ceremony. One grave fits all.

"Gorgeous" yelled back to the Lt., " I've found a live one !" The NVA regular was breathing and his eyes were open. He knew his fate and was waiting out his time, by nightfall he too would be riding with the Valkyries.

"Gorgeous" pointed his rifle at the prone soldier, "Should I put the dog out of his misery ?"

There was a long moment of silence. The Lieutenant didn't speak, no one said a word. "Gorgeous" took his M-16 off safety, the man barely blinked at the sound of the click.

" Don't do it !" It was Winston.

"Gorgeous" turned the M-16 towards Winston,
" And why do you want to save this fuckin' gook ? So he can come back again another day and try and kill us ?"   Juan tossed his lit cigarette at the nearly dead man, " He's right. Do you think this Charlie would do the same for us ?"

Winston felt alone. " You don't kill a wounded defenseless man. We're Americans, it's part of the Geneva Convention..."

" Rufus," who was carrying the radio, "call back for a gurney, we got a live one."

"Gorgeous" was steaming as he put his rifle up. He glared at Winston. There was nothing to say. He had no idea what the Geneva Convention was and didn't care.

Lt. Osgood had his men patrol the entire perimeter of the base camp, although one half

looked like nothing had ever happened, and the other half was a grotesque salute to man's ability to destroy himself. As they were halfway across, on their way back, feeling very relaxed and secure that nothing was going to happen, looking forward to sleeping away the afternoon; a terrible tragedy occurred. They heard the shot, and all hit the ground. It came from the inside of the perimeter. Rufus was on the horn as soon as he hit the ground, " This is Charlie One, what's that shot ? Have the NVA attacked ? Over."

" Stay put Charlie One, negative news at this time." The RTO from CP was always terse.

After fifteen minutes, the usual eternity, they were summoned to return. Three guys from the Second Platoon decided it would be cool to take some pictures of each other amongst all the dead NVA, and maybe find a war souvenir, so they climbed over the berm of sandbags and had a good ole time laughing and posing for pictures with each other. They acted as if it was a celebration, a grand reunion...perhaps they should start singing...they felt like they had single-handedly won the war. Coming back, the first guy that popped his head over the top of the wall of sandbags had a vision of a bullet, but only for a second. An artillery guy, who wasn't ever used to being on guard, fired the instant he saw him. It never occurred to him that any GIs would be on the other side of the perimeter, and he didn't hesitate to find out.

The other two GIS, after recovering from the shock of seeing their buddy's head blown off, started running to another point at the perimeter. They both started yelling with all the force in their lungs, "There's a gook inside the camp ! Charlie's inside ! Charlie's inside !" And screaming they pole vaulted over the sandbags, guns at the ready, and then they saw the GI with his head hung down low, another Wolfhound was taking his M-16, the platoon sergeant and the Top Sergeant were running over to him. The one GI fell to his knees...took aim with his M-16, and slowly, very slowly put his weapon on the ground, put his head in his hands and started weeping. The other ran screaming to the man from artillery, "You bastard ! You killed one of our own ! You fuckin' bastard, I hope you die in Hell ! I oughta kill you, you stupid bastard !" He was losing all self control as he charged the man and had to be restrained. It took three guys to hold him down, all the while he kept screaming at the man.

The Top Sergeant approached the man from artillery, " Soldier, I'm placing you under house arrest. Come with me."

The man kept his head down. He had nothing to say. He had committed the worst sin a soldier could do. It polarized the entire camp, all the infantry soldiers were ready to kill the dude from artillery, who was now confined to his bunker, probably the safest place in Nam for him. The Captain, and everyone else in the

command group, was trying to defuse the anger that had permeated the troops like a disease. Everywhere you could hear... "that motherfucker never looked ! That trigger happy bastard deserves to be shot ! Bad enough we have to deal with Charley, now we got an enemy on our own side...let's kill the killer..."

When the Chinook arrived with the backhoe it also brought ammo, food, and the mail, but mainly it defused the situation. Winston's care package from his mother contained cookies, candy, sardines, and a stack of Washington Post crossword puzzles. Something, anything from the world was such a welcome feeling. It was the connection that there actually was something other than a jungle and guys in fatigues. There really was something out there eight thousand miles away.

He also got a letter from Veronica. It even smelled like her.

Prince relaxed in the hot sun and read his letters from home, and while some slept, Rufus, Blackie, and "Gorgeous" were in the "head" bunker firing up some J's.

It felt like being inside a bird's egg, tiny, all brown and warm, with enough space for two eyes to look out and watch for unwanted sergeants. Blackie was on guard and handed Winston a J as he entered the dark bunker.

Rufus and "Gorgeous" were having a hot conversation, and Winston opened his care pack-

age to share the cookies, but reading his sweetie's letter put him in a trance, a reverie of an old memory...the night they got caught in a hot fierce Summer rainstorm, and removing their clothes in the down pour, a grassy spot near the parking lot became their instant Eden. It was fun. It was exciting. It was daring, and unforgettable. Rufus' rant snapped him out of it, and in seconds he was back in Nam.

Rufus was steaming mad, " Can't even dig that sight ! Not even ! Talkin' 'bout breakin' most foul ! I never want to see that scene again...and the shit is just beginning, Tet is still a few days away."

"Gorgeous" took a deep drag and handed Winston the J, " If you hadn't said something today, there would be one less gook to deal with." He spit against the bunker wall to emphasize his point.

" And that would make you a murderer, and we're soldiers, not murderers. Where I come from, which is the same place you come from, we don't kill unarmed people," and rapidly changing the subject he turned to Rufus, " hey man congratulations on getting the radio. Too bad it means you'll be closer to the Lieutenant."

Rufus lowered his voice, " Too bad Donovan had to die for me to get it, and I could give a rat's ass about the radio, it don't mean nuthin'." He put his fist out to everyone, " he was a good dude. We hardly knew him, but he seemed like

185

a real good man...when your number's up, your number's up."

"Gorgeous" was mellowing out. The heat, the exhaustion from the night before, combined with the pot was putting his mind in a psychiatric hot tub, " Fuck it, at least he'll never see another human wave attack."

"Lookey here, it was so unreal to see all those dead gooks, man, and to wind up as scrap in a human wave attack ? Oh wow ! I can't even dig it !"

" It is unreal...they came from the North and had to walk God knows how far through jungle and fantastic terrain...fire up that J Rufus...and they were trained same-same as us, and most of them drafted...and to end up hanging on the barbed wire...how would you like it to be your turn to lay on the barbed wire ?"

" Winston, my man, life doesn't mean near as much to the gooks. To die a glorious death, you're on a number one trip. Can you dig being a kamikaze pilot ? That's gotta be the baddest trip of all, but to the gooks it don't mean nuthin'. It don't mean a motherfuckin' thing."

" I still can't imagine it...there must have been hundreds of assorted bodies out there, and that one spot...you'd never know they were ever human. It's like a monster just chewed them up-...it was amazing...I've never seen so much blood. I think I'd rather walk point, at least it's not definite you're going to die."

" Oh man, don't talk the bad scene...I'm getting the death rattle...I feel it coming. We were lucky last night, it was the Third Platoon bit the bullet..." he paused, "...I feel it comin'."

" C'mon Rufus, don't get on that bad rap, you'll make me angry." "Gorgeous" voice was touching, pleading. For all his hatred and sarcasm, in this squad they were all brothers.

Rufus was in a nervous whirl, " I gotta get out of these next missions. I've been here too long, and those motherfuckers will never take me off line. They think I give them too much shit...I don't give them nuthin'. They won't be satisfied until I die. I'm amazed I'm still alive this long. Oh God, I gotta make it, but I feel it coming, somebody's gonna have to break my leg...I can't go out there anymore...my time is comin'."

" 'Gorgeous ', your turn to watch the portal." Blackie switched places with him.

" I'm steppin' out...I gotta figure some way to sham out of these next missions..."

" Don't we all." Blackie lit a square.

Rufus was exploding, " Man, I just know I'm going to die. I hate to tell you guys...but I just can't hold it back. I wouldn't be alive now if I didn't sham on my glasses."

" Don't rap like that Rufus. If anyone is going to make it, it's going to be you brother. I know you're going to make it, " Winston took a seminal drag on the J and passed it on, " don't let that gook graveyard get under your skin. I

don't get my rocks off either, looking at dead bodies, not like Juan...that was a real playground for him, and you would have thought Lt. Osgood had won the battle, the way he was acting.

" Yeah, he really dug that shit."

" He was trippin' on all those dead bodies, you'd think he killed them all."

Blackie interjected, " He's a dud. It staggers the imagination the only orders he's ever given we're already being carried out.Winston, you know they're settin' up trip flares on the dead bodies ?" He began to unroll some Kents (not worth smoking).

" Jesus ! What a detail ! I'm afraid I couldn't touch them...what a downer !"

"They figure the gooks will come back tonight and try and drag the bodies off. They've done it before. It'll probably be red alert tonight ." Blackie spoke monotonously, as if he was reading the sports page.

"The dude from arty," Rufus was getting gospel, "that dude from arty is going to fry in some kind of Hell, even if he has to make it himself, God rest his soul."

" You're being awfully kind to someone who was trigger happy enough to shoot without looking, " Blackie never looked at Rufus.

" Lookey here, this dude was a cruel fool, but you know deep in your hearts he never meant to kill him, and for that he's going to suffer...no fuckin' court martial can even put the

touch on the punishment he's going to put on himself...the man never would ever dream of killing one of his own...but he did. Amen."

" He may feel guilty because he fucked up big time, but the other GI checked into the Big Hotel today, and he shouldn't have...the dude was too hungry to shoot.."

" Gorgeous" snarled his words.

"...or too afraid. What was a guy from arty doing there in the first place ? They don't stand guard. That's weird." Winston was trying to Sherlock the situation.

" Maybe he was about to go souvenir shopping himself, " Blackie closed his eyes, savoring the smoke,

" there's all kind of dudes right now taking pictures, acting like heroes. There's a real smorgasbord of carnage out there for the folks back home to see...Winston, are you going to share those tootsie rolls ?"

" Getting the jones, huh ? Nothing like a little Mary Jane to whet the appetite." Winston tossed the tootsies around, "so what do you think will happen to that arty dude ? Will the military punish him ?"

Rufus laughed, " The military will probably transfer him to another unit and unless he says something no one will ever know, but you never can tell, the Army might court martial him. Either way he's goin' to pay."

" What makes you so sure ?" Winston in-

haled another tootsie.

" There was another guy, an infantry dude from Alpha Company, who broke foul and fucked up and accidentally killed his buddy. The nightmares wouldn't go away. He'd beast out in the middle of the night and start screaming, he would lose it during the day and not know where he was, and one afternoon he took his M-16 and put the barrel in his mouth. It was the only way to ease the pain," he paused, "I feel for the dude, I really do."

" I disagree with you Rufus, I'd put him in jail..."

"Gorgeous ", quiet while monitoring the small window to the base camp had to offer his opinion, " Roger that Blackie, I'd have him fry in the electric chair."

Winston ended this conversation, " Hey you guys, eat some tootsie rolls, there are a few left...what was the story on Lt. Osgood today ? He was on cloud nine, you'd think he was on R&R."

"Gorgeous" laughed, " The dude was trippin' ! God, he was diggin' it ! Consider Osgood can't even set up for ambush, he never knows where to put the various positions. If he ever pulled his head out of his ass for one moment the shock would blind him."

Rufus crushed out the J, " How you gonna act if the shit hits the fan, and there was no McAllister, and we had to depend on Osgood ? Freak on it !"

Blackie was stuffing another cigarette, tamping it down as he went along, " It was a strange sight today...it's hard to imagine they were all once alive, and they gave it up for a human wave attack. Osgood couldn't hide his smile...he couldn't stop himself. I wonder what he was grinning about, was he proud of something? It just couldn't be that funny."

" Maybe he was trippin'." Rufus knocked off the last tootsie roll.

" He's so square, his edges are showin'. I blew a J in front of him once and he never knew it." "Gorgeous" was laughing, " do you think Osgood is going to be a lifer?"

Winston jumped in, " I doubt it. He went to college, got drafted, went to O.C.S. and he digs the status but I don't think he could be buried in the institution. That's part of the scene anyway, doing a great job as an officer in the war and going home. Osgood doesn't have the spirit of the war like the lifers do, although no question he was diggin' it today, and he does go along with the program one hundred percent. Hey, it don't mean nuthin'."

Blackie fired up his freshly rolled J, " Maybe we should all hold our breaths until the Peace Talks come up with something."

" Maybe, maybe...I can get Juan to break my leg."

" Stop talking like that Rufus!" "Gorgeous" yelled at him, " you're right about one thing. If

anyone would do it, it would be Juan, if you paid him enough money, but you're going to be all right. Cut the jive, man."

" You got a roger on that 'Gorgeous' ! And Rufus, I know we'll still be here and you'll be on the Freedombird right on time," Winston took a hit off the J,"...anyway, it looks like a good day in the Nam to get stoned."

"Gorgeous" went to crash, while Winston, Blackie, and Rufus talked the afternoon away, and neither would let Rufus say one more word about his sense of impending death. When it came to chow time, they were so ravenous they relished "shit-on-a-shingle" the main course and even went back for seconds. Creamed chip beef, Army style, was more suited for filling potholes.

It was soon to be night, and having spent the last hour with the CP group being briefed about tonight, Sgt. Glover gathered his squad together on the bunker top.

" According to a Chieu Hoi (which literally meant 'I surrender ') they're supposed to hit again tonight." His tone of voice was the same as if he was ordering a hamburger from a drive-in restaurant.

" They got a Chieu Hoi ?" Dylan was flabbergasted, " where was he hiding ? In the shitter ?"

He was one of the NVA that got inside, had taken a round in the shoulder and crawled behind the Third Platoon's bunker and was waiting

to die underneath some sandbags. "Chuck" had interrogated him all morning to get the truth out of him, and his style would hardly be condoned by the Geneva Convention.

" 'Chuck' says they are planning to come back again tonight, so we have to get everything ready...lay out ammo and frags, open up some LAWS (light anti-tank weapon), as the Captain is personally going to inspect every bunker.

What happened last night is not going to happen again. Blackie you're to get a case of 79 rounds for your grenade launcher, and Dylan there's an extra barrel for your 60, and you and Juan should have a minimum of 10,000 rounds, each. Ordnance, behind the CP bunker is waiting for us to get re-supplied, so let's get moving and get this bunker completely squared away...and the good news is the whole company is moving out tomorrow to a battalion size base camp.

There would be no listening posts tonight.

Within a half hour there was enough firepower in or on the bunker to destroy a small town. There were clusters of frags with their pins straightened out ready to pull, about a half dozen LAWS combat ready, boxes of 16 ammo on each side of the bunker, a case of 79 rounds, enough machine gun ammo to string out a half dozen Christmas trees, and even cans of diesel fuel which, if necessary could be lit so that warships would know they are not the target. If the bunker took a direct hit by a mortar round, the

explosion would create a crater that looked like a B-52 had bombed it, and the Army wouldn't have to worry about dogtags.

" Well Sarge." Winston took in the panorama of armament, " it makes a great show if nothing else."

" Better safe than sorry," the Sarge maintained his cool attitude," I hope they don't hit us...but you never know."

" Our shit's together, but let's hope if they do hit, it's on the other side."

" Roger that." And Sgt. Glover left to take a shower while there was still light.

" Hey man, what's happening ?" Goofy grin and all, Dylan sounded like he was meeting a friend at the movies. The squad was all on top of the bunker, some sleeping already, some waiting, and Rufus on guard.

" Kind of scary out tonight," Winston sat down next to him.

" There's nothing to do but wait. Who knows when they're going to hit, it could be in an hour or 3 AM. Don't mean nuthin'."

Dylan joined them, " Might as well blow a bowl."

" Do you think it's safe ? I mean the Sergeant Major is prowling around. We're pretty exposed out here, and how do you deal with being high, if we get attacked ?"

" No matter, the wind is blowin' our way..." Juan was opening his care package from

San Antonio of canned chilies, tamales, bean dip, BBQ potato chips, and the proverbial staple...Tabasco sauce.

Dylan handed him the bowl, " When you hear the crack of a bullet over your head, it's an instant downer...like you never smoked. No worries."

There was something exciting about being so surreptitious about creating something invisible...getting high and no one knows.

" All the lifers will be checking out the bunker line all night. For sure, *they* want to make sure they are protected. They probably have as much ammo as we do in their bunkers." Dylan put the bowl back in one of the many pockets in his fatigue pants. Not caring if the First Sergeant saw him, he threw his socks into the shitter.

CHAPTER FIFTEEN

"The Humpty-Dumpty Chaplain"

They had no sooner finished, then this Humpty-Dumpty like figure approached them, armed with a humble smile, a Bible, and Captain's bars.

" Would you men like to join me in a moment of silent prayer, or if you like we can say a prayer together ?" He just stood there looking at them. With a very round face and a bald head it was like a somber egg nestled atop some very starched fatigues. He was a man that had never missed a meal in his life, with the girth of a Friar Tuck but all in all he was the perfect clone of Humpty Dumpty.

The three of them just looked back at him, speechless. The Humpty-Dumpty chaplain began to stare, but kept a calm expression.

Winston and Dylan stopped gaping at him, " No thanks, chaplain, I don't need a prayer. The Humpty-Dumpty chaplain was taken aback and simply stared at him, " How about you, GI ?" Dylan gave him his big goofy grin, " No thanks Captain, maybe you should try the next bunker." There was a pause.

" And you soldier ?" Looking at Juan.

Juan never looked at him, never said a word, just continued eating and shook his head.

The Humpty-Dumpty chaplain took one step towards Winston, " You know you have a lot to lose if the Bible is right."

If you die tonight, don't say I didn't tell you so !

Winston looked him right in the eye, " I guess I'll find out."

" Take this pamphlet, it's got something to say..."and the Humpty-Dumpty chaplain moved on.

" Man it's like our last night on Earth, they must really be expecting something...the chaplain going around to every bunker and saying a prayer." Dylan was getting nervous. They looked down to the next bunker and saw three soldiers with their heads bowed and the Humpty-Dumpty chaplain mouthing only God knows what."

Winston was bitter, " The Army is just too good to us, giving us a prayer...when a human wave attack is expected...what is this the Last Rites ? Why we poor li'l infantrymen are just getting treated too well. We don't deserve this."

" You know *he's* got an awful lot to lose if the Bible is wrong," Dylan pulled out his bowl and stuffed it.

Winston laughed, " That's right, he's dedicated his life to it. Funny if he found out that when you die you're going to some place no one knows about, and all that Heaven and Hell stuff is just make believe."

Dylan was "all there" with Winston, " Too many Christians have made too many wars."

" Since the time of Christ, and *long* before that, there's always been some kind of war. There's something about religion though that brings out the desire to kill, no matter the consequence. What a club ! Join or die ! But if everyone that was ever killed in a war stayed alive the planet would be huge. I guess it's as good as the Plague as a form of population reduction...next to Nazis, no one loves to kill on a grand scale than righteous Christians or righteous Muslims."

" It's very very sad."

" It'll never end."

" A prayer wouldn't hurt though." Juan spoke softly as he put down "Poncho" and opened up a can of tamales.

" I thought you were saving those for to-

morrow?"

Dylan was grinning.

" I'm hungry," and Juan started munching away,

" you want one Winston ? Put a little Tabasco on it, it'll make a man out of you."

" If I had known that, I would have started drinking it long ago."

" Why didn't you say a prayer when the chaplain came by ?" Dylan was all Cheshire Cat.

" That's not how I do it."

" I can't figure out why you're eating those tamales. I thought for sure you were saving those for breakfast."

" Hey Dylan, eat one...they're good." And Juan slapped him on the knee, " besides, you never can tell..."

Winston didn't say a word and merely set a match to the pamphlet the chaplain gave him.

The evening was nerve wracking...either the Top Sergeant or the Captain came by every hour to check on every bunker...but peaceful...in the far distance you could hear the sounds of combat, but whatever was going on, had passed them by.

◆ ◆ ◆

The organizers of Woodstock were making plans for the event, which would occur some-

time this year in August. The country was changing enough that an event like that *could* happen. The anti-war movement was spreading wildly, becoming adopted by the mainstream, and it was becoming a patriotic belief that it was better to end the war and save lives rather than try for a victory which seemed more and more illusive. Never had America lost a war...and to equate that with patriotism !

America was going through some major changes, a transformation into a new America. On the Great White Way The Great White Hope won the Pulitzer Prize in Drama and one of the greatest war heroes, who never went to war, won an Oscar, John Wayne. "Times, they were a-changin'," American women wore "hot pants" for the first time, and the youth listened to the Beatles' "Hey Jude", "Born to be Wild",by Steppenwolf, and Dione Warwick's "Do You Know the Way to San Jose ?" There was a questioning of everything, and one of the icons of the "Beat" Generation, Jack Kerouac, hit the road for the last time. Butch Cassidy and the Sundance Kid, Easy Rider, and Midnight Cowboy were filling theatres. Mario Puzo wrote The Godfather and Kurt Vonnegut's latest novel was Slaughterhouse Five. Vince Lombardi retired as coach of the Green Bay Packers, and computer bubble memory was developed. The new memory technology stored information when the power was turned off. A huge oil slick contaminates the shores of Santa

Barbara, and shortly Vietnam will surpass the Korean War in combat deaths.

Times were generally prosperous in 1969.

❖ ❖ ❖

CHAPTER SIXTEEN

Veronica's War With Men

Dwight, an intern studying to be a doctor, always looked at the newly arrived nurse interns as not just cohorts in medicine, but more of a menu from whom he could choose to seduce. When he saw Edith he pounced immediately, not knowing this blonde bimbo-like beauty might have claws. Draping his arms around her, enveloping her with his powerful masculine charm, he offered an evening of unrivaled pleasure.

Edith unwrapped herself from his tentacles and smiled...hugely, and then she slapped him so

hard he nearly hit the ground. Her remarks: " If you ever touch me again my friends will have you begging for castration. Are you capable of understanding my meaning ?" She grinned that huge Edith smile and sauntered off.

Normally Dwight liked a feisty resistant woman. It was a challenge, but he sensed that perhaps he should let Edith go. Elizabeth did not interest him, which left Veronica as the sole new candidate for his lust. After Edith, he decided to be a bit more cautious...and, his mother knew her mother. What a happy coincidence !

It began when Veronica returned home from school to see Dwight...tall, big bouquet of orange-red hair tumbling about his head, great grin, and saturated with poise and self confidence having coffee with her mother.

" Dear, have you met Dwight, my friend Erma's son ? He's going to be a doctor..."

She wanted to throw up. Her mother was infuriating her.

" Why yes mother, everyone knows Dwight." Sarcastically, " he has quite a reputation." Taking a deep breath, "So Dwight, do you know my fiancée Winston ? Just thought I'd ask, kinda a long shot."

" No. Is he studying to be a doctor ?"

" No. He's in the Army, in Nam, but I'm sure my mother told you that." She put her books on the table and raced upstairs to her room.

" Are you coming down dear ?"

" Sorry. Don't feel good."

Dwight apologized and left, but he had made up his mind...Veronica would be in his bed eventually. She would be a prize worth pursuing, and for Dwight a woman was a "prize."

Several days later, when she was walking home from school, out of nowhere Dwight appeared and offered to carry her books. The timing was if he had been stalking her.

" I know this is kind of corny, sorta like high school, me carrying your books, but it gives me a chance to talk. Sorry about your fiancée. I'm sure he's a great guy..."

Veronica interrupted, " what makes you say that ?"

" He'd have to be to be engaged to you."He grabbed her arm, " I just want to be your friend."

" Then let go of my arm, and I appreciate the offer, but I can carry my own books." She was close to a snarl, but Veronica had no clue that the nastier she became the more enticing Dwight perceived her.

It was a quiet solemn walk to her house. She did not say goodbye and he left.

Dwight was counting on Veronica being horny and giving in to his advances. He knew it had been, and would be a long time until she and Winston would get together. He'd be happy to be the back door man, as truly that's all he ever wanted...she was just another notch on the bedpost.

Although they passed each other at the hospital, with no conversation, and barely any recognition, it wasn't until several days later he once again appeared (at just the right moment !), and offered to walk her home.

" You're looking beautiful Veronica...as usual. Tell me, don't you want a friend ? Don't you ever get lonely ? Won't you let me into your life ? I'm not such a bad fellow, after all I am going to be a doctor."

" Dwight, I wish I had Edith's touch to make you disappear. You're a doctor because of the money. You don't care about women other than sex, and that's all you want from me. I can't stop what happens at the hospital, but please don't try and be friends with me. I'm in love with my fiancée and I'm true blue...so maybe you should move on to your next victim."

Dwight was tongue tied, but somehow he felt confident if he could get Veronica with her legs spread he would be her savior.

When she returned home her mother inquired, " I notice Dwight has been walking you home. What a nice gentleman. Of course, since he's going to be a doctor it's to be expected. I hope the two of you are getting along...he's welcome anytime."

Veronica wanted to throw up, " He's not a gentleman ! He's a stalker ! A sick man who should never be a doctor ! I hope I never see him here, and if you invite him into the house again

I'll find a new place to live !"

" And how will you afford that ?" Her mother smiled.

Veronica wished her father lived nearby, but he had left home years ago, packed up his veterinary business and started a new life. He paid for college, and occasionally sent much needed money, but he would be paying alimony forever. How anyone could put up with her mother was unbelievable, and it was too late to go and live with him.

" Maybe I can sell my body to Dwight. I'm sure he'd pay. That kind of thing appeals to a sicko." And Veronica went to her room to hide. She wouldn't see her mother until morning, and called Edith to get some advice about her situation. Edith suggested it was too sad her mother couldn't go out with Dwight, but on a serious note did mention she had been lucky with the creep...sometimes a slap is considered an invitation. Unfortunately there wouldn't be any new nurses coming to the hospital, so Veronica may have to come up with something clever to repel him. Give Helen a call was her best advice, and Veronica decided to do that tomorrow...she would play with her scrapbook organizing photos with text, making sure the key was quite well hidden.

In her therapy letter to Winston she did not mention Dwight. There was nothing he could do about it, and no sense bothering him. Everything

was hunky-dory in nurse world...couldn't be better...she wished the clock would move faster, but it still was just one day at a time. She put her arm around Louise, her faithful pet, and tried not to feel sad, before the sandman sent them off to dreamland.

CHAPTER SEVENTEEN

Tet

That morning the entire company got on an eagle flight to join Alpha Company in a significantly larger base camp. Winston was always thrilled by the eagle flights...first there would be the sound of them coming...getting the adrenalin moving...then there would be a few moments where the sound was everywhere and all you heard...and then wham ! They were visible ! Then they were landing on top of you at full tilt boogie. It would be a long flight, and with his legs draped over the edge Winston watched the tops of the trees, just a few feet below, go racing by in

a blur.

The new base camp was literally carved out of the jungle. It was huge, and the outside perimeter had its proverbial rows of concertina wire, and then like a wall the dense jungle encircled the camp. It seemed like an ideal location to launch a human wave attack. They could get close, very close, before commencing their attack. Winston got a sick feeling in his stomach, he knew he wasn't going to like this place. The company they were replacing were ecstatic to see them, they were smiling and waving their rifles as they hurriedly boarded the copters.

Inside, there was a lot more of everything...more artillery, mortar platoons, lots of picnic tables to eat on (which created a more casual stateside ambience), lister bags galore, and more bunkers with less space between them. They were constructed to do battle from the inside, they were lower to the ground and broader. They were arsenals unto themselves, and had wide portals for vision and sticking your weapon out to shoot. They would have the day off, there wasn't much to do as the bunkers were well fortified with C's, first aid kits, and enough ammo to supply four squads. Prince and Winston spent the morning walking around talking to other guys in the platoon and the company. It was like a family reunion.

The scuttlebutt was a huge human wave attack was supposed to hit tonight. The Kit Car-

son had been interrogating a captured NVA, and this was to be the big one of Tet, a military celebration of the New Year. Somewhere beneath the canopy of the jungle an army was resting up for the evening. It would be a tribute to the holiday, as important as Thanksgiving to Americans. They would be extremely determined to kill some GIs tonight. It had become an annual celebration.

Inside the base camp the artillery pieces were being stationed all around the camp poised to shoot point blank with those insidious beehive rounds. There was a feeling in the air that this would be the "big one", and all day long war stories were traded back and forth, which have a lot in common with fish stories, but that was what the sole conversation was...in essence, talking shop all day.

Winston and the rest of the squad were inside their bunker, the afternoon sun was too brutal to lay out on top, and even though the humidity was stifling there was a certain damp coolness inside the bunker.

" Well 'Gorgeous', do you think there's enough ammo to supply you ?" Winston was trying to figure out where to create a new "head" bunker.

" There's too much ammo in here, if an RPG got shot through that hole, we wouldn't know which side of Kingdom come we would land on." "Gorgeous" felt proud of his statement.

" Amen to that brother," Prince had had a productive day writing letters to all his relatives and his sweetheart, and was ready for some crash time.

" So Dylan, are you going to set up your 60 on top of the bunker as usual ?" Blackie's tone of voice was perfectly droll, as if he was inquiring about the weather.

" Not tonight. This bunker seems a lot more fortified than what we're used to, I think I'll stay inside, plus if the shit hits the fan like what everyone is expecting, being on top is going to be one dangerous position."

" Especially if you want your assistant next to you." Juan had made up his mind he wasn't going topside.

" You know that jungle looked pretty thick from the air. I bet those fuckin' gooks are hiding right now just outside the concertina wire and we don't know it." "Gorgeous" was his usual self.

Sgt. Glover walked into the bunker, " I don't think so 'Gorgeous'. There were three recon units out today, and there's not a NVA around for at least three klicks, and the jungle is pretty thick, it's slow moving out there, so if they attack tonight they should be on the move now, 'cause where ever they're comin' from it's got to be a long way."

" So Sarge, what do think of the new and improved bunker ?"

" It's something we don't have to get used

to anytime soon." He looked down at the floor.

" What do you mean ?"

" Our platoon is going on a platoon sized listening post tonight..."

"Gorgeous" was livid. "A platoon sized listening post ! I didn't think they came that way ! An entire platoon! Us ! *We* are going to be outside the wire, and when the shit hits the fan, *all* of us are going to run through three rows of concertina wire to get back in. This is the fuckin' Army's brilliant idea of a suicide mission, we have zero chance of surviving if they attack."

" According to Top we're going to be just outside the last row of concertina wire and we'll have easy access through the wire to get back in."

" Oh sure !" "Gorgeous" was screaming, " Jesus fuckin' Christ ! That lyin' piece of shit would love to send us out to see how many body bags he could tag. Top must be lovin' it. He's safe inside a steel reinforced bunker and we're the guinea pigs sent out to see if we can outrace Charlie's bullets tryin' to get back in. That's a real fuckin' downer." And he threw his helmet to the ground.

Holding his hands over his ears, he bolted out of the bunker, yelling, " My head is going to explode !"

" When 'Gorgeous' gets back somebody will have to tell him we leave shortly before nightfall, we'll be travelling light, but bring plenty of ammo."

" Sarge," Prince asked gently, " why, when a major human wave attack is expected would they send out a platoon sized listening post ? Why so big ?"

" Prince, I'm just passing out orders. I'm looking on the bright side, maybe it'll be like it was for you guys a couple nights ago. Listening post was the safest place to be."

" Too bad Donovan couldn't have joined us." Winston fired up a Kool.

" You know when your number is up, your number is up." Dylan grinned goofily, " Sarge," he paused as if to construct his sentences, " I don't like this. This is Tet and they will be coming at us with everything they got, and we are going to have to run, all of us...the entire platoon at once...through three rows of concertina wire to get back in. We better start praying right now they attack from the other side of the base camp."

Blackie had his grenade launcher cradled in his arms, and he rocked it like a baby.

Prince pursued, " The other company that was here, did they go through a human wave attack two nights ago like we did ?"

" No, they were by-passed. The NVA came to us...Bravo Company has been here a week and had no contact, they haven't seen so much as a sandal track."

" They seen nothing," Prince composed himself, "and they've been doin', like what man, nuthin' but recons and day bushes, and never

213

seen a single gook...and tonight is the celebration of Tet...ain't there a jumpin' good possibility the army from the North just might want to by-pass us ?"

" You're my man Prince," Juan was already acclimated to this mission being maybe his last, " If nothing happens tonight, I'll give you the first tamale from my next care package."

" Nobody really knows what's going to happen tonight. It could be just a sleepless night. Just because the Kit Carson probably beat the hell out of a captive doesn't mean it's going to be the truth."

" Prince, for a new man you offer a whole different side, "Dylan stopped smiling, " I really hope you're right. I truly do. Speaking for myself, Juan and I are going to hump beaucoup ammo."

" And frags." Juan would be carrying at least eight.

" I hope I'm right too, and all we lose is a good night's sleep," and looking upward, " and you fellas know I believe the Lord is watching over me."

" The fuckin' bad news is this could be our Alamo." Juan looked up from his whittling, " those guys knew they were going to die, and John Wayne was willing to give it up for the USA, but fuck John Wayne, I don't want to die for this..."

"...and John Wayne didn't die in the Alamo." It was the first time Rufus had spoken, " he went on to make other movies...if this is our

Alamo then we're in beaucoup shit...we're goin' out and no one is goin' to make a movie out of us...we be gone !"

Winston had to speak up, "We're not going to die, my man. We are going to make it !"

Dylan was an older veteran like Blackie, and he listened, and he paid attention, but the Nam was like God in proving "talk is cheap."

There was a true war story, about this GI who used to brag how invincible he was. He was more than tough, but a certified winner in life...and lucky, too. When he got out he was going to make a fortune and never have to think about the Nam again. He was invincible ! It was a major point with him that everyone knew he was the "man", and no NVA or Vietcong was going to do him in. His persistence and credibility grew the longer he maintained. He had survived eight and a half months in the field without so much as a scratch. In the Wolfhounds, during those days, that was a good stretch. Every new man would suffer under the bradaggio of how invincible he was.

One day a platoon of twenty-five men walking across a rice paddy were stunned and thrown to the ground when the 15th man in the line had stepped on a land mine, and in real life disappeared from the planet. They would be lucky to find enough to fill a body bag. No one else had suffered so much as a piece of shrapnel, and when they all got up and dusted themselves

off it was as if nothing had happened...no one was hurt, there was just a loud explosion...let's carry on...but quite quickly, obviously someone was missing, but who ? There was a bit of lostness to the explosion. There had been that split second of fear that that would be the last sound anyone would ever hear...it was mentally debilitating...after awhile they looked around...and they realized that twenty-four GIs had walked the same path as himself, step by step, but the "invincible" one would no longer be joining them at chow time. His number had come up.

❖ ❖ ❖

The Concorde had its maiden flight. Sirhan Sirhan testified he didn't remember killing Bobby Kennedy.
"Midnight Cowboy" would win the Oscar. The school teacher from Milwaukee, Golda Meir, became Israel's first Prime Minister, and thousands marched down the Avenue of the Americas in New York City, protesting the war.

❖ ❖ ❖

CHAPTER EIGHTEEN

Moods Swing

Veronica was depressed, which was odd for a Monday morning. It was her day off when she could escape and do some shopping, maybe go to a matinee, anything to avoid home or hospital. The weekend at the hospital was busy and free of Dwight, and tonight was gal pal night, but all she wanted in the world was a couple hours with her man; and she felt numb to everything...just walking through life with no expectations. Besides the pressure from Dwight and his ilk and the weight of her studies there were nights she just wanted to scream herself to

sleep...there was no escape from this pattern, the endless circle of a life caught in a maze with no exits. *Time* was both her worst enemy and hopeful friend...as the days grew long and heavy, each day would bring them one day closer to reunion, and the end of the "waiting life". As part of her day, practically the status of a hobby, she daydreamed her plans when Winston returned, and began to structure them in sequence of what's first, next, etc. and write them down. Winston would need to find a job playing the piano, but it didn't really matter...any kind of job to provide food and shelter would be grand, eventually he'd find a musical niche, he was too good not to, and once she became a nurse she could work anywhere.

These plans, which she only hinted at in her letters, but couldn't stop herself from mentioning, were the cement to her dreams...eventually she wanted to have a family, but just to start a life together that would be the genesis to her garden of Eden, every thing else would come together.

Her mother openly disliked Winston. Thought he was a lost dreamer who would never amount to anything, and was steadfast and resolute in finding Veronica a new beau, no matter how much she resisted, and felt eventually, as time stretched out its strangling tentacles hour by hour she would succumb. Loneliness does make strange bedfellows, but Veronica was de-

termined to be strong. To be hopeful.

That night she described to the girls her detailed plan for the scrapbook beginning with Polaroids from when they first met, interspiced with photos when they were children, accompanied by text mostly lifted from her diary.
The ending would be a humorous gathering of photos of their future life...a mansion symbolizing their future home, a pic of the Bahamas, Winston playing the piano at the Hollywood bowl. The girls loved it. She did not bring up Dwight. It would be nothing but aggravating.

Edith had a new boyfriend, the young owner of the local hardware store, Elizabeth still worried and was having no luck, and Helen had successfully avoided any rendezvous at McDonalds. She wouldn't mind having a boyfriend at least as a distraction, and someone not consumed with columns and numbers. Veronica loved the laughs, which were becoming scarcer by the day, and couldn't wait to hear Edith's new exploits with her new guy.

◆ ◆ ◆

CHAPTER NINETEEN

Alamo or Sanctuary

Dylan spoke up, breaking the atmosphere with a more practical reality, " So when is chow, Sarge ?" He beamed.

" At seventeen thirty hours soldier, and after supper we prepare for our night mission."

The squad emptied out of the bunker, chow time was shortly away, while Prince remained behind on guard duty. One half of the platoon was shocked they might be going to their death tonight, the other half totally numb and accepting it was just another military ordeal.

Lt. Osgood was trying to convince the Colonel that a platoon sized listening post was not

the way to go, but the Colonel was a West Point man, and didn't take much stock in opinions from second looeys out of OCS. " Colonel, sending a platoon sized listening post, when a squad can do the same job is a suicide mission. It's too many GIs..."

" Don't talk to me like that ! This is a military maneuver designed to give advance warning to the companies, and being platoon sized increases your chance for defense. If your people are alert and respond in a proper military fashion, there is ample time for them to get inside the perimeter. You are dismissed Lieutenant."

The entire "negotiations" lasted a minute.

Lt. Osgood just stared at him, saluted, and exited the CP bunker. The Colonel was too stubborn and too righteous, he always made sure to everyone that he was all West Point, and these were career moves...there would be other wars, this was just his first. When Lt. Osgood told McAllister of the mission he at first begged the Lieutenant to go back and plead for a smaller group...a squad is perfect size for a LP; but he realized the Colonel was a stubborn asshole, and, on principle, would never change his mind. He always thought the Colonel was a glory hound and now he was sure of it. After he informed his sergeants, he sat down and wrote a letter to his wife back in Georgia. If the attack was on their side, quite simply not everyone would make it back...if anyone. The Grim Reaper was going to

have a field day.

Chow was spectacular: fried chicken, mashed potatoes and gravy, corn on the cob, biscuits, and cake for dessert. "Gorgeous" was stuffing himself.

" Hey amigo, " as Juan lathered his food with Tabasco, "no one is going to steal your food."

" This could be the last fuckin' meal we eat..."

Prince joined them, " You don't know that, Charlie could just bypass and celebrate Tet somewhere else." His plate had six pieces of chicken and all the trimmings.

" You never know, or maybe they'll attack from the other side of the perimeter." Winston was with Prince.

Rufus had been toying with his food, he had no appetite, " Juan, if I give you a hundred dollars, will you break my leg ?"

Prince's sensibilities were piqued. Inside this Goliath of a man lurked a lamb, "Rufus, you are breakin' foul on me man, if anyone is goin' to make it, it's you..." The talk of imminent death was getting to him.

"Gorgeous" had to be involved in every conversation,
" Well at least you picked a good night, the reason why this meal is so good is it's because it's the Last Supper..."

" Put a sock in it, 'Gorgeous' ! And Rufus

stop talking like that." Blackie was getting rattled, an emotion seldom seen, and "Gorgeous" got up to get another plate of mashed potatoes.

While he was serving himself, he asked the cook, "Where do you wimps go at night when the gooks attack ?" He hated all cooks.

" We're on the bunker same-same you guys, and I don't take any shit from any fuckin' grunt."

" Oh sure, you REMF's must be real tough with a 16."

" You fuck with me and you won't eat again."

"Gorgeous" made a motion of dishing his mashed potatoes and gravy at the cook, then turned his back, and laughed.

" Juan, what do you think ? A hundred dollars."

" Juan, if you break his leg that'll make you an accessory to the fact," Winston was determined, "and Top will send both of you to the Long Binh Jail for trying to prevent someone from going into the field."

" At least I'll be alive."

" Hey man, Winston is right," Dylan grinned, " don't do it."

" And Rufus," Blackie seemed depressed, "c'mon brother, give it up. Quit with the bad rap, we're all going to make it. Tonight's going to be one hell of a night I think, and..." his voice softened, " we don't need that shit."

Juan pushed his plate away, " I don't know what the fuck Winston is talking about, but you only get in trouble if you get caught...I'll think about it." He looked at Rufus.

On the opposite side of the perimeter a young soldier was throwing a fit at his Lieutenant and the Platoon Sergeant. Alpha Company was, likewise, going to send a platoon sized listening post on the opposite side from them, and this man was refusing to go. He was screaming so loud the entire base camp could hear him, and Top was fast approaching with a medic close behind. He was waving his M-16 wildly in all directions, twitching and jumping so intensely no one could get close to him. Hysterically, he repeated over and over again he was never going into the field again. He had the look in his eyes of a man about to jump without a parachute. The entire base camp was silent.

Winston and his squad couldn't hear Top trying to calm him down and relinquish his weapon, and the screaming continued...They ate wordlessly and listened. There was a lull in the conversation then his scream could be heard from Hell to eternity, " I'M NEVER GOING IN THE FIELD AGAIN !" There was quiet as he raced inside the bunker, and then a long ominous moment of silence, and then the sound of one bullet.

In the microcosm of the base camp word spread cumulatively faster and faster, bad news can reach the moon before good news has time to

put its shoes on (to paraphrase Jonathan Swift), and soon everyone knew he had put his M-16 in his mouth and redecorated the inside of the bunker. He had stopped his fear.

There would be increased chaos and heightened anxiety in Alpha Company.

Prince, now on his sixth piece of chicken, " It's got to be something almighty powerful to want to take your life, rather than risk it."

" What in the fuck would want you to blow your brains out when the gooks are more than willing to ? It makes no fuckin' sense." "Gorgeous" was just fiddling with his cake, he had eaten enough for two.

" You know I'm the shortest man here, just 63 days, and I've never heard or seen anyone commit suicide...it just isn't done...and for good reason, Charlie is eager and willing to make that wish come true." Blackie never looked at his comrades in arms, and moved his food around on his plate.

" Why would anyone commit suicide ? It doesn't make sense." Winston was mystified, " the name of the game is to get through the year alive, it's that simple and to do it yourself !" This incident reminded him of the walk through the village where the mother with the dead baby screamed by...it was another perverted omen...but impossible to read...

Supper was over, time to saddle up, listening post was about to begin. The Lieutenant

checked out each soldier in his platoon, empha-
sizing the importance of combat readiness. As he
went down the line Sgt. McAllister followed him
adding his "lifer spiel"...this is for the good of the
country, etc.....and the platoon got nervous. They
were all well armed and ready to go, but...the
waiting was slowing down the hands of time,
the minutes were creeping long and slow...it was
painful.

McAllister barked out, " Smoke 'em if you
got 'em ! Orders are we don't set up position until
dark."
Nearly everyone smoked. Maybe it was a macho
thing, and for every Wolfhound it was the only
recreation on the planet. It was incongruous that
it might be bad for you.

Everything about this mission reeked of
insanity, while an entire platoon was exposed in
the twilight, the point man was cutting through
the concertina wire. By the time he got to the
third row, the darkness had slowed him down
and it took twice as long...and the platoon
waited... no one spoke, and as their destination
became dimmer... the adrenaline was beginning
to heat up. Each GI got grabbed by the barbed
wire, the gap wasn't supposed to be wide, and
it was impossible to get through without sacri-
ficing some blood.

Eventually, and everyone was in a hurry
scratching through the barbed wire, they arrived
at the edge of the jungle, and passing hand sig-

nals back and forth, they settled in. When they were in position, Rufus, the RTO, clicked in.

There was a long pause as Rufus handed the horn to the Lieutenant. It was the Colonel, who was looking at them through a starlight, " You're too close Lieutenant, you need to move further into the jungle."

Lt. Osgood dropped his jaw so quickly his mouth hurt. The agreement was to the edge of the jungle ! To enter this solid wall of black verdure would obliterate their chances of ever making a run back to the perimeter.

" My instructions from the Sergeant Major were we would position at the edge of the jungle." The Lieutenant was boiling. This Colonel was insane.

His voice was lower than it needed to be, " I'm the Battalion Commander..."there was a pregnant pause,
"those are your orders Lieutenant."

He handed the horn back to Rufus without the proper sign-off of "roger that." Lieutenant Osgood laid back against a tree reeling it all in. He was twenty-six years old, and would be making a decision in a moment that could change the lives of nineteen men..he knew the Colonel was watching them through the Starlight...it would be suicide if they moved outward...there would be no chance to run in. He motioned to Sgt. McAllister to come to him.. It was growing darker by the moment.

" Sergeant," he took a deep breath, "the Colonel has ordered us to go into the jungle."

The Sergeant wanted to scream. He hoped his wife really appreciated the letter. He passed the word on to Sgt. Glover and the other squad sergeants, but Lt. Osgood stood up and led the way. About fifty meters into the jungle he found a small bamboo clump, incredibly thick, and the entire platoon squeezed in, literally shoulder to shoulder. It was a perfect place to hide, it was so thick...except for the one spot they had to crash through to get inside this bamboo womb. There was no place to run.

It was Alamo or sanctuary.

Rufus clicked in they were in position, and the senior RTO from the CP group clicked back that everything was cool, the Colonel was done talking.

It became the night of the long wait, no one would speak, could speak, no one would move, everybody watched, the bamboo offered slits of vision into the darkness but as the night progressed it steadily became darker, and the Lieutenant kept prodding, no one slept, this was one hundred percent alert all night. A threatening moon was on the way. Time like dirty snails inching across broken sun dials in some long lost forgotten civilization ticked on and on...one second at a time...one long minute at a time.

And then they were there !

In one crystal synapse of energy, the

adrenalin roared so high the entire platoon felt like they could be levitated, although they simultaneously were trying to become one with Mother Earth. The NVA were running and stumbling furiously, the moon was half full, and the light in the jungle was so variegated, that one moment there's good vision and the next step total blindness, yet the NVA were *running*, high stepping, but also falling. There was a line of NVA on each side of their bamboo cloister, it was too thick to run through, and the entire platoon could see them as they swarmed by in the hundreds. It would only take one of them to see one of them, and all personal histories could be put aside. A careening footstep nearly stepped on Winston's weapon, he was bare footed, only inches away.

Rufus was trying to be as silent as possible clicking away the information the base camp had to know, hoping some fool wouldn't challenge him, pressing the horn to his ear as if he was gluing it to prevent the sound of a voice coming through. The sound of the footsteps was crushing their ears...it was the only sound, as an army raced by on both sides. There are no atheists in a foxhole, and while most hid their eyes lest they be noticed, some stared, and everyone said a prayer-...this situation was beyond their control...one tiny glance from an incensed stumbling racing soldier and the Big Hotel would be taking instant reservations. They couldn't talk, couldn't

move, they wanted to twitch...everyone was paralyzed...and then the sound of the stampede ended, and the knots began to unravel. Winston turned on his side, it seemed like forever since he moved..all time was suspended, there was no activity other than truly bated breaths so immersed in fear they covered their mouths. He looked up to see a straggler racing by at the same speed as his comrades, obviously oblivious to this group of armed men. Winston was on his back, and prayed not another straggler would scurry past his view...he had to exhale.

The battle had suddenly begun...the roar of artillery enhanced with the firepower of machine guns, 16's, and mortar rounds was deafening. Now they were hugging the ground again, to avoid the tracers just whizzing above their heads. If you reached your hand up, you risked tying your shoes one handed. The sky was falling and it was earsplitting. Once the loomy-loomys broke out, the night became a skyscape of constantly created suns, burning brightly as they slowly descended to the earth, a never ending cascade of illumination. It was like high noon...and the shadows through the dense bamboo highlighted everyone's face. It seemed like a convention of ghosts at a cemetery, all granite expressions... pale, ashy, hollow-eyed, helmets like skullcaps shading eyes so that their faces became indistinguishable.

The Lieutenant was yelling as loud as he

could into the horn begging them to stop firing the loomy-loomys in their direction. He was furious, and as long as they were illuminated, they would be reduced to target practice.

His screaming hypnotized them, " If you keep shooting loomy-loomys we will be dead ! Do you read me ?"

Then silence.

" This is Lima Papa 2, stop firing the loomy-loomys !"

There was another silence.

The Colonel was dimly audible over the sounds of the firepower in the background, and *he* was yelling,

" This is Charlie Papa 1, stay in position, the NVA have penetrated the base, we must continue with all resources until they are driven out and routed. Do *you* roger that ?" His voice was an irate roar.

Lt. Osgood put down the horn, and looked around at his men. They were all looking at him...with those quiet looks, and he had nothing to say. His head was spinning thinking of alternatives. Where could they move to ? This was as safe a spot as there could be. To move would be suicidal. The light flickering through the bamboo made the soldiers alternately disappear and re-appear in the shadows. It was a ghastly parody on danger.

In the changing light, like falling stars the shards of metal from the beehive rounds shim-

mered to the ground. They looked like little silver darting arrows...butterflies of war falling harmlessly to the ground. The sound of metallic rain put everyone on their backs.

The Lieutenant was sweating so intensely his shirt was sticking to him like a glove. He was scared. He took the horn from Rufus hoping to learn the status of what was going on inside the camp, bit it was mostly static with the occasional yell from the Colonel to " Stay with the target, maintain firepower."

Lt. Osgood thought to himself what a fuckin' cheerleader the Colonel was, safe inside his secure guarded bunker, constantly getting reports from the other platoon leaders but never so much as a check-in for him...it was as if they were already dead. He could hear him over and over yelling to maintain position, maintain firepower. The base was in chaos, there was shooting everywhere. The NVA that had penetrated the perimeter were like kamikaze pilots on R&R, darting in the darkness shooting at anything. One NVA knocked out an entire artillery squad before he was taken out.

In the morning there would be multiple dust-offs to take away the dead and the wounded. The legend of the Wolfhounds was paved in blood.

Rufus changed back and forth between frequencies to get a fuller picture of what was happening, to hear the communication between

squads and platoons, and after what seemed like living a page of eternity, the inside seemed clear of NVA...

Lt. Osgood grabbed the horn from Rufus, " They're running ! They're retreating ! Cease firing loomy-loomys ! They are approaching us !" It was Lt. Osgood's final transmission, as there they *were.* The lights were dimming as they huddled together inside this bamboo manger, everyone facing the ground, one eye out to see if the long arm of coincidence was going to grab them by the collar. This time some were running, many were straining to run, and many were either dragging themselves or a wounded comrade. All in all they were moving quickly, but not with the abandon they came in with. The petrified platoon listened and waited as the footsteps began to disappear, but they knew there would be stragglers, and they must continue the wait. The last ones out were the walking dead, their lives were measured in footsteps and a few died within yards of their bamboo sanctuary. In real time it was another twenty minutes before they got the word to move out and return to the camp, but it seemed like it was the time it takes to travel to Hell and back.

They were moving in the dark with Winston walking point, and the moon provided just enough illumination for him to creep through the concertina wire. It was difficult, painstaking, and no matter how meticulously he moved the

barbed wire away, it ripped at his clothes. They would never had been able to get back through in a timely fashion, unless they followed the style of the NVA, who were scattered in bits and pieces all over the perimeter and the concertina wire. After Winston had progressed through the initial row of concertina wire, Sgt. McAllister passed the order down for everyone to halt, and sent a message to Winston, "Beware the gooks in the moonlight, not everyone is dead that looks it, so crawl slow through the wire."

Winston followed orders and kept a low profile slithering in the dirt, and in the background he could hear Lt. Osgood on the radio affirming they were coming in and not to be trigger happy. The entire camp was galvanized, the bunkers were all weapons ready, loaded, and eager. There were dozens of casualties, and many deaths...and for the NVA, the cost would be tallied up in the morning. The Wolfhounds were incensed and frustrated, the NVA had gotten in despite all their planning and defenses, and the first dust-off was on the way...which would only be taking those that were going to bleed to death, the remainder of the wounded would receive bandages and words of good cheer, for it would be sometime after dawn, a couple hours away that the next dust-off would arrive. For Winston's platoon the feeling of safety and security was not to be. Their experience was meaningless, throughout the entire camp were wounded

GIs most just lying on the ground, some next to NVA, who were not all dead. It was a carnal catastrophe , with its own private cacophony of Hell.

There was crying and screaming and moaning and in the moonlight the soon to be corpses were trying desperately, clutching intensely, to keep their souls from leaving.

There were squad sergeants yelling at their men to stay on the bunkers and man their positions, medics yelling at the CP for supplies, platoon sergeants screaming to their people to be quiet and leave the wounded alone and return to their posts, and in the background the artillery officer was booming his voice repeating the co-ordinates over and over again for an artillery strike against the retreating NVA. The stench of gunpowder still clogged the air, practically clouding the moon...the only relief in sight would be the sun...there never was a human wave attack launched in open daylight...the dawn of a new day would be the end of Tet...but meanwhile, there was fierce bedlam creating the kind of chaos that would drive any man mad. Too much screaming and yelling, too many people praying they don't want to die, too much confusion...it was the perfect cauldron of war.

Nothing had changed but the faces for a thousand years.

Winston's platoon split up among two

bunkers, and once on top, even in the fractured moonlight, he could see where the NVA had made their road walking over themselves to get here, across the concertina promenade, which for some the road was forever face down in the dirt and the steel. Blood and guts mixed with the dust, as soldiers sacrificed their souls to create a living bridge for their comrades to trod on. For the first time it bothered him that this kind of determination might be undefeatable.

At night the scene was eerie, scary, and distant, but when the sun put the heat on, the whole scene would become monstrous and brutal, breakfast gore for the military machine.

Winston had never dreamed he would evolve into being a part of the machine...the universal eternal war machine where success is measured in death. But the acute stab to the soul was that he was not just a casual participant, he was part of the engine that moved the war along. There was no way out, and now surrounded by two companies of men, in unison,...bleary, exhausted, and strung out like live snakes on a cord in the sun...they wanted to twist, to scream...but the scenario was simple...you wait...for dawn's early light...it was still one hundred percent alert.

◆ ◆ ◆

Henry Cabot Lodge toasted the emissaries of North Vietnam. Paris, in Winter, was a pearly back-drop for the flow of champagne...the bubbles sparkle so much more in a landscape of light snowflakes, and they felt proud that the temporary cease-fire during Tet in Vietnam had been a success. Both sides reported very few casualties. Most newspapers reported what they said, and most readers believed their leaders, and everyone was glad there was a hiatus in the war. It was wonderful to be in Paris...the women, the cuisine...it was the "city of lights."

At dawn the first dust-off returned to pick up the wounded, all of whom were dumbed by shock and numbed by morphine. The ambulance helicopter was built to haul a crowd, the "docs" could strap numerous gurneys to the center post, plus the floor space. It would take more than one dust-off today though, the ride of the Valkyries was just beginning, and for the wounded it was a scary ride, not like an eagle flight. They were strapped down, tied to something...by default they were prisoners of war. Some would be patched up quick, maybe grab a few days of "sham time" and then be back in the field, and some would go back to the world and repair and

play "beat the clock" until their draft commitment was up, and then some would go back to the world to enter a VA hospital, an institution barely having caught up with the Korean War, and totally unprepared for the veterans of Vietnam who were disfigured and paralyzed...and young. There would be a reason for the high suicide rate.

Winston's unit wasn't going anywhere, it would be some other platoon's turn to do a sweep of the carnage. They set up guard duty, the same as nighttime, and one by one began to crash in the early morning hot sun.

On the opposite side of the perimeter Lt. Osgood was looking for his best friend, the Lieutenant for the first platoon of Alpha Company, that was the other listening post. Their bunker was empty, but it was early, and the way the Colonel worked, perhaps he had kept them still out there; so the Lieutenant climbed to the top of the bunker for a view.

From the landscape of gore it was obvious the NVA had attacked from this side as well. It looked like an ocean of blood with nothing but the wreckage of human forms floating in it. They were like ships in a perverted sea damned to an all too soon eternity. The knot in his stomach began to tighten at the sight. Nothing was recognizable, but he stared anyway.

Only two GIs from second platoon of Alpha Company had survived the crossfire, and

they had did it by pretending to be dead. They passed the darkness trying not to breathe, snuggling against their dead buddies, waiting for dawn to even put their heads up.When they first saw each other they both realized they were the only two survivors of a platoon of nineteen, and began running towards the base camp yelling "don't shoot us !"over and over again. They tore their fatigues to shreds sprinting through the concertina wire, wailing and screaming as if pursued by relentless ghosts. Lt. Osgood yelled to them to come on in. The men looked as if they had aged ten years, the lines in their faces seemed so pronounced, their eyes more sunken, hidden...and they collapsed as protoplasmic rubble at his feet.

Within the security of the base camp they momentarily regained their composure, and told the tale of their listening post. Lt. Osgood just listened.

They never had a chance. Their position was just barely inside the jungle, and the NVA seemed to come out of nowhere. The dash for the 2nd Platoon of Alpha Company from that point to base camp was futile, most were dead and overrun before they got to the first row of concertina wire. They had fought the best they could, but the NVA were literally rolling over them, and the massive machine gun fire, mortars, and then the artillery sealed their destiny...no way in...no way out. They knew they

were going to die, it was take as many with you as you could. None of these guys ever planned they would step out guns blazing without a chance in Hell of surviving, and one by one would disappear into the war. Only the Lieutenant was old enough to vote.

LT. Osgood felt sick. His best friend wasn't as lucky as he was, it was a suicide mission from the gitgo, and now he was going back to the world in a body bag. They had talked far too many times of getting back together in the states and reminisce about the good ole days. They both sensed that no matter how bad things seemed now, in ten years it would be a historical recollection. It would be looked upon as a good experience. The Lieutenant was at the nadir of his life...he couldn't imagine things getting worse.

He pulled himself together, " I'm sorry, but you two Private's are going to have to come with me and report to the Colonel."

They bowed their heads and followed orders. They had spent the night with seventeen corpses, formerly guys they ate, slept, fought, joked, and crapped together with; and both had heard everyone die...and not everyone died quickly...and both spent the night in the camouflage of the dead, hiding beneath a body, what was once a friend. The NVA had massacred them in their fiendish charge, and took shots at the bodies, in revenge, as they retreated.

They were infected with ghosts, the hor-

ror of the night was a tattoo on their psyche, and now that they were free...a madness was developing...they were beginning to relive the death-s...there were so many so quickly, and when the entire universe is your platoon, to lose them all so abruptly was like being orphaned out of the galaxy. As they approached the CP bunker both tried to stop the immersion of emotion, but by the time they were in the Colonel's bunker, both were in tears.

"Stop it !" The Colonel practically spit on them as he spoke. " Lieutenant, why are these men here ?"

Lt. Osgood, his eyes on fire from lack of sleep managed a return glare, " These men are the last two, the only two survivors of the Second Platoon of Alpha Company who were on listening post...I trust the Colonel would be interested in a report from the front." The men were reduced to blubbering idiots.

" Quiet ! Get hold of yourselves soldiers ! What happened out there ?"

The Colonel listened to one man between bouts of crying relate the massacre of the Second Platoon and then dismissed them. Lt. Osgood waited until they left, " I told you a platoon sized listening post was a suicide mission that no one could make it back alive," and he began to raise his voice to his military superior, "but you're the West Point man who know's best, what's a proper military maneuver..."

" You do not talk to me in that tone of voice, Lieutenant !" The Colonel's face was turning red with anger.

Lt. Osgood sat down without permission, and coolly looking up at the Colonel, " My best friend and seventeen of his men were slaughtered last night. Slaughtered ! You sent them there. My platoon lucked out pure and simple, because we fell into the perfect hiding place. Militarily we accomplished nothing, they were upon the base camp within one minute after we clicked in they were coming, and what did it accomplish ? They got in and killed and wounded...I don't know how many." He took a deep breath, and glared at the Colonel, " you could have been the Battalion Commander who sent two platoons to their deaths, but the record will state you sent just one."

" LIEUTENANT !"

" I wish to make a formal request to the General concerning your leadership. I want him to know first hand how you sent seventeen men to their deaths, and nearly another twenty...and for what ? To warn that an invasion was coming which you hadn't prepared for ? We would've been more useful inside defending the camp, not to mention there'd be a lot more live GIs." He stood up, " I don't care what you do to me, but I demand a formal meeting. He was exhausted beyond limits, his eyes were burning with pain, his legs were weak, and his heart was crying for

solace. He saluted and left without being properly dismissed.

The Colonel, just moments before had reported to the General how successful their effort had been against an overpowering well trained armed battalion (or two) of the North Vietnamese Army. He explained to the General there had been some wounded, and a few KIA's, but the human wave invasion had been successfully repulsed with the result of heavy losses for their side. Considering the Wolfhounds were vastly outnumbered by the enemy, the Colonel elaborated for the General their kill ratio was splendid, and most of all it was going to be a huge body count.

The General was pleased to hear the report. "Body count" was the magic phrase, the glue in the reports, the stat that kept the the war momentum propelled...the fuel of the war engine, the source of strength. The Colonel said he would report back to the General with the good news and the final tally later on in the morning, after they had done their sweep. In an immediate follow-up he requested a new infantry lieutenant to replace a courageous officer that deserved to spend the remainder of his tour in the rear.

Lt. Osgood went back to his bunk and privately cried himself into a coma.

By 1100 hours the Colonel had worked everything out...when he told the General about the sacrifice the second platoon of Alpha Com-

pany had made in defense of the camp, the General was impressed. An entire platoon died to save the lives of the entire base camp! They must have been courageous soldiers. He reported the body count as slightly under a thousand, and by morning tomorrow, after being back-hoed into a mass grave... no one would ever know. The General was altogether pleased with the Colonel's performance.

In the afternoon a Chinook helicopter would be bringing supplies, the back-hoe, and replacements. The Colonel had made arrangements for Lt. Osgood to spend the remainder of his commitment at Cu Chi, the division base camp. He would never load an M-16 again, let alone lead a platoon in combat. Getting on the Chinook would be the next closest thing to going home.

When the Colonel summoned him to his quarters, Lt. Osgood was thinking what kind of court martial defense he should get together. He was completely surprised at the Colonel's offer...amnesty for silence was what it boiled down to...he took the amnesty and for him the war was truly over, it was only going to be killing time...and no one in the Wolfhounds ever saw him again . He said good-bye to Sgt. McAllister and no one else.

CHAPTER TWENTY

A Gladiator Enters the Arena

When the Chinook landed in the base camp, everyone salivated, this was also the messenger bringing food and mail...the connection with the outside world. Along with all that was Lt. Osgood's replacement, a Second Lieutenant by the name of "Buck" Harris.

"Buck" was ecstatic to be back, especially this time of year, Tet, and after an invigorating briefing with the Colonel and the Company Commander, he was ready to carve himself a niche

in military annals. His first day back and the entire base camp was preparing for another human wave attack...and for him, it couldn't be better.

When Top introduced him to Sgt. McAllister, he saluted him as if he was a long lost brother, which in a way he was, as Lt. "Buck" was a sergeant his first tour in the Nam. He had spent most of 1967, part of 1968, with the Wolfhounds, and decided a career in the military was for him, and being an officer was the way to go. He loved war, the whole everything about it...the unification of men towards killing an enemy, the patriotism of all that was done under the aegis of defending one's country, and the pure thrill of high adrenaline in that every moment is a life or death situation. He had learned a lot his first time around, and he was one of those rare breeds of sergeants, who in the breadth of one hitch went from squad leader to platoon sergeant. He was good at war, he was born to it, and no intoxicant had ever been developed to parallel his feelings. He was on cloud nine that a human wave attack was predicted, nothing could be more challenging...if he had his way they would be doing hand-to-hand combat between the rows of concertina wire. The Colonel was going to love him. When he finished his salute, Sgt. McAllister felt he had been hugged.

" Platoon Sergeant McAllister, I would like to meet my men, please muster them up for me." He was militarily to the point, and Sgt. McAllister

caught on immediately, by the way he was addressed, that this was no college punk from OCS, (Officer Candidate School) although he was an OCS grad, and began to assemble the squads.

" Due to the nature of the alert, Sir, you will not be able to meet all the men at the same time, but I will introduce you to everyone in the First Platoon."

" It's very important that I meet every soldier that serves me, Sergeant. This is a very important war, and we must be both ready and *unified.* Perhaps you have already heard that I was a Sergeant, and I hope you don't feel betrayed that I went to a lesser calling," he smiled, "but I felt I could better serve the Army as an officer, just as you feel, I know, that the best you can do for your country is to be a leader, a platoon sergeant. I've been there, I *know* what it's like."

Chow time was minutes away and the men were half dead or half awake, exhausted from the night before and were in no mood for a meeting of any kind. Winston and Rufus were just about to find a place along the bunker line to blow a J.

" Okay Charlie One, listen up !"All you swinging Richards get in line and face me ! I want you to meet your new platoon leader, Lt. Harris..."

Juan interrupted, "What happened to ...Lt. Osgood ?"

Lt. "Buck" Harris spoke up, " He has been

reassigned to serve out his duty in the rear, I am Lt. Harris, and as of this moment you men are my personal responsibility. It is my honor to lead you all for the good of our country in battle, where we serve the Wolfhounds proudly and to the best of our abilities. Chow is about to be served, and shortly I will be meeting with each and every one of you. Gentlemen dismissed."

Winston looked at Rufus and they both thought the same thing...what kind of gung-ho bastard had fallen in their midst ? Lt. Osgood was always looking for a way to avoid combat, it was easy to see this second looey was just the opposite. While the rest of the platoon went to supper, Winston, Rufus, and Dylan stayed back on guard on top of the bunker, and decided to take advantage of the wind.

" Lookey here, you guys, did you know our new leader was a Wolfhound before ? This is his second tour, the first was a gung-ho sergeant. We are really going to miss Osgood."

" Roger that," Dylan grinned and passed the J to Winston and his fist to Rufus, "just what we need is some gung-ho motherfucker. I hope he doesn't do something stupid like volunteer us for listening post."

" After last night's debacle I can't imagine the Colonel being such an idiot as to send out listening posts again. We really lucked out big time, how we made it through the night is beyond me," Winston took another quick toke off the J (this

was not a cool place, especially with a new looey in the mix), " and those poor dudes from Alpha Company never had a chance. If the NVA didn't mow them down then 'friendly' fire did."

" They had no cover and no where to run, Jesus what a bum deal. They were slaughtered, and their looey was Osgood's best friend..." Rufus took the final hit off the J and tossed it over the bunker, "...and don't underestimate how much an asshole the Colonel is...the more of us die, the higher the glory count...the better he looks...the LBJ lookin' real good compared to ever doin' listening post again."

" I bet," and Winston lit up a cigarette. He always had a smoke after a J, "Lt. Osgood laid into the Colonel for his stupid orders and got himself transferred out of here. The Colonel fucked up big time. He should be court martialed for sending those guys to their deaths..."

Dylan had his usual Cheshire Cat grin, " But he probably will get a medal." He lit up a butt, " God, I hope we don't get another human wave attack tonight. I can't imagine that Charlie has got enough man power to do it all over again. He's got to be nursing his wounds, there were a whole lotta dead gooks out there this morning."

" Amen brother, but revenge is sweet, Charlie thinks we've been knocked for a loop, and maybe got us scared. He might just want to crawl back in the middle of the night and try again. You never fuckin' know..." Rufus crawled off the bun-

ker, and soon the trio was joining "Gorgeous" for dinner. He was gorging himself, climaxing the meal with apple pie and fast melting ice cream. Winston was amazed the Army could transport American made ice cream into the middle of nowhere.

" Hey Winston, whaddya think of the new looey ? A new shit kicker replaces the old wimp," "Gorgeous" burped. He had eaten so much he was beginning to dwell on the possibility of throwing up...and where to do it...he looked at the cooks, and grinned.

Winston picked up his tray, it was Salisbury steak, mashed potatoes, and green beans. Castaways on a deserted island would think twice before devouring this constellation of calories most cruelly configured. " You're wrong about Lt. Osgood. He was no wimp and he saved our butts last night. If he hadn't found that hiding place inside that bamboo hedge, we'd be having a conversation with the second platoon from Alpha Company. They didn't have a Osgood to find a camouflaged place to hide in and the luck of the draw went real bad for them."

" Roger big on that ! 'Gorgeous,' you look like someone that's about ready to explode, and brother we *all* pegged Osgood due wrong. He found us a nest where the fuckin' Colonel couldn't see us and neither could the NVA, and now the dude has been replaced by a second looey auditioning to be the next big war hero."

Rufus sat down next to "Gorgeous". " My God, this Salisbury steak is so mighty fine, back in D.C. we'd use it to pave roads with."

" Would you use the mashed potatoes on the shoulders ?" Dylan laughed, if anything, *he* thought he was funny, and dove into the potatoes, while Rufus sawed away at his steak.

A man from another platoon identified himself as Ellis, and interrupted them, " I heard about your new looey and I was with "Buck" on our first tour with the Wolfhounds..."
Winston was taken aback. "...and he was a sergeant that took chances and do anything for rank. He was constantly trying to fuck over the platoon sergeant...he was out of the Old West, hoping to make a name for himself."

"And this is your second tour with the Wolfhounds ?" Winston thought to himself he must be crazy, totally dinky-dau.

" You're probably wondering why I'm only a Corporal, but I had a bad time of it back in the world, and I figured here my chances are better to get my stripes back. I was an E-6. Things aren't going so well, but I'm the sergeant type, not like "Buck", who wants to conquer the world. I feel sorry for you guys."

Dylan drooled food at the man, " You two were sergeants together in the Wolfhounds ?"

" Roger that, we were both squad leaders in this same outfit, although everything has changed...everything... mostly the people, and

the way things are done. I think the new leaders of the Wolfhounds are a lot hungrier for a body count than the old ones were, which is why "Buck" is going to do so well with the current regime. Ellis looked at Winston straight on with his tiny, beady furry eyes, "Around this time two years ago ago, the Colonel, bless his heart, was talkin' to us men that a dangerous mission was all ahead soon...and before he could finish "Buck" jumped into the Colonel's face faster than a salute...he was ready and willing to go...where ever ! The Colonel was impressed, and because of "Buck" the platoon sergeant was obligated to volunteer the rest of the platoon. We were awarded the most dangerous mission at that time in the Wolfhounds...a LZ at dead dusk, setting up for a night ambush." He paused as he fiddled with his hands. He seemed nervous, "...some things never change, it was a hot LZ, *we* were the bush. But you wanna know something weird ? There was only one KIA in the entire platoon...it was the platoon sergeant, and guys ready for this ? Guess who was promoted the very next day to platoon sergeant ?"

Ellis was a squirrelly looking guy, sort of wiry with a dark complexion, he looked around as if someone was spying on him, got up abruptly and quietly returned to his bunker.

" Gorgeous" was so stuffed all he could do was crash. He didn't care if it was fifty percent alert or not, " So "Buck" Harris is number fuckin'

ten, I guess we'll find out. I know I didn't like him, but then I hate anyone that's a lifer, they all suck. I know the 'Assassin' is a member of our company, and I know he's not a member of the third herd...I wonder what he thinks of the new looey ? Don't mean nuthin', I'm grabbin' some Z's."

Blackie spoke up in his customary low voice. He was an old man, a short timer, the only one in the squad who knew who the "Assassin" was, " Well 'Gorgeous', you had chow with him and never knew it."

"Not that squirrelly sergeant-who'll-never-make-it !"

"Gorgeous" stood up, " Impossible !"

" I didn't say it was him, did I ?"

" So it was somebody else. Hell, I don't pay no attention to those other guys."

Blackie laughed a cold, cold laugh, " I only know who he is, because I'm one of the oldest Wolfhounds in the Company."

" You should be going off-line in ti-ti time," Rufus tapped his fist over his heart, " bet you're going to miss us brother."

" Like malaria I'm going to miss you guys."

" Bet you miss the cheap weed." Dylan laughed.

Sgt. Glover approached them, " The new looey wants to have a talk with us," he cleared his throat, "to address his men about the military consequences of tonight's possible human wave

attack..." he coughed again, trying to imitate the new looey.

"Gorgeous" flipped his butt in the direction of the cooks, " And to think I was constantly puttin' down Osgood as a true babysan, a fuckin' wimp."

" And now we have a gung-ho bastard," Rufus was chewing hard on his Salisbury steak. It was like chewing on a meat flavored rug, " just what this platoon needs...maybe he'll volunteer us for a night bush."

Dylan, likewise chewing on his steak as if it were a career opportunity, garbled, " Maybe the 'assassin' will wake up to the call."

" Except it's too bad he's not in our platoon," and Blackie pitched his plate at the 55 gallon drum, missing it badly.

Winston laughed, " Nice shot Oscar Robertson. I bet the rats won't touch that shit." Juan and Prince both pitched their plates, perfect slam dunks into the drum, and off to meet the wizard...

Lt. "Buck" was standing ramrod straight making idle chatter with Sgt. McAllister as Sgt. Glover had them fall to.

" Gentlemen, at ease ! Smoke 'em if you got 'em."

He approached Dylan first, " What's your name and where are you from soldier?"

" Private Dylan from Las Vegas."

" Ever do any gambling, private ?"

" I'm not old enough sir." Looking him dead in the eyes.

" Are you thinking of making a career in the military soldier ?" Dylan choked on his cigarette he was so taken aback, and turned away as if the man was on serious narcotics.

By the reaction the rest of the men gave, looking away, he knew these were all draftees biding their time like prisoners of war. This was valuable information for his leadership, he knew what draftees were like...they would do as little as possible and nothing at all if not directed. He continued down the line asking the same questions. They could care less, and could tell he could care less, it was just a military charade.

" Gentlemen, tonight once again will be full alert, and not only will we be manning the bunker, but along both sides as well. Everyone will be armed with extra ammo and be totally on the ready. The Captain and the Colonel will be inspecting the entire perimeter, and we will be combat prepared. Any questions ?"

Dylan gave him his weird grin, " Are there going to be any platoon sized listening posts tonight ?"

" No. The Colonel decided it wasn't necessary."

Sgt. McAllister took over and directed half the men to munitions while the other half took up positions.

Dylan turned to Winston and laughed, "

Full alert ! I thought it was going to be fifty percent. I can't wait to hear the snoring. Half these guys are already dead on their feet, and it isn't even dark yet."

" I agree. It's going to be tough to enforce tonight, but with our fresh new Lt. "Buck" we could be in trouble. He's had plenty of sleep."

" Fuck 'em," yawned "Gorgeous", " It's going to be impossible to enforce. This entire place is strung out and ready to crash. I personally can't wait for darkness. I don't give a fuck how many times "Buck" has to wake me up. We'll be on guard duty same-same usual, got to get some Z's."

" Amen brother," and leaning against the berm Blackie casually passed a J to him.

Sgt. Glover approached them.

Rufus, who had been setting up inside the bunker, surfaced, " Sarge, what's the word from my man Chuck ?Does he think the gooks are going to make a return dance through the concertina ?"

" The word from Chuck is that the group that attacked us last night is heading south, and as far as he knows there's no new force coming this way...but you never know with the gooks, and Chuck can't be everywhere, so we are going to be prepared."

" Sgt. Glover, so what's your take on 'Buck' ?"

" He is gung-ho, he's certainly not shy

about that. I just hope he doesn't get too crazy. You know my philosophy, let's all go home alive and in one piece."

Prince, who had been setting up Claymores while Blackie covered him had overheard Glover, and quiet though he usually was, "Amen to that Sgt. Glover. Let's all go home together. Amen."

Chuck was right.

The evening was peaceful, although "Buck" kept the adrenalin moving and everybody awake. By dawn the platoon was exhausted with nerves frayed and rolled together like some Gordian knot.

Blackie laid in the dust, drooling into the dirt, the morning sun was beginning to cook, but he didn't care, as half the platoon followed suit, and crashed into oblivion, with the other half not far behind.

◆ ◆ ◆

Spring, for the most part was rejuvenating America, "the world," with daffodils and crocuses making their flowery debut, and bringing that feeling of new beginnings, fresh starts, and the shedding of Winter's cold management. The planning of Woodstock was a sign that this was the year of the hippie. Music was changing, attitudes were being permanently altered, and with

these changes came divisions between the new and the old, the status quo and the emerging majority. America was like a new butterfly escaping from its cocoon, and like a butterfly it had no idea what its new world had to offer. In the world of Vietnam, all this was irrelevant, a butterfly could just as well be used for target practice.

◆ ◆ ◆

CHAPTER TWENTY-ONE

Phase One of the Attack

Love separated by 8000 miles was like being starved for a week, then teased with the aroma of a freshly grilled steak, the plate inches away, and then...poof ! It's gone. The only satisfaction in this twisted reality is the *hope* that love will be served and savored like a divine meal, with Venus the chef and Eros the waiter.

The letters went back and forth, reminiscing about the old days, making imaginary plans for the future...a vacation in the Bahamas, lying on the beach all day, having sex all night...for Win-

ston it was never having to ever hear the sound of an incoming mortar round, or a tracer cracking over your head, and for Veronica it was never having to run into Dwight again and hear his repartee of how gorgeous she was and the cure for her loneliness was a big strong man like himself. Veronica did not tell Winston about Dwight just as he did not describe the horrors of a human wave attack.

Lately the more Veronica resisted the more determined he became. The "subtle" remarks in the hospital hallways of how he could satisfy her missing needs, and that it would only take once before she'd be penning a "Dear John" letter to Winston repulsed her, but she never made eye contact, never said a word of reply. In 1969 the Women's Lib movement was just beginning to move out of the shadows and into the limelight, but it was a long way to go before there was strength in numbers.

When he nearly knocked her down, en route to her house, trying to get at her books, yelling he was just trying to be a gentleman and help her lighten the load, she had to drop her books and run. It was dark, very dark; the perfect element for Dwight to operate in. When he returned the books to her house, her mother remarked what a nice polite young man he was, and maybe since Winston was gone for so long, a nice male friend might be okay. It was if they had never spoken about Dwight. He was becom-

ing bolder and more aggressive. Veronica hid in her room and cried. The insidious poison of loneliness was making a toxic entrance into her soul, and being lonely can make you do things you might regret...but she was determined not to let the poison take control, as she missed Winston desperately. There was no substitute.

Just as Winston couldn't escape from Nam, Veronica was trapped in her own bubble. It could be perforated, but daily she made it stronger, more impenetrable...she would suffer inside herself, live with the tormenting loneliness and wait for the day that would surely, eventually come.

Winston wrote to his sweetheart about his companions, what they were like, and some typical days, but never describing the gore, or the fear of imminent death, or the wounds a heart receives when confronted with a scarring sadness. There are depths of sadness that leave scars that never heal. It was best to write about the past, or more importantly the future and what they could do together; and let the present melt into the past or slide into the future. Veronica got the glossed over version of Nam...not the one with ghosts in the body bags.

Every time there was a mail delivery he got a "sugar report" from Veronica. He could not repress his smile when he saw the letter, and even Prince was giving him a hard time (in a kidding way), as it was so blatant he was madly in love with this woman. He didn't care if she was writ-

ing about shoe shopping it was a balm to the tortured soul, and it would be the highlight of the week. The "sugar reports" told him everything was hunky dory. She was having fun being a nurse with her gal pals and kept busy patiently waiting for that magical "someday."

At the Monday night pow-wow Edith told Veronica one of her friends (an intern like Dwight) said that Dwight was bragging he would get Veronica in bed "one way or another."

Veronica's stomach was turning, " He knocked me down a couple days ago, saying he was just trying to help me carry my books. He scared me. I'll never walk home in the dark again."

Elizabeth chimed in, " He feels he's above normal standards and can get away with anything he wants. If he attacked you he'd say you enticed him...and it's a man's world."

Helen began downing her first cocktail, " Where's a castrator when we need him ?"

Edith, curling her blonde tresses with her fingers, " Unfortunately, the best way to sideline Dwight is to find a new target, which is no easy task but I told my new beau he has to find some good looking babe who wants to meet a potential doctor. In fact I made it an ultimatum."

" Dwight is a sicko. I feel for you Veronica, but I think Edith has the right idea," Elizabeth raised her glass, " a toast to girl power. We'll get this guy yet."

They clinked glasses.

Veronica, feeling a bit down trodden, " Thanks Edith. I guess things are going well with the hardware store guy..."

Edith laughed, " He has the intelligence to be crazy about me, which is why he'll find a new target for the creep, even if it has to be his sister." They all laughed.

Veronica took a deep breath, " Every time I laugh, I think how much Winston made me laugh, and how much I miss him (another long deep breath)...I don't know what I'd do without the three of you."

Helen was engulfing cocktail number two, " Hopefully not in jail for manslaughter," she laughed, " and speaking of laughs, why don't you bring your scrapbook next week."

Elizabeth, frowning, " Helen, c'mon..."

" I can get you some 'nice' pills at the hospital." Edith was grinning.

" If I was any nicer..."

Veronica jumped in, " we couldn't deal with the super sweetness !"

" Well said Veronica ! Besides someone has to keep you three blood and vomit types from crossing the line. Constantly being nice to people is not healthy, it makes one think of adopting raccoons as pets and bringing them home..."

Veronica and Elizabeth (in unison), " Helen, what would we do without you ?"

" Didn't I see you in McDonald's with some-

one the other day ?" Edith started them laughing again.

Any serious subjects were avoided and they laughed and joked and made fun of each other. It was like being school girls, but as they left, Helen, who was bothered by Dwight, a burgeoning doctor, who was really a stalker and misogynistic, told Veronica, "don't go anywhere alone where you are vulnerable until Edith finds a new guinea pig."

Once again, tomorrow would be the real world as they knew it, at least for another week.

◆ ◆ ◆

CHAPTER TWENTY-TWO

The Call of Doom

The month of March would begin in the Michelin Rubber Plantation. It would be a turning point for Charlie Company, the first platoon, and the third herd. A place of endless shadows and mottled sunlight, a world of satanic forestry where all the pretty trees had suffered at the surgery of the military.

It was their fourth day out, just circling around the rubber trees, setting up a bush, breaking down and repeating the maneuver. So far it had been an exercise in napping. They had not seen a thing, and the routine was making them

lazy. Rufus had a brand new Claymore and was tossing out balls of C-4 to everyone in the herd. It was breakfast time, time to heat up that can of scrambled eggs and ham. Conversation was low and whispered, when; with rice in their bowls and sandals on their toes they came garbling and gregarious, a group of five strolling down an ancient path. Through the rubber trees they sounded like a Vietnamese radio station. As the volume went up, Winston rolled over on his stomach, and Sgt. Glover motioned to the rest of the men something was coming, and Juan woke Dylan up. The "radio" added video and Winston saw them all together in the middle of the road, their weapons on their shoulders, talking and laughing, not having a care in the world. Winston's finger touched off his magic wand of violence, and eighteen rounds burst out faster than he could catch his breath. Dylan rolled over, still asleep, and began firing where Juan pointed him to, and the rest of the herd opened fire.

Poof ! No one would have known they were ever there except for a lone sandal and a hat and a bowl of rice. The bullets were merely a broom that scattered them away and "Buck" was furious. He had hoped it was a large force, and when Winston told him it was only five that he saw, he wanted to slap him across the face. Now their position was compromised with nothing to show for it.

Apostles of Mars under the whim of the

Court Jester, the third herd had come through again.

Rufus leaned up against a tree and lit a square. The rest of the squad stayed on their stomachs and kept an eye on the path and the trees around.

" Did you hear them ?" Winston turned to Sarge.

" I'll say. If that was an advance party, a bunch of scouts..."

" Then where's the birthday cake ?"

" They did sound like they were going to a party. Quite unreal."

Now artillery was peppering the area in a gross sense of overkill, a feeble rationalization of a pathetic situation.

No body count, but there was that sandal. McAllister passed the word along they would be moving out shortly. Some gum chewing cowboy from the second platoon wandered up to their position, " See you guys got into a firefight."

" Not really," Winston rolled over smiling, just some visitors for breakfast and they didn't like the menu."

" They didn't return fire." Sgt. Glover didn't bother to look at the guy.

" Wanna bet ? What's those holes ?"

Winston looked to see a stream of latex oozing down from a little hole about two feet above Blackie's head, and not to be the Lone Ranger there was one about two inches above his

head on the tree he was hiding behind.

The cowboy rejoined his platoon, and the third herd did a recon of the area...with only another Ho Chi Minh sandal (made from a tire tread) to be found.

It was a hot, hot afternoon in the rubber trees, and they sat and waited and smoked amongst the trees while just across the chalk, barely more than a hundred meters away, artillery pummeled its poison into a large hedgerow of bamboo covering nearly an acre, a suspected NVA camp...and no one spoke. Hunks and bits of shrapnel, the splash from artillery came whistling like miniature sirens down upon them. It was molten hot, and could set your clothes on fire, as well as produce an instant burn tattoo. Eventually it would stop, but they were too close to the artillery, and when it did the First and Second platoons would be crawling in to check the hedgerow.

The enemy's breakfast visit seemed nowhere particular or definite in time...it could have been years ago or just the moment before...it had that limbo yesterday feeling to it.

" Saddle up !"

They were the ugliest words Winston could hear. McAllister's eyes were urns of hate, his look gave Rufus the feeling he was scum...but he was good enough to die for him. The platoons' faces were granite facades, devoid of emotion...old men's looks in youthful wrinkles.

The two point men converged on the massive hedgerow merging into a single file. The bamboo was so thick they had to crawl, and with all that artillery pumped into it, they expected a cemetery of dead bodies...but they didn't have to crawl far.

Winston, in rear security, hit the dirt simultaneously with the rest of the Wolfhounds as the crackling of AK-47 rounds whizzed over his head. The bullets were every-where as the gooks were spraying the file.

Half the men were inside the hedgerow, with the remainder in the pathetic situation of waiting and watching and not being able to fire and not knowing what was going on inside the hedgerow. The blind following the blind in a blind...the NVA, although vastly outnumbered, were in control.

It was the ubiquitous horror show...there on the screen before Winston was non-lush green and yellow bamboo woven into an opaque mesh and in the center were men getting up and down with the crackling of the bullets, while in the background the sporadic yet constant symphony of the machine gun and its teammate the M-16 fired away. It seemed to be chaos.

Being the last man in the rear, Winston had a view of everything, and although something was going on in this surrealistic horror show, he didn't know what was happening. The men he could see were laying low, glazed in

sweat and smoke. Their eyes had that look of staying calm while watching Atlantis sink into the ocean. There was a certain flavor of lostness, but in the back of their eyes there was something forcing themselves to the reality of being there.

No escape.

Winston felt like he should get up and adjust the picture, then the screen seemed to open up, an alchemy of cinemascopic intensity. Some thing, some THING, was creeping, crawling, dragging up the path careening off the bamboo. It was a GI carrying some creature...some picture in the horror show...what was it ?

A white GI had lost an eye, and a soul brother had dragged him out of the bamboo. The wounded GI looked like his head had exploded in blood, while the brother knelt next to him, his arm around him, his eyes the eyes of a Viking, looking to some lost shore for his longboat.

Where have you been ?
What have you been doing ?
What world did you come from ?

Winston was watching it on the screen, a spectator apart from the phenomena...he wasn't with them.

The firing continued and he hugged Mother Earth, smoked cigarettes and watched and waited. And then from out of the mystery of the bamboo curtain another alien from another world stumbled from the hedgerow, led by an old man who kept picking him up and pushing him

along.

The word spread before his presence...

Sgt. Glover turned to him, " He's been shot in the nuts."

Winston said nothing and everyone in the file reached down and checked out the situation, as if Freud were sitting on their shoulders..there could be nothing worse except death.

The man was in nowhere.

He didn't even know his name. There was no pain on his face nor any categorical gaze, but a look into another identity. He was gone.

Just gone.

Winston's ticket had been punched for the horror show. He had never seen a man like that. The lines in his face had changed, he didn't look the same. Where his crotch should be was nothing but blood, his pants were soaked in crimson, and they laid him down away from the bamboo while a medic shot him up with enough morphine to make the sandman catatonic. Everyone kept checking their privates...the transformation from soldier to eunuch was too disturbing. The dream of returning to the world and seeing girls again was sliced to shreds. The man felt not whole, he was in pieces.

The NVA, which had survived the earlier artillery barrage had three bunkers amid the camouflage and protection of the bamboo, and they continued spraying the file. Dylan was on the verge of burning up a barrel, and Juan was

frustrated he couldn't get off a grenade through the dense verdure.

They needed to get closer.

* * the call of doom * *

It is always there and has always been there...the voice, the eternal call, in ships distant from shore and civilization...and inside every soldier, like an incurable cancer. In the mystery of an intense sun amid the invisible crackling of violence, Dylan and Juan heard the firm but clear, soul-less voice of doom. And they had no identity. Their souls were out of there bodies, aloof but caught up in the mystery stream. Their identities were frozen in time...but would be returned to them...the moment after.

Ride the pale horse...

They crawled like scared children over the quivering estranged soldiers playing mole with the ground. These men were immobilized by fear. All you could hear was the bullets and then the voice...but Dylan and Juan weren't crawling away, they were travelling to the enemy.

They were going to kill...

The second platoon's machine gunner, shrieking, exploding his voice in primitive torment...never saying a word, stood up with his wand of violence, and sprayed a barrage into the faceless bamboo. A bullet with "to whom it may concern" on it entered his earth form and he stopped doing everything.

And he no longer heard the voice...

Dylan and Juan, servants of the voice, started firing at the three bunkers, where the NVA, popping up sporadically from their holes of fire, were spraying the platoons at random.

They were going fast, actions were one step ahead of thought. They were captured in a power and stream of will that was resistant to their desire. They thought no dream or idea. Their will was the will of the voice.

Dylan's dragon never stopped spitting fire from its mouth, and Juan, in eruptions of inhuman hate began throwing grenades through the broken webbing of bamboo at the bunkers.

After the grenades it became quiet.

The voice was growing dim. And then they could no longer hear it.

The duo returned to their bodies, and lit a cigarette.

Where had they been ?
What did they do ?
No one knew.
No one could tell them.

The two platoons pulled back and provided security for the dust-off...the Cyclops soldier, and the man who felt like the unknown soldier, were loaded onto the helicopter, and in a rush of purple haze they were off across the treetops, beyond the horizon, and gone from their reality forever.

The voice of doom was still speaking in its eternal monotone but no one could hear it...and

in a mass of nerves and pent-up words, two files of soldiers backtracked out of the bamboo and across the chalk and into the rubber trees. Then the artillery returned. They set up a hasty perimeter and laying down and leaning against the brambly vestiges of a once great plantation they smoked cigarettes and made idle chatter, and watched the artillery explosions, dodging the splash as the birds of shrapnel came whistling down upon them. Winston touched a piece of metal about six inches long and an inch wide. It was so hot it was smoking and steaming, riddled with edges sharp as razors.

Then the jets and the air strikes began their show...taking their minds off all thought in particular...the noise was deafening and exciting. It was a military circus and they had free tickets.

The bombs were traditional in shape, and for a fleeting moment they could see them as they dropped, which was followed by huge clashes of the clapping of doom which drowned their ears and reverberated through the rubber trees, like the fading applause of the Grim Reaper. Then napalm, the silent messenger of cruel death hit the bamboo fortress, bursting into mountain high clouds of black-gray smoke laced with a crimson center, and the fire formed arms groping through the bamboo and into the crevices of the earth. Napalm would cling like glue on fire, a truly sadistic weapon of war.

The artillery returned, followed by the jets...there was no such thing as "overkill", but the realization they would be going back into the bamboo hedge again was painfully potent.

Winston knew that since he walked rear security the last time, he would be walking point. First one in...back to arena of death.

He felt very nonchalant.

For Blackie, he knew he was just a cog in the machine, a part programmed without emotion or suspense, and the scope of the phenomena was pure science fiction. He had no feelings about the situation, nothing mattered except getting through the day and being one day shorter. He had 47 to go...there was light at the proverbial tunnel. Smoking his menthols, mildly enraptured by the show across the street, Blackie turned to the sound of the metal behemoths creeping through the trees towards them...creatures from another strange universe.

Winston felt a burden fly away from his shoulders, and it was as if a vice had been removed from his breathing at the sight of the mech unit. He would not be walking point.

Blackie watched the metal behemoths (armored personnel carriers) creep and slither and wind through the trees. The large creatures paused as they began to re-supply the second platoon with water, and then they formed a line, a phalanx facing the bamboo, while the infantry units waited behind them. The behemoths

smoked and coughed their cogs...the noise was horrendous as the giant metallic beasts poured missiles into the bamboo...their long trunks spewed fire and noise, while slimy GIs poured oil on the beasts' trunks, and fed them with ammo, which they consumed as fast as sound.

And then in belches of speed and fury the phalanx of armored personnel carriers began knocking down the thick twenty foot bamboo. The behemoths razed the verdure to the ground while behind wandering pilgrims with weapons casually strolled, gazing at the destruction and mildly conversing in their earth language.

The behemoths uncovered some bodies, never cheering in their conquest but continued growling along...and rumbling and spewing smoke they disappeared from the bamboo back into the labyrinth of the rubber trees. Soon there was only a distant noise.

The smell of burning napalm on human flesh was raucous to the nose and for all the artillery, the bombing, the air strikes, and the cost of the Wolfhounds who would never return, there were only six dead NVA accounted for, although it would never be known how many had perished in their underground camp.

They could hear Lt. "Buck" screaming into the horn as the RTO buried himself in the bamboo as the first screaming round hit. Somehow the Colonel thought more artillery was necessary, and the platoons buried themselves in the

bamboo as the first screaming rounds began their descent.

" Abort ! Abort ! You are firing upon us !" "Buck" could've been heard back at the base camp, without the horn.

The round was off to the right creating only a fury of shrapnel . It sounded like the release of a huge flock of evil metallic birds, as they covered themselves with burnt bamboo to shield themselves from the burning steely wicked messengers of artillery.

And then it stopped raining artillery and began to rain rain...a deluge, a drenching mind numbing cold rain, thick as a curtain, dressing them in total wetness among the sickly burnt bamboo and mud.

For a mili-second Winston flashed back on his college days, and how irritating some of his professors were, and what a long walk to Shakespeare class it was , and then the memory went poof.

He couldn't tell Veronica what it was like to smell human flesh burning...at the moment he was sopping wet, with no where to go, marinating in a soldier's hell.

Rufus tried to keep his cigarettes dry, lighting one under his helmet. It was raining so hard it was hard to keep a smoke lit.

C'mon brother rain...
I'm a part of you...you're a part of me
Tell me a truth, brother

...am I going to make it ?

The rain momentarily stopped with a wisp and a lash of wetness, as well as the artillery, and Rufus got up with the rest of the file... and with the beat and tune of a fanatic gunship overhead, they exited from the bamboo back into the rubber trees, not to return again...for at least, today.

This day was over.

They set up, solemnly, for the night, their nerves were getting bundled together tighter and tighter, and like fetuses cramped in wombs of poncho liners they slept sopping wet huddled against broken trees in a military coma, as the cavalier and occasionally furious rain persisted.

In the morning they didn't care they were wet and chilled and exhausted, they were eagle flighting out in one hour. Some dry clothes and hot food and some sleep were waiting to be welcomed. They felt sorry looking at the fresh platoons exiting the eagle flight. Their clothes were still neat and they looked innocent. His group felt like old men as they took their places and sloshed into the helicopters and soon it would be powdered eggs and ham.

He spent breakfast talking to Prince, reminiscing about yesterday, events which seemed peculiarly distant already.

"Winston, beginning tomorrow I'm going to be humping the machine gun, opposite Dylan. And can you dig it ? I'm going to be an even big-

ger target. I know the good Lord must have intended it, so I'll take what is put on my plate, but I sure don't like it, I don't like it at all, and it's going to change my life."

" You're right about that brother. I'm next in line I think. Together we might be able to hit a barn door...but you're going to be fine...you're perfect for it, and you're cautious enough by nature that you won't be standing up playing John Wayne trying to wipe out a battalion of gooks."

" Amen to that...I'm all in for a low profile." He paused, looking at the ground, " that dude machine gunner that lost his balls was standing up trying to get at those gooks. He's headed for serious time, and he made a big mistake, a real big mistake."

" Roger that, that's why I know you're the man. You and the gun will dig each other in now time."

" Winston my man, yesterday was such a waste ! We spent all day getting some of our guys totally messed up or dead for six NVA !"

" Gorgeous," who had just finished slicking back his hair, admiring himself in his cracked mirror was eavesdropping, " That's the plan Wolfhound ! Anything for a body count ! Bet the Colonel reported a hundred dead gooks and a massive base camp destroyed instead of the six KIA among a few bunkers. It actually makes the dead guys look better, like they are dying for something." He started to laugh, sounding like a

snickering hyena.

Prince did not feel like getting into a heavy rap with "Gorgeous", took a last bite of breakfast and left abruptly. Winston did likewise heading in a different direction. Prince went to write letters. It was his therapy, he needed to write, and nothing else was as important. Winston found a solitary place on the bunker line, lit up a straight, and had a little talk with himself...the war was beginning to get under his skin. He was infected.

* Winston's Soliloquy and Lament to Sanity *

Soon we will be going out again...and again and again and again...herded and harassed into another mission...led by the mindless with no escape...until there are no more missions. If only I could pack up my memories and get the hell out of here.

I don't want to go. I don't want to go out in the field anymore. I never want to go again. I'm sick of it all ! I need to get away from guns...I've got too much piano in me that needs to be played...too much wandering not yet taken to meet up with the business end of a bullet.

Oh God, I don't want to go ! Why should I be one of the chosen few to risk my life for my country ? The old men on the Hill, who sip their coffee and listen to debate...they don't play the game...yet they make the rules. My country's freedom ? I'm not free.

What am I doing here ? How many more times will I attack my soul with this pathetic lament ? I am going insane. I am insane. I must be to be doing this. Twenty years from now who will answer ? Who will remember ? No one. Twenty years from now I could still be alive.

Everyone is melting into the same...we're all becoming the universal soldier...and we're all afraid.

Am I going to walk point tomorrow? Am I going to walk point forever ? My nerves are ready to snap...I just want to be a minstrel singing on some green path, not a soldier. What kind of country enslaves minstrels and forces them to be hunters ?

I know tomorrow I'm going to the Michelin rubber plantation...I'm not ready to throw down my gun...I'm not ready for a jail beneath the ground.

It will all melt down to a whisper on a wall. America is sick and we are the bleeding wounds that only death can heal...I want to look into the mirror and see a person...see a someone I can say hello to. Does America know what I'm going through ? Does anyone feel at all, do they know what it's like to go on a mission ? Does anyone care ?

I know I'll be going. I am insane.
Someday, I'm not going to go out anymore.

For reasons unknown to them the First Platoon did not go on a mission the next day, but in-

stead had light duty around the base camp.

They would get stoned for a change of pace. It was around ten in the morning and blistering hot already, as the sky people gathered in their bunker. They would get away from it all by getting above it all.

" Ho ! Ho! Ho! Santa brings sodas for good little boys, but don't open 'til Christmas Santa says. Ho ! Ho ! Ho !" Dylan was grinning like a son-of-a-bitch.

The sodas were ice cold.

Blackie started chugging a coke, "Where did you get these sodas...I'm gettin' a brain freeze."

" Let's say I have connections."

" Bravo to you !" And Winston took a can of root beer. There was salvation in a cold drink and Winston tried to savor it, but it tasted so good and so cold it went down too fast.

" Bring it home Santa," and Rufus grabbed a soda and started rubbing it across his forehead.

They passed the J's around. They were in a good mood, it was relaxing to have the day off.

" I got a letter from a buddy back in the world," Blackie puffed hard on the J, " and him tellin' me what's goin' on with him back in Chicago, and what's happenin' in the world..."

" Makes you feel really out of it..." interrupted "Gorgeous".

" Worse than that...it's like we're suspended in time...and nothing is real. We're not

a part of the real world. We're all here for a year, but our clocks stopped in the world when we left, and we won't be able to start the clocks again until we return. The world is moving but we aren't moving with it. It froze for us when we left. Nothing can be real for us, we're not in the same world as everybody else."

" I can dig it." Winston was on the same vibration.

" This world seems pretty fuckin' real to me, those fuckin' bullets that blew that machine gunner's balls off were fuckin' real..." Juan took a last hit and grabbed his poncho liner signifying he was heading for some crash time.

" Gorgeous" was playing with a stick in the dust, and running his hand through his hair, " Everyone of us probably thinks about the world every day. It's our dream, the place we're all going back to, but Blackie is right..what's happening over there has nothing to do with us. We're out of it, we're lucky to be reading the headlines. For us the world is just a carrot on a stick..."

" Tell me about it. I got 46 days 'til I'm sittin' on the Freedombird."

" I'm going to kiss the ground when I get back to Vegas," Dylan had his usual Cheshire Cat grin, " and I can't imagine Vegas changing..."

" Well, you just might be surprised," "Gorgeous" felt like Plato was sitting on his shoulder, " Vegas may not have changed, but all the people you knew have been doin' stuff without you...the

whole world is a distortion..."

" Well, I'm ready to find out." Dylan was as stoned as a duck.

" I dream all the fuckin' time about the world, I can't wait for the girls to see how pretty I still am...God ! I hate the Army !...but the world...it's just a distortion. It's not real anymore. Seein' bodies blown to shit, that's what real." He never looked up from drawing with his stick in the dust.

" Amen brother 'Gorgeous ' !" Prince as usual was as quiet as a cocoon until something moved him and his spirit would just emote and explode, " this *is* our reality, carrying a gun is our way of life, killing people is our job, everything else doesn't count. All we have is each other, and when we face the fact that being a Wolfhound is all we got...we all really need each other...but I can't stop the dream...of dreamin' of goin' back to the world...to see my future bride...it's what I'm livin' for...it's not to kill NVA. My mama didn't raise me to kill nobody. I'm countin' the days 'til I see my people back in Detroit. I'm not worried, I'll always be who I am."

Winston had never seen this side of Prince and was impressed with his eloquence, " The sad side to our reality," and he started to laugh, " is..."

" It don't mean nuthin'." "Gorgeous" interrupted.

" Worse than that, we are the players in

someone else's game and we have no rights, no say so, we're slaves of the machine."

" We may be the slaves, but we make it work..."

Blackie tried to continue...

" We're just as bad as the ones that call the shots. We play the game, we're as guilty as any warmongering general, we're the universal soldier...the one whom to blame...without us there is no war.""Gorgeous" was beginning to get hostile.

" So we're the scapegoats," Dylan looked stupid grinning like he was., " it don't mean nuthin'."

"...and there is no escape. " "Gorgeous" looked up from his doodling in the dust, and scowled at everyone in the bunker.

" And don't forget 'Gorgeous ', we're all expend-able..." Winston was trying to get "Gorgeous" to really go off.

Just then Rufus entered the bunker taking a J from him. He was about to unravel.

" SOMEONE HAS GOT TO BREAK MY LEG !" He pivoted and got right in Dylan's face, " if you tell Juan it's all right, he'll break my leg, but he won't do it unless you tell him it's all right." He sat down next to Dylan, put his head in his hands and began to cry. For a moment they were all paralyzed, then Winston went over and put his arm around him.

" Rufus, my main man, I _know_ you're

going to make it. If anyone is going to be sending us postcards from the world it's you. Goddamn, don't worry, you're going to make it." He spoke with a convincing confidence.

He reeled his head back, his body shivering, even though the temperature was in the high nineties, " I'm not going to make it." His voice was soft, as he stared out at some anonymous space, looking nowhere.

" Man, don't say that. You're going to make it."

Rufus had slipped into another world, a realm of his mind all his own, " I just know I'm goin' to die...I'm amazed I've lived this long...I never thought I would have...someone has got to break my leg. I've got to get out of this next mission...I just know it's going to be my last. C'mon Dylan, tell Juan he number one GI and make an easy 100 dollah."

Dylan could not look Rufus in the eye, he didn't know what to do, " I don't want to talk to Juan. This is between you guys, I got nothing to say about this." He realized it was time for him to leave the bunker and get some fresh air.

"Gorgeous" took a drag from the J and passed it on,
" Don't talk about death Rufus, things are bad enough already."

Rufus spit his words out at "Gorgeous", " I'M NOT TALKIN' ABOUT YOU !"

Winston got up, " I think I'm going to

write a letter and crash." This conversation was going nowhere. He left Rufus smoking a J by himself and heating up a can of beans and franks. Jesus would not have considered it the last supper.

CHAPTER TWENTY-THREE

Edith to the Rescue

Since the three nurses had different schedules they infrequently ran into each other at the hospital or school, so it was quite a pleasant surprise when Edith called. Veronica had just finished dinner listening to her mother's prattle. She had no idea what mother was talking about, her ears were tuned to the TV in the next room giving the play-by-play and the color commentary of another day in Vietnam. America was getting angry. Two hundred young Americans on aver-

age were dying every week, it would be nearly 12,000 for 1969 alone, and there was no end in-sight. The rhetoric of "winning the war" was becoming hollow.

" Hey fellow Nurse ! Guess what ? OK, give up ? My new beau has come through, and found a good looking babe who's dying to meet a doctor, which is what I told Dwight..."

" You what ! !"

" Yes, I called the creep up and pretended he was a human being, raving about this beauty that was dying to meet a good looking doctor, preferably young and single, who was friends with my boyfriend; and this Sunday we'd pick him up and the four of us would go to this fairly large picnic, hosted by old pals of John, my beau, and there'll be food and drinks and a great oppor-tunity to meet someone."

" Just beer and wine ? He asked.

" I told him all that and margaritas too. I could read his mind, that liquor would lubricate this woman's libido, and he thanked me pro-fusely, couldn't wait..."

" Edith, you are the rock of Gibraltar. This dis-traction sounds like it will save my life." Veronica started to clap and dance, waking Louise, ready to party. " You really went all out. I don't know how to thank you."

" What are friends for ? I know how seriously sick this man is. I doubt he'll become a doctor. I hope not. He will eventually end up in jail, mak-

ing the wrong mistake with the wrong girl."

" I can't wait to hear Monday night how everything went."

" Don't worry, John and I are on a mission. He said he always wanted to save a damsel in distress, and I told him now's his big chance. Hopefully, by the end of the afternoon Dwight will have forgotten your name."

Veronica was breathless. "You're a life saver...I'm going to call Helen, and tell her."

" Good deal. Elizabeth called me about maybe switching our schedule, so she's in on the 411. Talk to you Monday and give you the whole story."

When Helen heard of the plan she was ecstatic, " Who would have guessed that blonde bombshell was the only Einstein in our group. Genius ! Playing into Dwight's lust for conquest was perfect, let's hope the guinea pig falls for the real pig..."

" Edith said she was a looker and *really* wants to meet a doctor, so fingers and toes crossed. Elizabeth talked to Edith, and this Monday night will be a doozy. I cannot wait to hear what happens."

" Amen Veronica, if this doesn't work I'll enlist one of my accountant classmates to find a thug to beat him up."

" And what will that cost *you* ?"

" Probably dinner at McDonald's." She laughed. " To Edith ! See ya Monday night !"

CHAPTER TWENTY-FOUR

Darkness Becomes a Shroud

* * The Mission * *

Dylan had picked up some sham time on a sore foot, and Winston had inherited the machine gun, and betwixt reality and facade, he was having a giggle, "Hey Glover, look at this outfit...got to be the image of Pancho Villa, all these machine gun rounds wrapped around me." He was in a perversely good mood.

The platoon was assembling for an eagle flight.

Sgt. Glover was checking his gear for the umpteenth time. It was to be a three day mission,

which translated to a lot of C's and canteens. "You look like a real power figure Winston."

" I feel like a walking weapon, a human instrument of fire power."

Sgt. Glover surveyed the LZ, everyone was cluster-fucking, except he didn't see Rufus. " Where's Rufus, hope he's not calling in sick." Sgt. Glover joked.

" I hope he doesn't break a leg...he's really got something on his mind...he's getting the horrors."

" What do you mean ?"

" He thinks he's going to die." Winston had one of those " I don't know what to say expressions on is face."

Sgt. Glover didn't say a word, as he observed Lt. "Buck" escorting Rufus to the eagle flight.

The electric appearance of the eagle flight as they spontaneously and unanimously broke the horizon with a roar never failed to shoot adrenalin through the entire unit. The sound was deafening. They got on the choppers in the old mechanical way, head held down, hiding their eyes from the tornado of dust, and then, miraculously, they were in the air, once again on that magic carpet ride...and this time...? To where...? Everyone looked so old, and there was no talking on this eagle flight...there was nothing to say.

Rufus looked out at the bland treacherous

greenery of the Michelin rubber plantation and wondered what was waiting for him out there. He wasn't going back to D.C. He wouldn't be returning and setting the world on fire. His spark would never be seen. From the time they LZ'ed Rufus was convinced he was going to die...but in the back of his mind he thought if he could make it through this mission...it would be his last. He would figure out a way to get out of them, even if it meant he would have to go AWOL. Deep in his heart...he knew...he more than felt it...he knew it was just a matter of time...

As soon as the eagle flight landed, they divided into two files and began meandering their way through the plantation. Winston always had that feeling when they were dropped off that they were being abandoned. They were the lost boys waiting to be rescued by Peter Pan.

The afternoon was hot, slow, and uneventful; and as the evening debuted with a dusky darkness they walked through a deserted village, pillaged and decimated. It looked like the shadows were keeping it together. The atmosphere was pure gloom as the village offered too many fearsome niches for ambush. Even "Buck" was nervous as they walked past the dilapidated huts all painted with shadows. Twilight was transforming quickly into straight darkness, and as they moved into their night position, the opaqueness of a pure night began to blanket them. Rufus was too uptight, no one was reach-

ing him. The platoon silently nestled into positions and set up guard duties. In this darkness where no star could penetrate its light, it would be a freak occurrence if they encountered any movement by the NVA.

Tomorrow they would be sweeping all day and Winston was down to two canteens to last two more days. It wasn't going to work, but humping 5,000 rounds, many meals of C's, plus the 28 pound machine gun, and six canteens...one more canteen would break the camel's back.

He would be going to sleep thirsty, and drive himself mad dreaming about Dad's root beer, ice cold root beer.

The night was peaceful except for the usual enemy of the night...the simple mosquito. He always wrapped his towel around his head, double strength around his ears, but it was hopeless, the symphony of buzzing was ubiquitous.

Rufus awoke in the morning freaking on a spider web crisscrossing his face, which made him feel ensnared. Only a snake would've been worse. It was a snap horror, and nothing more, and he rolled out balls of C-4 for the squad to heat up their breakfast C's.

By the afternoon Winston felt like the bandoliers wrapped around his waist were merging with his skin, they had dug in and pinched, and step after step, he would have to live with the agony and think of other things. There was non-

stop swearing as the men tripped and fell among the miscarriage of nature. They were hot and exhausted and the twisted broken arms of the plantation was literally bringing them down. He only thought of water...and he was not alone. The rerun of this movie had become painfully old.

He thought to himself how stupid it was to wander around in circles through this sad decapitated land looking for contact...someone to kill, when all he wanted was a drink of water. The sad part of the equation was that if they made contact...they would get re-supplied with water. It was pick your poison.

He was driving himself mad.

The platoon took a break. It was an area of mottled shade and Sgt. Glover motioned to Winston that he was taking a nap, and he should stay on alert. Sgt. Glover laid flat on his back as he always did, with his towel covering his face, something Winston found suffocating just looking at him, but that was how he always slept. Even though it had to be hot and stultifying it did keep the flies off his face.

When Sgt. Glover awoke from his nap, ready or not, Winston wanted to talk, to chatter.

" Do you know I really trip off Rufus, he's a constant mind blow, without a doubt one of the greatest dudes I've ever met...one special guy, he helped me a lot when I first entered the Wolfhounds. But what really gets me is his obsession for death. Over and over again he says he's going

to die, he blew my mind with that rap the first day I met him, and I'm sure he's been saying it since last September, and this is March. That's a long time to live with a philosophy like that.

Sgt. Glover rubbed is eyes, he was barely awake, and hardly ready for Winston's diatribe.

Winston continued, " I think the reason he says he's going to die is to compromise with his real fear of death, something we all have in varying degree. He's really afraid, but it's easier for him to live with himself if he thinks he's going to die. It's like some people always count on the worst, so when it happens, it's easier to handle...but this is one worst where you're the last to know...and you're gone. It's weird to count on death as a means to holding onto life. Definitely Nam is going to have a lasting effect on Rufus..."

" Roger that Winston," Sgt. Glover was waking up,   " no one really gets out of here completely alive. I've known Rufus since day one...he'll never change, he can't stop the bad rap."

" It's going to take him some time to adjust to the world when he returns, but then you never know, he may adjust with a snap of a finger. I wish he wouldn't talk so much about death so constantly, but it's just so much a part of the Nam, death has a greater significance over here...but one thing I'm sure of...and I don't know why, but it's just something I feel, and deep down I just know, if anyone is going to make

it...it's going to be Rufus. I don't know why, but I just know. There's something about him...for all his pessimism, he's a survivor. It's strange. There are some guys that shouldn't be out here, the war is too much...I wish Rufus could figure out a way to get off line...but that's not going to happen...they're just plain not going to let him off."

Sgt. Glover shook his canteen. There was two swigs left, " Top has got extra glasses for him, he's maxed on shamming for broken glasses, and I think he's made Rufus his special case...no matter what, he's going to be in the field."

" Maybe he'll luck out and find something new to sham on. I hope he can..."

" Everybody gets some sham time sometime. I know come June, if I can't get off line I'm going to start shamming. I need a holiday." Sgt. Glover looked up to see Sgt. McAllister smiling at him.

" I'm going to take a shit right over there," he pointed with his shit paper to a clump of trees, " so don't shoot me. When you gotta shit, you gotta shit." He smiled and Winston noticed he had six rolls of shit paper, C-ration style, held onto his helmet by his camouflage band.

" Six rolls of shit paper, how often do you crap ? "

" Always be prepared, you can't run out of this stuff. You're shit would be weak. Weak, gentlemen. You'd be up shit's creek." He left on

his mission.

" There's something anal about him, but of course he's only a lifer, and shit is one of the most significant things in their lives. Your shit had better be in order, or together, and woe to the trooper whose shit is loose, hanging, or flaky. His shit would be dug in for sure." Winston ended his fecal diatribe.

As soon as Sgt. McAllister returned from his artistic expression, they saddled up. It was still very hot, and they walked and walked and walked. The trees had been so demolished by artillery they had lost the power of shade. They were walking in circles. Winston cut his hand on a bamboo shard, and the pain accentuated the burden of the machine gun on his shoulder and he sparked into a swearing oratory. Sgt. McAllister ran up front to yell in his face *not* to yell like that and that everyone was tired and thirsty and for him not to lose his temper...as he wasn't special. He wanted to spit on the rodent, but changed his machine gun from one shoulder to the other, didn't speak and kept on walking.

They were delirious with thirst, a now familiar consequence of multi-day missions, and he forced his mind to think of anything but water, knowing that somewhere in this forest of burnt and devastated rubber trees there had to be an oasis.

The new guy, B.B., walking point, found a bunker complex, freshly made. As they got on

line to check it out...*it* was discovered, a small spring all wet and gray complete with clumps of floating vegetation.

Ecstasy.

Those that were drinking were smiling and looking off into the distance, the glee soaking into their veins, and those that were waiting had the eyes of hungry animals. The nearness of water brought a sense of hope, a momentarily illusion of entering civilization, and Sgt. Glover, the Good Samaritan filled canteens four at a time for his squad. Winston put water purification pills in three of his canteens and drank the other. He could feel his strength returning, a shot of vigor...but meanwhile the bunker complex lay waiting to be searched.

Fresh tracks.

Only fresh tracks of Ho Chi Minh sandals and nothing more. The bunker complex had only recently been evacuated, and "Buck" decided to pull his men together for a little pep talk. As they huddled among the bramble of broken branches, feeling new life and invigoration in their blood thanks to the water, they listened to this disciple of the Valkyries.

He knelt down on one knee to be on eye level with his men, " Gentlemen, let's hope they are not so close they are watching us, but they can't be too far away." He paused, "we have the opportunity for a body count if we play our cards right and stay alert. That's what it takes. We

Wolfhounds have a reputation to maintain, and I don't want these gooks to get away, not if we can do anything about it. I want to be on the horn to the Colonel and tell him we uncovered a base camp and then followed through and annihilated their forces. It's what being a Wolfhound is all about. The key thing is we must be watchful and alert. We don't want to be the bush, we want to be the attackers." He paused again, glaring at his men, " now let's move out !"

Around and around they went and where they would stop no one knew. The sun was in broiler mode and Winston was getting strung out from getting cut by the fallen wounded branches. The plantation was in attack mode, as if all the wounded trees were exacting revenge against those that were destroying them. The sweat kept pouring into his eyes, but he was already burning all over. They walked and they stumbled and they fell, they got up and tripped and fell again; subdued into a trance by the hot sun and the monotony. When they broke for chow, he was so hungry he ate his entire C-ration including the fruitcake, which often could be substituted for a grenade.

They spun in circles all afternoon, the scenery had melted together, and even "Buck" was becoming numb to the routine. No one spoke. There was plodding, there was tripping, there was exhaustion piling on in layers as the day wore on. Some were a heartbeat away from

heat exhaustion and passing out.

It was a husky twilight among the disarrayed forest, and Winston was glad he wasn't walking point. The Colonel had given orders to patrol until nightfall, when normally they would have set up for the evening, hours ago. His military greed would cost them...they needed time to set up, and it wouldn't happen. As they began to move into their ambush site, it was a black gloom. Each man had to hold onto the shirt of the man in front of him it was so dark. No stars, no lights for a hundred miles, and the jungle canopy was like a shroud above them...creating an evil obscurity that clouded the mind, as well as one's vision. It seemed appropriate for the birth of Hell...Stygian and eerie.

He was so spent he just wanted to move into position and crash...they had walked at least ten klicks...walked ? Stumbled ! Through prickly branches and thorny bramble whose purpose in life was to hurt, and no one escaped from giving blood on this sweep. Quietly they melted into positions...it was so dark they had formed a very tight circle. Everything seemed normal except for the total blindness of the night. There were a few whispers, and then stillness...soon half the platoon would be in a deep sleep.

Winston and Juan immediately set up the machine gun on a very small berm, a roll in the ground, not much protection. There was no visibility so he had no idea what he was aiming at,

and once the thousands of rounds were removed, he felt he could fly. Together they clamped their bandoliers together. There were ten thousand rounds in one clip.

From out of nowhere...from within a fortress of silence, he heard the sound...a metallic sound. It was an instant shot of adrenalin. He took the safety off the M-60.

*Then it came...*the metallic sniffle of the AK-47 cracked over their heads...an occasional tracer showing how close he was.

Oh Jesus !

He was ten feet away...but where was he ?

When he stopped it was as if the lights went out.

Time exploded into another dimension...everything was going faster yet simultaneously a second seemed like a long stretch of eternity...he was on the berm madly spraying the area. The rounds were going everywhere, back and forth, a barrage against the atmosphere, the fire from the barrel illuminating the forest, and painting a Satanic glow on his face.

OH GOD, I'VE GOT TO GET THOSE MOTHERFUCKERS !

And then it jammed.

" Juan !" Winston roared in a whisper to him, " Fix it ! Juan, it's jammed. Fix it man, fix it !"

Winston was looking for a jammed round, but he was panicking, he couldn't see in the blindness. One moment he was a roaring animal

powering pure rage, a mad illumination coating his face...and his face alone...and the next, a deep dismal gloom awash in silence.

When Juan heard the sound of a grenade pin popping in the near distance he had two frags in the air before the gook grenade landed behind them.

It was a dud.

Juan crossed himself and said a quick prayer. He fiddled around for a moment with the 60, pulled out the links, cocked it...and put in a clip. He pulled the trigger and the silent thud, the soft click of the trigger not activating a round sent a solid cold ripple through Juan's body. He and Blackie started pitching frags wildly everywhere they thought the sniper might be.

Another gook grenade landed behind them. "Grenade !" The warning was a whisper. Everyone hit the dirt digging in.

The platoon tried to go subterranean.

Wham ! Winston knew he was hit. He felt his butt, it felt like someone had slugged it with their fist. He thought to himself, I must not be hit, I can't feel anything.

There was a tiny hole in his rear end, and he could feel the blood oozing onto his pants. He'd thought to himself, it's all right...just ti-ti shrapnel.

He felt relieved.

I'll get out of here.

I'll be dusted off.

Safety. I'll be safe...a dream wound...some sham time...I'll be off-line for awhile...oh God, a chance to get out of here...get away from this hell.

He buried his face behind the berm, he could see the flash of the muzzle of the enemy.

How
    Close
        Would
            He
                Come
                    To
                        Death ?

What strange invisible force had brought them all together ? Violence was in the air...the smell of it was overpowering...he couldn't see the sniper...where was he ? Was he still out there ?

He felt he was close enough to reach out and touch him...was he likewise as scared ? Did he feel that death was close to him ?

And then from the deep silence of the aftermath...the feeling saturated in the mystery of the unknown...words came to Winston's ears. They cracked the nerves like a descending into the purest of wild hells and his mind became a landscape of earthquaking emotion.

Oh God,
Would someone help me ?

They were just words from a distant voice, that seemed far away, just so very far away. In-

visible in the black verdure, he was only ten feet away from Winston. It was the worst sound, the most plaintive voice, and a plea to all humanity crying out in the dark...

It was the beginning of the trip back to birth...alone.

The first door is the final exit.

The medic and the platoon sergeant began to work on him, giving him morphine and trying to stop the bleeding.

It was quiet...just so quiet...his breath sounded like thunder...and then...only moaning.

The voice was unrecognizable.

A friend, a comrade, was hurt...but the voice sounded anonymous. Then he recognized it...he couldn't see him but his words were real enough to touch.

"Oh God, won't someone help me. I'm hit."

Then Sgt. Glover verified to him that it was B.B., he had been plastered with shrapnel from a grenade. His soul was slowly oozing from his body from a hundred holes.

"Dust-off ! I need a dust-off !" B.B.'s voice had the foggy texture of words coated in pain, but the core was crystal keen and pierced and ripped Winston's senses. The spectre was hiding in the camouflage of the night.

There was no way to get a dust-off through the night and the jungle into the rubber plantation...it was too thick. B.B.'s cards of des-

tiny would be played alone.

"I don't want to die ! God, please help me !"

He was screaming, and his voice echoed through the broken forest disappearing in the distance like a lost ghoul. The "doc" gave him another shot of morphine.

All you could hear was B.B.'s breathing, a heavy tumbling breathing. Intermittently he would cry out,

" Please God, don't let me die !"

He was literally gasping for breath, for life...there wasn't another sound among the Wolfhounds...they were waiting, frozen in frustration...the unheard bell of the Grim Reaper was tolling...he was coming for his due.

Winston's mind was a whirling dervish of distraught emotion.

What's going on in his mind ?

Does

He

Know ?

He started praying. There didn't seem much else to do. He prayed for B.B, but he was really praying for himself. B.B. was a cherry, no one really knew him.

He called out to God over and over again, softer and softer, until the morphine put him out of his misery.

Soon he bled to death.

There was nothing to do except wait...

Sgt. Glover crawled back to his squad's position, and broke the news to them. His voice was just above a whisper, " B.B. is dead..."

He paused, and in the darkness no one could see his eyes welling up with tears...he was having difficulty maintaining his rigid soldierly facade,

" Winston," and he put his hand on Winston's shoulder,

"Rufus is dead."

"What ! What did you say ? Rufus is dead ? Oh man, you're wrong, that can't be. I knew of all people that Rufus would make it back to the world...he had to..." He put his hands over his face, he was not ready to cry, "...how did he die ?"

" He got shot in the chest."

" Did he say anything before he died ?"

" No. He never spoke...he died immedi-ately."

Everyone knew Rufus and the word spread quickly. In this small group of men, isolated on an island of war, there was not a single dry eye among the mighty Wolfhounds.

His mind was tunneling out of this world...*oh God, where is my beautiful friend to-night ? Can he hear my thoughts ? What is he doing now ? How could he die ? Rufus* _was_ *my friend...no...is...how can a friend be a was ? What dreams will he have now ? The greatest of all super*

heads...he thought he was going to die, he said he was...and he asked us to break his leg but no one would do it...in fact ! I pushed against it...I was so sure this man was going to make it...if Juan had broken his leg we'd still be laughing with him...we'd all be getting stoned together weaving fantasies... what is it going to be like getting high without my main man ? Is there an angel in these dark woods tonight ? If there's a heaven I hope Rufus is going...I know he's checking into the Big Hotel right now, up there with the rest of the Nam heads...he thought he was going to die...he knew he was...how can you know about death ? It's the journey from whence no one has returned...he must have lived a few moments after getting hit...what was he thinking ? Did he know he was dying ? Was this the peace he was waiting for ?

Rufus was such a wild dude...he could have brought the world so much joy...could he see death ? Could he know he'll never be with us again ? Never is such a final word...never...not one more time...n-ever...Rufus has made the journey into the beyond and he was so young...did he die for nothing in this gloom ? What forces of destiny played out those bullets in Rufus' last act ?...did he know they were coming before they were coming ? How many seas will he travel before we see him again ? How could he know he was going to die ? Never !...never again breathe life...never...what's he doing now ? He must be blowing that evil weed somewhere...you just can't stop...not just never.

Winston started to cry. Soldier's tears...pillowy spools of liquid cascading down his cheeks, wearing creases in the grime...soundless. He was scared, and the tiny piece of hot shrapnel in his flesh was still burning. He had dumped a canteen of water on it and that had helped, but it was inside...it would take awhile to cool down. He was exhausted and adrenalized...they had walked so much today...they had gone so far to stop in this residence of death. In all the pockets of darkness in this gigantic rubber plantation, they had settled in where a sniper was waiting...a sentinel of the Grim Reaper whiling away the time, a soul collector on the cruel side of war.

A comrade and his best friend were lying still nearly ten feet away...a foreign object was on fire under his skin...and

where

was

the

enemy ?

Was the sniper still alive, still out there, waiting ?

The men that shared the death of B.B. and Rufus would never see their graves, but bore witness to the exit of their souls. It was driving Winston insane. Rufus was gone...but where was he tonight ? He was making the unknown journey.

It was quiet again. Not a word or a whisper was heard. There was no wind, no rustling among the perished branches, the only sound

was one's own breathing...the sniper had to be still out there, any movement in the darkness would translate into a thunderclap.

It was hushed, but for Winston there was *that* ringing in this ears...the echo of the machine gun. It was a soft ringing now...the bells of Hell, the chimes of death.

He would hear them again.

Am I next ?

Am I going to live through the night ?

The moon came up and washed the darkness from the landscape, and with the lunar illumination came a new horror.

He looked over behind him, and there in the pale light were the wrapped up corpses of Rufus and B.B..

It was like waking up into a nightmare, and the reality was there was no escape. It was a one-way road that must be taken. He stared at his friend, wrapped in the swaddling of his poncho liner. His face was covered...it must be suffocating for his soul...you couldn't see it was actually him...could he romance that camouflage blanket into a magic carpet ride ?

He looked at the mummified figures, and the tears flowed down his face.

His heart was broken.

He heard the crack of a twig, and Winston snapped out of his depression. He's out there. He could be hiding in the bramble just a few feet away. He was defenseless, the machine-gun was

just twenty eight pounds of useless metal. Juan heard it too and pitched his last frag in the direction of the noise and emptied a clip from his M-16. Once again, the entire platoon was energized.

There was not a break in the silence until dawn, it was perfect stillness. Winston kept looking at their masked bodies. He knew he should look away, but the strands of sanity were unraveling.

In the morning the sunshine brought the green back to the leaves...life goes on...the sniper had escaped in the night...and down the chalk the platoon carried the two bodies on biers of wooden staffs and blankets. They were completely covered up. He wanted to see Rufus one more time.

Just one more time.

Never.

Never.

The walk was slow and heavy, and he was glad to be at the end of the file. The piece of shrapnel had long since cooled down, it seemed unnecessary to have it looked at; but to exacerbate the situation, when he first put his helmet on, a spider was inside, which bit him, and now his hand was the size of a baseball mitt.

In the clearing, Sgt. McAllister popped smoke to signal the dust-off of their location, startling a gigantic snake. It's body was as big as a man's thigh, and it trampled the grass as it

slithered away. The bright green smoke wafted in the quiet breeze and in moments the dust-off arrived. They put the swaddled bodies on the floor and Winston got on.

Over the treetops they flew, the swirling atmosphere was energizing and he sucked on a cigarette as he tried to look out the doors of the copter rather than the covered bodies. It was a sad, melancholy flight...Winston could hardly hold back the tears...the three of them flying in the sky and where they would stop no one knew...and around and around goes the sing-psalm lopsided wheel of Fate.

He would never forget Rufus, and Rufus would always be with him.

Did he really know he was going to die ? Did he see death before death saw him ?

The lonely ride ended at the battalion base camp, and he tried to steel himself.

The two guys that approached the copter spent their time in the rear, they didn't know what "the field" truly meant. Their world of combat was war stories, and when they saw Winston...not expecting a "live one" the first one said, " I hear you all had a bit of trouble," and he pulled B.B. with the help of his comrade, off the copter and they tossed him into the back of a flatbed truck. This was every day for them, no big thing. Don't mean nuthin'. They tossed Rufus into the truck like a sack of potatoes, and Winston screamed at them, " That's my friend ! Treat

him with respect !"

They acquiesced and didn't say a word. They did this every day, but then Winston broke, and they weren't used to seeing that every day. He started to cry, to sob...everything was unraveling...he started to walk away...there was nowhere to go. He just kept sobbing.

The deaths were poisoning him.

◆ ◆ ◆

Back in the world the hippie movement was literally flowering. Free love was the anthem of the liberated woman. Hippies were developing their own culture...peace...love one another...get high. The marijuana leaf was a new banner and wearing your hair long was a walking statement of who you were. For many life was liberating and exciting...it was a brand new world. It was great to be alive.

The economy was healthy and the war protests were becoming more widespread and intense. The population was growing increasingly angry with the war, the mounting deaths and young men crippled for life were beginning to touch the hearts of America. On TV there were nightly reports of the violence and the casualties...it was becoming more real.

The Beatles and The Beach Boys rocked the music charts.

In Texas a young woman, barely twenty was giving birth to her first child, a son, and she was beaming with that Madonna like grace of giving birth. Outside the delivery room her parents were weeping, they would try and soften the blow, but they felt helpless. An Army Sergeant in full dress uniform had a mission to accomplish, and no circumstances were going to prevent him from his ordained task. On the day of her firstborn's debut into the world, she was told her husband had been killed. She had become a mother and a widow on the same day. She was B.B.'s wife.

CHAPTER TWENTY-FIVE

Ho Chi Minh's Rainbow Elegy

Several weeks later...

They were still operating in the same old zones. Today was in a jungle not far from the Michelin plantation and Winston felt he had been in the field so long he couldn't remember any other life. Blackie was no longer with them, he was killing out his days (he had less than thirty to go) in the rear at the main base camp. Nothing but light duty by day and beer at night.

The platoon was filled with cherries, and he didn't care. He was close to Prince and Dylan (who also was soon to retire to the rear) and

barely spoke to any of the new guys. They were just the new fodder in town. His nickname among the cherries was the "old man". After all, he was twenty-three...and a survivor.

It was the usual bush, the platoon separating into squads, somewhat close to each other, with the usual weather, with the usual attitude. It was becoming rote for him...just another day.

Dylan saw the two of them first. It was hot and late in the afternoon, and he and Sgt. Glover were the only two awake in their ambush site. They were hard core Viet Cong wearing NVA black pajamas, underwear (light navy blue), white Kressge -type plastic sandals, and toting AK-47's, some ammo...and a pocketful of ghosts.

Hot finger, wild eyes, and a couple hundred rounds later...filling a strange new horizon, Dylan saw that he had got one of them. Oh yes, it was quite a sight...enough for sore eyes...Dylan had performed a soldierly job on him...his birthday suit was in carnal disarray and with his milieu of unnatural holes Winston could see what made him tick. The bullets had sewn off his legs, the blood and cartilage glistened in the sun, his dark shirt a funeral bath of black crimson, and his head had caved in. He *was* a human...and there was his brain, a giant gnarled white-gray clump, just lying in the sand waiting for some compatriots of Humpty-Dumpty to put him back together.

His side had been shot innumerable times and

part of his guts protruded out.

This morning he was someone's friend and ally, after a menagerie of bullets had descended upon him...tomorrow he would be someone's nightmare. The cherries were in shock. For some it was their first death.

"Gorgeous" taking off his helmet and slicking back his hair, was standing over the kill, " Hey Juan, do you want to cut off his ear ? Make number one souvenir. Whaddya say ?" "Gorgeous" was laughing. His boots were mired in blood and sand.

Winston was disgusted, " They'll get you for that...it's disfiguring government property... know that ?"

That sent the rest of the squad laughing.

Everyone's getting their mind blown.

" C'mon Juan, cut his ear off. I know you want to do it." "Gorgeous" was laughing harder and harder, " how will they know a bullet didn't do it...and who gives a fuck ?"

Sgt. Glover was becoming nauseated of the situation and had his RTO ask the Lieutenant what he wanted to do with the body. He was ready to leave, but couldn't take his eyes off the disfigured gook.

Dylan laid back and smoked a cigarette, not looking at his kill, " Wow Sarge, a successful ambush ! Hard to imagine we got a gook and they didn't get us." He was all about himself.

Sgt. Glover got on the horn. He needed an

answer so they could get the hell out of there. What about the body ?

Does he want it rare or well done ?

Does his mother know what's in the front yard ?

" C'mon Juan, cut his ear off ! It's number one souvenir. Get beaucoup MPC from all those REMF's."

Juan went through his pockets and found only a letter and a photograph of what was probably his family...and the ghosts of dead GIs. He left everything alone, but removed the ammo belt, which was dripping in blood, and handed it to Sgt. Glover. It would be the symbol of the kill. They dumped the body behind some bushes, and Sgt. Glover using sticks in the manner of a spatula scooped up the lonesome brain and deposited it with the body. Juan scattered and spread out dirt over the pools of blood, threw the plastic sandals into the bushes, brushed away the tracks and presto ! No more dead gook. They returned to their ambush position.

"Gorgeous" was feeling punchy, "C'mon Juan, cut his ear off. It's not too late."

Why not both ears ?

The remainder of the afternoon was spent staring at the same space where the brainless gook had mistakenly wandered into their world. Fatal errors are odd sick bait, the mystical attraction would bring others. It would be just a matter of time before a new Viet Cong trooper would

be auditioning the trail. "Buck" did not want them to change position, which was not customary...after all if there were others nearby they would know their whereabouts. They would be stationary in their ambush site for the rest of the afternoon and all of the night until morning.

By twilight the squads' eyes had been blistered by the sun waiting for Godot, an afternoon of pain watching a single spot where no one showed up. All day they were focused on the trail, knowing there had to be a comrade showing up...someone was expected. When darkness came, he realized that if the Viet Cong were aware of their location, they were just a grenade away from going home early.

Except for the usual paranoia and nerves it was a night without incident and in the morning they rejoined the rest of the unit and eagle flighted back to the fire support base camp.

Rufus was becoming a scar on the past, the wound was healing...but Winston was getting those goin' home blues, and he and Prince had six months to the day before they would see the Freedombird. A minor eternity.

Arriving at the fire support base he and Prince learned they had earned some sham time and were going that afternoon to the division base camp at Cu Chi for their annual dental appointment. It could be three or possibly four days out of the field where there were movies every night, and beer, and sex if you wanted it. Yippee !

Cu Chi was a different world, ruled by REMF's, who were used to the amenities after a hard day at the office. They wore starched fatigues fresh every day and could catch a first run movie and drink beer every night. The war for the majority of them as they did the payroll, planned the meals, ordered the ammo, did the laundry, took the records, orchestrated leaves, etc. was just a job in a foreign country, with disturbing sound effects at night. Those B-52 bombing raids could be so unsettling some times it would interfere with the sound system of the cinema.

When the Chinook landed to drop off supplies, Winston and the rest of the shammers scampered into the chasm of camouflage that was the huge belly of the Chinook, and strapped themselves to the wall. He looked at Prince perched on a tiny seat, and they both laughed...it was so great to escape. Everyone had that look as if they had been blessed by the Cheshire Cat. Within an hour they were in Cu Chi, the birthplace of Ho Chi Minh, and the home of both battalions of the Wolfhounds, the crux, the heart, the genesis of the decisions of who would live...and who would die. The craps table at a casino in Vegas could have served them equally well.

The place was a city of GIs, and there were real buildings, a hospital, barracks like stateside, and mess halls that served hot food, separate fa-

cilities for drinking according to military status, and a movie theatre that would make Topeka, Kansas envious.

Winston looked for an outside shower, but Cu Chi had something else...women...nurses and donut dollys...so showers were located within the barracks.Prince went to the PX to buy stuff he wouldn't be able to get again: writing paper, good candy, some books, and Winston opted for the enlisted man's club to drink a beer. They would meet at the mess hall for dinner. Already he was feeling relaxed as if he was on vacation.

As he walked towards the club a Jeep pulled up next to him, slamming on the brakes, roiling up the dust over his clean fatigues.

" Hey lifer, want a ride ?"

He cleared the dust from his eyes and spat in his direction and then laughed. It was Blackie. " I thought you were back in the world ."

" Ti-ti time, seven days, hop in. I'll take you shopping." Winston grinned and got in. " I've been doin' some serious sham time. All day I drive this Jeep around and do a few errands. It's number one cool. Wanna buy some cansa ? I'm almost out." He put the pedal to the floor and they began racing around the perimeter, " I love to drive and be stoned, and I've been stoned all day every day since I got here...I can't believe I'm a one-digit midget, seven more days 'til the Freedombird."

" I'm jealous man, totally wishing I was you…" He could tell the nervousness of being so close to freedom made Blackie a lot more animated than his usual stoic self.

" Don't worry man, your time will be here before you know it…but these last days have been long, the longest days of my life…I got to get stoned to get through it." He stopped at the gate and flashed his pass at the MP's, they were heading towards the village outside the gate.

" Where are we going ?"

" This is a friendly village, and you can get anything you want," and in moments they were besieged by a cyclone of babysans, crawling over the Jeep pushing their wares.

" You wan pot ?" Babysan got number one."

" You wan pussy, beaucoup pretty, make dick wake up."

" You wan speed ?" He held up his hand with tiny vials of clear liquid adrenalin.

Blackie handled the negotiations and handed the babysan twenty seven American dollars. As he handed over the money he waved to the MP's, who were constantly patrolling the village. They would split a kilo of pot and each get a vial of Saigon speed. They waited about ten minutes for the babysan to return with the goods. Winston was nervous, the MPs were everywhere, but this was life in Prohibition ! He rolled up a J and they each swallowed a vial of

speed.

" Blackie, my man, aren't you nervous about getting busted, you being so short ?"

" First of all Winston, they know what's happening. There are a lot of jeeps coming into the village everyday, and secondly, some of them are making beaucoup bucks supplying the wild lieutenants and the flyboys. It's cool." He gunned the engine leaving a cloud of dust. The citizens barely looked at him, for them he was just another representation of how America was saving his country. And for Blackie, they were just gooks, he hated them all. Within minutes they were passing through the gate, where Blackie gave the MPs a big grin and a wave, as they never bothered to check if there might be a couple pounds of pot on board. Winston was paralyzed as the kilo was stuffed into his leg pockets. By the time they meandered into the perimeter, the speed was kicking in and they both felt really high, too high.

Neither was used to speed, and right from the first chattering of the teeth they realized they would need each other to get through the night, the amphetamine dose was too strong or too polluted. Winston began to chew on his wristband of twisted shoelace, " Blackie, I think we got some number ten speed...I'm as nervous as a jailbird. We're going to need some of this cansa and a bucket full of beers to bring us down."

Blackie slowed down as they began circ-

ling the huge base camp, and flipped Winston a ready made, " You're right about this shit, but the important thing is...it don't mean nuthin'." He laughed. Blackie's usual serious droll monotone was gone, he was liberated by the thought of freedom in just a few days.

" Roger that. I'm just diggin' being out of the field."

" Freedom brother ! Seven more days !" he extended his hand for the Nam handshake. " I'm never coming back . Never !" Blackie yelled out to the perimeter for all of no one to hear.

" I'm ready to retire. I feel like I've been carrying a weapon my entire life, and I'm only half way through. Day after day forever...will it ever end ?"

"Winston, it will seem like forever but your time will come, and you'll be pushin' a broom or maybe lucky enough to be toyin' with a jeep, and instead of countin' the days, you'll be like me, and be counting the hours. Don't worry-...don't mean nuthin'...it'll be ti-ti time before you're permanently off-line." He took a drag off the J and passed it to him. There was another jeep passing them in the opposite direction, with a Colonel in it, and they both saluted...everything was normal. Winston was fearful he would smell the pot, but everyone kept moving. He continued, " I hate to ask you this, but since B.B. and Rufus, has anyone else checked into the Big Hotel ?"

" No one that you knew. Lately anyone that has got blown away, is someone who was a cherry. I don't care and I don't know any of the new guys...don't give a fuck. Shit still happens and we know how to land in it, nothing has changed. "Buck" is still hungry for a body count and the Michelin is still sucking us in. I figure I'll spend the rest of my life walking around those rubber trees looking for Charlie. Jumping the subject, I'm supposed to meet Prince at the mess hall for dinner, but the last thing I want is food. I should check in with him, he is my DEROS buddy, we came together, we leave together, so let's say hello and good-bye and get a beer at the enlisted club."

The sky was beautiful with towering clouds reaching to the heavens through the ubiquitous blueness that immersed the afternoon...and then it began to pour. Mother Nature was auditioning for monsoon season, which was coming up soon, and although the sun was everywhere it was a torrential drenching downpour for about ten minutes. They were both sopping wet and didn't care, Blackie kept driving, and they both saw it and were amazed...there was a perfect rainbow extending from one end of the base camp to the other...the colors, all seven, were so strikingly brilliant and so close and the arc so perfect and distinct, Blackie stopped driving to marvel at the magic of Mother Nature.

The end of the rainbow was directly opposite them dissolving into a cloud of smoke. Blackie took one look at Winston and silently they agreed to chase the ethereal and find the end of the rainbow.

" There's a pot of gold out there Blackie, put the pedal to the metal." Blackie was moving fast but the sun was dissolving the miracle and the end of the rainbow was disappearing into a rising fog. By the time they got to the other side they could watch the last of prism's muse turn poetry into pure vapors...and in a stoned rapture saw the mighty colors dissolve into a sea of fog and haze...and then it was as if it had never existed.

Cu Chi was the birthplace of Ho Chi Minh, the leader and powerhouse of North Vietnam. Today, with the rainbow a signature of his ghost, and perhaps another strange omen, was the day he would die.

Prince joined them at the enlisted man's club and drank a soda while they pounded down some beers.

" Prince, you look like you're surviving the Wolfhounds pretty well..." Blackie was near drunk, and Prince had only known him as the serious cold ass stone soldier who rarely spoke at all, never sounding this animated.

" You mean I'm alive and still in one piece ?"

" Exactly. And you still don't smoke the

evil weed ?"

" Not me, ever. Don't need it, don't want it, won't be breaking' foul on me. Back in the Motor City I've seen beaucoup brothers thinks it's cool, it's hip, then get all messed up and do something stupid. Next thing you know it's the world lookin' through steel bars. I bet you won't be smokin' so much when you get back to the world."

" Roger that. I won't be able to afford it," Blackie laughed, "but for the next seven days I'm going to be nuthin' but flying on J's. I'm not comin' down until I get on the Freedombird."

" Blackie tells me there's a place behind the laundry facility where you can get a massage, and for an extra two bucks mamasan will give you a handjob."

Prince laughed, " Now that's something to write home about, getting your rocks off by an old lady."

" You do get a great massage, and I bet, big guy, that you go for the extra...you're no short timer."

The trio laughed raucously.

The evening was spent drinking beer, eating burgers...going out periodically for a discreet J...and reminiscing about the old days. They all talked about wondering what it was like to go back and visit their friends, and for Winston and Prince, the satisfaction of seeing their sweethearts again. It would be so great not to have to

get up early in the morning and carry a weapon all day.

In six days Blackie would learn why so many Vietnam vets committed suicide after surviving a year of Hell, or why some who hated the military rejoined. They couldn't re-enter the flow of time...it was more than just the passing of a year...it was never being able to catch the bus once it passed your stop. No matter how fast you ran, the bus kept moving, and screaming didn't help, you were forever simply too late.

All night, until Prince couldn't deal with their drunkenness, they buoyed their spirits with toasts and and pledges of promises of great deeds and fun once they returned to the world. Eventually the two realized they were so screwed up they should crawl back to the barracks while they still could. Besides, they might get into a fight with the REMF's, which would have been bad for one and all. Winston felt lucky "Gorgeous" wasn't with them, they'd already be in jail or a hospital.

In another day Prince and he would return to life in the field. They would never hear from or see Blackie again.

Sham time was short, Winston was hoping his teeth would fall out so he could return, but no such luck. When they arrived late in the afternoon their re-introduction into life in the field was quick and immediate. Memories of starched fatigues, a clean bed, beer and hot food

faded as quickly as the unloosening of a knot.

Sgt. McAllister greeted them in his usual cordial style. They were as welcome as a door-mat. " Well gentlemen, now that your teeth are clean I hope you're ready to be Wolfhounds again. Sham time is over."

" Good to see you Sarge." He spit in the direction of the shitter.

" Get ready to PZ in three hours." They could tell he was angry.

" Whoa Sarge," Prince dropped his mouth, " it'll be dark in three hours."

" Roger that soldier. Lt. "Buck" has volunteered us for a night ambush. We're back in the big bad Michelin for the night."

" You're fuckin' kidding me Sarge. That's insane, we'll be sitting ducks." Now Winston was getting angry.

Prince was feeling his stomach tie into knots. The platoon was fifty percent cherries, who could be considered as dangerous as gooks under unpredictable circumstances.

Dylan, Juan, and "Gorgeous" were on top of their bunker with a new man who looked strangely familiar to Winston.

" Welcome fuckin' back Winston," "Gorgeous" was on a rant, " guess you heard what the fuckin' looey has volunteered us for ?" He wanted to scream.

Juan was busy whittling as usual, and never looking at Winston, " Guess we haven't

seen enough action lately."

Dylan, grinning moronically, " Me thinks we'll see some shit tonight."

The new guy was an old guy, a transfer from the second platoon. They were having difficulty with him as no one could get along with him. He was totally anti-social, and their platoon sergeant asked McAllister if he would take him. "Buck" was more than glad to have an experienced soldier among his ranks.

When he looked into the mans' eyes, who made no sign of greeting him, it gave him a cold icy feeling. His eyes were squinty and furtive, they belonged in the head of a lizard. What went on behind those eyes Winston couldn't guess...they were evil. It felt like staring into the soul of Satan's disciple. He had the creeps and didn't want to hear "Gorgeous" rant about how screwed up tonight's mission was, and left.

It was a long restless afternoon before they got ready, and at chow Lt. "Buck" gave them a pep talk. He was so upbeat you'd think he was going to his coronation, " Gentlemen ! Tonight we are going to take the NVA by surprise..." Prince looked at him like he was on serious narcotics. The new man almost cracked a smile-...he was looking forward to the mission...he loved to kill. " It's about time we Wolfhounds took the initiative. They won't be expecting us and I hope to see a good body count by morning." He was practically dancing with exhilaration

and slapped Dylan and Juan on the back as if they were old school chums.

At twilight they were on the PZ and the adrenalin was running high, which kicked into overdrive when once again the fearsome ominous thunder of the eagle flight descended upon them. It was normal now for he and Prince...as if they ever knew another life.

The moon was out but the darkness made the Michelin look black, there was no definition in the forest, it was just a sea of a single shadow. The twin machine gunners on the copters were clipped and ready to go. No one except "Buck" and the Colonel liked flying at night.

There was a field fast approaching and the eagle flight, in perfect unison, descended like banshees into the clearing.

As they hovered and the Wolfhounds jumped into the grass the first shots came threatening across the open field from the forest. Their colored tracer rounds were a kaleidoscope of confusion. Sgt. McAllister was screaming to get down and get into position, but the attack was coming from all sides of the forest. The helicopter machine gunners were strafing the perimeter of the plantation, while making their exodus as expeditious as possible.

The deafening noise and raw stench of gunpowder was saturating the atmosphere. The air was thick and the night was black. They were firing everywhere at invisible targets. Then they

heard it, as the explosion rocked the tree line, the NVA had got one of the copters. It was a huge inferno that was blinding it was so close. They hid in the grass to avoid the blistering heat, and a cherry stood up screaming, " I'm on fire !" He was a torch of a target and fortunately the NVA put him out of his misery in seconds.

Lt. "Buck" was screaming to resume firing. Prince on one side and Dylan on the other were strafing everywhere. It was like shooting at ghosts...they could see nothing. The chaos continued madly, insanely for another hour, then it appeared the NVA had ceased their attack.

When they took assessment of the casualties, three unknown cherries were dead with another reaching out to the hand of the Grim Reaper. The "doc" was pumping him with morphine...but no angel of aeronautical mercy would be coming for him, no dust-off to rescue him...there was no saving Grace...he would bleed to death.

It was life in the Wolfhounds.

They knew the NVA were waiting, and had the enemy been armed with grenades the platoon would've been a carnal carnival of body bags.

In the morning they peppered the tree line with grenades and firepower, and then made their way into the plantation. They needed a new clearing for a PZ for an eagle flight to pick them up, as well as a dust-off.It was slow moving

carrying the four bodies and everyone took turns being pall bearers.

The hatred for "Buck" was only parallel to the praise the Colonel had for this man's courage and determination.

This was a brave Lieutenant who would go far in this man's Army. Risking life and limb to defeat the enemy was worth a medal. The fact that four GIs perished with no body count was irrelevant, it was still a successful mission...the enemy now knew they would go to any length to eradicate them.

The Colonel applauded "Buck" and wanted to know when he wanted to take his men out again on another night ambush. He was sure it would strike fear in the heart of the enemy. The next time they would arrive like drunken cowboys at a rodeo. The General had another opinion. The loss of a helicopter was costly.

After his meeting with the Colonel, "Buck" talked to Sgt. McAllister about the next mission. He was already excited about it, and as the sergeant listened to him, even though he was a convicted lifer, all he could think of was a transfer, or perhaps *he* should get some sham time.

The deaths of the four men meant nothing more to "Buck" than they contributed to the "glory count."

Without their deaths the war was meaningless, someone has to pay the price for victory. "Buck" gave no consolation speech to his men about the

mission. They were Wolfhounds...it wasn't necessary. He would sleep well tonight.

On the bunker top the remaining old timers gathered together to share the proverbial weed. If "Gorgeous" was deliriously angry before the mission he was now beside himself with fury. As they passed a J around "Gorgeous" ranted, " I'm going to kill this motherfucker. Someone has got to before he gets us all killed. The next time we're in the field and the shit hits the fan, someone has to put a bullet through his skull. It's our survival...what the fuck..." his words trailed off. He was exasperated.

Winston and Prince were numb, and felt helpless. They all knew "Buck" had crossed the line and a suicide mission could now be routine.

The new guy (but an old guy) they had tried to bring into their group, but he took one toke and just disappeared. Eventually "Gorgeous" became so down trodden he went numb as they passed a J around one more time and Sgt. Glover set up guard duty and they took up sleep positions. Their little cadre was grateful that it was nameless faceless cherries who died, and not any of them.

That night "Buck", rolling around in his sleep, awoke momentarily to the soft sound of a significant "ping". He fumbled, tiredly, with his poncho liner to find the source of the sound. Moments later he was decorating the inside of the bunker when the grenade went off.

The new man only shifted slightly in his sleep when he heard the sound. A smirk quickly crossed his face. The "assassin" had now officially joined the platoon.

The next afternoon the new looey was imported from the rear. The Colonel gave him his usual speech and tried to shape him in the style of "Buck," but this lieutenant was similar in the mold of Lt. Osgood, and it wasn't going to work on him. Sgt. McAllister gathered the men to meet Lt. Parchow who gave them his introductory speech. "Gentlemen, first of all I want to say how sorry I am to be your new platoon leader under the horrible circumstances of what happened to Lt. Harris. I hope the investigation will uncover what happened. Secondly, I am honored to lead an infantry platoon in the greatest group in the Army, the Wolfhounds." He was very tall, about 6'5" and lanky, with blond hair cut in typical military fashion, blue eyes, and although he was an officer, he was from California and was a surfer. He had a casual air about him, "...my philosophy is we do our job to the best of our ability...but we don't take chances. I'm not a risk taker. My responsibility is to ensure to the best of my ability that we all go home in one piece. Incidentally, smoke 'em if you got 'em. I'm not one for formality. I'm sure we can all work together. That's all." He shook everybody's hand and asked if anyone was from California. Prince and Win-

ston looked at each other and smiled. They, like everyone else immediately took to this guy. He was a breath of fresh air compared to the gung-ho attitude of "Buck".

The next day their first mission together was a sweep in an entirely different AO (area of operations) than they were accustomed to. It was huge fields dotted with patches of woods, dominated by rice paddies neatly squared off by dikes, which served as paths for the villagers as they tilled the paddies. There were huge water buffaloes fertilizing the crops everywhere.

Once dropped off by the eagle flight , they formed a single line and began meandering through the field which abutted a patch of woods and the village, a friendly one inhabited by peasants in the typical society of old men and women and children. They should have been nervous sweeping unfamiliar territory, but the new looey set the tone, joking with the men.

" Hey 'Gorgeous' ! The sarge says you're too pretty to walk point. You don't look so cute to me."

"Gorgeous" smiled and responded, " You're wrong sir, I am that pretty. Every broad in the world knows that."

Winston was the Lieutenant's RTO, listening intently to the radio jive from the CP RTO. The Lieutenant was completely in charge as Sgt. McAllister had stayed in the rear (at the last moment) with a bad foot.

" Hey Dylan," the looey smiled, " that machine gun looks pretty heavy, why don't you give it to Juan to carry. He's got a light load."

Juan turned and looked at him in disbelief, he wasn't accustomed to humor in the field, let alone coming from an officer. Dylan went through the motions of handling the 60 to him and one of the cherries was whistling. Winston hadn't seen morale like this in his memory...

...but it was to be short-lived.

The explosion knocked him off his feet blowing him backwards, careening his helmet into the cherry behind him. Lt. Parchow was lying on the ground trying not to scream. His foot had been blown off by a booby trap.

Winston started yelling into the horn, " We need a dust-off! Papa Lima has been injured," and he repeated the message over and over again.

" What are your co-ordinates, Foxtrot Zebra, roger that ?" The dry voice of the Command Post's RTO was completely nonchalant.

The "doc" took the lieutenant's boot lace and made a tourniquet, then pumped him up with morphine. Winston looked at the map and he might as well be trying to decipher the Rosetta Stone as figuring out where the hell they were. All the grids looked the same.

" Charlie Papa 2, this is Foxtrot Zebra," and Winston broke radio etiquette, " I don't know where the fuck we are. I think we're about two klicks north of the base camp. Roger ? This is an

emergency."

There was silence on the other end as the RTO was conferring with the officer in charge. " Foxtrot Zebra, arty will be firing a loomy-loomy in your general position, in just a few minutes. Give your position when you see it, out."

He hoped the Lieutenant wouldn't bleed to death, as it seemed an eternity before they saw the first round descend in the distance.

" Charlie Papa, bring it two klicks south, over."

Another loomy-loomy went off further away.   " Bring it south ! Get a dust-off in the air ! You're close enough !"
Then, although it was totally invisible, they all heard it, the tiny whistle crescendoing into a scream, and they hit the ground digging in for protection. It landed with a large thud about twenty feet from them. It was a dud.

" Stop firing ! You almost killed us with a dud ! Stop firing !" Winston was beside himself, but then they heard the sound of the dust-off and he popped a smoke grenade. It was Jimi Hendrix' favorite color...purple haze. Sgt. Glover took the horn and radioed in for an eagle flight.

The Lieutenant was gone. Never to be seen again, and now they smoked cigarettes and waited.

"Gorgeous " yelled back to him, " Can you believe our luck ! First time we get a decent looey and he lasts one day ! The next one will probably

be Adolf Hitler !"

The "assassin" was looking at the water buffaloes in the distance, thinking it would be fun to kill one of them, but he didn't, he knew it was taboo.

There wasn't much conversation while they waited. Tomorrow would be another day, and another lieutenant.

CHAPTER TWENTY-SIX

A Night at the Hospital

Just thinking about working the graveyard shift at the hospital was making Veronica sleepy. She would welcome Hypnos, god of sleep and son of Nyx, the goddess of the night, so powerful in mythology even Zeus feared to enter her realm, (but not her other son Epiales, the god of nightmares, although they often worked together).

It was a once a month experience and most times for most of the night nothing happened. It was difficult to keep awake sometimes, but life is unpredictable. Elizabeth would be handing her the baton, as she had the previous shift, and would probably be asleep before Veronica had completed her first round of check-ins. She

told Veronica that she was next in line for Edith's matchmaking/match breaking skills, as Edith was a magnet for men and she probably couldn't seduce a doctor delivering the mail to him naked...Hello! Hot nurse looking for a spouse! Read all about it! While Edith merely had to smile and they would be groveling at her feet.

Most patients were asleep, but the awake ones always wanted to talk, especially with a pretty brunette with an engaging smile. Everyone got some attention.

She would get up the next afternoon, about the time the picnic would be going strong. It was all she could think of...the eradication of her nemesis, and praying Edith had been a successful matchmaker. If Winston had been here this never would've been a problem, but he was 8000 miles away, and it was up to her gal pals to save the day.

Unknown to Veronica, Helen was on a date, for the first time in a long time; with a fellow grad student whose field was geology. They hit it off immediately when she began bombarding him with puns...do geologists sit in a rocker getting stoned, or do they iron out their faults? She said she was sedimental about geologists but was taking nothing for granite...and much worse. She could tell he needed some laughs and he was like putty in her hands.

Not too far away, Edith and John, her new beau, were driving back from the movies.

The hospital driver called into the ER saying he'd arrive in ten minutes. There'd been an auto accident, a dead female, and an injured male with severe head injuries. It was shortly after midnight. Veronica passed the message on alerting the doctor, and his intern, while she got the nurse. They were all in the smoking lounge, after all it was 1969.

The ambulance driver often would report *where* it happened, *how* it happened, but seldom *why* it happened...*should I ask an angel just how many of you can dance on a pin ?* It could be a gruesome job.

The woman was covered up, and Veronica pushed the gurney aside, the man was covered in blood as head wounds hemorrhage mightily, and the race began to save his life. While she and the nurse began to clean up the man and whatever the preparations the doctor ordered, Veronica had a chilling thought...was this John, Edith's new beau, whom she'd never seen ? And if it was so... *oh God was that Edith beneath the cotton shroud already journeyed to the other side ?* She remembered how she and Winston would double date with her and her latest flavor, and the laughs they had. Edith was not a big drinker, but a huge giggler, and more than once her date would realize this blonde bombshell was more than he could deal with. More than often in Winston's greenhouse mansion the three would

listen to him make music from touching ancient ivories from long dead ancients, and she and Veronica would crash in the bed and he would slumber in his reading chair (another chair & a table completed the furniture ensemble). Edith was the sister Winston never had and sometimes became a little too brotherly in her choice of men, but then what are friends for ?

It was becoming evident that the man (hopefully not her beau) was not going to survive...too much trauma, too much blood loss, and when the line went flat the doctor registered the time, covered him up, retrieved his wallet for identification and the John Doe went to the next to the last place he would go: the hospital morgue.

The dead woman was already there. It would be simple, especially at this hour, to uncover the woman's face...*it was driving her mad. Was this her best friend ?* She left to check on the patients on the ward. She had to keep busy...Veronica didn't know that Helen was out on the town with a date.

At 3AM there were still hours to go before sweet Hypnos would wrap her in his embrace. The doctor was napping, the nurse was smoking, and being the low person on the totem pole, Veronica was on the alert, and walked around the ward... and walked around and around avoiding the hospital morgue, which was only a floor away.

Somehow she knew.

343

A wave of crushing depression, a deep foreboding of what cruel knowledge was about to open up the abyss was about to happen *and she couldn't stop it.* Over and over again she told herself she would not go down the steps to that cold dark room, not open the door to peek at the silent immovable gurneys, not *go in.*

Once inside the room, no turning back.

She could feel a dark presence beckoning her to descend to the room of death. It was maddening, unrelenting, but which way to go ? To remain above and not learn it's Edith, not knowing...or the torture of knowing the unknown made real by simply making the descent into a room without a soul.

Veronica continued to stay occupied by straightening up the supply room, which was already neat and tidy; then going to talk with the head nurse, perhaps engage in some idle chatter. At the end of the shift, with the sun coming up, the " morgue men" as they were called came by to transfer the bodies to the main morgue down town.

Veronica, eyes blurry from stress and worry, stared at them as they placed them in the rear of their van. They returned the look as if perhaps this was her first day. As she approached them, he asked, " Is there something we can do for you, nurse ?"

Veronica did not look the man in the eyes, " Would you pull back the cover on the woman's

body...please."

Wordlessly he acquiesced.

When she stared at the face, Veronica took a double take, she looked different in death. She didn't scream. She didn't wail. It was Edith.

She didn't really begin to weep until she was safely alone in her room, with her loyal loving pet, Louise; and she cried and cried until she fell into a deep, coma-like sleep, but this time Hypnos brother, god of nightmares, Eliales, came to visit. When she awoke, early afternoon; the nightmare of seeing Edith's dead expressionless face was imprinted in her memory...the fuel for insanity. Calling Helen, who was as cheery as the ignorant after a fun date, brought everything back and Veronica cried, Helen cried, and they would meet tomorrow night as usual, and cry some more. After she hung up, she realized that the spectre of Dwight would be even worse, the picnic wouldn't be happening. She decided to sit down and write Winston a "sugar report" without telling him Edith no longer walked the Earth. It was going to be a long, painful day.

CHAPTER TWENTY-SEVEN

A Change of Venue...
Getting closer

It was a full moon in Vietnam the night Neil Armstrong walked on the moon, and listening to the events and his words on their tiny transistor radio, they stared at its brightness as the illumination highlighted the concertina wire and accentuated the shadows. They could imagine him thousands upon thousands of miles away walking on the moon, and what a safe place it was, and tonight basking in the full luminary bath, they felt more like they were a million miles away from the world.

Sgt. McAllister and Sgt. Glover were now short-timers killing time in the rear, and soon Dylan, Juan, and "Gorgeous" would follow.

Winston and Prince, who by now had es-

tablished more than a simple camaraderie, they were like brothers, were joined on the bunker top by Dylan, Juan, and a couple cherries, one who called himself "Gossamer Moses" (a prophet who could dance the light fantastic) and "Looney Louie" who had established a persona of being crazy, saying anything and doing anything, counting on being able to get over on the system. It wasn't working yet. The night he tried the sleepwalking routine, thinking that would get him out of the field, Dylan threw him down and put a knife to his throat. A stunt like that putting the squad in jeopardy was not tolerated...not in the Wolfhounds. It wouldn't happen again.

" Prince, don't you think it's amazing that we can put a man on the moon but they can't make peace so we can go home ?"

" Amen brother, 'cept you know goin' to the moon has got to be all fun and adventure and we grunts are nuthin' but a problem. Can you dig "Gorgeous" being drafted by NASA ? Very dinky-dau, beaucoup dinky-dau."

" It is a great feat though, to finally put a man on the moon, science is a wild bag."

" I can dig it," Dylan had his perennial goofy grin plastered on his face, " they are up there and we can't see them and they can't see us, and they are masters of the universe, and even though we can't see anything we do have free tickets to the show."

Winston laughed, " It don't mean nuthin'."

" It sure don't." Prince put his head on his helmet and stared at the moon. Soon he would be asleep and wake up another day shorter.

Man walks on the moon...Mankind plods on at the same old pace.

Within a few days the entire battalion would have a new AO (area of operation). No more jungle or Michelin rubber plantation, and no more firefights...they would be going south to the land of the rice paddy as far as the eye could see. A place with little vegetation, just small forests here and there, lots of swampland and villages scattered about the myriad maze of rice paddies.

It was the land of the booby trap.

While Woodstock played on during the month of August they literally holed up in friendly villages, still mostly deserted...and experienced monsoon. It rained everyday, and for half the month it would rain *all* day. And what a rain ! Anyone more than six feet away from you was less than a shadow...they were invisible. It was a rain that was more a flooding torrent from the sky. It could hurt you.

No one thought much, talked much about Woodstock. Although it had rained there and hippies frolicked in the mud, it was an event as relevant as an asteroid passing through the Milky Way. They, after all, were in a separate galaxy.

The platoon for the entire month never

went any further than to go from one village to another, where they would stay for a few days and literally live in hammocks.

It was a great time to sleep and read. Winston read the entire <u>Trilogy of the Rings</u> and then some. No one got injured, everyone got a little fatter...it was a lazy time. No more high stress time of human wave attacks or vicious killing ambushes, just walking along the rice paddy dikes... playing booby trap roulette. At night they had starlights, which enabled them to see in the dark although everything looked as green as Oz. For months nothing had happened, the platoon was the largest ever, and the times in the jungle and all the firefights were the "old days." It was a reminiscence, a nostalgia of what war was really like.

This was hiking in a group.

The monotony of the days was numbing. One day they were about to booby trap a dead NVA when a huge pig came by and ate his ears and cock off. He was on his way back North when he succumbed to his wounds from some battle in the Mekong Delta. It took about a minute for the pig to finish his snack. Winston never knew pigs had such a discriminating palette.

There was another instance when they could see a body heaving in the distance. It was so curious, they thought at first some NVA was taunting them, but as they got closer it got weirder, to see this human torso undulating back

and forth, in a high rocking manner over and over again, until they got close and could see millions of maggots inside the now exposed cavity devouring the guts of the soldier. The body was rocking so furiously it seemed alive, but was truly a dance of the dead. It was a vignette they all wished they could erase from their memory library.

When Winston and Prince had but 43 days to go, things began to unravel...the Fates of War don't like a stalemate...and one morning the 26th man out of 32 put the right amount of pressure on a land mine which then transported him into the next dimension. For everyone else it was still a walk in the park, nothing happened, nothing changed , except one guy had successfully auditioned for a body bag and got the part. It reminded him of the old war story of "Mr. Invincible."

In the afternoon the platoon encountered a booby trap in a small hedgerow near the trail. It was unusual as the trip wire was visible as well as the device itself. Normal procedure was for the grenade launcher to fire into the hedgerow while everyone else hid behind some cover, but this new buck sergeant with a wife and kids tells the current looey he can bust it with his M-16. He was the best sharpshooter in all of Arkansas, could hit the eye of an eagle in flight. The new looey, Lt. Canaday, now bored from months of non-warlike activity could give a fuck, and gave

him the nod.

In all of ten seconds he's dead. The bullet hits the booby trap perfectly and a piece of shrapnel the size of a match head enters his heart, and the only sign that he has been hit is the drop of blood on his chest. He looks perfectly fine except that he's not moving and there's no visible wound...his number was up.

The Lieutenant is berserk, this is not supposed to happen...a freak accident caused by improper methods, for which his leadership will be severely questioned...and with two GIs dying on the same day ! The zeal of a gung-ho soldier who was a crack shot had instantaneously created a widow with two small boys who will never know their father. It was too quick and too eerie...he looked like he was sleeping. A couple cherries were talking to themselves that it could've been them...anything can happen...this is a dangerous place...after all there's a war going on. Winston sucked on a cigarette and ignored them. This was nothing. It certainly was nothing to get all stressed up about...it's not like a thousand gooks are running at you over barbed wire and all they want to do is take your soul and separate it from your body.

That was stress...but things were different now, even the new guys seemed odder, some were doing heroin and some were drinking; and they all talked a lot about the world and what was happening...and it made him feel even more

remote and like a stranger...his whole life was being a soldier, carrying the machine gun, and the world was ever more a distant memory with a dim dream of the future. When the new guys talked about the new music, stuff he could hear on the radio, it seemed *they* knew what was happening...he was listening to the music...but not hearing it. He felt neither hip or young.

At dinner, he and Prince, now inseparable, usually dined apart from the rest of the platoon-...they were the old men...but they both agreed the best part of having 43 days to go was when they woke up in the morning there would be just 42 days to go. It was getting better every day.

" Prince, now that 'Gorgeous,' Dylan, and even Juan are gone it seems like we've been here an eternity...I feel ancient."

" You are. I at least look my age...you *are* the old man."

" Don't go and get dinky-dau on me. If getting older means getting shorter, I'll take it."

They did the Nam handshake, " What's the first thing you want to do when you wake up in the world ?"

Winston took a deep breath, " I can't wait to be re-united with the girl of my dreams, Veronica, who I know is getting some kind of pressure from other guys, who, of course want to sleep with her; as well as her mother who believe she shouldn't be squandering her youth, her looks...her future on some crazy guy who

wants to make a living playing the piano. I can't blame her but I got a gut feeling she's my mate for life...through thick and thin, and I believe she feels the same...and this part of our lives is certainly thin."

" Amen brother," Prince sighed, he'd been getting non-stop sugar reports from day one, and knew they were still tight, " I just pray that when we finally hook up with our sweet hearts all this will be like a bad dream...a very long bad dream, and we wake up and it's like nothing ever happened. Nothing changed. Like life is *normal*."

" My main man, are you sure you're not smokin' something ? I can so dig your philosophy. I'm with you...and best of all we're finally getting close, although it makes you nervous."

" Got that right. Even though I can't sleep, I can't wait for night 'cause the next day we're one day shorter."

Winston added, " I hope so, but doesn't it seem like a long, *long* time since we've seen the world ? I feel like I've been here forever, been doing this gig my whole lifetime, and it's all I know. Can you imagine waking up in a *bed*, touching your girl who's next to you ? Waking up with no mosquitoes buzzing around your face ! Imagine ! Breakfast that doesn't come in a can ! No sergeants in your face, no stupid looey trying to kill you for their glory, and you don't have to wear the same clothes every day."

" You're blowin' my mind Winston. It

does seem like this *is* the life, we were born Wolf-hounds, we be the Wolfhounds, and we die Wolf-hounds. There must have been a previous life, but I feel that if I don't clean my machine gun every day it's not a normal day. Yo daddy ! Is this what I'm going to do for the rest of my life ? I best not walk on that side of the street, 'cause I'm goin' back to the world and make a difference. I'm goin' to be someone."

Winston was playing with his meal, it was Salisbury steak, which was much more than a mystery meat disguised as food, it was an exercise regimen for his jaw.

" God, I couldn't cope knowing I would be a soldier the rest of my life...do you remember when the fuckin' looey decided we should camp out during monsoon in the rice paddies, and we slept in water, with water buffalo shit floating by ? That's the last time I ever lay down in water to go to sleep."

" And if the gooks were having a family reunion we wouldn't have known it. I didn't sleep much that night but at least my head didn't bob off my helmet into the crap filled water."

Darkness, like sneaky soft curtains summoned them to their bunker and as they sat atop the sandbag chateau, artillery began to provide the evening's entertainment. The choking smell of gunpowder was like a cloud immersing them, as they could watch the explosions in the distance. Some poor suckers were in contact and

hopefully the barrage of exploding pain from the sky would enhance their possibilities of living through the night. Something strange was going on as arty was simultaneously firing loomy-loomy rounds as well and they could see the pockets of illumination in the distance.

" God bless them. I'm glad I'm not out there, it must be a heck of a fire fight. Prince used a magazine as a fan to blow the smoke from his face, as arty was trying to set the sky on fire.

" They must be hungry for a body count to light up the jungle like that." He further clouded up the area with a cigarette.

" Or they are in deep hell."

" Anyway you cut it, better them than us."

" Amen to that. I'm too old for that kind of fire fight again."

The artillery explosions were made more visible, as they peppered the landscape, by the loomy-loomys which glowed like immense jewels in the distance and then would flicker and fade like a dying candle. The artillery rounds would hit the ground and transform into red clusters, puncturing the night screen like glowing crimson fingers and then would disappear. He lit up a J, this was the only show in town, he might as well enjoy it. Both he and Prince had stuffed their ears with cigarette butts, and even muffled, the noise was all pervasive. The smell of gunpowder was so thick it was all you could taste...and the show went on...riotously. Some-

one was dying out there, and every artillery piece in the camp was in danger of hot barreling. It was a helluva night show. They could only wonder at the size of the battle going on out there...and then it abruptly stopped...everything was stone quiet...and slowly the last of the loomy-loomys flickered out, and the entire base camp and everything around it became unmercifully dark. When the smoke had evaporated Prince went inside of the bunker, as was his life long habit, and crashed for the evening. Winston was sharing the top of the bunker with a bunch of new guys he barely knew and didn't care about. He flipped his J over the front of the bunker, he hadn't shared with anyone; laid down on his back and stared into the starless murk. Soon the new squad leader, Sgt. Strawberry, issued the order of guard duty. There were so many in the squad that Prince and he rarely had guard duty anymore, and if it happened they were either first or last. He missed Sgt.Glover, now back in the world, as this new sarge was humorless, with the leadership skills of a hermit crab.

He fell asleep wondering what peace was like back in the world...no ambushes, no artillery...and no Army ! Tomorrow he would be 42 days short.

He was getting those goin' home blues.

The next morning, there was a new lieutenant, who didn't bother to introduce himself, as, for a change of pace they eschewed their

habitat of rice paddies and took an eagle flight to Cambodia. The cover of <u>Time</u> that week advertised an article within that stated we would never enter Cambodia. We had no right to take the war into their territory, their boundaries had been diplomatically deemed sacred.

It was a beautiful eagle flight, the sky was an ethereal blue and Nature had made quite a show with clouds piled upon fluffy clouds reaching like muscular ghosts to the heavens, as the copters seemed to float through them, occasionally through holes in the sky like open doors, never so much as touching an untouchable cloud...like a magic carpet ride. It was a long trip and when they descended he was disgusted, the spell had vanished.

It was nothing but swamp as far as the eye could see punctuated here and there with bits of scrubby mounds of half dead shrubs. The copters swirled the water away from them as they jumped out into the muddy morass, and a third of the unit fell completely into the muck, which was just above the knees on Winston , and for the short guys it was waist high. The new looey had a shocked look on his face. This truly was stupid, where could there possibly be any gooks hiding out in this swamp ? They would proceed to the closest island, where some could eke out a spot to sit down, and as they made their way trudging through the black swamp they quickly learned this muck had apparently no animal life...no fish

to be seen...no frogs to be heard...no birds on the wing...except for a single species...leeches. They had been breeding for a thousand years and now they were ecstatic there was new meat in town.

Eventually, a slow slog, they got to a hedgerow, a small island, and when Winston saw a large snake sunning itself in the branches of a dead shrub, he thought of Rufus. The snake slithered away when they approached and once upon the "island" they would begin to burn off the leeches with a cigarette. A buddy would remove the ones from one's backside, but a leech on your balls or your cock was all yours, removed with the utmost care. As long as they stayed on this dead oasis they were free of these insidious creatures, but the Lieutenant could not stretch out the moment forever. He was disgusted, but he had his orders. While the Sergeant burned leeches that had gotten under his collar he gave the order to move out. They would traverse from "island" to "island" until the PZ point several klicks away. The swamp looked like the flatlands of Kansas, perfectly still and broad and expansive, but instead of corn there was nothing but a dark muddy sea. When they got to the next "island" they repeated the process of de-leeching, and the Lieutenant began to make it clear that this was idiocy. Everyone could hear him talking on the horn...he was far from subtle about his indignation, which scored points with the men, and Winston liked any officer who had some

spunk and would challenge the system. Unfortunately the eagle flight was going to pick them up at a pre-ordained time and location. They would need to wade through two klicks of leeches before rescue would arrive. It would be a long slow plod, with many dropping into invisible potholes, the slime coming up to their mouths. Most of the weapons were useless, but no one cared. This was the Army, the war...the way it was. No one argued, no one spoke...one step at a time. He smiled to himself wishing "Gorgeous" could have been there. The new looey would get an education and an earful.

Eventually it ended...a true exercise in stupidity, and it was difficult to crawl into the choppers they were so weighted down. The gunner looked at Winston and held his nose. The roar of the copter made conversation impossible, and he burned a leech off his leg and threw it at him. The GI reeled and never looked back.

Once inside the base camp it was an exodus to the showers and clean clothes, leaving a cemetery of abandoned leeches to die in the sun. It was evident in the showers that many had pulled the leeches off their bodies and there were blood bites everywhere...swamp souvenirs, little tattoos from Nature's aquatic parasite.

" Hey Prince, did you ever swim in shit back in the old days ?" Looney Louie was shampooing what little hair he had and making sure no itinerant leech was still looking for a meal.

Prince had little respect for this mouth, " No Louie, we dished it out, not like today, where we are forced to live in it."

" If I told my old lady we walked around in shit all day long gettin' devoured by leeches for absolutely no fuckin' reason, she wouldn't believe it."

Prince, exiting the showers, " Did you ever tell your old lady you were in the Army ?"

Winston and Prince ate at a corner of one of the picnic tables, and laughed about the day. They wanted to be isolated from the rest of the squad and the platoon. The camaraderie of the old days was gone...they just didn't care about bonding with the new guys.

" This mission, my brother, was..."

""...and you are my brother, using the term loosely."Prince laughed uproariously.

" And don't forget it big guy. Todays' farce was truly all Army pathetic, but all these cherries are thinking how stupid it was to march around aimlessly in a fuckin' swamp..."

" ...when we used to march around aimlessly and watch our brothers get killed, all these babies did was get bitten by a few leeches," Prince paused, " although those leeches were very very creepy."

" What did they possibly think we could find in that God forsaken shit hole ?"

" Lookey here, as Rufus used to say, do I care ? I'm so glad to be a two digit midget, and

getting shorter everyday ! And tomorrow makes 41..."

Winston laughed, " And who's counting ?"

Prince put his head back and ran his fingers through his non-hair, and laughed, imitating "Gorgeous", " I can't wait to eat my mother's fried chicken and her gumbo. A soup so thick it's like a stew, an old recipe from my aunt in Louisiana, and we never knew what momma put in it 'cept okra. Love that okra." He smacked his lips as if the bowl was before him.

" So, is all your family back in Detroit ?"

" Well, my daddy died when I was five, got the flu then the pneumonia, and momma said he went quick, which she thanked the Lord; but she had to raise me and my two sisters. My momma is one of those strong Christian women who can take an adversity and conquer it, although I know at times we lived on the charity of others, but momma went from a cashier to head of all women's clothing at our local department store, and momma knew everybody. She was strong and could make it work, and we went from poor to livin' good, but we've always lived in the same place. Momma loves Detroit, and can't give up the roots, and I hope to go back to the furniture store, where they promised me my job when I got back...but my older sister is going to college at the University of Michigan and I know she's going to run away and get married and burn those memories of Detroit. The drug dealers are

only a few blocks away, and who knows if things get screwed up enough, they'll be in our front yard..."

" ...and your mother will never move ?"

" Never. If a human wave attack hit our house, only then would she might consider di-di mauing. As grandma always said, the longer you live in the same place the deeper your roots go, and the deeper the roots the harder it is to move, and grandma lives next door, and intends to die old in her bed and as she says her next home is with the Lord."

" Guess you won't ever be leaving Detroit."

" No man. Not in my lifetime."

" All I want to do is find a nest for Veronica and myself...and I don't care where it is."

Sgt. Strawberry sat down next to them. He was only twenty with medium build and height and sported a pathetic mustache that looked like a caterpillar on chemo.
He was from Milwaukee, and had been jumping from one factory job to another with no satisfaction until the draft caught up with him. " Mind if I join you ?" He had a mouthful of food before he had even sat down at the picnic bench, " that sure was one disgusting mission," his mouth was so stuffed it was barely comprehensible, " you guys ever walk through shit like that in the old days ?"

Winston wanted to stuff his mouth with grub so he could properly respond, but he had finished his meal, "Nothing even close, I'm glad

to say."

"We hunted for gooks, not leeches." Prince finished his last bite and got up from the table. He didn't care much for the new sergeant, he didn't have the same character as Sgt. Glover...but then everything was different.   "Excuse me, but there's enough light left for me to write a letter."

Sgt. Strawberry barely looked up as he mouthed something through his food to Prince, "Winston, you'll be glad to know tomorrow we'll be returning to the rice paddies, and not back to that swamp."

"That's good news, maybe the Army is getting smarter."

"I doubt that. This man's Army will never change, and it could be we're not supposed to be in Cambodia."

He laughed, "...and we're not supposed to use weapons that fire a dum-dum round according to the Geneva Convention. I wouldn't put anything past the Army. They will do anything they can get away with that will get a body count."

"That's probably true. You can guess I'm no lifer."

"So why are you a sergeant?"

"I wanted to lead a squad in Vietnam, to see if I could handle it."

"But that meant an additional year of your life you gave up to the Army."

Sgt. Strawberry finished his meal, I'd rather spend more time with rank than two years as a Private, nothing personal."

" That's okay. When you're still wearing your rank I'll be a free man back in the world." Winston grinned, then laughed, and started to get up, " there'll be plenty of time for you to be a lifer."

Sgt. Strawberry, sitting alone, thought to himself that perhaps these short timers could use a little guard duty.

A monotony of missions later, Winston was down to 37 days to go, and with the sun barely making its daily debut he looked through the sky and dreamt of Veronica.

What was she doing today ? Is she all right ? Does she still love me as much as I love her ? I hope she's happy. In just a little more than a month we'll be together...I hope for the rest of our lives...God, I hope she hasn't found a boyfriend...and doesn't want to upset me with a "Dear John" letter...I am so lonely for her...the closer I get the more desperate I feel...we're almost there.

Eight thousand miles away on a dreary cloudy afternoon Veronica lay on her bed and stared out the window. They were both connected but not aware of the cosmic bond. She wanted Winston's arms around her to make her feel safe, to feel loved, to know he was her man. Dwight, since Edith's passing, apparently, had given up stalking her, and

now there were others, more casual, more subtle, less aggressive...but they would not leave her alone. Her mother continued to push her for a new social life...but all she wanted was her lover, and no one else. The solitude in her room was comforting yet heartbreaking...Veronica felt so alone...it had seemed to be so long...but soon, very soon they would be re-united, and it made her feel desperate...the anxiety of everything made each day seem like the long slow ride of eternity. Like Winston each night she prayed for sleep, Lady MacBeth's evasive friend, because the morning would bring them closer by yet another day.

Veronica was tired of crying, exhausted from worrying, and wondered if perhaps something had changed with Winston...did he have a change of heart and maybe didn't love her anymore ? In the dark recesses of her mind they're would always be a doubt but she knew, deep down, that that was impossible and unthinkable...their love could not be broken...they were destined for each other...that would never change. His tour was coming to an end...the year of infinite waiting was coming to a climax. Soon she would be leaving home for a new adventure with her man...if only it could be tomorrow ! !

Winston looked into the clouds and wondered what she was thinking...right that very moment. Could she feel the cosmic love for her coming from the invisible beyond ? Would she still love to

hear him play the piano for her ? He imagined a tune she always loved to hear..."Somewhere over the Rainbow" and imagined he could send it across the ocean on a mystical musical journey only Veronica could hear. Just a few more weeks, and after all this time it was simply a pittance in the cosmic clock.

Winston awoke from his "Veronica" trance, Sgt. Strawberry was motioning to the squad it was time to saddle up for another eagle flight. Not everyone was there and he was curious, "Hey Sarge, where's Billy Scissors and Christopher ? Isn't this a platoon sized mission ?"

" That's right Private, and I decided not everyone was needed, and those two will be cleaning up the bunker and policing the area..."

He got into his face. " Isn't it supposed to be the short-timers who are held back and not the guys who have been in the field forever ?" He looked at the Lieutenant, who looked away. " Prince and I have 37 days left in country, we should be the ones doing the piddlin' shit in the rear, not humping machine guns and shit !" He wanted to smash his face in...

Prince said nothing, wound as tight as a mummy in a tomb.

" Sergeant, get these men assembled." The arrival of the eagle flight ended all conversation, and to throw poison on the wound, a new guy would be humping the machine gun, Winston was going to be carrying the radio for Sgt. Straw-

berry.

They landed within sight of a village and the accompanying labyrinth of rice paddies in a flat territory of woodland and grassy field.

Sgt. Strawberry was filling in for the platoon sergeant, who was in the rear for dental work, even though he was relatively new, " Private Gundelach, you'll be walking point, men assemble into a single file..."

" Sorry 'bout that. No can do...I'm far too short and there's beaucoup cherries here, one of them can walk point. I've given it up." He started walking towards the rear.

" You're walking point Private Gundelach !" His voice was nearly screaming and his face was turning red, " now turn your ass around and get up front !"

Private Gundelach just looked at the ground and said nothing.

" You'll walk point Goddamn it !" He was fiercely yelling, " you will give twelve months of service ! Do you understand ? Twelve full months ! Now march your dead ass up front !" He sounded every inch the lifer he proclaimed he was not.

Gundelach looked to the Lieutenant for salvation, but the looey was going to back the sergeant no matter the idiocy. Plus, he hated them all, both the sergeant and the privates were all rodents as far as he was concerned. This new looey beat the draft by going to OCS after college.

As a college grad (Univ. Of Conn.) he felt it was proper to be an officer, wearing bars, and being a leader. His feelings about the war were irrelevant, the important thing was that <u>he</u> was an officer. His background as such determined that men who went into the military were officers, pure and simple, as enlisted men were scum. Both of his parents were lawyers, and he felt this would be a plus on his resume. Coming from a wealthy family further distanced him from the men, who he was obliged to lead; and wandering endlessly with little point to it, looking for God knows what, with a bunch of useless draftees disgusted him. This was a long way from the tennis courts and yacht clubs of Connecticut.

The whole thing was enough to send Looney Louie into a tantrum. He began screaming and squeezing his temples, " I'm going crazy ! This Nam is too much for me !" He dropped his helmet and began dancing around, and everyone started laughing and then tried to look away as if it were too surreal to watch. Winston turned his back on everyone. Looney Louie moaned and meandered through the platoon squeezing his temples. He screamed,
" I can't keep up with this vocabulary !"

" Get back in file soldier !" Sgt. Strawberry began to chase him which only heightened the comic relief of the moment, as Looney Louie ran circles around him and the others while yelling "Peek-a-boo" at him. Strawberry was losing it.

Eventually he stopped and got in line and saluted the sergeant.

Gundelach was smiling, " Okay, I'll walk point," he sneered at the sergeant, " it's just because I don't want to go to jail...it don't mean nuthin'." He marched to the head of the file, cocked his head back, and began a brisk pace. The platoon fell together as mindless as extras in a Hollywood war bonanza, Looney Louie picked up his helmet and started whistling, and they began to march as if nothing had happened. Except for the whistling, there was an eerie quiet to the platoon. No one spoke.

When they approached a canal, the sergeant was immediately ready to cross it. It probably wasn't deep, and Gundelach would find out, but the recent and fond memories of the swamp influenced the Lieutenant to find a detour. There were huge clumps of water buffalo feces floating in it, and it reeked like a cesspool.

The path along the canal was worn down, smooth from use, and there was litter of every kind and in abundance on both sides. Winston began singing a song from <u>Blind Faith</u> " I can't find my way home..." Sgt.
Strawberry scratched the ground with his foot and he exploded at him, " What are you looking for Strawberry ? Do you want to uncover a booby trap ? I'm getting too short for this kind of stupid shit." He started trudging through the litter and debris on the side of the path. It was filthy,

and Sgt. Strawberry looked at him like he was a fool...the path seemed safe to him. The air had no wind to it and the atmosphere was all stink, heavy and hot.

There were some rusty mackerel cans, little eight ounce jobbers buried halfway in the path, and Sgt. Strawberry leaned over to examine them.

◆ ◆ ◆

The Mets had won the World Series, and Charles Manson had decided to be his own lawyer. Jack Kerouac had found the end of the road, and Judy Garland found the end of the rainbow. Pres. Nixon appealed to the "great silent majority of my fellow Americans" to support his policies on Vietnam...while the body count exceeded the Korean War. Between two and three hundred GIs died every week, but America was dancing to disco and seeing such movies as <u>Butch Cassidy and the Sundance Kid.</u> The "world" was a great place to live.

◆ ◆ ◆

" Don't you dare touch those Strawberry ! You can blow both of us up ! Are you trying to be an idiot, or does this come natural for you ?" He was backing off from the sergeant.

Strawberry hesitated and then grabbed one of the cans and opened the lid. A weird kind of magnetism had drawn him to do it, and Winston fell back against some bamboo. " You just blew my mind Strawberry. Are you trying to find a booby trap ? You know the Third Platoon found three booby traps along this canal last week ?" He was going to put more distance between himself and this moron.

" Yes I know." He said the words very slowly as if his mind was on another planet.

Winston, since Strawberry seemed to be bewitched by something, commanded Gundelach walking point to keep a sharp eye on the path, and to be cautious.

Winston continued singing the song by <u>Blind Faith</u> that was stuck in his head.

BOOM !

That's just what it sounded like, a split second mind boggling explosion and for just that moment he could see the gray burst and then his nostrils were filled to the brain with the odor of gunpowder. His sunglasses jumped off his nose, his helmet fell off his head, and Winston reeled back...and then he was recovering...and time was slowing down...and he felt the pain in his neck and then it abated...and he turned to Gossamer Moses who was behind him and asked where he had been hit...and as he said it he knew he was alright...and told Gossamer Moses that for a brief second he had been really scared...he

couldn't see Sgt. Strawberry...Edmund the medic was kneeling beside him telling him he was okay...the phone from the radio was dangling on the ground, and Winston picked it up and good ole George, the looey's RTO was rapping like a banshee calling for a dust-off. He laid back and relaxed.

" Winston ?" It was Edmund, " you know you've been hit ?" There was blood dripping down from his neck.

" I'm all right. I'm all right. " He sat up regaining his composure, " for a second there I was really scared. It was really scary...I thought I had been hit in the neck. About half an inch higher and I wouldn't be lighting up this square...yeah buddy !" The "doc" began wiping away the blood from his chest and collarbone. " How's Strawberry ?"

" I managed to stop the bleeding with a boot string tourniquet, he's headed back for the world real soon and won't be back."

" So what the fuck happened ? The whole thing just knocked me on my ass." He took a drag from his straight, the adrenalin was beginning to ebb.

" He stepped on a booby trap, probably a mackerel can, and it blew his foot off half way up to his knee. When the surgeons get to him it'll probably be just below the knee." He applied an antiseptic to Winston's wound and he yelped, " looks like you got hit in the collarbone, Winston.

You're one lucky dude, an inch one way or the other and we wouldn't be having this conversation." He administered a cotton ball covered by a band-aid where the shrapnel was still in his collarbone.

" Oh man, two Purple Hearts and 37 days to go ! This is it. No more hassles. My last day in the field. I feel great !" The shrapnel itched and burned in his collarbone. The Lieutenant came over to check out the situation. " I'm done Lieutenant, two Purple Hearts in the Wolfhounds and you're out of the field. No more humpin' the radio, or the 60 ! I'm off line...c'mon dust-off !" His exhilaration was off the charts.

It was an "unwritten law" that two Purple Hearts earned you retirement from the field, but it still would be up to the medic to decide one's fate.

The "pathetic medic" was on the horn describing the nature of the injuries to the Company Commander.

The Lieutenant approached the medic, " Let me know if you want him dusted off, doc." The tone in his voice horrified him...he could tell he didn't want him dusted off.

" You've got just ti-ti shrapnel Winston." The "pathetic medic" meekly smiled at him.

It scared him. Escape was in the air and minutes away, and now, as the curtain closed the medic was going to keep the show alive.

" I want to know if you're going to dust

him off." The Lieutenant was becoming impatient.

" I'm never going to carry that motherfuckin' radio again, or anything else for that matter...again." And he delicately placed the radio on the ground and propped his rifle up against it."

Looney Louie came over to monitor the horn, " How ya doin' partner ? Oh yes, I can see you can get over with that. There's blood. I'm fuckin' jealous."

The "pathetic medic," after speaking with the Lieutenant came to his side, " That's just ti-ti man, they could give me some shit about dusting you off for that."

" I know it's ti-ti, you motherfuck, but it's enough, and it does hurt." He added a little extra sincerity to his plea.

" Let me know if you're going to dust him off." The Lieutenant was expressionless, but irritatingly persistent.

Winston took his finger and ran it across his wound, " This is blood. There's a piece of hot shrapnel in my collarbone..." he was spitting close in the medic's face, "do you think I can carry the radio with a piece of shrapnel in my neck ?"

" Okay. Okay," he turned to the Lieutenant, "I'm going to dust him off."

" Thanks doc. If it'll make you feel any better I'll tell them it hurt too much to hump the radio."

"Yes, tell 'em that. I'd hate to get my ass

chewed off for dusting off a man that wasn't hurt." He went off looking busy getting ready for the arrival of the dust-off.

He spoke to Gossamer Moses, " Can you believe that ! Doc was going to break ! Two Purple Hearts and 36 days and a wake-up ! he shouldn't have even hesitated...and what's with that looey, he didn't want to dust me off !" He was disgusted.

As the dust-off approached he waved to Prince, who gave him a thumbs up. The Lieutenant was signaling where to land, his arms held high as if his team had scored a goal, but George, his RTO was actually giving them instructions and motioned to the "pathetic medic" to pop smoke.

The two dust-off medics jumped off with a gurney and rapidly put Sgt. Strawberry on it. They looked like twins with their identical large mustaches and flight helmets. They were serious as stone. He sat on the edge with his feet dangling in the air, while Sgt. Strawberry lay next to him, his one leg a gory mishmash of protoplasm. He had a big grin on his face.

The "pathetic medic" had hit a home run. Sgt. Strawberry, perfectly straight and perpetually square was higher than a motherfuck on morphine. Just before the dust-off exited the scene, he caught a glimpse of his platoon in the field. The looey gave him an odd condescending smile, and half the platoon waved to him, most noticeably Prince, and he flashed them the peace

sign...and then they were gone...and for Winston he hoped it was nothing but good-byes and by-gones.

He lit a smoke as they passed over the fire support base, waving to the faceless GIs below. It was like Tomorrowland at Disneyland. They stopped to pick up another grunt who also had done the dance with a booby trapped mackerel can...and then it was off to fun city, the main base camp for the 25th division.

At the hospital the clerks checked him in and he couldn't remember his social security number. He wondered if they were going to turn him away. Sgt. Strawberry laughed at anything and everything. After being x-rayed he waited in the emergency room for the results. Only the Army would have an infantryman wait in an emergency room in Vietnam.

They came like the periodic migration of great birds, landing hard and departing quickly...the dust-offs were bringing the victims of the war out of the swamps and the villages under the scepter of the electric strawberry division. The doctors and the nurses barely had time to smoke a cigarette between dust-off loads. He thought to himself it couldn't be like this all the time.

There were two loads of kids, none above two feet tall, and some wearing only a T-shirt, few had sandals, and all of them had been hit, with some seriously wounded. All the babysans

had a totally blank expression. The fear had been washed out of them. They entered the hospital one at a time, stoically, except those with heinous wounds...who were hysterically sobbing...the eternal cry to be saved. It was too many at once for the staff to cope with, as usual it was worst first. The Viet Cong had booby trapped a school. Anything can happen in the Nam.

While he chain smoked an old peasant man and a GI, both with shrapnel wounds came in. He was feeling down, the shrapnel now was just a minor burn, but it was only 9:30 in the morning...it felt like midnight. Next, a dust-off dropped off a soul brother who was seriously fucked up...his whole body was contaminated with shrapnel and he screamed as if he was on the rack when the master sergeant stuck a catheter up his penis. A chaplain was coaching him on breathing, and eventually the anesthesia kicked in, but there was no hope...too many wounds, and soon Winston heard the now familiar death rattle. He was glad he was wearing sunglasses, his eyes were beginning to tear up.

Where were the x-rays!

He wanted to escape from this place, he was ready to explode...and then this granny in a nurses' uniform handed him the x-rays, and moments later a young doctor extracted the shrapnel and created a nice antiseptic ascot for him. It had sham time written all over it. The morning concluded and he hooked up with some dudes

and got stoned out of his gourd. The afternoon flew by in a peaceful sleep in the barracks.

◆ ◆ ◆

The concert at Altamont, outside San Francisco, would feature The Rolling Stones, and was an attempt to be the West Coast version of Woodstock, with the cream of the crop of rock 'n' roll that didn't make history on the East Coast. They wanted to show the Age of Aquarius what they could do.

It didn't take long for the concert organizers to realize they had a monster on their hands, and that all the mundane details such as traffic control, sanitation, and of course; security, were becoming more difficult to deal with. It was like some mythological beast, just when you thought you had it contained, a new head would emerge...and then they found this group willing to provide security...for free.

CHAPTER TWENTY-EIGHT

Goin' Home Blues

After the mission, Prince was taken off-line and joined Winston in the rear at the base camp. " Top", the First Sergeant, would do everything possible to make their last month as irritating as possible. He was an old lifer who liked his soldiers one way...young, white, and unthinkably obedient. First Sergeant Blastok hated college kids, they were no better than officers, and thought Prince was an uppity Negro. They would burn shit, clean showers, do KP, and pick up cigarette butts all day every day for the next thirty. This was his third tour...this was coming home for him...he hated the stateside Army, too much bullshit, but he hated this tour's breed of

GI as well. They were too much like civilians, a pathetic disorganized undisciplined group, the sheep that needed shepherding...the ones that needed protection...they couldn't survive without the existence of the Army...and the draftees were far below in status in his eyes than those who volunteered to audition for Valhalla...the true soldier. He was a soldier's soldier...all Army.

From now on the clock would be moving at a trudging pace, they were chrono-slaves: pushing and pulling at the hands of Time, constantly coaxing them forward, every second further was another moment closer to their new prologue.

No more ambush. No more. Never again. No more killing. Peace was on the horizon, the call of doom was waning, and without killing there was a chance for Hope. He had experienced his last eagle flight...never again would he ride the wings of the modern war chariot.

Everything in the Nam was becoming "a past", a "once upon a time", and ahead was the world and a brand new genesis. He couldn't wait to get his piano and re-enter the old world, his new world. The arts were exploding all over the planet...in sculpture, painting, theatre, and most of all for him...music. The 60's was the great incubator for this renaissance and he wanted to be a part of it.

But for the nearly 300 hundred Americans who died each week in Nam, the renaissance

would never happen.

He and Prince whiled away the days talking mainly of the future, punctuated with the reminiscences of "the old days" and day dreaming. For Prince he could only think of his girl, who was writing him a sugar report every day, and she was all he could talk about. His love for her was all consuming, and kept him going hour after hour, as they performed one menial dirty task after another. Winston felt like he knew her as a sister, her idiosyncrasies, her tastes, even her pet peeves. He laughed with Prince sharing his best friend's boundless joy. He was a lucky man, and Winston loved him more than just a brother, they were soul-mates who had survived Hell, and now together they would survive the cruel slowness of Father Time, as they toiled patiently waiting each day for the sun to sink into the horizon.

For him, he dreamed constantly of his nebulous future. He knew music was going to be the integral part of his life, but how the muse would manifest itself he was clueless...but then mystery was the magical fuel for his imagination...would he play in a band ? Be a solo artist ? Be an itinerant minstrel ? Only the baton of Fate could lead him in the right direction. It was exciting to believe that in a few long days the answers would be revealed.

The other cornerstone of his daydreams was love...he wanted what perhaps all men de-

sire...to kiss a girl who you're madly in love with, and is likewise in love with you, and make historical love with her, to fill her heart with ecstasy...and create a love that's binding and relentless. He couldn't see her face, but he could sense her body, feel her aura...know there is someone out there who would love him for who he was, and he could love her...and make her happy. At times the daydreams would drive him delirious ...he so much wanted to fall asleep with his arms around the girl of his dreams...but Cupid's arrows were still in its quiver...he was still in Nam after all...but now there was only eight more days to go.

Prince and he maintained their old habits, where Prince slept inside the bunker, and he slept on top; and Winston ("the old man") would chit chat with the new guys, but it was just idle chatter. There was no caring or friendship in the conversation, he only wanted to sleep and get another day closer to home.

While he laid on his back with his head on his helmet looking at the stars , his mind was a reckless menagerie of dislocated wild thoughts...death...beauty...a new beginning...eight more days...Rufus...suicide listening post...he was deep into those goin' home blues. A peaceful night in Nam is a pastoral night. Back in the world people stayed inside, watched TV, maybe dined out and went to some cultural offering, but rarely laid back and just looked at the sky. In Nam at

night it was the only show in town, and it was cinemascopic in grandeur. Every once in a while a shooting star would flash across the astrological panorama. In ancient times it was easy to comprehend that whole civilizations would be awed by the movement of the stars in the skies.

He thought of Rufus, and wondered what life was like in the Big Hotel. He couldn't purge Rufus from his psyche...the fact that he knew all along...from the beginning...that he was going to die...how could he know ? Is he looking down now and praying we survive ?

Is he in a better place ? Winston felt he had to be. The Big Hotel was filled with Wolfhounds who would never know fear again, never dread the Grim Reaper, and he hoped would only know laughter and good times for the rest of eternity. Rufus should've been sending him letters from the world, but all he was...was memories. He died in the jungle, just another statistic in the Army's soon to be forgotten glory count, but his ghost wouldn't disappear for him, and as he stared at the eternal skies he shed a tear for his friend, and wondered if the sadness will ever go away. Eventually his dalliance with the sandman would free him of consciousness, ridding him of thoughts of swimming in the wasteland of death and blood.

The morning was a Michelangelo of the sky. Pastels played with clouds fast and furious, it was a running rolling race of palette changes,

as dawn was game time for the Muses. Play while you can...the day was forthcoming, and the business of life and living was all ahead.

The early morning cool breeze brought the aroma of fried bacon, and the sounds of laughter from the gun pits, and Prince and Winston sat on their bunker and watched the change of day. It was one of those mornings where the moon was visible in the daylight, and huge Vulcan smithy gray clouds would float past both orbs washing colors away, leaving nearly white puffy pillows for the gods to sleep on. It was a beautiful morning.

Charles Manson went on trial for the murders he had orchestrated earlier this year. Insisting on being his own lawyer should've increased his chances for pleading insanity. The world would...at that time...find it shocking what a group of Satanic marionettes would do at the strings of an evil puppeteer. The world would watch and read about the trial. Nixon could not repress himself from commenting. People wanted them to die. Helter skelter.

Christmas was not far off.

CHAPTER TWENTY-NINE

Remember, Reminisce, and Repeat

They were one-digit midgets. Seven days to go.

Superstition rules, Murphy's Law prevails, and it became nerve wracking to realize they had gone so far and survived so much, it would be shameful and unfair for something to go wrong now. It would be like surviving from cancer and while celebrating dancing across the road, get hit by a school bus.

If paranoia begins as a tiny rivulet meandering out of a mountain, it was now a Niagara with crushing cascades.

Would something weird happen ? Would there

be an unexpected accident ? Could something go wrong ?

They were an isolated duo, the last dinosaurs of the "old" Wolfhounds of the Michelin rubber plantation and jungle firefights. Night after night, back and forth again and again they would dwell about their upcoming re-entry into the world and how different they had become.

Winston was no more a college kid, and Prince was much more than a furniture store manager.

He and Prince had never ever been hunters.

To click the safety off, to aim...to pull the trigger...the impersonal mechanics of killing...once totally unimaginable now seemed more than normal...but natural. It was the way things were served on the plate, and if you didn't want to starve...you played the game...it was like losing your virginity...once done the mystery is gone, and you're going to do it again.

He remembered the first pull of the trigger and how easy it was to fire again. Every modern war had to begin with a single bullet somewhere...for someone, and it seemed that bullet would metaphorically never stop ricocheting across the universe. One shot fits all.

In 7 days he would never touch a gun again, but he couldn't erase from his mind that it seemed imponderable to walk around and *not* have a gun in your arms. Every day, all year,

all the time...yet he remembered walking around and never contemplating a weapon as a basic piece of wardrobe. What was life going to be like in the new prologue ? Winston agonized to himself that he would be ready. It would be a return to the good old days...what else ? Can't be the Nam, so it must be the world. Living the life in the world...just the thought made him dizzy...he was eager to return and molt his GI skin...but what if he had changed too much and the world wasn't ready for him...or the world had been moving too fast and he was some orphan trapped in a time zone ? Forget the revolution ! It was time for a renaissance, at least a personal one.

That night looking out across the rows of barbed wire, steel waves in a pillaged sea flowing out in a glistening tide in the moonlight, disappearing into the rice paddies in the darkened horizon, the duo listened to the radio intermittently playing Christmas carols amongst the usual menu of rock'n'roll; and they contemplated the future. In a few days what seemed like eternal damnation would only be memories.

" Prince, you remember how Rufus, from the first day I met him, always said that he would never make it..."

"...and he fulfilled his destiny. It was meant to be."

" I think that's a fact...but did you ever doubt that you wouldn't make it ? " he cupped his

smoke in his helmet , even though there probably wasn't a VC or NVA around for miles.

" It ain't over yet, but tomorrow...say hallelujah ! Five days and a wake-up ! There were some bad days back then, and I had my doubts. There were some days I'm amazed anyone got out alive."

" We've been lucky." They both laughed very quietly.

" How 'bout you Winston, did you ever think the Grim Reaper would come by and punch your number ?"

He hesitated, sifting the days through his brain, " No man, not really...you never know, but I always thought I would make it...but then I believed Rufus would make it."

" Anyway how, soon we'll be sitting in a restaurant eating pizza and drinking cokes in ti-ti time...and I'll be with my sugar."

" Prince, you're going to be on cloud nine."

" Roger that, my sugar has been true to me and I've pledged my heart to her. I can't wait to get married. It will make this year of Hell worth it."

He smiled at his only friend, " That's so cool Prince. I can't wait to be back in Veronica's embrace...just to look into her eyes will be a reward all in itself."

Prince laughed, " You got it as bad as I do brother," stretching out his large frame, " I'm crashin' Winston. The fastest way to get to six is

to close your eyes."

" Roger that."

After Prince went down inside the bunker, he was alone with his thoughts...he remembered a firefight back in the Michelin, back in the day when just mentioning Village 13 brought a nervous wince, when he carried the machine gun on rear security and thought he had killed five gooks, but the firefight became too intense so they never checked it out.

Pull the trigger.
See the smoke.
Watch souls disappear.
In the wink of an eye.

He could only perpetually wonder if he played the hand of God. His mind was a murky mire of madness. It had been a year of death and souls lost to the chilling, deepening embalming sea, always growing darker...a mysterious extinction. Death was always near. He wished he knew what he had done...he wished he didn't care.

It was a year of human wave attacks... people walking over themselves for the right to die.

It was a year when the moon would encounter footsteps from aliens from another planet.

Woodstock was peace and love.
Manson was murder and mayhem.

Between the horizon and the cruel steel whiskers of barbed wire there was another beginning.

Six more days...

Next **week**...another world.

It don't mean nuthin'.

                    Run

   Spot

    Run.

Next **week**...

Driving a car..

Veronica...

Beer in a bar with friends...

Sleeping in a bed...

No sounds of artillery at night...

Sleeping in...

Reading a book in the park...

It still seemed too unreal and far, far away.

First Sergeant Blastok started Winston and Prince on their morning detail of washing pots and pans on KP, then after a police call of the entire base searching for cigarette butts, they would burn shit. After lunch they would clean weapons stored in the tiny armory, and perhaps clean a vehicle or two.

The numbered days piled up like seismic waves on the Richter scale. Each day became progressively more intense, longer (although they did the same tasks day after day), and nerve wracking. It seemed odd to see their platoon re-

turn from a mission and not be a part of it. They were tourists in the war machine and he felt deep down he should be out there with them.

After all, it had been his whole life, but watching from afar, on the other side of the looking glass was a good thing. The military umbilical cord was as tough as any Gordian knot to sever and Winston felt for them, but they had many pages to go, and for him the book was closing. He made idle chatter with his fellow grunts, but now there was a distance between them. Maybe he didn't care anymore, his mind was slipping away into the next world.

Their roles in this theatre was all them...he felt like the complete spectator.

Even Prince was getting edgy, nervous; the clock was not moving fast enough for him. The days were getting longer as they got shorter. He couldn't sleep at night...too many nightmares...too many expectations. All he could think about all the time was his home and family and his sweetheart. He wanted to walk the streets of Detroit, wave to the people...eat real food made by black people. Over and over again he dreamed of watching TV with his sugar, eating pizza...waiting for momma to to fall asleep so they could neck on the sofa. And soon they would have their own place. His image of her face and body was as solid as a tattoo on his soul, there was no chance of forgetting...the memories were in his bloodstream, enclosed and never

ending. Soon the memories would collide with reality. God, he couldn't wait...it couldn't be soon enough.

CHAPTER THIRTY

Chicken Little's Revenge

And finally the long year rolled into the last day...DEROS (date of estimated return from overseas) day...an electric morning that felt like Christmas, the 4th of July, and your birthday all rolled into one. As soon as Winston and Prince saw each other they gave each other a gigantic hug.

THEY DID IT !
THEY HAD SURVIVED !

They wanted to pinch each other, it was too unbelievable, too good to be true. In a few hours they would be leaving...
and never coming back.

At breakfast on the last day in the Nam, Prince and Winston said their jubilant good-byes

and good lucks to their fellow Wolfhounds. The current GIs cared just a little, they felt simultaneously jealous but glad for them...they earned it...but their world was seeing that their ass got to make that walk to the bus that would take them to the airport and that final rendezvous with the Freedombird, same-same Winston and Prince. Looking at the two, all they could think of was that someday that would be them.

THE LAST DAY !

Their smiles were un-erasable and uncontrollable. It was a surge from within that was out of control...

THIS WAS SKY DAY !

The single day they had fought for all year long...the appointment book on the calendar read destiny day...they were going home. Everything seemed like a crystal clear world...freedom was finally no longer a lure in the distance, it was almost a breath away.

Good-bye and hello.

It was sky day !

Prince wore a smile so deep and broad you'd think he'd given up his face for it. This was the happiest day of his life. He looked at Winston as they began the walk to the bus pick-up. There were no words to describe his spirits and no words were needed to be exchanged to confer their feelings, his feeling of bliss precluded his

feet from touching the ground.

The horrid memories of the cruel bitter deaths they had witnessed, the seas of dead bodies, the fear of dying, the myriad ambushes and search and destroy missions...all of that was disappearing...the war was over...and as they walked they felt lighter as those heavy feelings began to evaporate.

Winston fired up his last J in the Nam, " Prince, want a first toke ?" He laughed.

" We're a football field away from me never seeing Nam or dope." Prince picked up the pace, they could see the dilapidated blue bus parked along some palms. There was no real reason to hurry...they would undoubtedly wait once they got on board.

But they would be on board...just one step away.

Prince was whistling some song Winston had never heard before. He had never even heard Prince whistle. It seemed like the music was everywhere. Complete exhilaration. He flipped the J, exhaled a mighty cloud, and began dancing to Prince's aria. The atmosphere was all peace, music, and pure glee. Never had he felt so relieved or so ecstatic.

A soul brother in a jeep sped by them and Prince raised a clenched fist to him. The man in the jeep was an M.P., a military policeman, the right hand man of law and order and sometimes of God.

He did not return Prince's clenched fist. The M.P. slammed on the brakes of his jeep and began backing up.   Winston felt the adrenaline tangle up in his stomach, a churning sickening feeling.

" Hey ! What's that I smell ?"

There was a long pause. They both were dumb-founded. The M.P. got out of the jeep and approached them closely.

" Hey brother, I don't smell a thing."

The M.P., much shorter but athletically built, looked up at Prince, his face no more than a foot away,

" I'm not your brother. I smell pot...where is it ?"

" Hey man, I don't touch that garbage, c'mon we're leavin' today. We sky in fifteen minutes...this is our DEROS day."

Winston's nerves were unraveling.

" Get in the jeep ! Both of you !"

" Oh man, he's right. He's never touched the shit. It's me, c'mon let him go."

The M.P. was expressionless, " Get in the jeep ! !"

Prince started yelling, " We've been here a year. This is our day. It's sky day, our last day...you can't do this to us. Oh God, please."

" He didn't smoke anything. I did. Let him go. You'd be punishing an innocent man."

The M.P. walked past Winston as if he was dirt and found the barely smoldering J and picked it up.

He put his hand on his pistol and glared at them. Winston pleaded with him, " Get righteous brother, let him go. I just said it's all me. He's never smoked. He can still catch the bus to freedom." He looked into the eyes of the M.P....it was like peering into the cold heartless soul of a reptile, " please let him go."

" You are not going anywhere today, except the jail at M.P. Headquarters." He unhooked his pistol and pulled it out. It wasn't necessary, but he wanted to show them how tough he was. He felt righteous...he was doing his job...perhaps he would get a commendation...and he loved playing God...they were nothing to him. He repeated himself, " You two are not going anywhere today."

He looked at Prince, his face was a funeral of dead dreams, and he looked at the M.P.. He wondered if he made a run for the bus if he would shoot him. He wasn't going to risk it...this power infected bastard would nail him in the back before he was down the hill.

Using his pistol as his magic wand he motioned them to get into the jeep, and then handcuffed them together, and radioed in that he was bringing his prey into M.P. Headquarters.

" Do you know we're Wolfhounds ! We're infantry for Christsakes ! You're busting us for a lousy J and stopping us from going home on the Freedombird ! We were leaving today !" Winston was hysterical. " This is nothing man. It's

not worth our freedom. Nothing but smoke !" He screamed into the M.P.'s ear, " You have no fuckin' compassion !"

Prince looked down at the floorboard, where his spirits were, and murmured loud enough for the M.P. to hear, " You got no heart. You're right...we're not brothers. You got to have a soul to be a brother."

The M.P. turned around and looked at them, not saying a word. He had gold mirrored sunglasses on so all they could see was themselves. He stomped on the pedal and a mountainous dust cloud seemed to follow the jeep. From the rear it looked like a magical hazy cloud had captured them and taken them away, and disappear was what Winston wanted to do.

The jeep was jumping madly in the pot hole infused dirt road. He wanted to cry, " Prince, Prince, I am so sorry. I don't blame you if you never forgive me. It's all my fault."

When Prince turned to look at Winston they both saw the blue bus disappear around the corner and soon out of the base camp and...gone. That made it deathly official. They missed the bus. No freedom. They were once again trapped in Nam.

" It's okay man, they can't keep us for long, we've done our time," he shook his head, " but who could believe it ? The NVA have at least some compassion...
who'd guess we got Satan's man to come and take

us back to Hell."

" I can't believe it's happening either...of all times for an M.P. to drive by...on our final day...and I had to celebrate with a final joint..." He put his head in his hands, " I'm so sorry."

" Freedom is going to be another day." Prince looked away, his eyes were filled with dust...a great camouflage for tears. Inside he was breaking up, the world had just imploded, and there was no where to run, no where to hide...and now, no way out.

When they got to the M.P. Headquarters they were frisked and placed inside the "cage." It was an all metal box with a window the size of a shoebox, a cement floor, a toilet, and a cot.

Winston sat on the floor and alternately apologized and tried to be upbeat that the military couldn't, wouldn't do much to them...maybe a little humiliation, a bust in rank and then they would be going home in a few days. Just losing "the day" was punishment enough.

Prince couldn't imagine a worse fate then what they were experiencing this moment. In a few hours their Freedombird would be leaving without them. He did not want to talk and laid down on the cot. He didn't want to hear Winston either. He had put them in this cage, but Prince did not hate him for it...a horrible coincidence, the most horrible experience in his life...and his deep Christian faith told him that forgiveness was a mighty virtue...and he would survive. He

had suffered through everything else this year, he would take whatever came his way and conquer it, but for the moment he was spinning a cocoon around himself as he withdrew into his own private world. If Winston was talking he couldn't hear.

The M.P. Headquarters was all abuzz that the two GIs in the cage were on their way home before they got busted. To a man they agreed the sergeant did the right thing in busting them, and his superior lauded him for his conscientiousness. After all it was against Army regulations to do drugs. Over mess that night it would be the focal point of conversation, a philosophical debate over who might have looked the other way seeing how it was their last day in the Nam. They would never see them again. After all...it don't mean nuthin'.

They spent a restless, sleepless night in the cage, and in the morning the personnel sergeant, a total mental collapse; the lifer clerk who would never see action in his career, his arms festooned with tattoos like "death before dishonor " opened up the cage door with a heavy jailor's key. He belonged in the Middle Ages. " Gentlemen !" He paused, " I'm taking you back to the Wolfhounds. Get up !"

They were handcuffed, and placed once again in the rear of the jeep. Besides the personnel sergeant was a private armed with an M-16. The entire trip back to the base camp he watched

them ready to shoot if they attempted to leap from the moving vehicle.

No one spoke.

Winston thought to himself. This was just the beginning of the humiliation exercises.

When they arrived at the camp no one spoke a word. Their fellow Wolfhounds barely looked at them...silence was everywhere. It was too mysterious, they weren't supposed to be here...it was like seeing specters return from the dead.

◆ ◆ ◆

Perhaps because they had volunteered for free, and it seemed cool, the concert organizers with the blessing of their premiere act, The Rolling Stones, were ecstatic the Hell's Angels would be the security force for the concert. They were armed with clubs and knives, and some had guns...and they were drunk and flying on acid. It was hardly the recipe for the promotion of peace, love, and flower power; more the equivalent of the Nazis "guarding" the Jews. No one in their right mind was going to interfere with this group. If there were going to be any fights or skirmishes it was because they had started them. Most of the concert goers, many who were equally screwed up kept their distance. Fear and flower power...not a good karma cocktail.

CHAPTER THIRTY-ONE

The Last Letter

Veronica was on cloud nine. Her favorite walk was to the mailbox, and today she was well rewarded, as it contained a letter from Winston telling her he had only 6 days to go...and next week he would be calling her when he arrived in Oakland. One week ! She could not believe her eyes...after this brutal long, long year the wait would be over...her new life could begin. Her mother could tell by her expression she had received banner news fromWinston . She was happy it was coming to a conclusion as well.

As was her usual custom, she sat down at her nightstand and re-read the letter...then

paused to gather her thoughts...look into her mirror...make a wish...and read the letter once more. *This was an exceptional letter...* nothing but good news and high hopes, with the complete affirmation of his unfaltering love for her. Every woman in the world would cherish a letter like this, and best of all this time next week they would finally be together. Veronica decided she would go shopping for a new and spectacular dress, something that would make Winston's eyes pop out. A dress that a man would remember what she wore on that day, the day he returned, twenty years from now. It would be sexy, but classy...he would be proud to have a love like her.

As part of her letter reading and writing routine she always said a prayer, and began to compose her response. This would be the final letter. He should get it just before he leaves.

❖ ❖ ❖

Seeing their dazed expressions, First Sergeant Blastok smiled at them, speaking the first words upon their return,
" So you stepped on your dick." He wanted to laugh. He thought it was funny.
Winston looked at the ground, " It was all my fault. Prince doesn't smoke pot."
" Well welcome back to the Wolfhounds

gentlemen. Your squad leader will issue you a couple M-16's. You're going back to the field *today.* This afternoon your eagle flight will take you back to the swamps." He grinned.

" We did our time...we got our Purple Hearts to show for it. C'mon Top, let us burn shit for awhile...or anything else. This isn't fair." Winston was livid.

" What kind of sadist thought this was fair ? Just keeping us past our DEROS is hell enough...but to go back to the field !" Prince was trembling trying to control his anger, " how long will we be out there ?"

" The CO came up with the punishment, so it's up to him how long you're in the field. He figures this punishment sets a good example for the other men. Pot smoking is against Army regulations." His smile grew more cinemascopic, " it probably won't be more than a couple weeks. You're dismissed."

The platoon treated them like visiting ghosts. They were supposed to be on their way to the world, not awaiting an eagle flight to the swamps looking for a suspected school of nurses for the VC.

Once again they were issued weapons and Prince went inside the bunker to be alone. His "sugar" would be expecting him home in a couple days, he didn't know what to write to tell her he was being delayed. Winston related the episode to the men in the squad. They offered

their condolences and unanimously agreed the punishment was too severe. Jail time and being busted in rank was far superior to returning to the field and one more time bucking the odds and the spin of the wheel of Fate.

They both were scared. Neither could eat. On the PZ the sniper tossed Winston the smoke grenade to signal the eagle flight. It was purple haze, his favorite. The Lieutenant was happy to have them back on board, to him nothing had really happened; he grinned his phony I-really-don't-care grin, " We got a cherry today, first day in the field, maybe him and the other new guys will learn something from you two."

Winston scowled at him, and thinking to himself, " You motherfucker ! How'd you like a grenade up your ass ?!"

Even slaves can escape, can run away, but there was nowhere to run, no where to hide; and soon the roar of the eagle flight, the harbinger of their arrival filled the air. It was like liquid fear and he and Prince were drowning in it.

The cherry was on the chopper with Winston, and being his first eagle flight he was typically paralyzed with fear. His was due to ignorance, Winston's was just the opposite...he knew what he was getting into. It seemed strange to be on an eagle flight with a man that had a year to go when he had a year in country, but today they were simply soldiers in the field. Just another day in the war.

He was home...it was if he never left, as if there never was any other kind of life. The cherry didn't know he had just opened the door, and in Nam, for some the first door is the final exit. The cherry would find out...positively definitely.

He lit up a straight, then fired up another and handed it to the cherry. The roar of the blades drowned out all conversation. Winston tapped his fist on his heart and shook the guy's hand. No one relaxes on their first eagle flight, but he could see he had given the guy a spoonful of hope, and for the first time the soldier thought that just perhaps, death was not going to be the second he jumped out of the copter.

Winston screamed to himself, " **What am I doing here ! !**" He could've repeated that over and over again, but here he was, the Atlas that had let the world slip off from his shoulders.

◆ ◆ ◆

A young kid, college age maybe, at the concert at Altamont thought it would be so cool to dance to the music of the Rolling Stones with The Rolling Stones, *on stage.* It was so cool, he would tell all his friends. The music was so loud his girlfriend couldn't hear him yell in her ear he was going forward to the stage. He started waving his arms high and back and forth, gyrating his hips as he maneuvered through the crowd in

front.

The Hell's Angels began to take notice.

CHAPTER THIRTY-TWO

Dwight

Her mother was out of the house having lunch with one of her friends, and Veronica felt relaxed knowing she would have an entire stress free afternoon. Louise frolicked as the two skipped to the mailbox. She wasn't expecting a letter...but you never know...

When she returned ready to make some lunch and work on the scrapbook (although all it needed was some fine tuning) she screamed when she entered the kitchen.

It was Dwight, sitting nonchalantly at the kitchen table.

" I never got to tell you how sorry I was about Edith. I know she was your best friend..."

She screamed, " GET OUT ! WHAT ARE YOU

DOING HERE ?" Veronica was shaking.

Completely non-plussed, Dwight calmly spoke, "Perhaps you could use a friend. You know I've always liked you, and your mother likes me too. In fact she's having lunch with my mother." He stood up.

" Get out now ! You're sickening !"

As he began to approach her Louise got back on her haunches and began to snarl.

Dwight laughed, " Pretty ferocious dog you got there. I'm really *scared*." His laugh turned more raucous, as his presence became more threatening, " You know Veronica you really should give me a chance, you might forget that piano playing loser you're waiting for."

" Stop ! Don't come closer ! When Winston returns he's going to chop you up and feed you to the fishes..."

Grinning repulsively, " Maybe he won't be coming back...that's why I'm here." He was slowly, steadily forcing her into a corner. " C'mon Veronica, you know you want it. It's been a long time...I think you'll forget that piano player once we get together."

She screamed as loud as her lungs would allow, and he momentarily backed off...paused...and lunged. He was big and strong and it was easy to rip her blouse off, as he began to press against her, tearing the hasp off her bra; and then he felt it. Veronica had pulled a simple kitchen steak knife from the drawer and poked

him in the side, drawing blood. He was more startled than hurt, " C'mon baby, give me the knife. I know you aren't going to use it. You're not going to hurt your lover boy..."

He grabbed for the knife and by sheer accident Veronica had seriously slashed his wrist. He screamed, grabbing his arm and ran. It looked like a suicide gash. He turned looking at her. It would need a tourniquet and she could do it. She pointed the bloody knife at him. It was a clear message, and squeezing his arm he ran to his car. He'd make up some story at the hospital.

Veronica slumped onto the floor completely drained of all energy, while Louise licked her face to comfort her. She knew she should call the police...but it would be her word against his, and he was the one slashed. It was a man's world...if he called the police she'd be in jail before nightfall.

After what seemed like an eternity she composed herself and buried her ripped blouse in the trash can, cleaned up all the blood, and decided to tell her mother nothing. There was nothing to be gained. Her own mother would've sided with Dwight.

An hour later her mother returned, " Veronica dear, I was having lunch with Dwight's mother, when he came in with his wrist all bandaged. It seems he seriously cut it helping a friend sharpen his lawn mower. He said he could've bled to death."

Veronica feigned a yawn, " How sad. Too bad

it wasn't his throat instead of a wrist..."

" Veronica ! How can you say that ? He's a nice boy...and, *he's* going to be a doctor. I wish you would give him a chance."

Veronica just stared at her, thinking to herself, "if you only knew," and went to her room with Louise. Looking at the scrapbook with childhood pictures of the both of them positioned as if they had met in kindergarten was cute and funny. The entire project, her first artistic labor of love chronicled their lives from birth to the present, including a letter he sent and the pictures and text showed their inseparable bond, and what a strong future lies ahead.

In about a week he would be home. It seemed like forever, and Veronica was nervous and scared...the next few days would be crushing... waiting for the wait to end.

She told Elizabeth and Helen about Dwight, and hoped she wouldn't run into him anytime soon. She was not sure what she might do.

CHAPTER THIRTY-THREE

More than Just a Dream...

Their destination was a swampland that was actually deserted and abandoned rice paddies. Much of the area had been so decimated by B-52 strikes that an observer from outer space would have surmised that some mad gods had destroyed the area playing tic-tac-toe...the round bomb craters and the square paddies...a marriage made in the military.

The sky was as massive and awesome as ever, and the air was always cool in the sky. Below were the swamps...the wasteland...the kind of place that could be the birth of the Earth, everything a shade of green except for the dead brown drowned trees, the occasional skel-

eton in a sea of slime. Hedges had grown along the paddies giving some parts an English garden look, except there would be a swamp between the hedges rather than flowerbeds. It had an eerie feeling to it, Winston would have preferred to land in the jungle knowing the possibilities, rather than this no man's land where there is no reason for life. He associated swamps with leeches, and nothing more.

This was going to be another stupid, exhausting, idiotic mission, but hopefully a harmless one.

Yesterday, he and Prince had had a conversation with the Company CO about how long they would be out in the field. The Commander said they could be free that moment, as far as he was concerned, but the Battalion Commander had set the length of punishment and today would be their last day, tomorrow they'd have seats on the Freedombird !

He thought to himself, " We are looking for a school of nurses for the VC, in a place where the only life form is a leech. Is there anything wrong with this picture ?" It might have been funny, if it wasn't so disgusting and pathetic.

The eagle flight began to hover over the swamp, and as if on cue they dropped like marionettes with their strings cut, into the slime.

The expression on the cherry was laughable to Prince and Winston...they were veterans...as the squad leader pushed him off the

copter and into the swamp. Everything but his rifle and his head had been submerged. When he arose, not truly appreciating his baptism into the Wolfhounds, he was completely slimed and soon auditioning leeches. His weapon was dry, and his brain was spinning. He was a long way from Kansas.

Neither Winston or Prince were concerned, the news from yesterday was exhilarating ! Winston felt all the hate, the bad karma, everything evil wash away with the sunshine. He couldn't stop grinning as hope had conquered his soul and filled him with happiness. In but a few days he would be with Veronica ! It would be over !

He yelled over to Prince, " Hey brother ! Look at my feet ! Do you see them touchin' the ground ?"

Prince grinned back, " I'm feelin' it brother. I can feel the Lord has saved us. We got just ti-ti hours, just a few more hours ! NOT DAYS ! I'm not gonna lose this grin...I can almost feel my sugar melting in my arms. We're finally at the end !"

" Amen Prince ! We arrived together, we leave together...I'm on cloud nine...I'll never forgive myself for putting you here trudging through a swamp, when you should've been home..."

" It was evil Fate, bad luck. Who knew a scumbag MP would just come by, and then wanna play God with us, but it's done, it be OVER.

I forgive you Winston, we'll always be brothers."
They continued trudging, the rest of the platoon
had no clue why they seemed so happy.

The platoon organized into two files and
proceeded with no particular direction in mind
as they stumbled across the shattered crumbling
dikes. All he could think of was escape...but tomorrow he would be skying up.

Just this one last day.

He felt he had been doing this forever and
still it was one day at a time.

After but a short distance they came upon
an unexpected treat, a stand of wild sugar cane,
which was quickly cut into foot long pieces and
distributed. He could chew on cane all day, it
had a unique sweetness to it. They wandered
back and forth across the dilapidated and bank-
rupt paddies. The only way a school of nurses
could survive out here was if they had gills, at
least that was what Winston was thinking until
they encountered a hooch still standing in a
hedgerow. There was no vegetation around it...
someone had to be occupying it recently. The
area had ample enough high ground to build
underground bunkers and they approached with
a greater sense of trepidation.

The cherry's face was the perfect portrait
of fear.

Every step could be his last. Prince's expression had changed...he wasn't talking and did

not wish to be spoken to. Winston lit up a smoke and increased the distance from the man in front of him. This area was practically guaranteed to have trip wires hooked up somewhere, and one casual wrong step could buy a ticket back to the world. He would be overly cautious, someone else could be the lucky winner in booby-trap roulette.

The two files encircled the area and slowly got closer and closer to the hooch. The point men were perspiring the size of pearls. He and Prince held back as the point men entered the hooch.

There was no telling how many had been there, and apparently it had been used recently, the tracks did not appear to be old, but not a single molecule of rice remained. They presumed they would have detonated a booby-trap by now and the platoon took advantage of the higher ground and took a collective break to burn off the leeches...and then back into the wasteland. In the distance, beyond the large crater created by the B-52 strike, now a perfect circular pool the color of mustard algae green, evenly lipped all around with a mound of dirt was another hedgerow larger than the one they just checked out. That was their next destination.

He kept chain smoking, the mosquitoes were a plague...no amount of bug juice was going to deter this army. There were too many of them.

The usually bored lieutenant was thinking this might be fun and games. Leeches and

mosquitoes...lions and tigers and bears, oh my ! A small entrance fee to participate in the war. He hoped they would encounter this secret hiding place and ideally engage in a firefight with their protectors. He had never killed a gook, and a notch on his gun would mean more to him than a medal.

Both Winston and Prince were blind to the scene, all they could see was love's reunion. The bonds of war were about to be broken and Freedom had released Cupid to do his job. There was an inner glee hard to control within each of them.

The large hedgerow they were approaching had three dilapidated hooches artfully camouflaged by vegetation. "Gossamer Moses" suggested to the Lieutenant that he recon the area with his grenade launcher to try and blow up some booby traps.

Neither Winston or Prince cared whatever "Gossamer Moses" and the lieutenant were talking about...they were in another world, their private universes, where war did not exist, and a year's dreams were about to come true.

The Lieutenant would have nothing to do with this precautionary maneuver...it would spoil his fight...and once again the platoon slowed up the pace as they trudged closer to the hedgerow, knowing each step further was one step closer to the likelihood of booby traps. "Gossamer Moses" vigorously continued to press the Lieutenant for permission to recon the area,

but he was not listening...or caring.

The sound seemed to come from the far reaches of Hell...the atmosphere had been silent except for the ubiquitous droning of mosquitoes.

It seemed to erupt out of nowhere.

The nearness of it was frightening...

The cherry had set off a booby trap, a grenade attached to a trip wire. The expression on his face was complete shock and horror...he spun like a dervish in the slime, the explosion blasted him deaf. He screamed awaiting the onslaught of pain...but none came...he felt lost, his ears were consumed with the chimes of Hell. All he could sense was this deafening ringing, a tolling that seemed to crescendo in volume. The cherry put his hands over his ears trying to make it stop...he was the perfect model of Munch's <u>Scream.</u>

The entire platoon went chaotically numb diving this way and that along the crumbling dikes, seeking refuge from the invisible fear. The cherry melted into the slime and began to cry, but he was unhurt...and he couldn't stop the tolling.

The Grim Reaper was on the move...

◆ ◆ ◆

The young black man continued to dance his way to the front of the stage. He was having a great time. This was so cool to get up

and dance with The Rolling Stones. The Hell's Angels began to approach him. People everywhere were on their feet yelling and clapping with the music, which was deafening...all other senses were drowned out...the crowd was oblivious to this pack of wolves closing in on their prey...only those very close by could hear him screaming when the Hells Angels began kicking and stabbing him. At first it seemed he was being welcomed into the group, dancing and jumping to the sounds, and those behind him weren't sure what was going on. The music was so loud his screams were like punctuation among the crescendoing guitar riffs. They stabbed him over and over again...fifty one times until he was dead.

The Rolling Stones watched from the stage...they were performing one of their greatest hits.

◆ ◆ ◆

Winston's helmet had fallen off as he gaped at the cherry...then a million thoughts and dreams raced through the panorama of his mind as he looked down. All loose ends were coming to a conclusion. All beginnings were climaxing into a finale. The last door was opening...time was freezing...the next dimension with its new sun... was dawning. Winston tried to look at Prince...it

was all happening too fast...

...the pain was all immersing as the shrapnel from the grenade had blown off both his legs, the explosion of blood into the swamp drained his soul blocking everything off, as Winston sank into the mire...

and like

the quick unloosening

of a knot...

He was dead.

Prince threw his helmet off and screamed.

He started running towards Winston, the tears were flowing like a blinding fury down his cheeks and he kept screaming Winston's name over and over again. The platoon were like statues frozen in the wasteland, no one moved, all eyes on Prince.

" It isn't fair !" He screamed. A year in country... moments from freedom...and now he was plodding and stumbling the long final feet across the swampy paddy to rescue his friend.

But he knew Winston was dead.

He roared to the entire platoon, and to the entire world, " It isn't fair !" He screamed loud enough to wake the Valkyries. " **IT ISN'T FAIR !**"

When he got to the dike, only yards away, the reality hit him his best friend, his true soul brother, was beyond rescue. Winston was lying face down in a pool of blood. The circle of blood grew larger and larger in the green slime sea.

Everyone was still, the platoon was mesmerized in shock...and then as he got close to pull his friend from the wasteland, Prince triggered the other booby-trap, the grenade sending him flying into the air.

He had checked into the Big Hotel before he landed in the swamp. The Grim Reaper had collected his bounty and Prince joined his soul with Winston and together they set off on their final journey. The goin' home blues were officially over...the song had been played out...

The men pulled them out of the slime and covered them with poncho liners while they waited for the dust-off to come and carry them away. They stared at the motionless bodies, moments earlier filled with life and hope...and no one spoke. In the Big Hotel the trumpeter began the slow mournful dirge of "Taps"...they were soon

◆ ◆ ◆

The Rolling Stones continued playing "Sympathy for the Devil". The volume was so loud few could hear death's tolling bells, which rang steadily across the planet.

◆ ◆ ◆

Veronica, as usual, was eager to make that

walk to the mailbox...sometimes there was nothing, but when there was a letter ! It would make her day, raise her spirits...put air in the balloon of Hope, give strength and credence to her will to stand by her man...and most of all add fuel to the fire...that sometimes flickered, that was her love forWinston. She didn't expect a letter today...but you never could tell, after all...he would be home soon. It was always an enjoyable stroll to the mailbox, a temporary escape from her mother's glare, perhaps a letter that always added another thread of steel to her armor, that fortified her love for her man. Her thoughts were all consuming about Winston, every hour, every day and now with their reunion being so close... nearly every second...and their future. After a long year the reward would be even more satisfying. All her dreams would be coming to a conclusion, the reality of a new life was only a few days away... she would dance to the mailbox. It was a day blessed with pure sunshine, not a cloud in the sky; the perfect day to be consumed with hope and happiness.

She would never give up, never give in to outside temptation, they would be the "forever" couple, the Rock of Gibraltar twosome no one could ever separate.

As she approached the mailbox she saw Winston's
mother walking towards her. She smiled and happily waved to her. She felt like skipping and

singing.

Her expression was not reciprocated, and Veronica could feel the numbing sadness as she came closer. She was carrying something, and Veronica knew what it was.

She sank to her knees, put her hands over her face, and began to weep.

There was nothing to say. His mother tried to speak, but could not, and handed her the neatly folded flag. Her eyes were drowned with tears.

Veronica huddled the flag to her bosom like a newborn, and began walking. She kept her eyes straight forward, never looking at people as she walked along the sidewalk, tears slowly cascading down her cheeks. No one could look into her soul, her eyes were clouded over. She moved with a steady deliberate pace, the pace of a woman who knew where she was going and wouldn't be stopped.

It was but a short walk, but still time to think, and Veronica had no hesitation in her purpose. It was time.

When she got to the bridge...she wiped her eyes, cleaned her face, took a deep breath, and stepped over the railing.

People near by knew what she was doing. No one spoke.

Veronica unfurled the flag, let it fly...and blew a kiss...and without a second thought, or a single glance backward she jumped into the sky.

Her leap of destiny. It was simultaneously deeply poignant and sad...and pure ecstasy. Time had stopped and became a new dimension. It was over and a new beginning in seconds.

Somewhere in the vast eternity two souls bonded together...the final exit opened a new door...they were finally together.

The war was over.

THE END

Made in the USA
Coppell, TX
04 January 2026

68210446R00252